THE HEROIC SAGA OF THE KENT FAMILY AND THEIR COUNTRY, AMERICA

Millions have thrilled to the story of the Kent Family and the founding of a great dynasty that was to stretch across our vast land. Now, here are the magnificent stories of the Kents—from Philip Kent's desperate flight to the New World to the agonies of Gideon Kent's forbidden love—taken from *The Bastard, The Rebels, The Seekers, The Furies, The Titans, The Warriors,* and *The Lawless.*

Here, too, is the story of their beloved country—the painful and glorious struggle—the saga of a mighty, new nation. A chronicle of America—its wars, its ways, its politics, its people—told in seven condensations, seven original essays, and over 175 illustrations. An unforgettable panoramic portrait in words and pictures of the stirring times in which the Kents lived and loved and died.

ABOUT THE AUTHOR

ROBERT HAWKINS was born in Highmore, South Dakota, in 1923. After graduating from Trinity College in Hartford, Connecticut, he began teaching at the Hotchkiss School, in Lakeville, Connecticut, as master of English and French. In 1947–48 he was a special student at the University of Edinburgh, Scotland, and has more recently spent a year and a half in England and Italy. He is the author or coauthor of several books on literature for students, and coauthor of *Landowska on Music*, a distinguished collection of writings by the world-famous harpsichordist. When he is not teaching or writing, he avidly pursues his hobbies—cooking, ornithology, mycology (the study of mushrooms), and studying wildflowers. He is now senior master at Hotchkiss.

ABOUT THE ARTIST

RON TOELKE was born in Queens, New York, in 1947. He graduated from the State University College of New York at Buffalo in 1970. He took painting and sculpture courses and has a particular interest in drawing and painting subjects from American and military history, costume and fashion history, and the decorative arts. Ron is a founding partner in a graphic-design studio in Chatham, New York, where he and his wife, Barbara Kempler-Toelke, live in a refurbished barn.

The Kent Family Chronicles Encyclopedia

With condensations of
the John Jakes novels and
essays about America
from 1770 to 1877

Prepared by Robert Hawkins

Drawings by Ron Toelke

Produced by
Lyle Kenyon Engel

THE KENT FAMILY CHRONICLES ENCYCLOPEDIA
A Bantam Book / November 1979

ISBN 0-553-13383-7

Published simultaneously in the United States and Canada

Bantam Books are published by Bantam Books, Inc. Its trademark, consisting of the words "Bantam Books" and the portrayal of a bantam, is Registered in U.S. Patent and Trademark Office and in other countries. Marca Registrada. Bantam Books, Inc., 666 Fifth Avenue, New York, New York 10019.

PRINTED IN THE UNITED STATES OF AMERICA

0 9 8 7 6 5 4 3 2 1

Table of Contents

Foreword

Many people have asked me to try to explain the popularity of the Kent Family Chronicles. Readers could do it far better than I. All I can offer are a few suppositions, based on what I've read in literally thousands of letters.

The Kents are the kind of people we would like to see more of in America today. They are by no means perfect, but the best of them are courageous, idealistic, and patriotic without being blind to the country's mistakes and flaws.

They exemplify our still-unequaled tradition of liberty and opportunity. They endure the worst life can offer, but they never lose faith; at least not for long. And in a day when so many families disintegrate under various pressures, the Kent family manages to survive.

If a novel is a writer's child, this book could be called a grandchild. I didn't write it, yet it springs directly from the continuing story of the Kents—and I have more than a passing interest in it.

Robert Hawkins, senior master and instructor in French and English at the Hotchkiss School, wrote the text. Mr. Hawkins's summaries of the novels are concise, his sketches of each historical period colorful and, in short space, exceptionally comprehensive. The illustrations by Ron Toelke supplement and enhance the text, depicting people and things of each historical period with accuracy and great charm.

It's my hope that the volume will add to your enjoyment of the Kent Family Chronicles.

JOHN JAKES
Hilton Head Island
June 20, 1979

Preface

During the past few years, millions of Americans have had the pleasure of feeling their history come alive in John Jakes's phenomenally popular series of novels, *The Kent Family Chronicles.* First in the books, then on television, people have seen the events of our past history firsthand, as it were, through the eyes of successive generations of Kents, from Philip Kent on down.

In a successful work of fiction, people and places can be vividly presented. At the same time, much inevitably must be omitted—for instance, all those aspects of a historical period which the characters themselves are not aware of. In order to fill in some of this background for John Jakes's readers, and thus to enrich their knowledge and experience of American history as well as the Kent chronicles, this book has been prepared.

It presents, first of all, a series of essays (one for each of the first seven of the Kent novels) dealing with the events and times through which members of the Kent family moved, from the period just prior to the American Revolution down to the post-Civil War period—roughly 1770 to 1877. Some subjects of these essays are closely related to the Kents' own fortunes; the evolution of printing and publishing in America is one such topic. Other subjects are related, but not quite so closely. The evolution of American architecture, for instance, was not something with which the Kents were deeply involved; a discussion of the kinds of houses they lived in, however, can surely enhance our view of them as living characters. Finally, some attempt has been made to provide odd bits of social history—"kitchen history"—that might reveal little-known aspects of the Kents' times.

In addition to the essays, there are condensations of each of the Kent novels. For readers already familiar with the series, these short digests will serve as a reminder of the action in the novels. For people not familiar with the series, it is hoped that the digests will spur them on to reading the novels in all their exciting detail.

An indispensable companion to the written material in this book is to be found in the highly evocative and historically accurate drawings by Ron Toelke, prepared expressly for this volume. Here are the people and their surroundings, their houses, costumes, tools, weapons, and conveyances—all recreating vividly the living world of succeeding generations of the Kent family.

When Lyle and Marla Engel asked me to consider writing the essays and condensing the novels of the Kent series, I had been for some years involved with teaching and writing in fields other than American history. In addition to teaching English and French, I had edited several books and journals; produced three textbooks, including one on poetry; anthologized the writings of Wanda Landowska, the harpsichordist; and in general had been rather more aware of European history and culture than American. Then I began reading *The Kent Family Chronicles* and realized that I had been neglecting a story as thrilling as any told by Gibbon or Macaulay or Prescott or Lecky.

I must now admit that I see a certain parallel between Matthew Kent and myself. Matthew Kent was an expatriate. He took himself to Europe to further his own development as an artist and remained indifferent (even hostile) to things American. Like him, I was immersed in personal pursuits, the immediate activities of a busy secondary school as well as various writing projects, and because of this was in a sense an expatriate, though technically resident in America. Having since been inspired by John Jakes not only to become interested in American history but also to read more deeply in the field, I must wonder what might have changed in Matthew Kent's life if he had had a John Jakes to stimulate his interest. Perhaps he would have developed the same regard for his country's history that I have reacquired for mine. I hope that this new interest on my part is reflected to some advantage to readers of this book.

ROBERT HAWKINS
The Hotchkiss School
June 5, 1979

The Kent Family Chronicles Encyclopedia

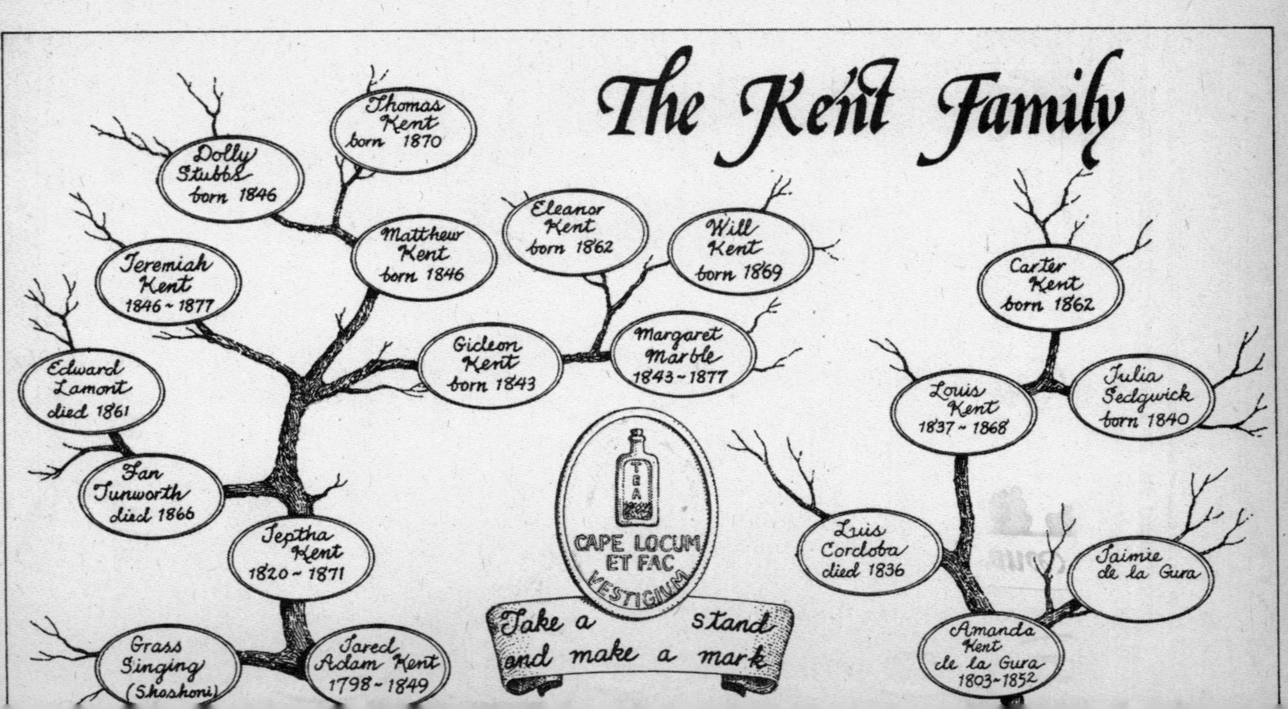
The Kent Family
Thomas Kent born 1870
Dolly Stubbs born 1846
Matthew Kent born 1846
Jeremiah Kent 1846 ~ 1877
Eleanor Kent born 1862
Will Kent born 1869
Gideon Kent born 1843
Margaret Marble 1843 ~ 1877
Edward Lamont died 1861
Fan Tunworth died 1866
Jeptha Kent 1820 ~ 1871
Grass Singing (Shoshoni)
Jared Adam Kent 1798 ~ 1849
TEA
CAPE LOCUM ET FAC VESTIGIUM
Take a stand and make a mark
Carter Kent born 1862
Louis Kent 1837 ~ 1868
Julia Sedgwick born 1840
Luis Cordoba died 1836
Jaimie de la Gura
Amanda Kent de la Gura 1803~1852

Abraham Kent 1775 ~ 18?
Fletcher 1778 ~ 1801
Judson Fletcher died 1778
Peggy Ashford McLean Kent died 1800
Gilbert Kent 1783 ~ 1812
Lebow died 1813
Andrew Piggott
England 1771
France 1771
Anne Ware 1753 ~ 1778
Phillipe Charboneau Kent 1753 ~ 1801
Lord Roger Amberly died 1775
James Amberly Duke of Kentland
Marie Charboneau died 1772
Lady Jane Amberly
Kingdom of Great Britain and Ireland
Bristol
London
Kent
Paris
Kingdom of France
Auvergne
Kingdom of Spain

The Bastard

A CONDENSATION OF

The Bastard

1770–1775

BOOK 1

In the spring of 1771 Marie Charboneau and her seventeen-year-old son, Phillipe, left the squalid inn which had provided them a meager living in the Auvergne. They were going to England to appear before James Amberly, Duke of Kentland, Phillipe's father. Marie had formed a liaison with the nobleman years ago when she was an actress in Paris and he was making the "grand tour." Although the duke had never seen the son Marie had borne him, he had not forgotten him.

Now word arrived from England that the duke was seriously ill and wished to see his firstborn son. Marie was not loath to leave. She was passionately dedicated to seeing Phillipe reach that station in life to which his heritage entitled him, and it was not to be found in this backwater of France.

The year 1770 had already brought changes to Phillipe's young life. Because of a certain swagger in his demeanor, Phillipe had inspired the enmity of neighboring toughs, who had cruelly assaulted him. Shortly afterwards he had rescued from those same ruffians a boy in a cadet's uniform, the Marquis de Lafayette. By the end of the year, a friendship had grown up between the two that was later to be resumed in America. Gil, the name by which Phillipe knew the marquis, rewarded him with a sword and scabbard, which were to become cherished heirlooms in the family established by Phillipe Charboneau in the New World.

Shortly before their summons to England, where her son would meet the duke's legitimate son and heir, Marie had revealed to Phillipe his expectations. In a letter witnessed so that it would constitute a binding legal document, the duke had acknowledged Phillipe and pledged that the boy would receive an equal share in his estate. The letter was stored in a small casket which Marie guarded with all the tenacity of her fervent spirit.

Late in April Marie and Phillipe found themselves in the Kentish countryside, where the Amberlys had their home. At Kentland they were received by the duchess, who made no attempt to conceal her hostility. She refused to allow Phillipe and his mother to see the duke, maintaining that his health was too perilous to admit visitors.

Before their interview had ended, a haughty young man appeared. Phillipe knew instinctively that this was Roger, his half brother. With him was a girl so beautiful that Phillipe almost gasped. The duchess presented her son and his fiancée, Lady Alicia Parkhurst.

The days of waiting to hear from the duke passed slowly. To fill the hours, Phillipe helped with chores around the inn and took walks through the countryside.

One afternoon in the woods he heard the sound of hoofbeats. Astride a black stallion was Lady Alicia. She informed him that his father's condition had not changed. As they talked, Phillipe became increasingly aware of Alicia's physical presence. He placed his hand on hers, and their eyes locked. Soon they were tumbling on the grass, arms entwined, kissing, Phillipe thinking his tongue tasted of wine. They began to let their hands explore.

By the end of May there was still no word from the duke. Phillipe enjoyed further meetings with Alicia, and soon there was no intimacy the two lovers had not experienced.

One day a carriage arrived to carry Marie and Phillipe to Kentland, where they were ushered into the duke's presence. Upon reaching his room, Marie rushed toward him, but was restrained by a physician who shut the door against mother and son.

The Kentish summer wore into August. Then late one evening Phillipe heard that the duke had died. He and his mother hurried to Kentland. Marie ran past the footman, only to be confronted by the duchess. Roger screamed, "Leave this house, you French scum!" and struck her with the silver head of his walking stick. Marie fell, exclaiming in pain. Phillipe sprang at Roger and dragged him outside. After a violent struggle he seized his half brother's stick and brought its silver head down again and again on Roger's right hand, crushing the fingers, destroying the hand.

Aware that they had to flee the wrath of the Amberlys, mother and son prepared to leave the inn at once. Their landlord advised them to lose themselves in London.

BOOK 2

Phillipe and his mother spent their first night in London in St. Paul's churchyard among beggars who set upon them and would have killed them had it not been for two sturdy figures who drove off the assailants. Victims of fever and fatigue, both Phillipe and Marie collapsed during the struggle.

They awoke in the home of Solomon and Emma Sholto, whose two sons, Esau and Hosea, had rescued them. The Sholtos were Whig printers, politically opposed to the arrogance and indifference of Tory families like the Amberlys. Kindly Solomon Sholto invited Phillipe to enter his printing business as an assistant. The young Frenchman worked industriously, and in a short time became a skillful printer.

One Sunday Marie and Phillipe joined the Sholtos on a barge trip down the Thames and were attracted by an unexpected sight—a middle-aged man, swimming vigorously. He was none other than the American Benjamin Franklin, who was in London as a colonial agent. Solomon Sholto spoke glowingly of Dr. Franklin, whom he knew personally.

Inspired by Solomon's stories of Franklin's accomplishments, Phillipe borrowed books on the American colonies from Mrs. Sholto's lending library. He inquired into the American character by means of a collection of essays published under the title *Letters from a Farmer in Pennsylvania to the Inhabitants of the British Colonies* written by one Dickinson, a Pennsylvania lawyer.

Phillipe decided he was a partisan of Dickinson and his American brethren—if only because they seemed opposed to the sort of high-handed behavior that had brought the visit to Kentland to such a tragic outcome.

The colonies were hardly ever out of Phillipe's thoughts; he was convinced that he and his mother should emigrate. It remained, however, to persuade Marie. Somehow he hesitated to bring the subject up. But one day in April of 1772 an unexpected visitor to Sholto's shop took the matter out of his hands.

"Lad, come up front!" the elder Sholto called. "I promised to introduce you to a colonial, didn't I? Well, Ben Franklin's come by."

Addressing Franklin, Sholto said, "Phillipe shows an aptitude for the printing trade. He's most anxious to talk with you and to read your *Observations Concerning the Increase of Mankind.* Our two copies, alas, are gone."

"Then come by my lodgings and we'll accomplish both

objectives. May I ask, however, the reason for your interest in my paper on population in America?"

Sholto answered for him. "Phillipe's considering going there rather than returning to France."

Phillipe glanced at Marie and saw the anger in her eyes.

As Franklin departed, he called out, "Mr. Charboneau, don't fail to call." When he was scarcely out of earshot, Marie bore down on Phillipe. "Will you destroy me after I have surrendered my whole life for you?"

Two days later Phillipe visited Franklin, who fired his interest in America. "Should you decide to go," Franklin said, "let me know, and I'll give you a note of introduction and recommendation."

A few days later Mrs. Sholto casually mentioned that a stranger had appeared in the shop. One of his eyes was covered with a black patch; the other had a mean glare. He wore a dirty coat that might have once been orange.

Mrs. Sholto's birthday fell on a Saturday in April, and they all, Marie and Phillipe included, drove to Vauxhall Gardens. After a picnic supper, they listened to the orchestra in the park. But within a few minutes, Phillipe announced that he wanted to walk. The spring air, the music, and the muted laughter of lovers wandering the mazy paths had brought disturbing memories of Alicia. He hoped a little physical activity would dispel them.

Pensive, he failed to hear, until they were close behind him, footsteps approaching with unusual speed. Phillipe turned. He saw a tall man in an orange coat.

"I have a present for you, sir, from the one to whom you gave a ruined hand," said the man as he drew out a pistol. Phillipe had time only to fling himself forward onto the ground as the pistol roared. He felt a sting as the ball grazed his left temple.

The stranger dashed out of sight.

Against Marie's violent protestations, they left without delay for Bristol to secure passage for America. Phillipe worried about his mother. Her consuming passion for him to remain in England and claim his share of Kentland made him desperately afraid for her sanity.

On the post road to Bristol, Phillipe saw from his seat on the roof of the coach a horseman a short distance behind. Simultaneously, two other riders appeared from a thicket ahead.

The coach guard raised his blunderbuss but then let it drop. The driver was already slowing down, unwilling to press his luck against a trio of highwaymen. One of them, Phillipe noted, had one eye and wore a dirty, faded orange coat.

The one-eyed man gave the driver an empty smile. "Captain Plummer, sir, at your service."

Captain Plummer and his two men called all the passengers out, but the dazed Marie did not move. "Assist our reluctant passenger," Plummer commanded one of his cohorts.

As the man bent toward Marie, his body blocked the line of vision between Phillipe and Plummer. Phillipe struck for the man's exposed middle with both fists and then whirled him by the shoulders as Captain Plummer positioned himself to shoot. His pistol blew a hole in the man's neck. As Phillipe threw himself to the ground for safety, the driver's blunderbuss roared and the third highwayman toppled from his saddle. Meanwhile, a fellow passenger had pinned Plummer's arms. Phillipe reached for the fallen man's pistol and fired. With a scream, Captain Plummer arched his back. Over his left ribs the dirty orange coat showed a black-edged hole from which blood spurted.

Phillipe and Marie obtained passage on the *Eclipse* bound for Boston. Her master, Captain Caleb, was a reliable and God-fearing man.

Marie's physical and mental state worried Phillipe as never before. Her agitated mental state and the rough seas were taking a double toll from her low reserve of strength.

Seven days out Phillipe realized his mother was dying.

He awoke in the darkness of their tenth night to hear her call, "Phillipe, I will never see this America of yours."

"Yes, you will—if you'll only help yourself to live!"

"To what purpose? Your father is dead. So is everything I held out as a hope for you. But I know you made the best choice—the new country. You have the youth, the heart for it; I do not."

Phillipe Charboneau kept a vigil for the next twenty hours. At the end of that time, the woman of Auvergne was dead.

On the morning of July 6, 1772, Phillipe walked on the deck of the *Eclipse*, thinking of the words Captain Caleb had spoken after his mother's burial at sea. "I'd suggest one final separation from the past. Why not start as a new man entirely? Take a new name."

With every other important tie severed, his name was his only link to his past. He needed something that belonged to both worlds to carry him through the gigantic transition rushing to meet him. He therefore decided to Americanize his Christian name and to acknowledge his origins by shortening his father's title to Kent. Philip Kent. From now on he would be known by no other name.

BOOK 3

Nothing could dampen Philip Kent's eager anticipation as the *Eclipse* entered Boston Harbor, but by nightfall his mood had begun to change. Hunger had forced him to scavenge through a litter heap where he found oyster shells from which he scraped bits of clinging meat—his first meal in his new country. "An event to remember," he thought ruefully as he pocketed one of the sharp-edged shells. He spent his first night in the new country sleeping in a haystack.

Philip woke shaking with fever. The next few days he trudged about Boston, eating garbage and sleeping where he could. He began to be conscious of King George's soldiers, who were everywhere in the city.

One evening while Philip was wandering around, a British captain and his lieutenant whirled around a corner and crashed into him. Weak and feverish, Philip stumbled and fell in the muddy street. His fall caused mud to spatter over the spotless white breeches of the captain.

"The clumsy young bastard!"

"We'll make him pay for a laundress," said the lieutenant as he grabbed Philip's collar and pulled him up. "Come round to the headquarters of the Fourteenth West Yorkshires in the morning. Here, hold on!"

Philip had pulled away. As he did so, he knocked the restricting hand away.

The lieutenant slid his sword from its scabbard. He flicked Philip's sleeve with his blade and then raised it to lay open Philip's face. But Philip had presence enough to hold the lieutenant's sword arm off while he grabbed the oyster shell from his belt and raked it down the lieutenant's left cheek.

The captain began to unlimber his sword just as a man seized Philip's arm. "Need assistance?"

Philip, staring into the face of a lean, black-haired, middle-aged man, could do no more than nod as the lieutenant advanced, sword up, commanding, "Stand aside, sir; I'm going to gut him through!"

The gaunt man shook his head. "Sirs, let me inform you that the Salutation"—he indicated the inn just up the street—"is crowded with my friends. I guarantee you a substantial number of Bostonians will be after your heads before three blows are struck. I have some ability at summoning them out. I am Will Molineaux."

"Molineaux, the leader of the whole damned liberty mob?"

"Yes, sir, the same," he laughed, as the captain and his lieutenant disappeared around a corner, almost at a run.

Molineaux led Philip into the Salutation, where the landlord, Campbell, played host to those who were active in the cause of liberty. Upon hearing how Philip had handled the captain and his lieutenant, Campbell promised Philip food and lodging in return for work.

Campbell obviously liked the young man. After observing him for some days, he said, "I think you have the makings of a fellow who might wear this some day!" Campbell tugged at a chain from which a medal gleamed. On it, an arm grasped a pole, on which perched a peculiar-looking cap. Engraved on the medal were the words *Sons of Liberty*.

Philip often waited upon a group of men who gathered regularly in a private room in the Salutation. Among these was Benjamin Edes, a printer, to whom Philip said one day, "If you've ever a need for a devil..."

"Constantly," Edes sighed, gauging Philip, "I can't hold 'prentices. Most of 'em are frightened of running afoul of the king's justice."

The following morning Philip called on Mr. Edes and began as a boy-of-all-work around the shop.

As the summer of 1772 mellowed into autumn, Philip was promoted to setting type. Samuel Adams was a frequent visitor to the shop, usually arriving with a new diatribe against the king. Abraham Ware also came; his essays were almost as inflammatory as those of Adams. And Paul Revere brought political cartoons.

One morning Philip, alone in the shop, looked up to see a young woman entering. She was the daughter of Abraham Ware and had come with copy from her father. Philip suddenly felt a physical response that had lain dormant for months. But the girl showed him only a haughty disdain. The next morning Philip set off for Ware's house on Launder Street with the proof sheets of Ware's article. A servant informed him that her master and his daughter might be found in Mr. Knox's bookshop.

At the bookshop Philip found Mr. Ware and his daughter talking with a Captain Stark. When Anne noticed Philip, she brushed past the elegant young captain, who was trying to arrange a meeting with her. As she cordially greeted Philip, he said in an undertone, "Your behavior is somewhat different today. For practical reasons?"

Her flush admitted guilt, but he didn't mind her strategy. The warmth of Anne Ware's expression delighted him. Suddenly she asked, "Do you have a decent suit?"

"No, but I'll get one."

"I should be pleased to have you call, provided you have a proper broadcloth."

Philip hoarded his shillings. A few days after the beginning of 1773, he was outfitted in a suit of broadcloth complete with a neckerchief, hose, and buckled shoes. So one Sunday afternoon he called on Mistress Ware.

Looking serene and beautiful in a white gown, Anne gave Philip a smile that concealed just a tiny bit of amusement. Philip's new clothes itched, and he fidgeted. Embarrassed and not quite knowing how to deal with this kind of encounter, he had the urge to flee. Later when Anne said, "I thank you for coming to call, Philip," they stood close together for a moment, bodies nearly touching. "You're welcome to come again." He found himself replying, "Thank you. I will."

In the months following he became a frequent visitor at the house on Launder Street. Summer brought intensification of the crisis between the colonies and the Crown. Anne Ware was exhilarated by politics, and it annoyed Philip that she cared to talk about little else.

In an attempt to divert her from her preoccupation, Philip asked Ben Edes for a Saturday afternoon off in September so that he and Anne could picnic. But even as they climbed toward their picnic site, Anne continued to talk about the Cause, as she termed the resistance that would be mounted against the recently imposed threepenny tax on tea.

"Anne," he said, "I've something to tell you."

"What is it?"

"That I care for you very much, that I want you very much."

Flushing, she answered "Let's go to the top. The mutton won't be good if we don't soon..."

"Anne."

On November 27 the *Dartmouth*, the first of three vessels on the way to Boston with the hated cargo of unjustly taxed tea, was sighted. The following night Philip and Benjamin Edes labored late on a broadsheet which urged every "friend to his country, to himself, and to posterity... to make a united and successful resistance to this last, worst, and most destructive measure of administration."

Since that day in September Philip had avoided Anne. He was not entirely sure whether his reaction had come about because he was in love with her and feared it or because he wasn't.

Two nights after the *Dartmouth* anchored, Philip awakened. Smoke? He jumped from his bed and dashed into the shop. Flames were shooting up from a stack of papers. The fire, though not yet large, illuminated the front door, which he could see was half torn from its hinges. He raced behind the press, seized the bucket of sand kept there for just such emergencies, and emptied it on the burning papers.

By the time Edes arrived, the blaze was extinguished. "Sharp work!" he said. Reaching under his shirt, he pulled out a chain bearing a medal like the one Campbell had shown him. As he looped it around his startled assistant's neck, he said, "You earned it with what you did tonight!"

"Philip, you know there's to be action tonight. Are you with us? It may be dangerous." Ben Edes spoke these words on December 16. "What's your answer?"

The younger man grinned. "Do you think I'd miss it?"

When Philip arrived at Ben Edes's house, he found it crowded with young men dressed in costumes ranging from blankets to women's shawls. Edes led him to a table laden with axes and hatchets. Choosing one, the printer pressed it into Philip's hand. "Tonight, my boy, you'll be a noble savage. Don't be surprised if you're required to use this on something other than tea."

The "Indians" had their rendezvous near Fort Hill. They marched towards Griffin's Wharf, where Edes's group boarded the *Dartmouth*. Other groups charged down the dock to the *Eleanor* and the *Beaver*, which also carried tea.

As the first of the canvas-covered chests was raised from the *Dartmouth*'s hold, Philip and two other men hacked it open and spilled its contents into the water. Then they threw the empty chest overboard and went on to the next one, until the entire cargo had been dumped.

Halloos from the other two ships indicated that work had been finished there, too. Philip didn't know what to make of the whole affair. Certainly there would be repercussions. But all he really wanted to do was to go back to his room and sleep.

As he began trudging home, he suddenly heard footsteps behind him. Glancing back, he saw two British officers. One was Captain Stark, whom he had seen at Mr. Knox's bookshop. Philip flung off his blanket and ran, but he hadn't gone two blocks before he knew he couldn't outrun them. Philip turned into an alley and stumbled. From there he saw Stark drawing his sword. The other officer hadn't been able to keep up and had been seized and jostled by an angry group of citizens. Stark had been too fast for them.

On his feet, Philip started running hard again, but Stark was gaining on him. Without warning the captain launched a forward thrust. But Philip ducked, and throwing himself at the grenadier's boots, he pulled him off balance. Scrambling up again, Stark lunged, raised his right arm, and brought his blade whipping down. At the last moment Philip jerked his head aside, and the blade only grazed his temple. Managing to free his ax from his belt, Philip swung it full force and chopped through Stark's trousers into his thigh. Stark managed to hobble forward for another thrust of the sword, but Philip kicked him in the belly.

Stark's hand opened, and his sword dropped; he moaned and sank to his knees. Philip snatched up the sword and rammed it through Stark's midsection.

Then he bolted away to Ben Edes's shop.

He heard distant rapping. The knock came again. Then another. This time it was accompanied by a voice. "Philip?"

He whirled, ran up past the press, unlocked the door, and jerked it open. A figure shivered in the December wind.

"Anne!"

"I had to see you. When I heard you were with Mr. Edes—well, I can't properly describe everything I felt. I have been so miserable ever since that afternoon we had our picnic. Why didn't you come calling again?"

"I thought it best not to. Now I think I should see you back home. It's after three o'clock."

"Not just yet . . ." She touched his cheek and gasped softly. "What's that? You're cut."

Philip revealed what had happened. "Here," Anne said, "sit down and let me clean you up a little. Pull your shirt off."

As he did, he noted her surprise at the sight of his liberty medal.

"I didn't know you wore one of these."

"A present from Mr. Edes for dousing a fire a few weeks ago."

Carefully she scrubbed away dried blood, and he relaxed under her ministrations. Then he grew conscious of an itching under his right foot. He pulled off his boot and tilted it. He laughed as a little cascade of tea poured out.

"I think I should save this—a souvenir of my career as an Indian." Anne watched amused as he poured the rest of the tea from his boot into a small green bottle. "Another Kent family heirloom."

The girl stood up slowly. She said in a quiet voice, "I want you for a lover, Philip, with no conditions, no promises, no pledges." In the corners of her eyes, tears began to glisten. But she was smiling, too, as she unfastened her dress and pushed the bodice and sleeves down and her linen shift along with it.

Later, yawning and whispering and holding hands, they walked through the December morning to Launder Street.

A few days later Knox, the bookseller, made a surprise visit to Mr. Edes's print shop. He was recruiting for the Boston Grenadier Company. It took little persuasion to convince Philip to enlist.

At last Massachusetts was to be punished for destroying the tea the preceding December and for long, open rebelliousness against Crown authority. The Boston Port Bill had passed Parliament. It forbade the loading or unloading of any cargo in Boston harbor. George III would reopen the port only when the duties on the ruined tea, as well as the cost of the tea itself, had been paid in full.

In addition, Governor Hutchinson resigned his post and was replaced by General Thomas Gage, who enforced even stronger Crown rule in Boston.

In August Lawyer Ware left Boston to attend a Philadelphia congress of representatives from the colonies to decide what was to be done about the Intolerable Acts. Before departing, Ware sought out Philip. "You know I'll be away for several weeks and that my daughter and Daisy, our cook, are alone with that redcoat who's billeted in our home. He's a lumpish creature, though not a bad sort for a Tommy. But I want to speak to you on another subject. In my absence call frequently at Launder Street. Look after Annie as only a man can."

Sergeant George Lumden, the redcoat Mr. Ware had mentioned, was just under thirty, shy, almost humble. Around him Daisy O'Brian was positively fluttery.

The sergeant had chosen military life as a means of escape from poverty. As he sat in the kitchen of the Ware house, he discoursed on the soldier's life and the cruelty of commanders.

"Got a tyrant in charge, do you?" Philip asked.

"Lieutenant Colonel Amberly."

Philip said quietly, "Do you know this Amberly's first name?"

"'Course! It's Roger. Roger Hook-hand. He has this crippled right . . ."

One night as Philip sat with George and Daisy, Lumden suddenly asked, "Can I speak to you in confidence?"

"Of course."

"I've been thinking of leaving the army. Deserting."

Daisy nodded emphatically. "George and I wish to be married."

Lumden put in quickly, "It's not cowardice on my part. I've just no stomach for going into battle against those whose only crime is holding fast to what belongs to them and is being taken away."

"Understood," Philip assured him. "But let's discuss the practical problems."

"Leaving Boston, you mean?" Daisy asked.

"Yes. It's either Roxbury Neck or the river."

It had to be the Neck. Lumden could not swim. Crossing the Neck required a disguise, but George and Daisy had already planned that. It needed another person, however—one to pose as George's nephew. Lumden would play the role of an oafish farmer being assisted home because he had not restricted his consumption of rum.

Once free, he would hide at Daisy's home, a farm beyond Concord. If Philip would find a reliable lad to help with his plan, George would reward Philip with his musket and bayonet.

They decided that George should disappear after muster on Saturday night. Philip hired a boy at the Green Dragon and instructed him to arrive with a cart and horse to meet George at Launder Street. Philip would wait for them at the Neck.

That Saturday, Philip was at the Neck as planned, but the boy and Lumden never appeared. Fearing some foul play, Philip ran first to the Green Dragon, then to Launder Street. As he rounded the corner where Lawyer Ware's house stood, he saw a strange horse tied in front of the house. Creeping up the steps and peering through a gap in the drapery, he caught the flash of an officer's scarlet tunic inside and realized the hired boy had betrayed them. He backed down the steps and stole out to the barn, where he found Lumden hiding.

A scream came from the house. It was Anne's voice. Philip bowled past Lumden and snatched up the sergeant's musket. In seconds he had detached the bayonet, and with the glittering steel in his hand, he dashed across the yard and up the back steps as the cry rang out again.

He reached the parlor doors and heard the sounds of a struggle. Then a voice that dredged up memories of depthless hatred hit him. Philip pried the doors apart and stepped into the dim light of the parlor. The officer turned. "My God! Charboneau!"

"Charboneau?" Philip repeated. "You're wrong, Colonel. Charboneau died in England. Charboneau's mother is also dead—because of your harassment. It's a man named Philip Kent you must deal with now!"

Roger freed his blade from its hilt and ran at Philip, who had no time to think, only to react. He twisted aside as Roger's sword gouged the door. Roger's midsection was fully exposed by the force and extension of his lunge. Philip brought his right hand up and stabbed the bayonet into Roger's belly.

Quietly Philip commanded, "Daisy, get George."

Philip and George dragged Roger through alleys away from the house.

"I'm going with you, George," Philip said. "That's the only way you'll ever escape now."

They decided that Lumden would play the role of an incoherently drunken yokel. Philip, acting as his cousin, would lead him past the sentries. The plan succeeded remarkably well, although there was one tense moment when one of the guards spied blood under the arm of Philip's surcoat. Philip invented a story having to do with getting his cousin away from voracious Boston whores, one of whom was, he fabricated, "kind of cut by accident. She bled a storm."

BOOK 4

Philip and George walked for two nights and half the intervening day before reaching the O'Brian farm, where they were greeted by a ball from a musket held by a middle-aged Negro. "Honest folks don't come sneakin' into farmyards 'fore the light's up." This was Arthur, a freeman who worked for Mr. O'Brian.

The farmhouse door opened, and Philip saw a short, rotund man emerge. After some difficulty in convincing Mr. O'Brian that they were friendly, Philip and George were invited into the house.

O'Brian had found himself not only with a hungry

Boston patriot, who was at the moment possibly being sought by the king's soldiers, but with a deserter who wanted his daughter's hand in marriage. Smiling, he said, "Arthur, let's feed these scarecrows. I guess I'd best become acquainted with Tommy here, since it appears I may be stuck with him, like it or not. As soon as they've eaten, you can put 'em to work."

January turned into February, but still no message arrived from Boston. By this time Philip had met O'Brian's neighbor, Colonel James Barrett, who was readying the Concord militia and companies of minutemen in the event of hostilities. Philip was soon training with them.

In early March the Concord patriots heard that the Crown had declared Massachusetts to be "in rebellion." Acting accordingly, General Gage sent soldiers to Salem to seize arms stored there.

Philip remained preoccupied with the lack of communication from Anne. By the second week in March he had decided he would attempt to reenter the city.

While he was preparing to saddle the mare O'Brian had offered him, he heard Arthur call, "George, Daisy's here!"

Not only had Daisy arrived, but Anne and her father, too; they were waiting for Philip at the tavern in Concord.

Philip called, "Tell Mr. O'Brian I've gone to town to see—" He stopped suddenly, looking at Daisy, who was staring at him.

"Daisy, what's wrong?"

"There—there seems to be fairly certain evidence that the officer—well, the one who came to the house the night you left, isn't . . ."

"Isn't what?"

"Isn't dead."

Philip stalked into the tavern, saw Anne, and wrapped her in his arms. Despite the joy of their reunion, Anne was ill at ease.

"Amberly was apparently found where you left him, unconscious, but not dead. He was removed from Boston a few days later," Anne explained. Then she gave Philip a letter which had arrived only hours before she and her father had set out for Concord.

The top of the letter read, "Philadelphia City," and bore a recent date.

My darling Phillipe,

I have arrived at the home of my aunt and her husband, Mr. Tobias Trumbull. In the next chamber Roger lies unconscious, perhaps already in the throes of death.

We agreed that in the event military duty in the colonies resulted in any serious injury he would communicate with my aunt if possible.

My aunt forwarded the news to me, and I have come to Roger's side. Last night he was awake long enough to talk with me.

He named his assailant.

I write the truth. I want nothing more than to see you, speak with you.

I do not know whether my husband named you his assailant before he was borne here. I think not. My aunt and her husband do not know of you, of that I am certain.

I beg you to come by any swift means to Philadelphia. I beg you to answer my pleas. But come—even if we may meet only for a day.

For God's sake come, my darling!

Alicia

"Are you going to run to her the minute she commands?"

"I don't know."

"My God. You're actually considering it. Well, go and be damned!"

"Anne, you know I care for you."

"Stop it! We've nothing further to talk about."

"Yes, we do. There's no other way to put the past to rest but to see Alicia one last time."

As Philip clattered down the stairs, Lawyer Ware

glanced up from his chair in Wright's public room. "Kent, a word! Anne's been sickly of late. I have a suspicion as to why she—"

But Philip had already stalked out into the rain.

The journey to Philadelphia was without incident. Upon arriving, Philip realized that the solution to the riddle of his future hadn't yet presented itself. Of the two women Anne was by far the more sensible, but she also represented uncertainty, the peril of this struggling country. Alicia stood for everything he had been taught to desire all those years in the Auvergne.

Philip had no trouble locating the Trumbull residence, where he found on the front door a somber wreath trailing black crepe ribbons. He penned a hasty note to Alicia: "A friend desires to know the cause of the household's bereavement. P. Charboneau."

Within a matter of hours a tall servant arrived at the inn where Philip had put up. "Tomorrow," he said, "there will be a room waiting for you at the City Tavern." Upon arriving at his new quarters, Philip was shown to a large, airy bedroom and informed that his bill would be handled by someone who wished to remain anonymous.

Later that evening Philip was aroused by a faint knocking. It was the same tall servant. "Come with me, if you please."

"Where?"

"To a coach where a lady awaits."

As the servant preceded Philip down the creaking stairs, he chuckled lasciviously.

Philip was tempted to run, but he heard a voice saying, "Phillipe, you're safe and there's little time."

"Alicia?"

"Of course."

Philip was aware of a faint lemon fragrance and a stronger smell of claret. His hands circled her waist while she held his cheeks and hungrily brought her mouth to his. The kiss was long and full of the wine taste of her breath. "I want to be alone with you, Phillipe. I want us to be alone the way we were before. I'll marry you, Phillipe Charboneau, and God damn what any of the rest of them say."

The coach stopped, and Philip climbed out and stood under the April stars. As the coach departed, he thought he heard a low, cutting laugh. A laugh of pleasure. Certainly . . . of victory.

He went to his room and flung himself on the bed, trying to think everything through. Instead he slipped into sleep and dreamed, not of Alicia, but of Anne Ware.

Six days passed. Philip was continually worried about Anne. He wanted to leave but could not. He cursed his own indecision and Alicia's hypnotic influence.

At length Philip set out for the Trumbull residence determined to force a confrontation with Alicia. As he walked, someone called out to him.

"Sir, a moment. Aren't we acquainted?"

Philip turned to see a stout, elderly man with spectacles. It was Benjamin Franklin.

"Mr. Charboneau, isn't it? I remember you from London."

Philip accompanied Franklin to a tavern to hear him discourse on the state of the colonies. "I wish," the statesman said, "I knew where all the turmoil will end. We're a powerful people here in America. Should the ministers decide to test us to the limit, I think they will be mightily astonished."

"Do you think the ministers will, Doctor?"

"Given George's determination—yes. His Majesty's not an evil man, but he's a bad, misguided king. And there's not a person who'll gainsay him: not North, not Dartmouth, not Kentland, not . . . What's wrong, Mr. Kent? You're white as ashes."

"You spoke a name. I'm not sure I understood—Kentland?"

"Aye, James Amberly, the Duke of Kentland. He was gravely ill a few years ago, but recovered eventually and came up to London to take a place in the government."

Philip stood up suddenly. "Dr. Franklin—you'll pardon me—there's something I must do—"

Philip ran through the streets to the City Tavern, where the landlord stopped him, "Mr. Kent, you've a visitor upstairs!"

He bounded up the stairs and found Alicia. Her bare shoulders shone golden in the glow of a single candle.

"Why didn't you tell me my father is still alive. Why, Alicia?" He bent her wrist. "Tell me, God damn it!"

"Please. Please don't hurt me, darling. The duchess hatched the scheme."

Philip dug his fingers into her scented flesh. "You knew that my father wasn't dead!"

"Phillipe, the past doesn't count. Roger's gone—your father is alive—we've found each other!"

"Alicia, the past counts very much in your case. Roger's dead. The duke is living. And I'm his only heir."

"If you return to London and show him the letter . . . Phillipe, you do still have the letter?"

"What if I answered no? Suppose I sent it down to the sea with my mother's body?"

"Tell me the truth!" Alicia cried, one small fist raised to strike. "That letter can mean a whole new world to you!"

"And you."

"You said you wanted to be what your father was! It's within your reach."

"I do realize what's in reach, Alicia, but I have one small doubt, one tiny doubt that tells me you wouldn't offer your endearments, your vow that nothing else matters but our being married—unless, unless I had the letter. Good-bye, Alicia."

Philip suddenly realized he was within sight of Concord. He didn't know the exact date. April seventeenth? The eighteenth, maybe. He rode into the village and dismounted at Wright's Tavern. The hostile eyes of

Lawyer Ware locked with his.

"Back at a most inauspicious time," the little man barked. "I presume you wanted to flee from danger—and your shameful actions."

"I went on necessary private business. Is Anne inside?"

"Whether she is or not makes no difference. Don't try to see her again. If my daughter is, as I suspect, carrying your child, I'll find you wherever you are. And I'll kill you!"

Not many minutes later he turned the mare into O'Brian's farm and drew Daisy aside. "I need to see Mistress Anne, but her father wouldn't permit it," said Philip. "Can you slip in and give her a message?"

"Of course."

"Tell her she has my love. And, Daisy, are my things still stored in the clothes press?"

She nodded.

Philip went to the clothes press and rummaged in it until he located the leather-covered casket. Opening the lid, he drew out the document on top. He replaced the casket and walked swiftly to the fire. He stared at his father's letter and then consigned it to the flames.

Philip and O'Brian had arrived in Concord at dawn to meet a small group of about a hundred other men, all drab in their plain shirts, their farm-muddied boots and trousers. In the east they spied what seemed a great red serpent crawling along the road. Several hundred grenadiers and light infantrymen were preceded by musicians with fifes and drums. That flood of armed redcoats would be sweeping into Concord before another hour was up.

The sun rose higher.

The British companies advanced across the bridge, but the whole action seemed hesitant, as though the British hoped to bring the colonists to heel without violence. Just before eleven a black plume of smoke climbed into the sky. The British were burning buildings in Concord.

A few minutes later Philip heard the command to load with ball.

Suddenly the muskets of the kneeling front rank of the central British company exploded.

It had come.

Philip fired.

He reeled against the kick of the musket and saw an infantryman at the far end of the bridge spin and sprawl.

Philip knew an era had ended and another had begun for him and for all the shouting, cursing Americans who leveled their weapons and fired on the king's soldiers.

By noon the British expeditionary force had taken the road back to Lexington. Concord lay quiet in the April light.

Men were running everywhere, jubilant. Someone in the crowd seized Philip's arm. It was O'Brian. "Come along, Philip. We'll chivy them all the way back to Boston."

No sign of Anne. Not anywhere.

"Philip?"

He turned.

Her dress was stained; her hair was tangled. Tears welled in his eyes as he ran toward her. He swept his arms around her, kissing her unashamedly in the smoky sunlight.

Then Philip headed out of Concord with the other men. How would England react now? With armed might, surely. Unrestricted and unrestrained. Only in that way could the king hope to put down this rebellion in the cause of freedom.

No matter. He would follow the road from Concord wherever it led. And come back to Anne and see their baby born.

England in the 1770s

Background to THE BASTARD

The novels of *The Kent Family Chronicles* are an ingenious blend of fiction and history, in which made-up characters like Phillipe Charboneau live side by side with real people like Benjamin Franklin. Since John Jakes wants us to sense the flow of history in early America, he has wisely chosen not to interrupt his story in order to spell out historical accuracies. However, the *Chronicles* have so whetted the appetites of readers and TV viewers alike for knowledge of America's past that it might be useful to supplement the novels with some information of everyday life in the years they cover.

The Bastard covers the period from 1770 to 1775. Life in England in those years was, owing to the insularity of that nation, different in style, if not in substance, from life on the Continent.

As for life in America, styles there were by and large what English styles had been some years before—a phenomenon referred to by social historians as "cultural lag." It took time in the days before the instant communication of radio, telephone, and television for ideas and fashions to cross the Atlantic. For instance, witch-hunting had been virtually abandoned in England two decades before the Salem trials in America had even begun.

Early in *The Bastard* Phillipe and Marie board a vessel at Calais bound for England. Remember that Marie was French and a former actress. Her clothes, therefore, may have been old-fashioned and threadbare, but her Parisian background and theatrical training would have kept her from looking dowdy. Over her linen undergarments she supported a series of hoops called a farthingale, over which she wore a voluminous skirt. Such skirts were wide and cumbersome and made going through doors difficult. Fashionable women were a dozen years in advance of Marie and had already begun to give up the farthingale.

Marie's white silk bodice was even more old-fashioned than her farthingale. It still fastened in the front, not in the back, as the Paris fashion had now decreed for some time. It was reinforced with whalebone, which encircled the body, even across the breasts. Over these garments Marie wore a *contouche*, a long shapeless cloak that gradually widened downward. This particular garment had long since gone out of fashion, but in the Auvergne clothes ceased being worn only when they were too threadbare to hold together. Marie's stockings were her best linen; she could not afford the silk hose of the *beau monde*. Her shoes were plain. Even had she had the money to buy elegant shoes, there would have been no shoemaker in her village skilled in making the dainty high-heeled slippers worn by women of quality.

If Marie's costume bore some semblance of elegance, Phillipe's had none. His clothes were those of any Auvergne rustic—homespun knee breeches with a fairly broad front flap, supported by shoulder braces. Over a coarse linen shirt he wore a simple waistcoat that laced across the back to the shoulder blades. His outer garment was probably a coat of the riding sort; his hat was a shapeless piece of felt. Marie had knit his thick wool stockings; his boots were heavy and ill-fitting.

The vessel that carried Phillipe and his mother to

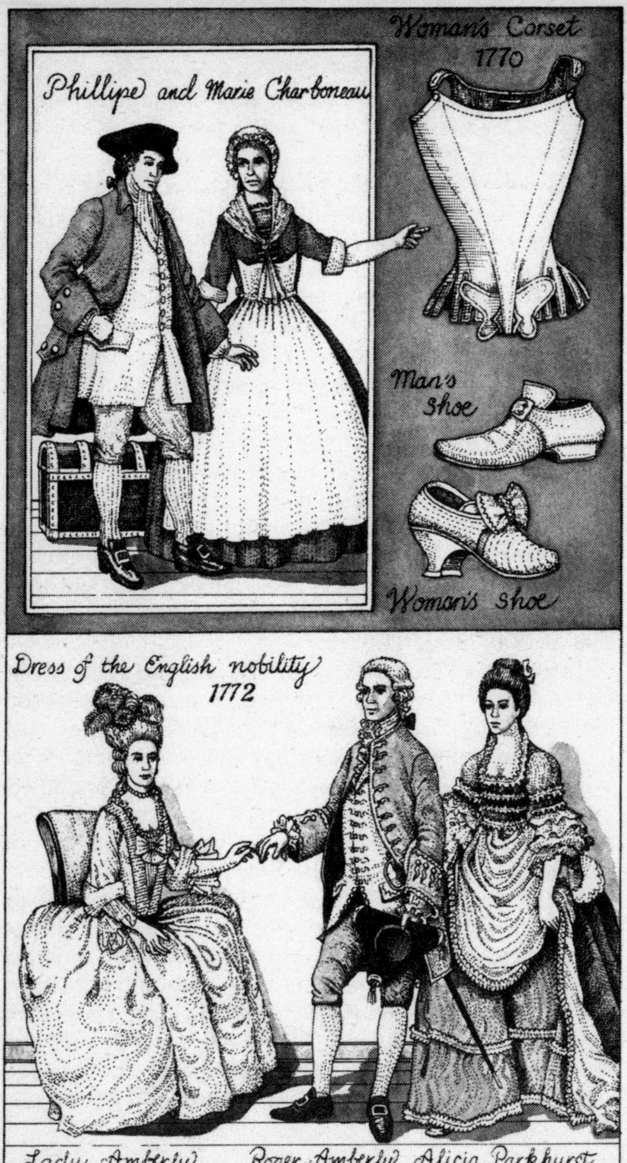

Woman's Corset
1770
Phillipe and Marie Charboneau
Man's shoe
Woman's shoe
Dress of the English nobility
1772
Lady Amberly
Roger Amberly
Alicia Parkhurst
Ron Toelke 79

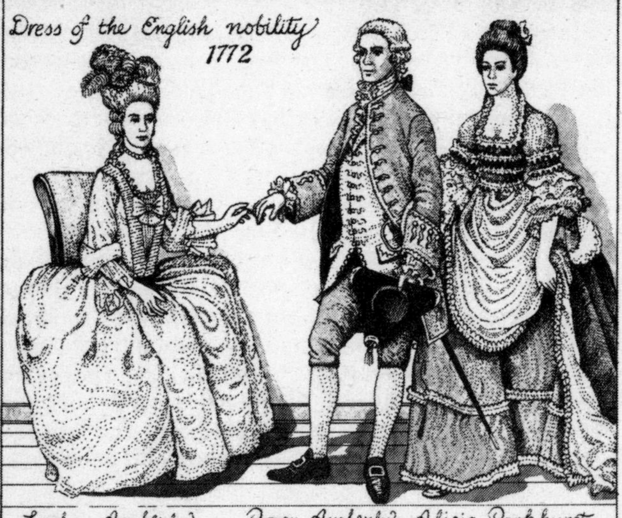

England was an ancient sloop that was scarcely ship enough to withstand the rough seas of the treacherous English Channel, or *La Manche*, "the sleeve," as the French called it.

Passengers—rare at most times—shared space with the cargo carried by these rat-infested tubs that were a challenge to even the most stalwart sailor. Phillipe's youth and vitality saw him across the twenty-mile stretch of water, but Marie suffered greatly during the crossing.

Upon disembarking, the travelers put up at an inn whose incredibly low rates would today tell us something about the quality of its accommodations. Romantic accounts have given us pictures of snug chimney corners with blazing fires reflecting on shining paneled walls; rosy wenches carrying tankards of ale; serving men with vast joints of beef and whole saddles of mutton. Not so. Inns were as a rule drafty and appallingly filthy. Sleeping arrangements were primitive; complete strangers often had to share vermin-infested beds. Service, such as it was, was surly. Food was usually poor stuff, crudely prepared. The ale was thin and bitter.

Inns were a kind of last resort. Sarah, the first Duchess of Marlborough, was so loath to patronize them that she had sizable dwellings built, each staffed with servants, at intervals of a day's journey so that when she went to visit a favorite granddaughter, she could always sleep under her own roof and avoid the horrors of a public inn. The granddaughter in question lived a week's journey from Blenheim in Oxfordshire, the Marlborough seat.

Had Marie and Phillipe had a long journey to Kentland, they would have gone by diligence, a public stagecoach, on roads that were, although vastly superior to those of the first decades of the century, still rough and forbidding and beleaguered by highwaymen. These men were not the handsome swashbucklers of romantic poetry, but the desperate cutthroats of fact, who were the terrorists of their day. Diligences moved at a good pace,

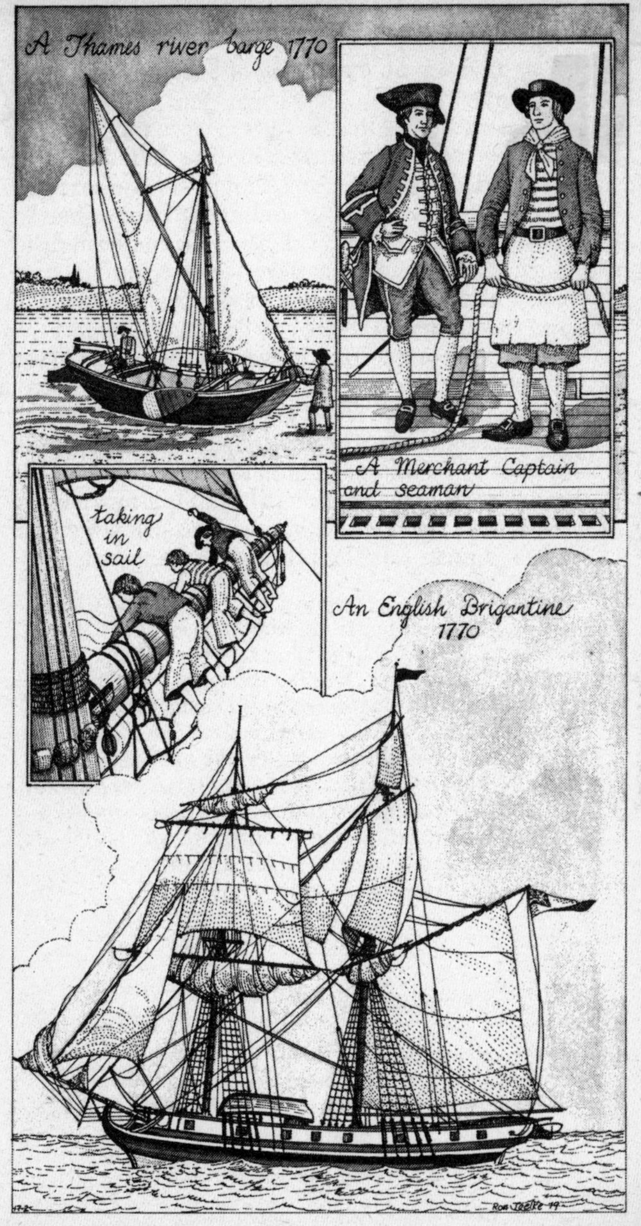
A Thames river barge 1770
A Merchant Captain and seaman
taking in sail
An English Brigantine 1770

about eight miles an hour, but at best provided an uncomfortable ride.

If the many barges that plied the rivers and canals of England had carried passengers, Phillipe and his mother would have ridden comfortably, though slowly. But there was no room for human cargo among the freight, usually grain—in particular barley, which was used extensively to make malt for ale and beer. Early in the century Daniel Defoe estimated that five-sixths of all the grain grown in England was barley.

Except in the West Country, where cider and perry, a liquor made from pears, were drunk, ale was the native drink of English men, women, and children at every meal. Only later in the century did spirits, tea, and coffee make strong inroads on ale consumption.

Benjamin Franklin records in his autobiography his observations of the drinking habits of his fellow workers at Watts's, a great London printing house.

> I drank only water; the other workmen, nearly fifty in number, were great guzzlers of beer. On occasion I carried up and down stairs a large form of types in each hand, when others carried but one in both hands. They wondered to see, from this and several instances, that the Water-American, as they called me, was stronger than themselves, who drank strong beer. We had an alehouse boy who attended always in the house to supply the workmen. My companion at the press drank every day a pint before breakfast, a pint at breakfast with his bread and cheese, a pint between breakfast and dinner, a pint at dinner, a pint in the afternoon about six o'clock. I thought it a detestable custom, but it was necessary, he supposed, to drink strong beer that he might be strong to labor.

If the eighteenth-century Englishman suffered from addiction to ale, it was nothing compared with his sufferings caused by gin. Gin was an urban more than a rural vice. It has been reckoned that toward the middle of the century, every fifth house in London sold gin. Phillipe and his mother unwittingly, when they first arrived in

An English Inn and yard, 1770
A canal aqueduct spanning a river ~ England, 1765
A highwayman holding up a public coach, 1770
Ron Toelke '79

London, wandered among gin-crazed derelicts and were only miraculously saved from being robbed and murdered by them. The misery caused by gin was well documented in accounts of the day.

Coffee had appeared in England during the reign of Charles II (1660–1685) and was drunk mainly in fashionable coffeehouses. It did not become the household brew that tea became. By 1760 tea drinking had become a national habit and a corrective to the consumption of spirits and beer. In 1784, thirteen million pounds of tea were consumed in the kingdom. It was the beverage of all classes. And it was drunk with sugar, which was now on every table. In Shakespeare's day, two hundred years earlier, sugar was a luxury in limited supply.

The eighteenth-century Englishman did not forgo the pleasures of the table. Travelers from abroad—no doubt Marie and Phillipe too, when they were in London with the Sholtos—were astounded by the quantity and quality of fish and red and white meat on the table. Vegetables were eaten in abundance, and were those we know today—potatoes, cabbage, carrots. But the pride of place on the English table was held by sweet dishes and puddings. An ordinary dinner might well consist of a leg of mutton as well as a brace of ducks. A very elegant dinner served at Christ Church, Oxford, in 1774 comprised a first course consisting of "part of a large cod, a chine of mutton, some soup, a chicken pie, pudding and roots, etc. Second course, pigeons and asparagus, a fillet of veal with mushrooms and high sauce with it, roasted sweetbreads, hot lobster, apricot tart, and in the middle a pyramid of syllabubs and jellies." A dessert of fruit followed, along with Madeira and red and white port wines.

The middle-class household was carnivorous, whereas the poorer among the cottagers were likely to taste meat only on the rare occasion when a rabbit fell into their snares. Many lived on bread and cheese, a diet occasionally relieved by vegetables, tea, and beer.

When Phillipe and Marie visited Kentland, the atmosphere, to say the least, was hardly conducive to a leisurely examination of that enormous establishment. We can assume, though, that they were aware that it was extensive, that the serving staff seemed limitless, and that the gardens were undergoing some kind of renovation.

Perhaps some imaginative conjecture about the history of Kentland would be in order. Like so many of the great houses of England, it was probably not of a piece. The oldest portion of the house might have been built by the original owner three hundred years before, during the reign of Henry VI. (And even that forebear had probably built on foundations of a Saxon keep which had been destroyed during the eleventh century by invading Normans.) As families prospered, houses were enlarged. During the Tudor period several oriels, or projecting bay windows, were added, along with elaborate new stables and a second courtyard, so that by the reign of Elizabeth, Kentland had lost all of its medieval primitiveness. A ha-ha, or moat, was dug during the reign of James I, and one seventeenth-century duke, no doubt, ordered fanciful topiary work. All but the ha-ha was gone by the time of Phillipe and Marie's ill-fated visit, for the present Duchess of Kentland had retained Capability Brown to transform the grounds into grassy slopes and broad vistas.

The serene vistas of Brown were in striking contrast to what the present duchess had done with the interior. Inside, her taste could well have leaned toward the Gothic, which was so admired at Strawberry Hill, the Twickenham estate of the gossipy, epicene Horace Walpole. Seventy years before, we can imagine, in the reign of Queen Anne, the public rooms of Kentland had been decorated in the prevailing classical style; the duchess of that time had brought Grinling Gibbons to the house to execute his marvels in woodwork, and the house was replete with paneled recesses in which blue and white jars stood on elegant stands. Some of the furniture was of mahogany, which was beginning to be imported from the West Indies. The present duke's mother would not have changed a thing, but her daughter-in-law had lavishly redecorated in the "new taste" with its dark, fussy massiveness and romantic unrestraint. The delicacy and symmetry of the early decades of the eighteenth century had been sacrificed to a fashion, it would seem, altogether appropriate to the dark machinations of the duchess's mind. Gloom and shadows had replaced light and grace.

No one was certain, but it was generally agreed that Kentland contained over two hundred rooms. Nobody had ever bothered to count them. Whatever the number, the place required an army of servants, ruled over by a tyrannical domestic hierarchy. The duchess dealt only with the housekeeper and the butler; they in turn managed cooks and maids, footmen and pages. A factor supervised gardeners and farmers, herdsmen and shepherds. Order was kept, service was efficient, and life was lived at its fullest at Kentland when the duke was well.

The outstanding feature of Kentland was its library. The present duke and his forebears were by virtue of their position literary men. The first duke, who had perhaps received his title from James I in return for generous loans, was a poet of modest accomplishment and a generous patron of poets, whose works, often dedicated to him, lined the shelves at Kentland. They were handsome, leather-bound volumes stamped with the Kentland arms. In addition there were English, Latin, and Italian classics. Illustrated quartos of travel and local history filled other shelves. But none of those added in the eighteenth century compared in excellence of printing and bookmaking with the tomes of the preceding century.

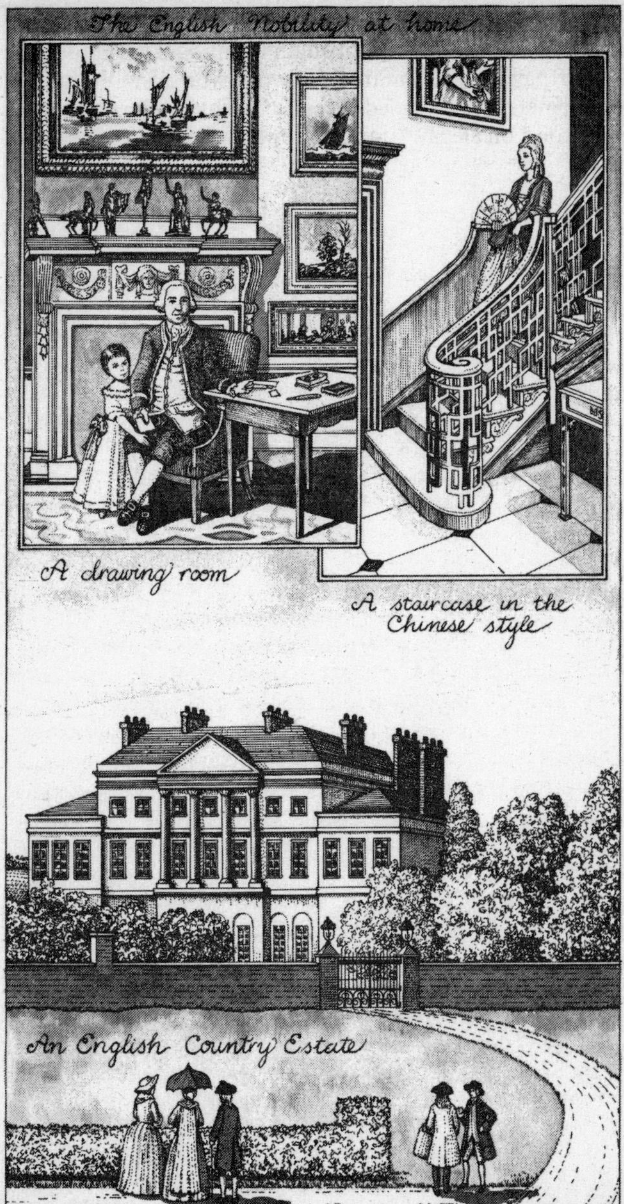

The English Nobility at home

A drawing room

A staircase in the Chinese style

An English Country Estate

Nor would any succeeding century produce more beautiful books.

There were other great houses in Kent, the county known as the Garden of England, and the people who inhabited them enjoyed life with a zest that will not be seen again. Hunting, endless meals, games, a passion for the classics and English and Italian poetry, good talk, gambling, infidelity—these were the activities of the upper classes.

Though lofty poetry of classical and modern times was the mainstay of erudite conversation at the tables of gentlefolk, there was an equally important—and more democratic—avenue of literary endeavor in the eighteenth century. The *novel*, although not an invention of the period, certainly reached its ascendancy at this time. It abounded in all forms, from enduring literature to the worst trash, and it was the staple of lending libraries such as the one Phillipe would find at the Sholtos' in London. Many of these novels were mediocre indeed: long romances in epistolary form, more or less bad imitations of Samuel Richardson's *Pamela*. The plot, such as it was, was usually built around the seduction, early in the action, of a pretty serving maid by a profligate aristocrat. They then spent the remainder of the action deliciously regretting their transgression in a welter of heavy-handed moralizing.

Of such stuff were the trashy novels of the eighteenth century, but it must not be forgotten that some of the greatest novels in English were also written then. Richardson, along with Tobias Smollett, Laurence Sterne, and Henry Fielding, made the novel that literary form which writers ever since have found particularly effective for showing disturbing social forces at work in society. *Tom Jones, Tristram Shandy, Humphry Clinker,* and *Clarissa*—all written in the eighteenth century—are among those titles that are the glories of the English novel.

The verses most widely read in England, and in America too, at this time were the works of three poets who died shortly before Phillipe and Marie arrived in America—Chatterton, Young, and Gray. There were, to be sure, many other poets read and quoted, but none so widely as these three.

At the age of fifteen, Thomas Chatterton had perpetrated a magnificent hoax on a nation that was becoming aware of its own antiquities. Chatterton claimed to have found ancient English verses in a chest in an old church, while in actuality they were compositions of his own fertile imagination. His forgeries were so convincing that even Samuel Johnson, who was known as the Great Cham of English literature, was convinced of their authenticity. When Chatterton was exposed two years later, chiefly through the efforts of Horace Walpole, his chagrin was so great that he committed suicide.

Edward Young's *Night Thoughts*, which is seldom read today, and Thomas Gray's *Elegy Written in a Country Churchyard*, a work still known and loved, were two long poetical works greatly admired by eighteenth-century readers. Young's poem is a lugubrious contemplation of death and the grave containing a few memorable lines, but with little else to recommend it to today's readers. Although the subject matter of Gray's work is similar to that of Young's, it is handled with an artistry and grace that assure it a prominent place for all time in English literature.

No view of eighteenth-century literature could be complete without mention of Dr. Samuel Johnson, who was lexicographer, poet, novelist, critic, and, above all, conversationalist. He was ardently Tory and held no brief for the rebellious colonies in America; he would not have allowed himself the company of the Sholtos and their Whig friends. Nor, indeed, did he often frequent county circles, Whig *or* Tory. A thoroughgoing man of the city, he unleashed his wit most often in London coffeehouses and homes. "When a man is tired of London," he said, "he

Fashionable London : Bloomsbury Square 1775
"Poor Jack" the street seller
The Chimney Sweep and his boy
A London Street 1770

is tired of life; for there is in London all that life can afford."

It was to this London that Marie and Phillipe fled, escaping the wrath of Roger Amberly and his mother. The city they saw upon their arrival was growing quickly—though more rapidly in bricks and mortar than in population, as people left the crowded lanes of the old city for the newer parts of the town. The disorder, corruption, and cruelty that had been common in London earlier in the century were beginning to be replaced by an increasing sensitivity to the brutalities of life. For this new awareness much credit must be given to John Wesley, a priest in the Church of England. He was fifteenth of the eighteen children born to the Reverend Samuel Wesley, rector of Epworth in Lincolnshire, and his wife Susannah. His social awareness and work among the poor brought him into disfavor with the Church, notable at the time for its worldliness and lack of social concern. Wesley eventually fomented a fundamental change in attitude that helped save England from the political upheaval that was to befall France. Methodism, as Wesley's doctrine was later called, appealed chiefly to the middle and lower classes. It engendered vehement religious enthusiasm. Its adherents recoiled with horror from the anti-Christian tenets that were associated with the revolution in France, and the English turned their backs on anarchy.

The established church at this period was not without its great and godly churchmen, but there was a certain secularism and cynicism that pervaded the institution. The Lords spiritual (the bishops) were as wordly as the Lords temporal (the peers of the realm). Bishops' palaces were often as lavish as noblemen's seats and were maintained along the same lines. By and large, most prelates had little social, political, or even spiritual influence. They and the great Tory families were mutually supportive and were content to maintain the status quo. When it was reported to George III that John Wesley was making too great a stir in the staid Church of England, the king's solution to the problem was the terse retort, "Make him a bishop!"

The lesser clergy were lesser models of their superiors. Many were younger sons who profited from rich benefices and the corrupt practice of holding multiple livings—that is, one man would receive the income from several churches simultaneously, while leaving the actual work of the parish in the hands of an ill-paid curate. Such rectors participated fully in the world of fashion. There was a whole group known as "the hunting parsons." Perhaps the most famous among them was the Reverend Jack Russell, who developed his own private breed of hunting dog. The Jack Russell terrier is well known in England to this day.

England, in short, was a worldly place. Though the inner light of Methodism shone, outward signs of grace were few. And nowhere was this more true than in London. When Marie and Phillipe arrived there from Kent, they were greeted with a host of appalling sights. Though perhaps a splendid place for the likes of Dr. Johnson, London was a miserable place to be poor. Deaths in the metropolis exceeded births. Poverty, overcrowding, filth, drunkenness (encouraged by the grain interest), violence, neglect, child abuse—all contributed to the sorry state of many of England's subjects.

The eighteenth century was an era of building, but many of the new houses appearing in London streets at this time were destined to collapse, frequently because of defective bricks. The demand for bricks had increased the price of clay so greatly that bricklayers adulterated their product with the debris of the streets. Much of the property in London belonged to the Church or other corporations. Those with only a life interest in estates were concerned merely with immediate profits and cared little about their tenants' well-being or the permanence of their properties.

It was possible for a house to be occupied by people of varying degrees of prosperity and even of different classes. The very poor—street vendors and charwomen—lived in the cellar or in the garret. (Among working-class people it was fairly common for an entire family to live in a single room.) Changing bed linen three times a year was considered by many excessive. Blankets were never washed; they were used until they fell apart. From three to eight people often slept in one bed. Whether one lived in a cellar or a garret, no change of air was possible.

The accommodations in the middle part of the house, although uncomfortable, were superior to attic or cellar rooms by virtue of being drier, lighter, and airier.

The eighteenth century was an age of careful social distinctions. Lines, as Phillipe learned less painfully than others (because of the kindness of the Sholtos), were drawn between the artisan and the laborer, the master and the journeyman; and nowhere were distinctions so carefully drawn as they were in the matter of wages. A laborer usually made about ten shillings a week; journeymen earned upwards of fifteen shillings. Phillipe's good fortune had led him to the printing trade, and printers were among the better-paid London journeymen. They frequently made a guinea a week—more than twice the wage of a laborer.

Although such wages seem pitifully low by today's standards, purchasing power of money then was very different too. In the 1770s the coarser cuts of beef cost three and one-half pence a pound; lump sugar cost seven pence a pound. A breakfast of bread, cheese, and beer was twopence.

Working hours were long, usually from seven in the morning to eight at night, with an hour off for dinner. In busy seasons shops would remain open until ten or ten-thirty.

But of all the shocking conditions that existed in the back rooms to the shops that Phillipe and Marie passed, the worst were those endured by parish children—abandoned, illegitimate orphans thrown on the not so tender mercies of the parish. At as early an age as possible these children were apprenticed for a long period of time—some males until they were twenty-four, some females until they were twenty-one or married. Many of the apprenticeships were little more than legal sanctions for child enslavement. Parish apprentices had few opportunities to enter any but the least skilled and worst-paid branches of trade.

The relationship between the master and the parish apprentice was, at best, unsatisfactory. The apprentice fee of five pounds paid by the parish to the poorer sort of master was a temptation to the needy to take apprentices whom they could not provide for. Having secured the fee, the master often found it desirable to rid himself of the child. He might achieve this by mistreating his apprentice so that he would run away, or by tempting him into the kind of misconduct that would justify the cancelation of the indentures without having to return any of the fee. Sometimes he would arrange to have the unwanted apprentice kidnapped and sent to an American plantation. More than one youthful apprentice died from starvation and beatings.

Parish children were often apprenticed to trades so poor and disagreeable that no one else would be apprenticed to them. (It was not unusual to hire them out to rogues to beg or pander.) No children were more forlorn than the little climbing boys, or chimney sweeps.

Boys as young as seven were forced up chimneys at the risk of being burned or suffocated. Always black and in rags, they were social outcasts, considered no better than beggars or thieves. They were molded by their masters and were sometimes even encouraged to steal. Finally in 1773 there was an investigation into the plight of these climbing boys, but it was not until 1816 that any legislation was enacted to protect them.

But all was not abuse and misery. There were pleasures—reputable and disreputable—to be had for all classes. One of them, for the rich, was to see and be seen.

In the seventies, fashions had become extremely lavish, and men as well as women were very clothes-conscious.

London in the eighteenth century was, as it is today, a city of parks. Each offered a particular attraction—Hyde Park with its riding ring, Kew with its gardens, St. James's with its walks where the fashionable might be seen.

The most celebrated place of amusement was Vauxhall Gardens. To this celebrated pleasure spot the Sholtos and the Charboneaus went to celebrate Emma's fiftieth birthday. Vauxhall was open only during the spring and summer months, but was considered one of the finer sights of London. In the center of the gardens, which were laid out formally, a large orchestra played. Surrounding the orchestra were Chinese kiosks furnished with chairs and tables. Here parties supped and listened to music. The Sholtos knew that food was not inexpensive at Vauxhall, so they frugally brought their own repast.

Among the pleasure gardens, Vauxhall was unique in that all classes mingled there. Anyone who could pay the shilling entrance fee was admitted, from the aristocrat to the apprentice out for an evening's fun. The atmosphere was occasionally a bit rowdy and at times boisterous. Any young woman who walked alone or without an escort of the opposite sex was sure to encounter trouble. With drink flowing freely and women for the asking, fights and brawls occurred frequently.

London was a city of crime. In the haphazard arrangement of lanes and alleys that lay behind the main thoroughfares, the dregs of the population holed up, coming out at night like beasts of prey to steal, pilfer, and terrorize. Youthful gangs with fanciful names, such as the Mohawks and the Black Boy Alley Gang, terrorized the streets. These boys—often of noble birth—amused themselves by rolling old ladies in barrels downhill or by beating up decrepit watchmen. Less dangerous, but in greater evidence, were shoplifters and pickpockets, some of whom were very young. There are records of "infant thieves," usually children taught to beg and steal in order to provide money to furnish their mentor with gin.

Closely involved in the world of crime was prostitution. The procuress and the pimp were well-known figures in the underworld, often operating for affluent patrons under cover of the *bagnio*, the eighteenth-century version of a Turkish bath. Each was ruled over by a madam whose title was *mother*. Brothels of the more fashionable sort were found near St. James's; less exalted establishments were to be found everywhere in the city.

Phillipe was no doubt often solicited on the streets of London. The number of streetwalkers was said to be near fifty thousand. They took their customers into low taverns, where rooms were reserved for them. Most of the streetwalkers were poor men's daughters, and most were between the ages of twelve and sixteen.

Marie did not live to see the America that so ineluctably drew Phillipe away from Europe and his mother's vain hope that he would find his rightful place in the aristocratic society of England. She died on the dreadful passage to America, a voyage of some six or seven weeks aboard the American schooner *Eclipse*, and she was buried at sea. The captain, Will Caleb, a good man, kindly suggested that Phillipe change his name in order to put the past behind him and to greet the New World. So it was that he became Philip Kent.

The Boston that Philip found, that July morning of 1772, was one of the busiest ports in America, though it was then only the third-largest city in British America, after Philadelphia and New York. The town was laid out on a hilly peninsula, connected to the mainland only by a soggy natural causeway (which later became known as the Neck). The Neck provided the only land approach to Boston; none of the filling and leveling that was to be accomplished later, during the nineteenth century, was to be seen. The town itself retained few of its original seventeenth-century frame buildings, most of which had

Sam Adams of Boston
1775
British soldiers
on Boston Common, 1774
Faneuil Hall on
Dock Square
King Street, Boston, 1775~
the State House is at center.
Ron Toelke 79

been destroyed by fire. Brick structures had replaced them; many of these still stand today and serve their original functions.

Philip arrived by boat, as did most travelers, and had to walk a goodly distance past numerous wharves and docks before reaching the actual shoreline and streets. The streets had been named some years before, and there were excellent maps of the city. Philip, however, could not afford one. He learned the lay of the land by wandering through the city looking for work. Although the narrow streets might have appeared little better planned than cow paths, they had in fact been laid out in the accepted English pattern. All led to central squares where business and government were transacted.

Many notable features of present-day Boston were there in Philip's day. Two were especially significant—the Common and Faneuil Hall. The Common, a forty-five-acre tract, was more than a delightful public park in the eighteenth century. It provided pasture for cattle and a training ground for the Massachusetts militia. Faneuil Hall, a building later enlarged by the famous Boston architect Charles Bulfinch, provided market space on its ground floor and assembly rooms in its upper stories, functions it provides to this day.

It was in Faneuil Hall that Samuel Adams harangued the Sons of Liberty to action. They were actually a motley crew of artisans and common laborers whose frequent acts of vandalism the passing years have sanctioned as patriotic. There is, for example, little to justify their wanton destruction of Governor Hutchinson's papers some ten years before their heroic defiance of the Crown at the Boston Tea Party.

The hue and cry raised by the "Indians" of the Tea Party was in fact a cry for a brave new world, a whole new realm of social and political conditions. Or so it was for the more radical of those Bostonians at the harbor. For more conservative souls, the issue was still freedom within the context that had always existed: a loyal but

KENT & SON
TEA
PRINTERS
Philip Kent Efq., Proprietor,
North Side of the TOWN-HOUSE
and Oppofite the Town-Pump, in
Corn-hill, BOSTON.
18th century printing
leather inking pad
Inking the press
lead type
Benjamin Franklin, printer
Ron Toelke 79

independent colony of free Englishmen wisely left by their sovereign to manage their own affairs three thousand miles from the mother country.

The Boston that Philip found, then, was a mixture of old and new, conservative and radical. Most institutions, whether legal, ecclesiastical, social, or moral, were patterned after those of the mother country. A few were very old, for a new country; both the Boston Latin School and Harvard College were nearing their sesquicentennial (150th anniversary). The ties of Boston to England were strong, though not so strong as those of Southern planters. The well-to-do of Boston and the South tended to imitate slavishly English behavior.

But ties to England were growing tenuous, and within months of his arrival, Philip was to see many English institutions become distinctively independent and American. He was to know before long that America was unique.

The Rebels

A CONDENSATION OF

The Rebels

1775-1781

BOOK 1

The temperature that blazing afternoon was well above one hundred degrees. Philip Kent, jammed in a redoubt with several hundred soldiers on Breed's Hill in Charlestown, had a vision of his death.

Philip Kent, born near the village of Chavaniac, France, 1753. Died Saturday, the seventeenth of June, in the year 1775—

No! he thought, anguished. Somehow he would come through, somehow he would live for his wife Anne and for their child soon to be born.

He hadn't slept all night. He was exhausted, starved. That the colonies he had adopted as his homeland would dare to challenge the armed might of the greatest empire the world had known since Rome was madness.

After that day in April when he had been reunited with Anne, Philip Kent had experienced an almost euphoric joy that lasted several weeks. The British had run back to Boston. And an American army—ragtag, poorly organized—had encircled the city.

But today, wave upon wave of British soldiers swept up the hill, capturing the redoubt. At day's end came the cry "Retreat!" The colonists fled, Philip with them.

Philip was physically exhausted, not from work, but from boredom and constant worry about Anne. She was near her term and had not been well. Philip got to see her once or twice a week if he was lucky.

Finally, at a quarter past twelve on September 29, 1775, in Watertown, Massachusetts, she was safely delivered of a son, who was named Abraham for Anne's father.

Judson Fletcher was a tall, elegantly handsome young man with a long, sharp nose and just a slight softness at the edges of his mouth. As he rode the lanes of Caroline County, Virginia, he thought about his boyhood friend, George Clark, who was two years younger than Judson. George had discovered that Fletcher was something besides a typical tobacco planter's son. In fact, Judson loathed his father's plantation, Sermon Hill. He much preferred studying with George the geography of the heavens, and where the heron hid for protection, and how to identify objects and details of terrain at twenty miles.

They had traveled to fairs in Richmond, where they had spoken with men who had tramped the wild country west of the Blue Ridge Mountains—the Blue Wall, Virginians called it.

In 1772 George Clark had wandered out that way. He had a courage Judson lacked. Also, George was not in love with a woman he couldn't possibly win.

She had been Peggy Ashford, respectable, while he had been—still was—Judson Fletcher, something less. She was all grace and gentility, a perfect lady, whom he had loved since he was seventeen. He had courted her—all with the growing disapproval of the Ashfords, for Judson's nature asserted itself in frequent public drunkenness and brawling. Finally the Ashfords had forced Peggy to stop seeing him. It was heartbreaking for her, but she was a dutiful daughter. Then Seth McLean had stepped in. And ever since Judson had behaved like a gentleman; he kept his distance. To him Peggy Ashford McLean was something of a saint.

Sermon Hill was five thousand acres of prime tobacco land worked by five hundred male and female slaves. The whole agricultural economy in which Judson had grown up was based on the grueling physical labor of these slaves. The institution of slavery had grown so entrenched—producing fear and repression on one side, submission and hatred on the other—that an eventual confrontation was, Judson saw, inevitable. He wished he were out beyond the Blue Wall with George Clark. No laws, no incipient rebellions, no Peggy to haunt him.

The owner of Sermon Hill, Judson's father, Angus, was a tiny-boned man of sixty with a pointed chin. Despite his age, his slight frame suggested great strength. Judson could never remember a time when there had been tenderness between himself and this man. His father had always treated him sternly—demanding more than a boy could give. (Of his mother, Judson could remember next to nothing. She had died when he was four.) Judson had resigned in defeat by the time he was ten. He could never be as strong or as pious as Angus expected him to be.

Furthermore, being the second son, he could not inherit and hence was less important than Donald, who was ten years his senior.

At thirty-five, Donald was a gout-ridden member of the Burgesses chosen to represent Virginia at the Congress in Philadelphia.

Judson hated his father. He took pleasure in tormenting the old man. After one particularly acrimonious encounter, his father yelled, "Something in yourself has ruined you, Judson. Better to shoot any child you'd father than let him live his life with your devil's blood poisoning him."

Devil's blood. Try as he might he couldn't scoff away the uneasy suspicion that Angus had struck a vein of truth. The only way to blunt the fear was with drink.

Donald Fletcher, a steady-minded but phlegmatic man, returned to Sermon Hill for a brief holiday. In Judson's opinion, Donald didn't look well. He had gained weight, and his normally soft face was puffier than usual. Donald had married late, at thirty. His wife died in childbirth thirteen months later, and the child died with her. After that Donald's only pleasure seemed to lie in his involvement in the political affairs of the colony.

"Jud," Donald said one day, "this siege between you and Father will only come to a bad end. You need to leave Sermon Hill for a while."

"To go where?"

"I must return to Philadelphia. I lay abed three weeks during the last session. I'd like to go north confident that if my strength fails, someone trustworthy could be appointed to fill my seat."

"You mean I'd be your replacement? I'm flattered you'd even consider me, Donald, but I doubt very much that members of your delegation would welcome someone like me. Can you just wave your hand and appoint me to attend in your place?"

"Naturally not. You'd have to be duly elected to the delegation."

In the second week of September Donald Fletcher, heartened by a letter from his friend Thomas Jefferson, returned to Philadelphia.

Judson remained at home. He was dining with his father one night in November when their overseer, Reuven Shaw, interrupted their meal with news that one of the curing barns was afire.

"Afire?"

"Yes, sir. The niggers been jumpy as hell."

Angus leaped up. "The niggers set it?"

"Who else, Mr. Fletcher? Half the bucks ain't in their cabins."

The renegade slaves were loose, not just at Sermon Hill, but out in the countryside.

That made Judson run like a man demented to the

stable, where he flung a saddle on his roan. He rode fast towards Seth McLean's house, and as he reached the front drive, he saw that it was not the barns burning, but the slave cabins. The front door of the great house stood open. On the floor lay Seth McLean, hacked to pieces by a field knife. Judson raced upstairs and found Peggy lying on the floor. A young black bent over her, his trousers around his ankles. Desperately the slave lunged at Judson; but his trousers hampered him, and he stumbled. Judson caught the sweaty chin. The young slave saw what was coming. As his mouth opened, Judson shoved the muzzle of his horse pistol between the man's teeth. . . .

In December Donald wrote that the gout and pleurisy were afflicting him, and that he would be returning home. As Judson left for Philadelphia to serve as Donald's alternate in the Congress, Philip Kent was laboring eastward through snow and ice. He was returning to General Washington's Massachusetts headquarters with fifty-eight pieces of heavy artillery which had been captured from the British.

"Anne? Annie, I'm back!"

Yelling at the top of his voice, Philip Kent climbed the stairs of the house in Watertown. He stopped, paralyzed by what he saw hanging on the door—a wreath of black crepe. Fear for Anne and little Abraham flashed through his mind. When the door opened, he almost wept at the sight of Anne's fatigued face.

"The baby's well," Anne said quietly. "He's sleeping now."

"Then it's your father. Oh, Annie—"

Abraham Ware had died peacefully in his sleep two weeks earlier. Anne described her father's final illness, his burial, her anxiety when no word came from Philip.

"There is one happy circumstance in all this grief," Anne added, "Papa left what money he had to both of us. He said we should use it to start your printing business one day. He thought well of you, Philip; he really did. He wanted you to know."

At his table near the fire, Judson Fletcher was sweating out the dark brown ale he had swilled. Certainly it was a select group from the Congress gathered at the City Tavern this rainy evening in late January, 1776. Around him were politicians whose names were known in every one of the colonies—Benjamin Franklin, John Adams, Thomas Paine, the Lee brothers, Thomas Jefferson.

But Judson was anxious to get away from this augustly populated room and return to his rented quarters. He hoped Alice wouldn't choose to spend the night with him. She was a damned attractive wench, of course, a welcome diversion despite certain puzzling quirks of personality and a past that was a total mystery. But he didn't want Alice tonight. He wanted no companion save Mr. Paine's *Common Sense*.

Judson had undergone subtle changes in attitude since arriving in Philadelphia. There had been a period of confusion—a couple of weeks of familiarizing himself with the routine of the Congress, of sitting in his first committee meetings—but confusion and all, those first two weeks had brought Judson a great sense of pleasure. He relished association with important men.

Judson climbed the stairs to his musty parlor and opened Paine's pamphlet. He read the whole book in an hour, relishing its polemical savagery. So rapt was his attention that Judson didn't hear the light footfalls on the stairs or the soft clicking of the latch. In a moment Alice entered. Throwing back the cowl of her cheap cloak, she was as lovely as ever. And as drunk.

She was a peculiar girl, a strange admixture of feigned refinement and gutter frankness. At times she moved with the grace of the finely dressed ladies of Chestnut Street. But unlike those ladies, she had a direct, unconcealed interest in matters sexual. She knew how to stir Judson.

She drank too much, much more even than he did. On

occasion she used foul language, but it sounded awkward. She was ruining herself physically and mentally, and she couldn't be more than twenty-three or -four.

In the Congress the radicals continued to press their case. Finally North Carolina empowered its delegates to support a declaration for independence. And at a meeting of the Virginia House of Burgesses in May, that colony followed suit. Judson felt a deep sense of pride that it was Virginia that had provided the means for Congress to act. Thomas Jefferson, known for his ability to write, was chosen to prepare the necessary statement to submit to the Congress.

Judson hoped Alice would visit this evening. He was anxious to tell her what had happened, even though he knew she wouldn't be very interested.

In the deep shadow on the corner opposite his lodging-house, Judson paused. Across the street he saw a very tall man leaning against a brick wall.

Alice seemed in a playful mood. Judson drank, and she drank. Then they tumbled into bed.

Somehow their lovemaking had an unusual effect on him. Ordinarily he went right to sleep afterward. Tonight he was tense, but not unpleasantly so.

Musing, he was a fraction late in hearing the stealthy footsteps on the landing. The door crashed in, the fragile latch booted to pieces by the hulking figure Judson had seen earlier.

"Stand fast. I have a pistol!" said the intruder. "Get up and go to the inside wall. Any delay, and it will be my distinct pleasure to kill you. If you remain quiet, you'll come to no harm." The tall man called toward the door, "She's here, sir; it's safe to come in."

A portly, elegantly dressed man of middle age entered. He gazed at Alice. "My God, smell the wine on her. Sir, if you've debauched her—"

"Debauched her! She's a tavern whore!"

The portly man bent over the bedside. "Alicia, it's Uncle Tobias come to take you home."

"Alicia?" Judson repeated. "Her name's Alice."

All at once Alice sat upright. Her voice was a mixture of terror and fury. "What are you doing here, Tobias? Get away—get out!"

"What am I doing here? I'm taking you back to Arch Street."

"I'm where I want to be! Leave me alone!"

"I want an explanation," Judson said to Trumbull. "You claim to be her relative—"

"My wife is her aunt. She is Mrs. Alicia Amberly, widow of an officer in His Majesty's service and daughter of the Earl of Parkhurst."

Facing Alice, he said, "You will come home for care."

She spat in his face.

Trumbull turned pleading eyes to Judson. "In God's name, sir, help me!"

Judson shook his head.

"I am here by choice!" Alice screamed.

Judson gestured toward the door. "I think you'd better leave. At once!"

"You'll do nothing?" Tobias Trumbull said, livid.

"Nothing."

"I—" Trumbull swallowed. "I do have one recourse. I can demand satisfaction."

Judson eyed the overweight man. "You're not up to a duel."

"Then you'll deny me satisfaction?" Trumbull asked. "You're a coward, is that it?"

Stung by the insult, Judson shouted, "Goddamn it! If that's what you want, send your second."

Judson crawled into bed. When he awoke after sunup, Alice was gone. Every trace of clothing, every indication that she had been in the room, had disappeared.

Concern for Alice had lessened Judson's interest in the Congress. He spent a large part of his time searching the city for her. The days dragged, and there was no communication from the Trumbull household. Then one of Judson's fellow Virginians took him aside and told him that Trumbull's challenge had become a choice item of gossip. It was hoped some settlement less scandalous than a duel could be worked out. Judson promised to do what he could.

He wrote Trumbull, offering to reconsider his challenge, but the proud Tory only demanded satisfaction more strongly than ever. Alicia could not be found anywhere. The Trumbulls feared for her safety and blamed him. Judson knew that if he went ahead with the duel, he would be asked to withdraw from the Virginia delegation.

At first light on July 3, 1776, Judson Fletcher faced Tobias Trumbull in a grove beside the Delaware River.

The Tory wheezed, "I ask you one more time, sir, where is Alicia?"

"I haven't seen her, and I don't know."

"Liar! Damned liar!"

Pistols held muzzle up, the two men took their positions.

Trumbull's pistol discharged; Judson heard the ball whiz past a good yard from his chest. Judson's ball caught Trumbull in the side of his temple.

Despite the fairness of the duel, Judson had no delusions about the stories that would be circulated. Philadelphia would be hot for him now.

Weary, he unlatched the door to his quarters on Windmill Street. There before him was Alice, all filth and rags. "Is my aunt's husband . . .?"

"Dead. I gave him a fair chance." As he reached her, she uttered one short wail and dashed past him. He ran after her, shouting her name; but she eluded him in the morning mist.

He searched in vain for the remainder of the day. The next morning he read in a newspaper that Alice's body had been found floating near a pier, apparently a suicide.

Judson sat alone in his rooms drinking, wondering if he himself wanted to survive amidst the wreckage he had created, but he lacked the strength to expunge his guilt by doing away with himself. Outside, bell boys passed frequently, shouting that the text of the independency declaration had finally been approved by the Congress. It was Thursday, the fourth of July, 1776.

Despite the horrors of the past days, Judson couldn't help feeling a shiver of pride at the thought of what had been done in Philadelphia.

By early afternoon on the eighth Judson was riding south along the Delaware, bound for Virginia.

BOOK 2

Home on leave in February, 1777, Philip Kent stood with his wife at their front gate, bidding farewell to visitors. He noticed a curtain stirring at a downstairs window of the clapboard house next door.

"Old busybody's watching us again."

Anne laughed. "Mrs. Brumple is a dear lady, Philip. Eccentric, but dear. She's been very kind and helpful."

"Well," said Philip, "do you think she would care for Abraham for the day if we went to Boston tomorrow? I want to look up Ben Edes." Ben Edes was the printer for whom Philip had worked before he joined the army.

The young couple found Ben Edes busily working his handpress, publishing the *Gazette*. Perusing a copy, Philip's attention was drawn to an advertisement for sailing crews placed by a Captain Caleb, the kindly master of the *Eclipse*, the ship that had brought Philip from England.

"He's going into privateering in a big way. He's got two

ships armed already. He's trying to raise money to build two more," Ben Edes explained. "Depending on his luck at sea, he and the people who buy in stand to lose a lot—or get rich."

"Philip," Anne said, "I think we might go along and look up your old friend."

"Whatever for?"

"To see whether we might put a bit of Papa's money to work for us."

In his office, Will Caleb made a deal with Anne and Philip, who invested one hundred pounds in each of his two new ships. As they were leaving, they met a tall, swarthy man whose arrogant expression repelled Philip.

"Excuse me, Will. Didn't realize you had visitors."

"Investors, Malachi," Caleb said. "Mr. and Mrs. Kent—my associate, Captain Rackham."

"Pleasure," said Rackham, bowing. Philip noticed how the man's eyes worked their way from Anne's face to the outline of her breasts.

As they walked down the stairs, Philip said, "Anne, I disliked that Rackham fellow on sight. A low, scurvy sort."

"I agree. I didn't care for the looks he gave me."

By now Judson was thoroughly tired of Lottie Shaw, but he had had no other place to live when he rode home from Philadelphia the preceding summer. Lottie had set herself up in business, granting favors to any planter's son with a few shillings in his pocket. Judson had gone to see her, and they had reached an agreement, one helped along by Donald's sense of responsibility. Judson's brother had made a bargain with him: "Don't flaunt yourself all over the county, and I'll return from time to time." He had fished in his coat and pulled out a small purse.

On one of his visits, Donald brought Judson word that Peggy McLean had returned home, her health and composure having been reasonably well restored. She had heard about the depths to which Judson had sunk and had written Donald to ask if there was anything anyone could do to help.

"Maybe I'll answer in person. I haven't seen Peggy since Seth was killed."

Reasonably presentable, Judson rode up the lane to the McLean plantation the following Tuesday.

Peggy wore white silk. She was still slim, elegant, heartbreakingly lovely. Without knowing how it happened, he touched her. He was drowning in the scent from her skin. Against all prudence and judgment he leaned down to kiss her neck. The rest would never have happened if some impulse hadn't caused her to weaken just one instant. Swiftly she reached down with her right hand to grasp his and pull it around her. Clumsily he pulled her into an embrace, taking her prisoner, his arms around her waist. Suddenly she clasped her arms around his neck. He picked her up and bore her to the lounge.

Pacing his cabin all that long night, Judson seethed with shame. He had virtually raped her. In the dawn he penned Peggy a single sentence: "I abjectly beg your forgiveness."

A few days later, a black rode over with an answer to Judson's note:

> All shame and responsibility must be shared equally. I deem it wisest and safest that we do not ever see one another again. P.

On a stifling day in August, 1777, Philip stood in the ranks on a parade ground near Philadelphia. He had trouble seeing the brightly uniformed officers cantering toward the Massachusetts companies. Of course Washington was immediately recognizable, but the two men beside him were unrecognizable blurs until they drew up.

Philip gasped at the sight of a long-forgotten face—youthful, aristocratic, a face he'd first seen near his mother's inn when he had come upon a thirteen-year-old boy struggling with two assailants. The boy had been born to the French nobility, destined for a military career: the Marquis de Lafayette, who recognized Philip immediately. And thus was resumed a friendship begun many years before in the Auvergne.

Judson Fletcher rode like a man pursued. "What if I'm too late? What if he's gone?" The day before, Donald had dropped a casual remark that had sent Judson speeding south: "Your friend George Clark has been at Williamsburg for a fortnight."

At that moment Judson felt as if a door had opened—perhaps the last one remaining for him.

Now in the October dawn he pounded into Williamsburg and walked through the tavern entrance, where he met George Clark head-on.

"Judson . . . ?"

"Hello, George. Donald told me you were here. I rode most of the night. I've thought a good deal about what you used to write in your letters about the open country in the West. I'd like to be one of your men. I want to go to Kentucky."

"I don't think you quite know what you're asking."

"I can do it. I know I can."

"I need steady hands, sharp eyes."

Finally it was settled that Judson would join George Clark, but with one stipulation—he must give up all liquor. He was to be back in Williamsburg in exactly three weeks. "If you're not here," George warned, "I won't wait."

The next morning at dawn he set out for home. The golden radiance of the October sunrise filled him with a mystical feeling. He wished he could tell Peggy where he was going—and with whom. It might make her think a little better of him. But the idea was academic. According to Donald, Peggy hadn't been home for the past four weeks.

Ahead he saw the familiar curve of the road near home.

He let the horse find its own way to his dooryard, where he pulled up short. A lantern glowed inside the cabin, and he heard a woman's voice—Lottie. But she was supposed to be in Richmond. They had quarreled, and he had ordered her out.

Judson dismounted. Lottie's voice had gone silent all at once. Why was she back?

The door opened. He saw her right enough. She was standing beside someone else—a man who blocked Judson's entrance. "Mr. Carter and me, we're livin' here now," Lottie said. "You'd better not make any fuss about it."

"Don't intend to, Lottie. I'm going to mount up and leave you and your business associate."

Suddenly Judson saw how badly he'd miscalculated the extent of her feelings. Lottie's hands were clamped on a horse pistol. The hammer fell. Judson ducked, but not quickly enough. The ball slammed his left side, knocking him from the saddle. He floundered in the dirt. He heard his horse clatter away down the road. The dirt of the dooryard rushed up toward his blurring eyes, bringing the ruinous dark.

All through the horrors of the winter of 1777–78 at Valley Forge not one letter arrived from Anne. "Annie, for God's sake write me. Else I can't go on here. I just can't go on," Philip thought. During the cold and hunger, he had dizzying visions of Anne and little Abraham sitting by a cheery fire in Cambridge. At least they were safe and warm; at least they would survive. Finally, in April, a letter written by Anne the preceding November reached him. In the midst of endearments and news of their son Anne reported that Malachi Rackham had written her "another distressingly impertinent letter, which Mrs. Brumple, who is now moved in, considered alarming in its tone of familiarity."

In Cambridge, a few evenings later, as April rain pelted

the village, Mrs. Brumple collected her cloak to pit her Christian courage against the elements and attend her prayer circle, where reading scripture was combined with sewing shirts for General Washington's forces.

"You're certain you don't mind my leaving you this evening, Mrs. Kent?"

Anne smiled. "You're the one who's going to get soaked, not I."

Anne kindled a small fire in the parlor and then sat down to her mending. A loud knocking startled her. Who could be calling at this hour?

More knocking. Louder.

"I say, Mrs. Kent, are you at home?"

"Oh, my God," she breathed, recognizing the voice.

"Pardon me for just walking in, but I thought it possible you didn't hear the knock," said Captain Malachi Rackham.

"Captain Rackham, it should be evident many times over that you are not welcome here."

"We have private matters to discuss. *Gull* anchored in Boston Harbor last Sunday. We took a mighty handsome prize off the Carolinas. The total proceeds came to about half a million pounds."

The sum stunned her, leaving her confused and uncertain about how to proceed. If he wasn't lying to her, the prospects were dizzying, and she ought to know the whole story.

"Fetch me rum, and I'll be happy to share the details."

"I'm sorry; I've nothing to give you."

"Ah, Mrs. Kent, that's where you are quite wrong." His smile left no doubt about his meaning.

"Get out," Anne said, livid. "At once!"

He grabbed her wrist, and Anne raked his face with her free hand. Rackham struck her, and she staggered crying out, "Madman!" Again Rackham struck her. She tumbled at his feet, stunned. He leaned down and jerked her head up by a fist of her hair. "I want to tell you about your property, your investment, Mrs. Kent." He yanked her head, and Anne screamed deliberately, hoping to attract attention outside.

"Be quiet!" Rackham shouted, smashing the side of her head with his fist. Anne fell, struck her temple on the floor, moaned, and then lay still.

Anne awoke to the sensation of motion and the sounds of water lapping against hull planks and an anchor chain being pulled up. She opened her eyes; she was lying in a ship's bunk. She shifted her throbbing head and saw Malachi Rackham.

"Wondered how long it'd take you to liven up. Been an hour since I brought you on board. Give us a kiss."

This time Anne Kent screamed the wild wail of hysteria. But Rackham only laughed as he climbed on top of her.

She awoke sometime near dawn. She had not been hurt so terribly in all her life. Anne felt almost destroyed by the repeated punishings Rackham had inflicted on her all night long. As she tried to climb from the bunk, the *Gull* rolled and she fell. It took her almost two minutes to pull herself to her feet. Through the oval stern windows she saw the steep-sided hills and valleys of the ocean—and no land anywhere.

She hammered on the door. Tugged, wrenched. It was bolted on the outside.

Then out of her pain emerged rage—rage and a determination not to surrender to despair while one breath was left. Rackham would return to the cabin eventually. But how could she get out of the cabin? Only by eluding him. Disabling him even. She began searching for a weapon.

Remembering something, she stared at the overhead lantern. Then, whimpering a little because the effort hurt so much, she knelt on a table and seized the lantern.

Soon after, she lay in her bunk, her body curled not

only to feign sleep but to hide her left hand which held a shard of lantern glass.

The bolt rattled.

"Having a spot of rest, my girl?" Rackham's hand closed on her left shoulder. Anne shot out her left hand and tore the sharp edge of the glass across his face once, twice.

Malachi screamed and slapped his hands over his face. The glass had pierced his left eyeball. Anne ducked as he flailed at her and dodged by him. She almost made it to the door. Then the deck tilted sharply, and she lurched backwards against Rackham. He grappled her around the waist, and they fell together against the window, which burst outward on impact. Both of them plunged toward the boiling white of the wake.

BOOK 3

A clock ticked in Judson's mind, hurrying him another mile and then another. It woke him every day, and he would be up and gone, ignoring the healed wound in his left side that still ached when the air was cold. George Clark had said he would depart from the fork in April or early May, 1778.

He was proud of having come this far alone, proud of surviving on sheer persistence, with not one drink of liquor since he had left the Tidewater. He had summoned up resources in himself long unused. There was deep satisfaction in finding them still present. Yet even that pride was fading as he plodded on foot, fearing, knowing he would be too late.

Lottie and Carter, the man who was living off her diminished earning power, had left Judson in the damp autumn leaves along a creek. Somehow he'd stumbled away from there, and was staggering along the road to Sermon Hill when a field hand spied him and summoned help. He was borne to his father, who sent for a physician and permitted his son to remain at the plantation in one of the slave cabins until he recovered—or died.

Judson awoke in the cabin to find Donald perched on a stool beside his pallet. "You'll kill yourself for certain if you flop around that way."

"I promised to meet George Clark in Williamsburg."

"You what? You've been lying here the best part of two weeks."

"When I am able to leave, I still intend to follow George."

"By yourself? That's insanity."

"Maybe, but I am going. I'll settle with that Shaw bitch first, though."

"You'll be spared. Father sent drivers searching for them with pistols and muskets."

"I'll be goddamned."

"Why should you be surprised? Blood outlasts everything—including hatred."

"But the old man thinks I've a bad strain running in me. Devil's blood, he calls it."

"He has the same kind."

On a bright morning in late March, Donald stood at the river road with his younger brother. "You're not the same person I used to know," he said.

"Of necessity," Judson replied. "I guess we drive out our demons the best way we can. I don't really know where I'm going. That's a splendid declaration of purpose, isn't it?"

"It's an honest one. I'll take care that Peggy McLean be told."

"Is she back home?"

"Yes, but she's been staying in; evidently in poor health again."

"What's wrong?"

"Her manager professes not to know, but he did let slip something about a trip she took up in New England."

Judson reached the rim of a gully ten feet deep. Weakened by heavy rains, it gave way under his left boot. He toppled over and struck the bottom, his left leg bending back under his right knee. His leg was lanced with an excruciating pain. Bracing his hands in the mud beneath him, he straightened his left leg. The fierce pain exploded again. Damn! He had twisted something badly.

He attempted a few steps, only to give up in agony. Every wasted moment spelled ever more certain failure to find George Clark at Pittsburgh. He'd crawl on. . . .

Philip's musket felt slippery in his hands as he squinted through the steaming air. It was June, and he was somewhere west of Monmouth Court House, New Jersey. His hands almost worked independently of his exhausted mind: he loaded, fired, dodged instinctively whenever he heard a ball hiss through the leaves. He was spent, so spent. All that kept him here were two faces—a woman's and a child's.

Warning shouts. Musket fire exploded behind him. Another musket blast obliterated the rest. Philip felt something thump his right calf, then searing pain. A moment later his dazed mind knew that something had pierced the top of his right boot, something large and hurting that was lodged in the flesh inside that boot. Then he saw the redness pouring through the place where the ball had penetrated the leather. "My God, I'm hit!" he thought with a curious, light-headed detachment.

Philip woke in the inferno of a medical tent. He tasted rum in his mouth. Bit the ball when ordered, as unseen pincers dug into the flesh of his calf just a few inches above his ankle.

"Got her out nice and clean. Hold steady now. We're going to cauterize it."

The heated metal touched his skin. He started to scream. Rough hands seized the injured leg, held it. His calf and foot, numbed by the searing iron, felt curiously thick. The surgeon's sticky face peered down. "We're wrapping your leg, and we have a crutch for you. One of your messmates is outside. He'll help you walk."

Before a week passed, Philip knew something was seriously wrong with his right leg. The doctor dressing his wound told him to test his weight on the wounded limb. Philip fell over in a childlike sprawl.

"I think," said the doctor, "internal tissue may have been damaged. A great tendon, possibly. If it doesn't heal properly, you may have difficulty walking."

"For how long?"

"For life. At least there's one benefit. You'll be mustered out very promptly now."

The doctor's prediction proved partially correct. Philip had started getting about without a crutch. The injured leg no longer caused him much pain, and the wound was healing; but there was permanent damage. His foot was stiff, lacking natural springiness. He had a noticeable limp.

The doctor had also confirmed that Philip was no longer fit for fighting. Before many more days he would be free to return to Boston.

Forgetfulness of all that had recently transpired came with concentration on the two much-wrinkled letters he pulled from his pocket. One was in a man's hand; the other in a woman's.

One was from Mrs. Brumple. Phrases leaped out to sear his mind: "distressing events . . . a seafaring gentleman of your acquaintance has called and believes he may have some clue to the perpetrator of this act of abduction. . . . I will care for your son Abraham devotedly until some resolution of the situation is affected."

The second letter was from Captain Will Caleb. It told the rest of the dreadful story.

Judson continued to move through the busy square with the sleepwalker's gaze and gait. He seemed not to hear any of the clatter of the river settlement. In a hoarse voice he asked, "Is George Clark here?"

"Try Semple's Tavern right down there."

If he could only relieve his thirst with a drink of rum to ease the tension, to moisten his parched throat.

As he entered the tavern, he saw men seated at a table.

"Have any of you seen Colonel Clark?"

"He's lookin' to supplies. He expectin' you?"

No one invited him to sit down. He supposed he couldn't blame them for that. He might be a Tory spy. Still, the rejection rankled.

With effort he shuffled away to an unoccupied table. The tap boy appeared beside him. "Something, sir?"

"Bring me a rum."

Then after many more he looked up to see George Clark's face—surprise, bewilderment, disappointment, and finally disgust. George saw him drinking and walked out.

Judson had only two courses—either to slink away and hide until George departed down the Ohio or confront him and try to explain the circumstances that had caused him to break his vow. When Judson thought of the distance he had come, the hardships he had endured, there was really no choice. He had to find George and confront him.

Near the head of a landing, he found him. George turned and said coldly, "I never expected to see you, Judson. When you failed to arrive in Williamsburg—"

"I was shot. A light wound, but I couldn't leave until I recovered."

"I am afraid you traveled here for nothing."

"For nothing?"

"You gave your pledge—the only condition under which I accepted you."

"What the hell am I supposed to do, George? I've left everything behind."

"All I can do is invite you aboard my boat and pour you one more rum."

As they approached the craft, George raised a finger to keep Judson silent. Up the plank sidewalls the trap lay back, open. George bent close to Judson's ear. "Someone's inside, where I keep my public orders locked. I don't care to jump through the trap and surprise our visitors in the dark, but maybe we can flush them out into the light." George leaned forward and started hammering on the sidewall of the flatboat.

Hands shot up through the open trap, and the lithe figure of an Indian crawled onto the roof. George leaped up onto the rail and then to the roof. He caught the intruder's hunting shirt and held on by sheer strength while Judson painfully gained the roof.

With a guttural yell the intruder yanked a knife from his belt and swiped at George's throat. Releasing his hold, George jumped backwards. He skidded and sprawled. The Indian reached for his English dragoon pistol. George was a target too large and too close to miss. Judson launched himself hard and fast. Instinctively the Indian swung. The pistol discharged at close range. Judson doubled as the ball struck him in the gut.

George regained his feet and caught the Indian. He wrenched one arm around the spy's windpipe; with his other hand he pressed his knife to the captive's throat. He flung the man into the hands of others and rushed to Judson.

"You took that shot deliberately, Judson."

The initial violent pain had subsided; it was replaced by a steady ache. From the waist downward he was bloodsoaked.

"You"—speech required immense effort—"you would have gotten it otherwise."

Faces drifted through his mind. A wrathful Angus, a disappointed Donald. Butchered Seth and Alice drowned. Peggy, lovely Peggy.

And there was George. There he could be proud. He had helped one of Virginia's finest captains to set out and to extend the boundaries of a new nation. That could be written down in the meager column opposite the much longer, blotted one.

Slowly he closed his eyes. His head lolled to one side, a faint smile fading away.

On a spring afternoon in 1779 Philip Kent and his friend, the Marquis de Lafayette, climbed Breed's Hill overlooking the Charles and the Mystic and Boston Harbor. Philip spoke, "If business doesn't improve, I may go out of the trade altogether."

"What?" Gil exclaimed. "You're only just started. If you abandon your enterprise, what will you do? Printing is all you know!"

"That's true. But without Anne, I have damned little heart for it."

"My friend, it saddens me to see you grieving so deeply," Gil said. "It makes you sound like an old man of seventy-five. Come. I would like you to accompany me to a supper party in my honor. Since I am a married man, the kind family issuing the invitation have arranged for my partner for the evening to be quite advanced in years. There is, however, a young widow without a suitable companion. The young woman is from Virginia. Her name is McLean."

The Marquis de Lafayette would return to France on the morrow. Having earlier promised to deliver a letter to Philip's father, he now resorted to blatant bribery: he would not carry the letter if Philip would not accompany him to the party. All this was an attempt on Gil's part to revive Philip's purpose and direction, which had failed since Anne's death.

Philip's anxiety was back full force, heightened by a continued sense of betraying Anne's memory, and he was not a little irked when Gil said, "We are calling for Mrs. McLean where she boards her child. She is staying at our ultimate destination, the home of our hostess, who is her aunt."

"You've paired me off with some panting bitch who's lost one husband and is desperate to trap another to support her brat!"

"I am assured that the young woman's daughter was born well after her husband's death. Born out of wedlock, I suspect."

"Then I've more in common with the baby than the mother," Philip growled.

Peggy McLean appeared all at once on the upper landing. Over her shoulder she carried a howling infant, angelically beautiful with fair hair and pale blue eyes. But the beauty was marred by the infant's rage. The mother was elegantly gowned, with dark hair and fair skin. Her pretty features showed her distress.

"My apologies. Sometimes Elizabeth is so uncontrollable. I'd swear she is an imp tutored by Satan himself." Her smile was dazzling.

Perhaps the evening wouldn't be so disastrous as he'd imagined. He even caught himself eyeing the swell of this young woman's figure under her coat.

October 19, 1781, the British surrendered at Yorktown.

At Sermon Hill Donald Fletcher had taken over the operation of the plantation; his father had died the year before from a paralytic seizure.

The former Peggy McLean's property had been placed on the market. She was away on one of her frequent trips to Boston when the plantation went up for sale. She returned in early December. To the astonishment of the entire district, she brought with her a husband and two children. One was her husband's son by his first wife. The second was a little girl just a few years younger, who was supposedly related to Peggy's distant kin in New England.

All smiles and blushes—looking healthier than he'd seen her in many years—Peggy Kent invited Donald to call. He found himself enjoying conversation with the fellow Kent. At one point their conversation was interrupted by the sudden arrival of the two children. One was a stocky, dark-haired boy of six; the other a bad-tempered but lovely little girl of three. The girl caused so much commotion that Peggy seized her and carried her out bodily. Fortunately, neither Philip nor Peggy noticed the thunderstruck expression on Donald Fletcher's face.

He understood at last Peggy's long absence in New England before Judson's departure to the West. She was bearing this child, Judson's child. Elizabeth had Judson's bright eyes and bore a facial resemblance to him. She had also inherited Judson's violent tendencies.

So now an angel-faced little harridan was carrying the Fletcher blood to Boston. *Thank heaven,* thought Donald, *I won't be around in fifty years to see what havoc that's wrought!*

America During the Revolution

Background to THE REBELS

The beginning of the Revolutionary War is traditionally said to be the Battles of Lexington and Concord in Massachusetts, on April 19, 1775. Likewise by tradition, the end of the war is regarded as having occurred on October 19, 1781, when Cornwallis surrendered his entire army to Washington at Yorktown in Virginia. A treaty was not signed, however, until September 3, 1783, in Paris. During the war there were squalid skirmishes and a few glorious battles, fought all the way from Quebec to Savannah, from Boston to the Mississippi.

The first glorious battle was Bunker Hill—it was actually fought on Breed's Hill in Charlestown, Massachusetts—June 17, 1775. Philip Kent was there, as he was at Lexington. The untrained, uncoordinated militia repulsed two British charges and inflicted heavy losses on the king's forces. The British were successful in their third assault simply because the Americans had run out of powder. Although the British won the day and were in control of Boston for the time being, the psychological advantage belonged to the Americans, who were greatly strengthened in morale by this demonstration of courage and fighting ability.

In March of 1776 General Washington took command of the Continental forces and managed to obtain some heavy guns through just such maneuvers as involved Philip Kent at Ticonderoga. He was then able to force the British to evacuate Boston and to retreat to Halifax, Nova Scotia.

In July of 1776, two days before the Declaration of Independence was signed in Philadelphia, the English general William Howe landed unopposed on Staten Island with several thousand men. A few days later his brother, Admiral Lord Howe, arrived with a battle fleet. The remainder of that summer British soldiers and supplies continued to arrive on Staten Island, until there were more than thirty thousand armed troops there.

Washington was nearby with almost as many men, but they were chiefly militia, the least effective of the American forces when it came to pitched battles. Another American disadvantage was that Washington was less experienced than Howe. As a result, the American forces were soundly beaten by the redcoats on August 27, 1776, in the Battle of Long Island. This marked the beginning of a series of humiliating defeats for Washington's men. Howe had pushed them all the way across New Jersey; by December he had chased them to the other side of the Delaware.

Then Howe made a tactical error. According to accepted rules of Continental warfare, he called a halt for the winter. Washington did not. He hit the English hard. On Christmas night, 1776, Washington crossed the Delaware. With few losses to themselves, the Americans captured a thousand Hessians, German mercenaries fighting for the English. As at Bunker Hill, the outcome of this feat, the Battle of Trenton, had greater psychological than military importance.

The following year General Howe showed some very poor judgment. He had his subordinate, General Burgoyne, lead an expedition from Canada down the Hudson Valley with the intention of isolating New

18th Century Fortification in America
Fort Ticonderoga in New York
Handle Cartridge
Load Cartridge
Draw Ramrods
Cock Firelock
Fire!
Musket Drill for Infantry in the 18th century
The American Army at Brandywine Creek, 1777

England; but since New England communicated with the other colonies almost exclusively by sea, there was little to be gained by such a maneuver. In the meantime Howe captured Philadelphia, where there were many loyalists to receive him enthusiastically.

Burgoyne did not fare so well. His march was through hostile country. The militia and Continental troops besieged him all along the way. On October 17, 1777, the British commander surrendered at Saratoga, New York. This is considered by many to be the turning point of the war. It won foreign assistance for the Americans, because the prestige the British had so long enjoyed in Europe was considerably tarnished by the fiasco of Burgoyne's ill-considered Hudson Valley campaign.

Two months before the Declaration of Independence, the colonists had asked for and received a million French pounds from Louis XVI. They collected an equal amount from Spain. But they needed more than money; they needed military assistance. The Congress sent Benjamin Franklin to France to seek it. The redoubtable Philadelphian knew how to handle the French, and in turn they loved him.

The result of Franklin's efforts was a brilliant diplomatic victory that brought not only France but Spain, a year later, into the conflict. The Spaniards, however, proclaimed themselves allies only of France; they never asserted their allegiance to the Americans, presumably because they had too many colonies of their own in the New World which might have followed the revolting colonists' example.

France sent both men and ships. The Comte de Rochambeau arrived with six thousand soldiers. Seventeen ships under the command of the Comte d'Estaing followed by twenty-eight more under Admiral de Grasse gave the rebels a navy. Heretofore their only sea defense had been provided by privateers.

The French entered the American War in June of 1778, but not until somewhat later were there any decisive battles for them to engage in. Meanwhile,General Howe had been replaced by General Henry Clinton, and the British offensive was shifted to the south. The English subjected coastal towns to heavy raids while mounting offensives against Georgia, which they recovered in 1779. By May of 1780 Clinton had taken Charleston, South Carolina, with its garrison of five thousand men. He then rushed north in an attempt to rout the French, who were moving against Newport, Rhode Island, which the English had occupied since 1776. The southern campaign was left in the hands of General Cornwallis, who commanded an army of eight thousand. He moved northward rapidly and dealt a stunning blow to the Americans at Camden, South Carolina, on August 16, 1780. As he passed on through the interior, Cornwallis encountered stiff opposition from the militia.

In October of 1780 Washington sent General Nathanael Greene to consolidate the American resistance, which was striking at Cornwallis in a series of quick attacks. While Cornwallis pressed on toward Virginia, Greene shifted his raids to the south, where he not only prevented the British from coming to Cornwallis's aid, but caused them to turn their attention to retaining the important coastal cities of Savannah and Charleston.

Greene's maneuvers allowed Washington to isolate Cornwallis at Yorktown, Virginia. With the aid of French forces, which outnumbered the Americans two to one, commanded by Philip Kent's boyhood friend, the Marquis de Lafayette, Washington forced Cornwallis to surrender his army of more than seven thousand on October 19, 1781.

Not all of the war by any means was fought in the original thirteen colonies. Action in the West, an area from the Appalachians to the Mississippi, was geographically extensive and militarily decisive, and no one was more important to it than Judson Fletcher's boyhood friend and hero, the canny George Rogers Clark, whose younger brother's expedition in 1804 with Meriwether

Lewis fills a memorable page in American history.

It must be remembered that the colonists were not yet Americans; they were Rhode Islanders, Pennsylvanians, Georgians. George Clark was a Virginian. To him the war in the West was not only important to the military strategy of the Revolution, it was a means of bringing material gain to him and to his fellow Virginians.

Clark advocated carrying the war into enemy country in the West. It would keep enemy forces there that might otherwise be deployed against the Americans in the East. He could eliminate posts where the English provided Indians to fight against Virginia.

The war in the West was a brutal and often shameless conflict conducted against small British detachments and against Indians hostile because of years of white expansion. It consisted of murder, raids, and retaliation that had been going on for years before Concord and would continue long after Yorktown.

Clark had to rely on all kinds of ruses, since he lacked men, supplies, and money. In 1778 his successful attack on Vincennes on the Wabash was achieved by concealing his men from view in the hills but grandly displaying their banners. The enemy were thereby convinced he had more troops than he actually had.

The campaign in the West made a significant contribution to the Revolution and an extraordinary one to the United States. Out of that area of the West that figured so prominently in the war, seven new states were eventually carved—Kentucky in 1792, Ohio in 1803, Indiana in 1816, Illinois in 1818, Michigan in 1837, and Wisconsin in 1848. West Virginia did not achieve statehood until her separation from Virginia at the time of the Civil War.

In this stop-and-go war, the American forces were organized like the British—infantry, artillery, and some cavalry. The regiments were composed of regulars, whose two or more years of enlistment were controlled and paid for by the Congress, and colonial forces, such as Philip Kent's Twenty-Ninth Massachusetts, which were supported by the separate colonies. Colonial enlistments were usually for a year. There was a third group, the militia, recruited for a few weeks or months and locally maintained. The least skillful among the troops, they were important because their large numbers kept the British from occupying much land beyond the major cities.

The militiaman, as likely as not, was a farmer who had no uniform. A private in a colonial regiment was issued one. His dark blue coat had red facings, cuffs, and turnbacks. His breeches were also dark blue, while his waistcoat and yarn stockings varied in color. He wore his black felt hat turned sideways, apparently to facilitate shouldering his musket. He carried a single-strap knapsack, a leather cartridge box, and a canteen.

The American line officer also wore a dark blue uniform, but with white facings, cuffs, and turnbacks. His black felt hat, which was not worn sideways, bore a black cockade, to which a white one was added after France entered the war as a gesture of gratitude and as a mark of respect for the new ally. He wore a kind of close-fitting coverall of white wool, linen, or canvas. His officer's sash was scarlet.

George Clark's men wore a round hat quite often adorned with a buck's tail; the "coonskin" cap didn't become popular until after the Revolution. Their fringed hunting shirt and coveralls were usually of heavy linen, only rarely of leather. They not only carried the famous Pennsylvania, or Kentucky, rifle, but a knife, belt ax, powder horn, hunting bag, bullet-loading block, canteen, and tote bag.

Most American naval fighting was done by privateers. The ordinary seaman looked much like his British counterpart. His flat hat was black. Over his waistcoat he wore a gray or green jacket, and around his neck a kerchief. His trousers were not unlike the plus fours

American Rifleman
1780
A Light Dragoon
of the
Queen's Rangers
1780
A Loyalist Corps
Americans ambush a British patrol
in the Carolinas, 1780

favored by golfers at a much later date. A service pistol and a straight-bladed cutlass were his arms.

American dragoons, today called cavalrymen, wore green coats faced with red and red waistcoats. Deerskin breeches with knee wrappings and heavy boots added to their dashing appearance. The helmet worn by these horsemen supported a crest of white horsehair. Their arms frequently included a Brown Bess as well as a saber.

The arms borne during the War of Independence were basically variations of the flintlock, ascribed to a smith from the Normandy village of Lisieux, one Marin, who was born about 1550. He combined features of the Dutch snaphance—a springlock carrying a flint—with those of the pistol traditionally carried by bandits of the Pyrenees; but he added to them an invention purely his own. He made the sear, the catch in a gunlock that holds the hammer at cock or half-cock, to work vertically, rather than laterally as it did in all other flint arms. The change was significant because it not only strengthened the action, but permitted a safe half-cock position.

Many different models appeared to suit the requirements and tastes of each nation that adopted it. The English, in applying the vertical sear to their particular lock, produced the Brown Bess, which played an important role for over a century in British history. The origins of its name are uncertain, but the brown part of it surely springs from the browning of the barrel and the walnut of the stock.

A barrel was browned to deter rust and to avoid glare. It would seem, however, that the browning was often removed by soldiers who found a shining barrel much more in keeping with their uniforms and glistening buttons.

The Brown Bess was produced in several models during the one hundred and twenty years of its official use. All were similar—brass mounted guns with .75-caliber barrels fastened by pins to sturdy stocks.

Despite their long barrels, they balanced well, and their locks did not break easily. When Americans began manufacturing their own muskets at the beginning of the Revolution, they naturally produced the Brown Bess, too. So for a while the fighting was mainly Brown Bess against Brown Bess.

The French musket was always the chief adversary of the Brown Bess. It was lighter, with a caliber of .69. The barrel was fastened to the stock by iron bands instead of by pins, allowing a lighter, more graceful stock without loss of strength. The pan was brass, which does not corrode as easily as iron. As French support of the colonies increased, the American rebels abandoned the Brown Bess in favor of the French flintlock.

The flintlock musket was popular because of its strength, its dependability, the speed with which it could be loaded, and the bayonet which it supported. In the hands of a careless operator, flint ignition could cause frequent misfirings and flashes in the pan; but if a soldier cared for his gun properly, he had a highly dependable weapon.

Speed of course was important. The paper cartridge, which became universal during the early years of the eighteenth century, made loading a quick process. An expert shot could sustain a rate of fire of one shot every fifteen seconds. That did not leave much time for aiming; but in eighteenth-century warfare the standard formation was the line of battle, which made aiming of secondary importance. Two or three rows of men would stand shoulder to shoulder, one line immediately behind the other. A few feet behind them was yet another row—"file closers" they were called—to take the place of casualties. In this formation soldiers would march within range of the enemy, deliver a volley, and then charge. Opposing soldiers took the attack in this same formation. They would wait until the charging enemy was within range and then fire a volley or two before the enemy was on top of them. There was little aiming at targets. The idea was to

American cavalry saber
Officer's spontoon
A bayonet
Paper cartridge
Cartridge box
An American soldier biting a cartridge
Hunting Pouch and powder horn
Frizzen
Comb
Flint
Cock
Spring
Pan
Lock Plate
Trigger
A Flintlock Musket
17-8
Ron Toelke 79

lay down a field of fire through which the enemy had to pass.

When the forces closed in on each other, they used their socket bayonets. These were fitted over the barrel of the musket and were locked in place with a stud and slot. There was an elbow that bent out at a right angle and a straight blade, usually triangular in section. Thus with one weapon a soldier could fight at a distance or hand to hand.

Another weapon, the blunderbuss, was a very effective instrument—in expert hands. Regardless of the size or shape of its muzzle, the blunderbuss spread shot out: at forty-five feet, the spread was twenty to thirty-six inches; at sixty feet, forty to fifty inches. A large blunderbuss could take a load of sixteen buckshot and a charge of one hundred and twenty grains of black powder. Such a load made this gun excellent defense at close range, not only in warfare but at home or on the road.

The arms used by Judson Fletcher and Tobias Trumbull in their duel were pistols, also constructed on the flintlock principle. Few firearms have attracted more interest than dueling pistols. They were the work of the most skillful gunsmiths. They had to be fast and accurate, which meant that the bore had to be true and finely polished to carry the ball directly to its destination. The barrel was usually about ten inches long, octagonal, and exceptionally heavy for the very practical reason that the aim would less likely be affected by a nervous hand. To avoid glare, the mounts were iron or steel—brass only rarely and silver almost never—and were browned like the barrel. Stocks were without ornament or carving except for checkering on the grip. The relative plainness of this pistol was intentional; it was felt that any decoration might be distracting just at the wrong minute.

The first "Kentucky" rifle—the kind George Clark taught Judson Fletcher to use—was developed, ironically, by the pacifist German immigrants of Lancaster County in Pennsylvania, who improved on a rifle they

English leather water bucket
Handspike
Worm or Wad Hook
Rammer and sponge
Canister shot filled with musket balls
Howitzer shell
Cast iron round shot
Linstock and slow match
American Howitzer c.1779
American Artillery in action 1778
17·9
Ron Toelke 79

had brought from Europe. The primary use of the rifle was for hunting, but it soon found its military place in the French and Indian War and in the American Revolution.

As the westward march progressed, the makers of these arms accompanied the frontiersmen to satisfy the demand for this superior, graceful weapon which became the standard gun of hunters and soldiers. By association it became known as the Kentucky rifle, although purists today would like to call it the Pennsylvania rifle. At first it was simply known as the American rifle. Whatever its name, its accuracy and reliability were not surpassed in an area where marksmanship was vital to survival—to bring food to the table and to defend oneself where any tree might be concealing an enemy. A boy began handling a rifle as soon as he could hold it steady.

Shooting matches were commonplace entertainment. The turkey shoot, still held today, was very popular. A turkey was tied behind a log, and the contestants had to try to induce the bird to show its head and then hit it. The first man to do so won the turkey as a prize. There were beef shoots too. Contestants would aim at a target; the man with the best shot would be awarded the best cut, and so each round continued until the entire animal had been disposed of.

The barrel of the flintlock rifle was usually octagonal, although the older design of an octagon rounded out toward the muzzle persisted among some makers. The octagonal pattern was heavy at the breech, tapering gradually toward the muzzle, where in some models it was slightly flared. The facets of the octagon were about three-quarters of an inch at the breech and five-eighths at the muzzle; the barrel was forty-two or -three inches long. It was customary to engrave the maker's name and hallmark on the top facet. Bores were rarely less than .35 or more than .60. The number of grooves varied with the maker, but six to eight were the most common. The front and rear sights were attached by slipping them into dovetail slots on the top facet of the barrel. The lugs on the bottom of the barrel had either round holes or rectangular slots through which metal pins passed to hold the barrel to the stock.

The single most characteristic feature of the Kentucky rifle was a box carved in the right side of the stock, with a sliding cover, for storing small tools, extra flints, and the greased patches used by American riflemen. The cover of the box was usually brass, although some in other metals existed.

Ordinarily, we can only surmise when and where the seeds of revolution are sown, but we know that our own was nurtured in particular, favored places. Not least among them was Virginia. That the "establishment" of the most *English* of colonies among the thirteen should be a leader in the revolutionary cause is not as ironical as it would seem at first. There were reasons both economic and philosophical that impelled many Virginians of gentle birth and good education—Washington, Jefferson, Patrick Henry, the Lees, the Randolphs—to become leaders in the struggle for independence.

The belief that English aristocrats were the first settlers in Virginia is one of those historical fictions—harmless enough, but the facts are better. There is no denying that Virginia in the eighteenth century became the "aristocratic" colony; its first families had, however, with few exceptions, sprung from middle-class stock. Judson Fletcher's father's simple antecedents were historically, if not morally, correct. The aristocratic character of Virginia developed with the colony; it was not something that had been transplanted.

Economically it was supported by large plantations, slave labor, and extensive trade with England. Politically it was engendered by the absence of a middle-class and sustained by its peculiar method of appointment to office—one based on wealth and social position. Socially it was fostered by the ever-increasing wealth of the planters, whose style of living was modeled as closely as possible after that of the great landowning families of England.

The Virginia plantation in the eighteenth century had much in common with a feudal estate. The planter, like the baron, because of his isolation came into infrequent contact with his neighbors. His close associates were his servants and his slaves; for companionship he turned to his family. Just as a chivalrous regard for women had grown up among feudal lords, so it developed in Virginia for the same reasons. The role of the Virginia planter's wife was an exalted one, unmatched in any other colony at the time of the Revolution. She was her husband's constant companion and the mother of his children, also constant companions. On her shoulders fell the responsibility for the management of a large household, which was not a casual operation. She directed an army of servants and saw to their needs. Her importance was recognized, and homage to her was an important part of a social code that was uniquely Virginian.

This social code was recognized by other colonists as something special. The importance of Virginians in the Continental Congress during the Revolution and afterwards was no accident. Nor was it by chance that of the first five presidents four were Virginia planters.

This capacity for leadership was due in part to life on the plantation. From his early youth the Virginia gentleman's business was to command. The plantation, again like the medieval barony, was an independent community whose members looked to the owner for direction and obeyed him implicitly as he directed them in the maintenance of a complex enterprise. His task was to command; never was he in a subservient position.

Commercial relations with England had, of course, an important influence on the daily life of the Virginian democracy. Their household items, their coaches, even their clothes were imported from England. Young men were frequently sent to Oxford and Cambridge, even long after the establishment of William and Mary College. The

Virginia's Capitol Building in Williamsburg 1775
A Slave
A Slave Cabin
The Manor House of a Tidewater Virginia Plantation, 1770

ideas and habits acquired by these young gentlemen exerted a considerable influence upon society in the colony.

Despite the Virginians' tenacious adherence to English things and behavior, society was different in many respects from that of the mother country. There was no town life with its coffeehouses and political and literary clubs. Distances discouraged the county life, which was such an important part of society in England.

As the planters increased in wealth in the eighteenth century, they built magnificent houses which they furnished elegantly. Most of these mansions were constructed of brick made at the site. The rooms, usually few in number, were large, and the ceilings were high. Cooking, baking, and washing were done in buildings separate from the main house. It was not unusual for the grander establishments to have a schoolhouse if there were young boys in the family. It would serve also as a dormitory where they would be overseen by their tutor. And of course there were slave quarters, mean one-room accommodations some distance from the main house.

If the exteriors of these mansions were magnificent, the interiors were opulent. Floors, mantels, and stairs were often of polished mahogany. Furnishings were usually imported from England. There were not many pieces, but they were elegant.

Silver was much admired, and there was a great deal of it. There were pictures, not only family portraits, but even paintings by Italian masters.

Travel in the Tidewater during the seventeenth century was mainly by boat. Plantations were never far from the river, so there was little need for roads, and those that existed were wretched. Overland travel was made on horseback. By the middle of the eighteenth century, however, roads were greatly improved, and vehicular travel was more common. Even so, the Virginia gentleman continued to ride, and his mounts were the finest to be found in the colonies.

Coaches at the time of the Revolution were elegant and extremely costly. The bodies were carved and adorned with crests and coats of arms and were highly varnished. The interiors were lined with excellent cloth that was quilted. The windows were of the best glass, and the floor was carpeted. Every gentleman had one. It was drawn by four horses or six and was attended by liveried slaves.

Apparel was also elegant and costly, and in the latest English fashion. A gentleman's wardrobe contained clothing of rich fabrics—damask, velvet, the finest broadcloth, gold tissue, plush—in scarlet, green, pink, and blue trimmed with lace. His lady wore brocades, taffeta, and satin in winter and cambric, muslin, and lawn in summer.

Gold and silver lace adorned the cocked hats worn by gentlemen. Their cold-weather coats had large cuffs and knee-length skirts stiffened with buckram. They were well lined. Hose was silk in summer and fine worsted in winter. There was no underwear.

Women adorned themselves with necklaces, Brussels lace, and handkerchiefs of exquisite material. They wore silk gloves and mitts, satin shoes and silk hose; muffs, furs, and tippets warded off the cold. Hats were elaborate—black or white beaver with feathers. Quilted bonnets were worn in winter. Indoors every lady wore a cap festooned with ribbons. Her dress was shaped with stays and buckram and hoops.

It appears that much thought and time were lavished on wigs, perukes, and hairdressing. At times highly fanciful, if not grotesque, creations resulted, and milady frequently endured great discomfort on ceremonial occasions in order to have a particularly elaborate hairdo.

Men were clean-shaven, and periodically sent their wigs to be dressed, albeit wigs for men were slowly going out of fashion. The succeeding mode was to queue or club one's natural hair and wear the tail with a ribbon or in a black silk bag. Hair powder and pomatum were used liberally.

The aristocratic Virginians set a lavish table based on the natural bounty of the region—game, birds, and fish. The seas had not yet been overfished, and lobsters, crabs, and oysters, not only in enormous quantity, but in enormous size, were abundant. One wonders if a lobster almost the length of a man or an oyster a foot long would be particularly succulent. Domestic fowl and livestock were abundant and when not served fresh were salted, smoked, and pickled for future use.

Cereal grains were widely cultivated in all the colonies. North Carolina sent rice north. Pennsylvania grew wheat; it did not thrive in the inhospitable soil of New England, where rye grew better. But Indian corn, or maize, was then, as now, the great American cereal. Indigenous to the New World and easily grown in most of the colonies, corn found itself presented at the table in numerous forms, as did the potato, another indigenous food. The Virginia aristocrat used these gifts of the earth to prepare a cuisine more refined than that of the other colonies.

Each eighteenth-century plantation maintained vegetable gardens, berry patches, and orchards, raising those plants that their forebears knew in England. Nutritional standards were high, the result of available foods combined with instinct.

The Tidewater planter favored those wines drunk by the English gentry—Madeira, port, Malaga. Alicia Amberly's favorite drink, claret, was not much in vogue. Rum was widely drunk and in various concoctions. Hard drinking prevailed among the Virginians, as it did elsewhere in the colonies. Of course tea and coffee were drunk as well as chocolate, although the last beverage much less than the other two.

It was only natural that tobacco was widely smoked and snuffed in Virginia. In addition it became a substitute for money. The Virginia clergy received part of their salaries in this commodity.

The colonial Virginian did not by any means live by bread alone. Libraries were a regular feature of the mansions of the aristocracy. They contained the books one would expect to find in an English nobleman's home—Greek and Latin classics, histories—as well as tomes practical for Virginians, such as Wing's *Art of Surveying* and *The Laws of Virginia.*

Music was not neglected by the planters. Their homes contained various instruments—virginals, which later gave way to the larger harpsichord, violins, guitars, flutes, oboes, harps, and harmonicas. This last instrument was much esteemed by the Virginians, some of them becoming virtuoso players of it.

Of all the refined pastimes dancing was admired most; dancing masters made a good living in the colony even in the seventeenth century, and by the time of the Revolution dancing schools were common. The colonists danced minuets, jigs, reels, and country dances.

Seth McLean had, like most of his fellow planters, an overseer, but Angus Fletcher did not. The temperaments of the two men explain why this was so. Angus was not a trusting person, and an overseer was generally entrusted with the management of the entire plantation. Many, like Peggy Ashford McLean's Williams, were so competent and trustworthy that they took all care and responsibility from the owner's shoulders—an arrangement important to the Revolution and the establishment of the Republic. For many planters devoted the leisure time this system afforded them to the arts and to study, and so Virginia developed a particular brand of political philosopher in the likes of George Washington, Thomas Jefferson, Patrick Henry, James Madison, and John Marshall.

Donald Fletcher shared their spirit, if not their vigor and genius. Even Judson Fletcher was not without that political and patriotic sensitivity that was the portion of the tidewater planters of Virginia.

If Virginia and Massachusetts were leaders in the American struggle, it is not surprising, then, that

Philadelphia, a city between the two, was selected as the site of the Continental Congress. Indeed, a glance at a map of colonial America shows that Philadelphia was a focal point for all the colonies, from Massachusetts to Georgia. It was a trade center as well as the distributing center for all mail dispatched among the colonies.

But the fundamental reasons for the distinction Philadelphia attained in the 1700s lay in its origin in the preceding century. Charles II wanted to do something for a friend, Sir William Penn, who as a soldier and sailor had earned the gratitude of his country and king. That gratitude extended to Penn's son, also named William, when he asked for and received from King Charles a grant of land in America as a refuge for his fellow Quakers, who were being persecuted in England.

The first members of the Society of Friends arrived in the place that was to become Philadelphia in 1682 with their leader, the younger Penn, who was a remarkable man. He is remembered for his piety and liberal-mindedness in an age notable for its worldliness and bigotry. At a time when Europeans regarded the Indians as beings slightly less than human to be exploited, Penn regarded them as landowners whose rights were to be respected. As long as he lived, there were no Indian troubles in Pennsylvania. Above all, Penn was a reasonable man who put his stamp on the colony. His rule of religious tolerance not only prevented Pennsylvania from succumbing to the religious fanaticism and bigotry of some of the other colonies, but also made it attractive to persons of moderation and reason. No wonder that a hundred years later another reasonable man, Benjamin Franklin, should choose Philadelphia as *his* city.

When Philip Kent and Judson Fletcher made their visits to Philadelphia, they were in the richest and most populous city in the colonies. Benjamin Franklin had been a citizen since 1726 and had seen Philadelphia grow from a city of eleven thousand to a metropolis which with its environs numbered forty thousand. This extraordinary growth was the natural result of a prosperous society and a continuous accession from without, notably of Scotch, Irish, and German immigrants.

Philadelphia merchants carried on a flourishing trade with the West Indies and Europe, even going as far afield as Leghorn, Italy, to carry sugar and return with carpets and other household furnishings. Although this Italian connection and others like it were not commercially important, they were culturally significant. Philadelphians were rich in ideas as well as in things.

The provincialism of Boston was impossible in Philadelphia. The citizenry were cosmopolitan and liberal. Even so, society was not particularly democratic. The government was in the hands of the rich. Those who benefit most from affluence do not readily espouse causes that may upset the status quo. In the city of the Declaration of Independence there were, ironically, many loyalists. Tobias Trumbull was not unique.

Personal property in excess of fifty pounds—a considerable sum—was a requirement for the vote. It kept matters in the hands of rich merchants; most of these were Quakers, although by 1776 the Society of Friends counted for less than a fifth of the population. Only one male in fifty had the franchise, the political power of the rich which enabled them to check economic competition from below. The opposition of the rich to the relief of debtors was a constant source of bitterness and trouble before and during the war. Class distinction was evident, but the population was growing and changing too fast for it to become entrenched as it had in Virginia.

In addition to its north-south and international commerce, Philadelphia had a western trade catering to country people. To supply their needs, there were numerous retail shops and small manufacturers as well as large concerns. Philadelphia's shipbuilding yards were the most extensive in the colonies. There were also wagon factories, a shop for the manufacture of fire engines, several rum distilleries—in other words, all the business one would expect to find in a strategically placed, rapidly growing city.

Some of Philadelphia's public buildings were impressive, but by and large they lacked the distinction of those found in other sizable colonial cities. Carpenter's Hall, where the Continental Congress sat, was the meeting place of America's first builders' association. It, like other public buildings, including the State House and Province House, later called Independence Hall, was modeled after contemporary English buildings, which we now group together and call Georgian architecture. Shortly before 1776 the Philadelphia streets, which had been carefully planned to intersect at right angles, were paved; they had been lighted as early as 1752. The more than five hundred public pumps along the main thoroughfares supplied citizens with their water and strangers with impressive evidence of early city planning.

Around the middle of the eighteenth century, Philadelphia boasted some one hundred and twenty licensed taverns—all the way from wharfside groggeries to the politically famous City Tavern, where Philip Kent was lodged. These institutions were not merely drinking places; rather, they took on the nature of clubs, each with its own particular character. Loosely knit groups of customers would gather in them regularly to dine, drink, play cards, and talk. From these taverns developed a number of carefully organized clubs, which by the time of the Revolution had become a distinctive feature of Philadelphia society. They had shifted their emphasis from being purely convivial to benevolent, social, philosophical, or political purposes. They became powerful means for fostering public projects and directing public opinion. When the time came, they played an influential role in various ways in Philadelphia's contribution to the Revolutionary War.

The American Revolution frustrates those who see all revolutions primarily as class struggles. It cuts sharply across all divisions—class, regional, religious, and ethnic.

The Philadelphia Waterfront 1775
Carpenter's Hall
The Pennsylvania State House (Independence Hall) 1776
Ron Toelke 79

The social structure was so fluid that in most colonies, Virginia being the notable exception, social distinctions rested on the winds of chance and local opportunity. Some members of the community were richer than others, but their positions could be readily reversed with no effect on the structure of society. This mobility gave rise to political disputes, but never to class struggle.

Of course, one absolute clan division did remain—that between freeman and slave. It is estimated that about a million Americans, or a fifth of the population, were slaves in 1776. The irony is inescapable in a revolution fought in the name of freedom. To be sure, measures had been taken to free slaves, but only in states where slaves were so few in number as not to constitute a labor force.

For all its failures, for all the discrepancies between ideals and accomplishments, the American Revolution wrote a glorious page in the history of civilization. It disproved the old assumptions that some men are born to ride roughshod over others, that things always have to stay the way they are. It proved that man had the imagination and courage to challenge oppression. By so doing it revolutionized the world.

The Seekers

A CONDENSATION OF

The Seekers

1794–1814

BOOK 1

August 20, 1794. Near dawn, Abraham Kent, nineteen-year-old son of Philip Kent, crawled out of his tent, somewhere in the Northwest Territory. For a moment, he wondered if he would see the dawn of the twenty-first, for today promised a battle.

Abraham was thankful that his father's business had prospered sufficiently to permit him to become an excellent horseman. Otherwise he would never have been accepted for General Wayne's dragoons. Whether General Wayne—admiringly called Mad Anthony ever since his daring exploits during the Revolution—stood a chance against the tribesmen waiting somewhere up the Maumee, Abraham could not say.

Abraham had enlisted two years before, leaving his home in Boston because he and his father Philip were not getting on well. Philip had wanted his son to attend Harvard and then join him in the family business, Kent and Son, Publishers. They had had loud and lengthy arguments on many other subjects too, including politics. But Abraham loved his father, even though he found him unbearably opinionated, and deep down he knew that he wanted to excel in the impending battle chiefly in order to have an accomplishment to show his father.

Shortly after seven, Abraham swung his mount into line behind his troop's senior officer, Lieutenant Stovall from Maryland. A reputed sexual deviate, Stovall was unpopular with the men, and his manner was condescending.

The battle along the Maumee was fought and won in under half an hour. It was won by superior numbers and specifically by the dragoon charge against the Indian flank. Seven or eight in Abraham's troop had died, including the detested Stovall.

Abraham felt that the battle had brought him a little nearer to manhood, but the experience was not as glorious as he had imagined it would be.

By December the Indians surrendered. Thirteen months later Abraham Kent received his release from the army and returned home to face his father.

There was a magnificent dinner in honor of his homecoming, with all the family present. At the head of the table sat Philip Kent; at forty-two his strong features had acquired some of the lines of age. Across from him was his second wife, Peggy Kent, gentle and lovely, Abraham's stepmother. Between Philip and Peggy sat Gilbert, their son, just eleven, fragile and intense. And beside Abraham was Elizabeth Fletcher, Peggy's child by the mysterious, violent Judson Fletcher of Virginia, now dead.

In recent years, Philip had demonstrated a hard shell of conservatism and had developed an aura of confidence, power, and even arrogance that was intimidating. Elizabeth's dislike of her stepfather's manner and opinions was clearly evident. From childhood, she had shown a certain recklessness and defiance, and now, at seventeen, she was no different. But she had grown up.

She was no blood kin of Abraham's, yet Abraham found himself disturbed by the sensual thoughts she inspired in him.

After dinner father and son retired to the sitting room, where they had a brief and unsatisfactory talk about Abraham's future.

"I am relying on you to join the printing house," Philip said.

"But Papa, wait! I'm not certain that's what I want to do with my life."

"Be kind enough to tell me what you have chosen to do."

"I haven't decided yet."

"You don't know what you want to do, yet you already know my proposition is unsatisfactory. Odd."

Abraham had thought a great deal about the future. He wasn't content to fit into the mold prepared for him by Philip. In many ways his service in the Northwest had unsettled him, showing him that the world was not confined to paper and presses, which were all he had known as a child.

Borne down by weighty thoughts, Abraham climbed to his room on the third floor and pushed the door open.

"My God!"

"Sssh!" Elizabeth, within, put a warning hand to her lips. "Don't be a ninny and make noise, or you'll spoil everything!"

She was clad only in a nightdress of filmy material, Abraham noticed uneasily. She went to the bed, whose coverlets were turned down, and plumped herself on it.

"Sit with me and talk. There's no one else I can talk to in this house." In her lovely face there was a look of reckless disregard for propriety.

"Abraham," she said, her face close enough so that he could smell the sweetness of her breath, "you understand what your father is trying to do to both of us, don't you? He wants to trap both of us, with his notions of respectability. We must fight him together. Secretly."

Any doubts Abraham might have had about Elizabeth's purpose in coming to his room were soon dispelled. By an act which Philip would have considered reprehensible, she could defy the authority he sought to exert over her. Abraham had felt some of the same pressure in his painful interview with his father. Thus he was willing to let the instincts of his young man's body have their way, joining the girl in this private, ultimately pleasurable form of protest.

In the weeks that followed the new year of 1796, Elizabeth visited Abraham by night whenever she could. No one suspected. Soon Abraham realized that he was no longer merely defying his father; he was falling in love with Elizabeth. He loved her in spite of all he knew about her—her rebellious blood, her delight in defying accepted standards.

The young couple soon decided they would marry and escape Boston and Kent and Son. They would begin their life together in the Northwest Territory.

When Philip heard of the young couple's plans, he reacted swiftly: "Madness! Absolute *madness!*"

After protracted argument Philip managed a compromise: he and Peggy, Elizabeth and Abraham and Gilbert would travel to Philadelphia and points south. He hoped that the cosmopolitan life of the new country's capital would beguile Elizabeth and Abraham and dispel the allure of the frontier.

The family arrived in Philadelphia in April, and were received by President and Mrs. Washington. Then they continued south to Peggy Kent's native Virginia. Along the way it became evident that Elizabeth was not a good traveler, for she experienced fits of nausea every few hours. Abraham began to wonder: would she be suited for a life in the West?

Since Peggy had known Thomas Jefferson in her

youth, she persuaded Philip to accept an invitation from the man whose democratic leanings were opposed to Philip's own Federalist views. Philip later regretted visiting Monticello.

"I believe our country's future lies, not in the East, but in the West," Jefferson said, and upon learning of Abraham's intentions, added, "I'd encourage you to follow your instincts, young man. They're correct."

That night Abraham and Elizabeth announced their determination to stick to their original plan.

Philip burst into a rage. After an acrimonious interchange he limped from the room with his arm around Gilbert's shoulders. "At least I've one son who won't turn his back on me."

Stunned and hurt, Abraham watched the two depart. Elizabeth moved closer to Abraham and buried her head against his chest. He could not see her eyes, ugly with triumph.

On a Saturday in July Abraham and Elizabeth were married before a company of Boston's notable citizens. Philip looked glum, and Abraham found the ceremony difficult to endure.

After the ceremony, Abraham managed a few private words with his father, at which point Philip thrust a gift of five hundred dollars into his hands.

"Five hundred! A gift like this when you don't even approve the match?"

Philip stiffened. "Are you trying to say you refuse the gift?"

"No sir, of course not. I'm extremely grateful for—for an expression of your love."

Philip's voice broke as he embraced his son. "God keep you, Abraham, and your dreams."

Abraham and Elizabeth began their wedding trip to Salem with a stopover at a country inn. As a ferry bore them across the Charles, Elizabeth grew pale and pressed a hand to her stomach.

"It's nothing, darling, don't worry. Only a minor dizziness caused by the excitement of finally being married."

But Abraham saw that her face was still white as they stepped off the scow.

In the weeks that followed, Abraham and Elizabeth traveled down to Pennsylvania and then headed west across the Alleghenies aboard one of the great cargo-carrying Conestoga wagons that regularly traveled the high road. The driver, Leland Pell, a loutish fellow of the lowest sort, got drunk and tried to rape Elizabeth. Enraged, Abraham attacked him and killed him with his whip. Elizabeth and Abraham took Pell's wagon the rest of the way to Pittsburgh.

Abraham and Elizabeth arrived in Pittsburgh in late fall. After disposing of Pell's horses and wagon and seeing to the delivery of his goods, they decided to make the rest of their trip by riverboat. But that would not be possible until spring; in the meantime they sat out the winter in a tiny room in a boardinghouse.

In February Elizabeth discovered that she was going to have a child.

At a wagon camp Abraham met the Clappers—Daniel and Edna and their children Daniel Junior and Danetta. Clapper had left his New Hampshire store some years before and moved west with his family. He planned to set up a store in the Ohio country and had with him a wide assortment of goods, from bolts of cloth to kegs of nails. He intended to sell his wagon and team and invest in a one-way ark to travel down the Ohio, and he and Abraham struck a deal.

On a brilliant day in April the Clappers and the Kents began their comparatively easy journey. Indians no longer posed much of a threat in that part of the country. In fact, about the only real hazards were sawyers, submerged logs whose upper ends rose and fell in cycles of twenty to thirty minutes.

One evening as Abraham and Daniel sat talking, they felt a violent impact. With a great crunch, their ark wrenched broadside to the current, and as the bow came around, it lifted sharply on the port side and then slammed down.

"We musta hit a sawyer, Pa," Daniel Junior cried.

"Danetta!"

The cry came from Edna Clapper. She was kneeling beside Elizabeth.

"She fell when we hit. Danetta! In God's name, will you hurry? Mrs. Kent is losing the baby!"

BOOK 2

On a gray, thundery afternoon in May, 1799, Abraham was planting corn. He glanced at the cabin, a windowless twenty-by-sixteen-foot building; in it were Elizabeth and their baby, Jared Adam, born the preceding autumn. He regretted now the location of his property, some four miles from Fort Hamilton, for although Indian raids were infrequent, they did occur, and usually at some distance from a fort or village.

Abraham and Elizabeth were just as much prisoners of their surroundings as they would have been had they remained in Boston. They had mortgaged their lives to twenty acres along the Miami River, and they were consumed with the tasks of sheer survival. Elizabeth was scarcely ever in good humor now.

It might be different if Elizabeth were stronger physically, tougher mentally, Abraham thought. But, of late, she had seemed so tired, even to the point of neglecting little Jared. She admitted that she hated the country they had chosen and that she had no courage left.

One day after a particularly distressing period of depression and inertia, Elizabeth talked of her father. "He was peculiar—wild, and brave in some ways. But weak in others. He ran from whatever he disliked. Perhaps his nature was strength and weakness in one. Mama calls it Fletcher blood, and I have it. But I don't want it to hurt you, or baby Jared."

"How could it?" Abraham asked tenderly.

"Well, Jared has the same blood, doesn't he?"

Some time later Clapper decided to move on, and he suggested that Abraham take over his store. With an animation he had rarely shown of late, Abraham said he thought it would work. He could sell his farm to one of the new families arriving in the spring and use the money to buy out the store. Elizabeth too was enthusiastic, and both of them looked forward to the coming change in their lives. On April 1, 1801, their hardship would end.

On March 25, the Indians came, at dawn—two of them, an old man and a young warrior, looking for whiskey. Abraham grabbed his rifle and went to drive them off.

Abraham threatened to shoot if the two did not leave immediately. In response, one threw his war club at Abraham, who lunged out of the way. In three long strides, the Indian recovered it. On the ground, Abraham braced his rifle against his hip and fired. The Indian fell.

"Abraham!"

Elizabeth was outside. *Why had she not stayed inside?* thought Abraham. The old Indian's musket roared.

"Elizabeth, no. No, Elizabeth!"

An unkempt man of about twenty-five trudged up Beacon Street in Boston, early in July, 1801. With him was a tow-haired boy whose face looked pinched and gray. They knocked on the door of one of the more substantial homes on the street.

A mobcapped girl opened the door. "Beggars are not allowed here."

"I am Abraham Kent. I live here. I wish to see my father."

"Sir . . . sir . . . Mr. Kent died in his sleep on the last day of April."

With the death of Philip Kent, Gilbert, his younger son, now eighteen, had been thrust into control of Kent and Son. Gilbert felt he had to demonstrate to the world—and to himself—that he was worthy of the task. He was, in reaction to his father's Federalist bias, a Jeffersonian, a position not popular or even common among Boston's merchant families.

On a warm summer's day in 1803, Gilbert, tall, slender, and impeccably clad, made his way toward Kent and Son. He was in excellent spirits until he reached the main entrance, where he saw bloodstains on the cobbles.

Upon investigating, Gilbert found that his half brother Abraham, now employed by Kent and Son, had been involved in a fist fight—and not for the first time. Drunk again. He would have to bring Abraham into line.

Gilbert sympathized with Abraham, but he could no longer tolerate his brother's sullen, destructive behavior. It stemmed, no doubt, from guilt over his wife's death, the rift with his father, and sheer discontent with himself. Perhaps a change of scene . . .

All at once Gilbert remembered that Meriwether Lewis was captaining an expedition to the West. Abraham had soldiered with Lewis under General Wayne and also with the younger brother of George Rogers Clark.

He would speak to his half brother as soon as he returned from whatever den he had crawled into after this latest fight.

Beyond that, he would have to gain his wife's consent to the plan. Harriet, one year older than her husband, was eight months pregnant, a fact which only exacerbated her disapproval and dislike of Abraham and little Jared. The boy was impertinent and rebellious, behavior that Harriet attributed to his Fletcher blood, for Gilbert had described Elizabeth to her in detail. Despite Harriet's feelings about Jared, when Gilbert proposed that they keep the boy so that Abraham might go off with Lewis and Clark on an expedition to the West, she agreed to the plan. Anything to rid the house of Abraham.

Abraham eventually dragged himself home, where he listened sourly to Gilbert's suggestion.

"So you're proposing to send me west again. I know Captain Lewis won't accept me. I am not in the excellent health he demands. During my various jaunts around town in search of a bit of amusement, I've spent time with certain women. I've caught the pox."

"My God!"

"I expect you—and Harriet above all—will want me out of the house now."

"I won't let you leave."

"You have no choice. I'm going up to get Jared." He reached for the decanter and glass that had been set beside him.

"You're not going to take him."

Weaving a little, Abraham jerked the library doors open. Harriet stood before him.

"Well," Abraham said. "It seems I have secrets from no one." His face grew ugly. "I'm going to fetch my son. You'd be wise to stay out of my way."

Abraham started for the staircase. Hampered by her swollen belly, Harriet lurched after him.

"Help me, Gilbert!" she cried. "You can't let that filthy creature touch the child."

As Abraham ascended the stair, Harriet managed to catch one of his boots. Abraham kicked out. Gilbert leaped forward to catch her. Harriet shrieked, "You seem to have—a skill—for harming—women with unborn children."

"God damn you!" Abraham howled. He shoved Gilbert aside, bent, and lashed her cheek with the back of his hand.

Gilbert heard the thump as her head hit a riser. She slid to the hard floor and lay still. Gilbert *knew* Abraham was going to strike her again. He spun and ran, jerking Philip Kent's sword down from its pegs over the mantel.

As Gilbert came towards him, Abraham tried to scramble out of the way, but the blade hacked his left cheek and then glanced off. Unreasoning terror had driven Gilbert to attack—he who had never used a weapon in his life.

A maid who had heard Harriet's outcry ran in and knelt at her mistress's side.

"Mr. Kent, I think the child's coming."

Gilbert commanded, "Run for Dr. Selkirk! Run!"

As Gilbert slowly raised his head, he saw his half brother on the stair. His bearded cheek was bloody and one hand as well. On the landing above, Gilbert could see Jared, accompanied by a frightened serving girl.

"Leave this house at once," Gilbert cried.

"I want my son."

Abraham climbed toward Jared. The boy jerked back, cowering against the skirts of the maid.

"Jared?"

In a hushed voice, the maid said, "For pity's sake, sir! Leave the poor child alone."

Abraham turned, descended, reached the front door, and stumbled down the front steps into the rain.

Gilbert Kent's daughter was born towards dawn, a difficult but successful birth. The girl was named Amanda.

On a steamy morning in August, looking more haggard than any of his employees had ever seen him, Gilbert Kent looked up from his work.

"Yes, Mr. Morecam? Any news?"

"No, sir. It's the same as the last five days. The boys we hired spent all night searching. There's no sign of Mr. Kent."

"The boys aren't doing the job. Hire men with horses. Check every printer in the state. I want him found."

Gilbert looked out the window. He reflected that there was but one source of joy left to him in the world. Amanda.

Gilbert knew that he had let a beast loose within himself that July night. In a peculiar way his outburst had drawn him closer to Abraham. They were more alike than he had ever expected.

"Find him," Gilbert muttered. "Find him."

But every man he hired failed. By late September he concluded that he would never see Abraham again.

BOOK 3

Harriet's concern for Jared had only been pretense. In the years that followed Abraham's disappearance, she repeatedly demonstrated her true feelings of hostility toward Jared. Slowly, after much pain and inner turmoil, the boy became resigned to his position in the house. His uncle Gilbert was kind to him, but Jared remained an undesirable outsider.

One day after a particularly stormy encounter, Harriet exclaimed, "I'll have you out of this house!"

Jared beamed. "That would suit me *admirably!*"

But he needed a destination—a means of escape—*something*.

Finally, in a talk with his uncle, Jared expressed his distress. With affection and understanding Gilbert explored possibilities for the future, and when he suggested a career in the burgeoning American navy, the idea appealed to Jared's restless nature. Yet fear remained: what if he failed? He wouldn't! He swore to that silently, fervently.

July 26, 1812. Boston's own frigate, *Constitution*, was anchored in Boston Harbor. The next day Jared heard the crew roster had not been filled. He ran most of the way to the recruiting office.

The officer in charge was a young lieutenant, slender and tanned, about twenty. And almost too handsome. His brown eyes had a languid quality. Somehow the officer made Jared self-conscious; his eyes had a disturbing way of focusing on odd places—on Jared's mouth, his hands, and once, he was sure, his groin. . . .

The lieutenant praised the navy, and Jared concurred, saying that he had no desire to join the army. "My father was a soldier—"

The lieutenant broke in. "So was mine. Where did he serve?"

"In Ohio, with Wayne at Fallen Timbers. . . ."

"Remarkable! My father was there as well. Got himself killed, poor wretch. Well," said the lieutenant, moving closer to Jared and squeezing his shoulder, "we have something in common."

Jared jerked away. The lieutenant's eyes widened. "Well, I see you have a ready temper. You'll have to curb that, or it'll be curbed for you."

The lieutenant completed the required forms, and Jared's hand shook as he signed them. After he had left the recruiting office, he looked at the parchment. The young officer's signature was at the bottom. *Hamilton Stovall, 6th Lt. U.S.S. Constitution.*

By his own choice, Jared went to Long Wharf alone the next morning, putting everything at Beacon Street out of his mind, from Gilbert's prideful good wishes to his cousin Amanda's sob. He carried his personal items in a small canvas bag; these included a gift of a knife of Spanish steel.

Constitution carried a complement of thirty boys—rowdy youngsters who slept in canvas hammocks on the berth deck. Exchanging opinions about the officers, they referred to Lieutenant Stovall as a "mean, dirty sod."

Jared was assigned to the officers' wardroom, and was lucky to have a likable companion assigned the same job—a boy of twelve, Oliver Prouty.

One day after *Constitution* had put to sea, Jared was sent with lunch to Lieutenant Stovall's quarters, where the officer was supposedly indisposed. Jared put the meal down and stepped backwards. "If that will be all..."

"Not quite. You will sit down." He perched on the edge of his bunk and dropped his hand on Jared's knee.

"Take your hand away."

"What's this? You giving orders to me?" The fingers caressed his leg.

"I'm just telling you—take your hand away or—or I'll kill you."

"My God, Mr. Kent. That's incredible brass. But I admire it. You've got spirit."

Jared was convinced Stovall was deranged.

"We are much alike, dear boy. We will be intimate friends—commencing now. Come now, no more sparring. Pull off your trousers and climb into that bunk."

Jared shot from his chair, throwing Stovall off balance. He had the door halfway open when Stovall's fist struck the back of his head. The boy fell, and Stovall's hands reached for his throat. There were voices overhead. Jared reached down to his waist and jerked his Spanish knife into view.

"You touch me again, and I'll cut your face to pieces," he whispered.

Stovall turned pale and cursed, and Jared knew he had struck a vulnerable spot—Stovall's vanity.

A knock at the door. "Captain requests all officers to the wheel at once. We've sighted—"

Jared jerked the door open and bowled past the goggling master's mate.

Still limp from the scene in Stovall's cabin, Jared joined the other boys in scanning the horizon.

Oliver Prouty said, "You're white. What the hell's wrong?"

"I . . . I had to pay a visit to Stovall's quarters. He tried to . . . I had my knife out."

"You're in for it!"

"Captain Hull will have the cat on my back as soon as he can."

"Well, Hull won't put his mind to anything till we've learned whether yonder ship is friend or foe. Suppose we do engage, and enemy metal puts Lieutenant Handsome out of commission—or that something else happens to him."

The stranger was the British *Guerriere*, and by five o'clock she was engaged. At first Captain Hull refused to commit himself, but at length he ordered the sailing master to lay alongside the British vessel. Broadside after broadside was fired from *Constitution*'s guns, inflicting heavy damage. The two ships were so close that their lines became fouled, and a party from *Constitution* prepared to board the enemy vessel.

A good twenty feet away, Jared spied Oliver Prouty. He was at the fringe of the boarding party when a chance shot from *Guerriere* blew away the back of his head.

Suddenly a hand grabbed Jared's arm. It was Stovall; he held a pistol at Jared's forehead.

"They'll think it was a British ball, won't they, Mr. Kent?"

Jared swung his cutlass. The lieutenant dodged, and Jared's blade cut the breaching rope of a nearby cannon. The runaway cannon rumbled towards them. Stovall, slipping on the deck, fell on the cannon's muzzle. He screamed as his face slammed against the breech below the firing pan. The odor of burning flesh was overpowering.

On August 30 *Constitution* dropped anchor at Long Wharf in Boston. Standing on the deck, Jared saw Stovall being carried down the gangplank on a litter.

Though Boston did not favor the war, a tide of well-wishers was on the wharf. One filthy woman—a whore, Jared was certain—darted in front of the boy.

"I'll pleasure you for half the price—special rate for the brave lads from Boston's frigate."

The woman's companion laughed. His voice was slurred with drink. "Leave him be, Nell. The lad's not old enough to buy what you're selling."

Jared looked at the woman's pimp. He was about forty, unkempt, foul-smelling. His face was covered with sores, his right eye milky with blindness.

The pimp extended his hand. "Privileged to meet any of the lads who... Boy—? Would you tell me your name?"

"Why?"

"Because you resemble..."

"Prouty. Oliver Prouty." It was the first name that popped into Jared's head.

"Oh, mistake then." But as he moved away, the pimp murmured, "He lied to me." His voice was more sorrowful than angry.

As Jared walked to Beacon Street, another voice challenged him. It belonged to a girl, lounging in the shadows.

"Are you off the Boston ship? I could make you happy to be on land again."

Jared had nothing of value to offer, but she said she would accept one of the two bracelets of tarred cordage that he was taking home from the ship. They passed together from the blue shadow of the street to the deeper shadow and mystery of her shabby ground-floor room.

At Beacon Street Amanda opened the door and squealed with delight when she saw Jared.

"Here, Amanda. I brought you something, a bracelet of rope from *Constitution*. I made it myself."

Gilbert returned later, looking thinner, and said, "Do you know they're going to give you a parade down State Street and a dinner at Faneuil Hall?"

Several hundred men had gathered in Faneuil Hall to dine, smoke, and drink toasts. Only the hardiest boys from the ship kept pace with the heavy drinkers; Jared was not among them, but he perked up when Gilbert rose to make a toast.

Gilbert held his glass aloft.

"To unconditional victory. We have suffered..."

Gilbert swayed. His left hand jammed against his chest. He toppled, dragging china and tablecloth after him as he slid to the floor.

BOOK 4

In mid-July, 1813, as Harriet sat before her mirror combing out her long, dark hair, something stunned and angered her. Gray hair. Gilbert was responsible for it. He'd wrenched her whole life away last December when he died.

It had been a dreadful ordeal, but she had got through it, only to be plunged into another: Jared's homecoming. Harriet found him infuriatingly self-assured; she could no longer intimidate him.

Harriet herself had succumbed relatively early to the marriage proposal of a man she had met only in March. Mr. Andrew Piggott was urbane, polite, and accepted in the best circles. But before her wedding night was over, she realized what a ghastly mistake she had made, what a ravenous beast she had married.

In the autumn of 1813 hostilities with England appeared to be drawing to an end, but Harriet Piggott was little interested. A battle was being waged in her own household. Piggott not only drank excessively, he gambled recklessly. And to finance his play he had wagered one of the presses of Kent and Son. There was no way to stop him, for no agreement had been made before the marriage to limit Piggott's access to Harriet's property.

Amanda feared her stepfather. One afternoon when Harriet was out, Piggott became violent when Amanda could not say where her mother was.

"I'll punish you as you've never been punished before," Piggott cried, pinning Amanda to the wall.

"Punish her for what, Andrew?" asked Harriet, appearing at the door.

Amanda escaped his grasp and hurled herself at her mother. "He was making me tell where you had gone. He said he's going to pack."

Harriet's tone was almost happy. "You're leaving, Andrew? Good. Take all your belongings. I've instituted a bill of divorcement. Henceforth my name is Mrs. Kent."

"Well, your name's all you'll have henceforth. I have recently lost heavily at gambling with two gentlemen from Maryland who are in metal refining—pig into wrought. They accepted my notes wagering the assets of Kent. Because of my losses, you no longer own Kent's."

"You lost . . . everything?"

"They're taking possession this very afternoon."

Harriet rushed distractedly out of the house. She did

not see the heavy dray lumbering along the street. In a moment she lay at the curb, her neck broken.

"I don't believe it!" Jared cried.

"It's true, and it's legal, Mr. Kent. You are now working for me."

Two men, elegantly dressed, stood before Jared at Kent and Son. All he could see of the younger was half a face. A white silk bandana covered the rest.

"Mr. Kent and I are old acquaintances," said Mr. Hamilton Stovall. "Ever since my untimely separation from the naval service, I've laid plans for a return to New England. This is my agent, Mr. Walpole."

Jared cried, "You goddamned, conniving..." and sprinted for the stairs.

His rage was out of control. He pulled out a pistol he had bought when Piggott first began to gamble away Kent and Son. He then tore into the office once used by his grandfather. He jerked open the door of a small stove and began tossing in anything that would burn. Then he tipped the stove forward, his face breaking into a ghastly smile as the flames spread.

Stovall and Walpole appeared on the landing outside. Jared aimed his seven-barrel pistol. It went off a second after Stovall had wrenched Walpole in front of him. Walpole shrieked and fell back to the landing.

"Murder!" Stovall cried as Jared ran for the rear stairs. "The boy's done murder!"

Snow was falling heavily as Jared ran into the house on Beacon Street and up to his room. Murder was murder. He'd be arrested if he didn't run.

The door opened suddenly. It was Amanda. "Why are you putting things in the bag?"

"Because I'm leaving. You musn't tell Aunt Harriet you saw me."

"Mama's dead!"

The boy was speechless. Amanda flung her arms

around his neck. "Please don't go away and leave me, Jared."

"I'll take care of you. At least I'll try."

Twenty minutes later two figures emerged from the darkness around the entrance to the Beacon Street house.

Hamilton Stovall watched Kent and Son burn. A man ran up to him and said, "Walpole's going to pull through."

"Has anyone seen the Kent boy?"

"No. I expect he's fleeing for his life. He undoubtedly thinks Walpole's dead."

"Let him," Hamilton Stovall said.

Jared and Amanda put miles between themselves and Boston. Jared had no clear destination in mind. In Pennsylvania, they managed to secure a place on a wagon heading for Pittsburgh.

There the boy found work in the boatyards. With the wages he earned working fourteen-hour days, he and Amanda rented accommodations in a shabby boarding-house. His cousin was maturing rapidly. Her face promised beauty in adulthood. She had ripened to the point where she attracted the stares of older men.

In February, 1814, Jared and Amanda went by boat down the Ohio to Louisville, where they planned to round the Ohio falls and head downstream again to New Orleans. (Jared had resolved never to go west, where his parents had found only unhappiness.)

In early March, they set off along the Cumberland Trail. They spent their first night in the open in a pounding sleet storm. Jared awoke the next morning feverish. They continued their trek, Amanda leading Jared by the hand toward a cabin she spied ahead.

The cabin belonged to a family called Lincoln, who took them in for two weeks. Jared had beaten the disease, he thought, but after leaving the Lincolns, he was sick twice more.

One day in mid-May Jared awoke to see a lean man

hunkered beyond what was left of the fire. Beyond him a horse fretted.

"Morning, boy. Hardly expected to find two youngsters camped in these woods. My name's Reverend William Blackthorn."

The man was polite enough, but for some reason Jared felt an instantaneous distrust. The preacher's sunken greenish eyes strayed past him to Amanda.

"We're leaving," Jared announced. "The fire's yours."

"You don't look well, boy. Are you sick too, girl?" Blackthorn brushed his fingers across Amanda's forehead.

"Don't you touch me!"

Jared's hands dropped to the hilt of his Spanish knife.

"I'd hardly say your behavior's Christian, boy."

"And you don't act much like a preacher," Jared replied.

"I am. I'm also the best free-for-all fighter in Tennessee." Dropping his pretense of cordiality, the man said, "Give me that canvas bag."

As Jared jerked out his knife, Blackthorn grabbed the boy's arm and twisted. The knife fell into the fire. Jared lashed out at the older man, but he was no match for his strength. Blackthorn pitched him onto his side, and he blacked out.

When Jared awoke, the man and Amanda were gone. Guilt overwhelmed him for a moment. He had let her be kidnapped.

Jared stood up, still dazed from the beating, and began to walk. Just as he recognized the thundering sound of a horse's hooves, he realized that he had staggered directly into the stallion's path. The last thing Jared saw were hooves slashing down toward his head.

"Well, his eyes are open, Miz Rachel. Fever's gone too."

"I'm not so sure the young man will be thankful to be

awake when the judge comes home," the young woman said, pulling a corncob pipe from her teeth. "You nearly lamed his prize horse yesterday."

"Yesterday! I've got to find my cousin. Mrs.—?"

"Jackson. Rachel Jackson. Judge Andrew Jackson's wife. You'll obey the doctor's orders and speak to the judge tonight."

He obeyed, for he was too weak to travel. But he vowed he would kill Blackthorn.

A few days later, Judge Jackson, who had been one of those responsible for having Blackthorn run out of Nashville, brought discouraging news. Blackthorn was heading toward St. Louis. Sensing Jared's determination, he asked, "Are you sufficiently well to ride, Kent? If so, I'll have a horse for you at sunrise. Consider that I'm making an investment in the punishment of the good reverend with a horse, food, sturdy clothing, and five dollars in gold."

On July 20, 1814, Jared Kent approached St. Louis. Though he wouldn't be sixteen until the fall, he felt twice as old.

He questioned everyone he met, but there was no news of Blackthorn and Amanda. Then one day he heard of a Wilford Black. Something in the man's description suggested Blackthorn. Here on the frontier a man could use any name that was convenient for him. This Black was reported to be living at Mrs. Cato's.

Mrs. Cato's establishment stood on a dark, grubby street. As Jared approached it, he heard men shouting, laughing, and cursing; women shrieking; and furniture being broken and glass shattered. He entered to find a melee. A dumpy woman was attempting to bring about some order—obviously Mrs. Cato.

Attracting her attention, Jared said, "You have a man here—Wilford Black?"

"Still here. Upstairs. Second door on right."

The governor personally took Jared's deposition the next morning. The boy repeated the story of Amanda's abduction and what Blackthorn had said as he was dying about selling her to white traders heading for Sioux country.

Jared was acquitted on the ground of self-defense but was given ninety days in jail for disturbing the peace and was told that at the end of that time he was to remove himself from St. Louis and not to return.

EPILOGUE

Amanda Kent opened her eyes. She was lying on one of three beds arranged around the tepee wall. Remembering where she was and why, she lunged up to a sitting position, all at once feeling the thongs that bound her dirty wrists and ankles. The traders had brought her here and sold her to a tall, well-built Indian, who now stood gazing at her.

She looked at the bracelet of tarred rope—her last tangible link with Jared and the past. She knew she would never see him again, but she would wear it until she died. She thought two connected thoughts, thoughts which gave her hope that one day she would escape from the snare in which fate had trapped her:

I will live.

I have found a way.

I will live.

The Young Republic

Background to THE SEEKERS

In this era of instant communication and diminishing distance it is hard to understand how separate and remote each of the original colonies was from the others in attitudes and practices. They all came together, sometimes reluctantly, in the 1770s to fight a common enemy; some two decades later, by the time Abraham and Elizabeth had begun their westward trek, sectionalism threatened to break up the new American nation. All the old divisive forces—local quarrels and jealousies that had divided the colonies before 1776—reasserted themselves. Conspicuous differences existed between the East and the West, and a North-South conflict had begun to cast its ominous shadow in the uneasiness generated by the continuation of slavery in the South.

The East-West conflict was caused primarily by the extraordinary growth of population of the new country and the vast tracts of land available. In 1700 the population of the colonies, excluding Indians, who were never very numerous, was about 250,000; in 1800 the population of the new American nation was estimated at 5,000,000. The Kentucky-Tennessee area alone saw its numbers increase from 10,000 in 1781 to 110,000 in 1790.

The growth in the West was helpful to the East in preventing social problems that result from overcrowding, but it fostered other conflicts. It created citizens whose needs were different from those of other Americans, but who had to surrender their political interests in order to attend to those needs. Representation did not keep up with expansion; hence governing bodies remained under the domination of Easterners, who frequently neglected the needs of Westerners.

That the Union did not break up by the turn of the century was due in a large part to the realistic appraisal of human nature of the Founding Fathers and the political mechanisms they set in motion.

In 1788, for the second time since the Declaration of Independence, Americans attempted to establish a government acceptable to all sections of the country. The first effort, the Articles of Confederation, had failed because the body proclaiming them, the Continental Congress, which sat from 1774 to 1789, at no time had any real power to enforce them. This lack of power resulted from the fact that separate colonies—even after becoming states—kept their hands on the purse strings. Sordid contention over land claims by speculators in disputed territories plagued the Congress. Many of its members owned shares in speculative companies, and this caused conflicts of interest.

The only power in the federal government, the Congress, grew feebler while the states grew stronger and became contemptuous of its authority. They violated the Articles of Confederation by ignoring the nation's treaties, by waging wars with Indians, and even by establishing navies of their own. The states were like rebellious, headstrong children—older, more confident, and better established than their family head.

As state governments grew stronger, they grew (in the opinion of leading citizens) more irresponsible. An interstate convention was called to discuss problems resulting from the postwar depression. At this meeting, held in Annapolis in 1786, a movement grew to consider a thorough overhaul of the Articles of Confederation.

The outgrowth of the Annapolis convention was the Constitutional Convention, which convened in the State House in Philadelphia May 25, 1787.

Historical research has shown that the motivation for the convention was not entirely patriotic. Economics played a great part. Be that as it may, a formidable group of fifty-five men were convened. Washington, who was chosen president of the convention on its first day, brought authority and dignity to the proceedings. The venerable Benjamin Franklin was there too, but most of the delegates were young men. Thomas Jefferson and John Adams were conspicuously absent, both being in Europe at the time. Samuel Adams and Patrick Henry were not there either—and probably all to the good, because they had grown old and politically reactionary. The Federalists, who were responsible for drafting the Constitution, were conservatives favored by Philip Kent. Abraham supported the liberal faction, the Republicans, whose champion was Thomas Jefferson.

The issues that made these early Americans cast their vote with one side or the other were matters more of temperament than of principle, a fact dramatized in *The Seekers* by the political differences that were a source of contention between Philip and Abraham. At the risk of oversimplification, it can be said that the Federalists were in favor of a strong executive branch; some even wished to adorn it with the trappings of a monarchy, much to the dismay of the democratic Republicans, who wanted power to reside with the States. Since the Federalists represented the Establishment, they were understandably loath to see political power pass from their hands, because with its disappearance financial power would leave too.

Despite political uncertainties, the nation was forging ahead economically. No one demonstrated the fact more dramatically than enterprising New England shippers, who were discovering new markets for old and new products all over the world. On August 30, 1784, the first American ship to visit China arrived carrying forty tons of ginseng, the herb *Panax quinquefolius*, esteemed in China for its medicinal properties. At the time it was found abundantly in America from the eastern seaboard to the Missouri River. Asian sources were disappearing. American business men secured tea and other marketable products from China in return, making a sound profit.

No corner of the world remained untouched by these enterprising Yankee traders, nor was any commodity too exotic, provided it made money. Salem, Massachusetts, became the peppercorn capital of the world. This spice was in demand everywhere. In 1805 Salem exported 7,500,000 tons of peppercorns.

The ingenious Yankee was making himself felt all over the world. A good example was Frederic Tudor, from a prominent Boston family, who developed means of storing ice so that there was minimal melting. He was soon shipping ice cut from clear New England ponds all over the world, making a huge profit. He designed an economical icehouse for the tropics and with his partner, Nathaniel Wyeth, invented an ice cutter that greatly expedited the operation.

Jared Kent could without doubt have become one of these Yankee entrepreneurs, or he could have entered the family publishing house; he chose rather to enlist in the newly established United States Navy.

In 1794, during George Washington's second term as president, the Congress began taking steps toward creating a navy by authorizing the construction of six frigates (later reduced to three). The last ships of the old Continental Navy had been sold ten years earlier. In the summer of 1797 the three new vessels—the *Constitution*, on which Jared served, the *United States*, and the *Constellation*—were launched. They were considerably larger than their English and French counterparts.

The *Constitution* was as long as a ship of the line, but

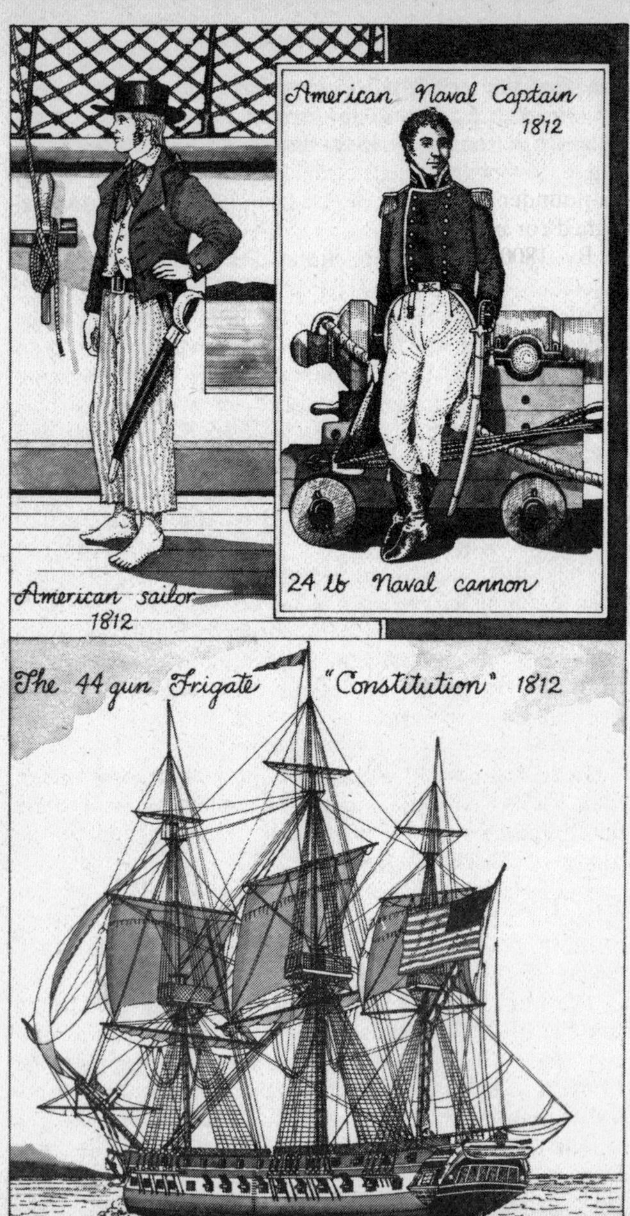
American Naval Captain
1812
24 lb Naval cannon
American sailor
1812
The 44 gun Frigate "Constitution" 1812

considerably less broad of beam. Her mainmast soared 180 feet from her deck. She carried thirty 24-pounder guns in her main battery, instead of the 18-pounders which normally armed frigates. On her deck were twenty 32-pounder carronades—stubby, short-range guns designed for close combat.

By 1800 the United States fleet had grown to a respectable force of thirty-four ships. But in March of 1801, when Thomas Jefferson, an avowed pacifist, took office, all ships in the service were sold except for the *Enterprise* and thirteen frigates, seven of which were laid up in reserve. Pay was severely cut, and the naval officer corps was reduced to 9 captains, 36 lieutenants, and 150 midshipmen. (Until the Civil War the highest rank in the United States Navy was captain, though the courtesy title of commodore was given to an officer who commanded a company of ships.)

With the War of 1812 the navy came into its own. Indeed, most of the action of this two-year conflict took place on water—first at sea, and then on Lakes Huron, Erie, Ontario, and Champlain.

The Treaty of Ghent, which ended the war, was signed on Christmas Eve of 1814, but word did not reach America in time to prevent Major General Sir Edward Pakenham from marching on New Orleans in January, 1815. His veteran troops were utterly routed by General Andrew Jackson's sharpshooters.

Jared Kent was not temperamentally suited to the classroom. His lively spirit rebelled at the rigidity of formal education, and his frequent truancy was his only means of protest.

Opinions vary as to the quality of the education Jared rejected. Primary and secondary education had not altered greatly in the North from the system—if indeed it could be called a system—the Puritans had put into effect shortly after their arrival.

The very young boy or girl's first academic experience

was at a dame school, where elderly widows or spinsters, who usually knew little more than their pupils, taught children their letters with the aid of hornbooks—the alphabet and a few simple sentences on precious paper protected from grubby little fingers by a sheet of transparent horn.

Grammar schools were for boys chosen on the basis of social status and ability in languages necessary to the study of theology and the humanities. The first of these was the Roxbury Latin School, still in existence today, which opened its doors in 1635, a year before the founding of Harvard. The only courses taught were Latin and Greek. When, one hundred and sixty-four years later, the school shortened its course from seven to four years, the only courses taught were still Latin and Greek, with all recitations conducted in Latin. A few grammar schools taught English and arithmetic, but for the most part the curriculum was predominantly classical until after the Revolutionary War.

Generally, girls were given very little academic training after leaving a dame school. Any further education for them was directed toward accomplishment in dancing, music, painting, and needlework. Occasionally they might also learn a few words of French.

By the last decade of the eighteenth century, the academy had begun to displace Latin schools. They prepared the young not only for college, but for business and the lesser professions. Their curricula varied remarkably and might include algebra, geometry, trigonometry, surveying, geography, logic, elocution, English, commercial courses, and quite often a course in science. They even admitted some girls.

The quality of teaching also varied, depending on the interests and finances of the community. There was no established system for hiring teachers, so the selection was haphazard at best. Pay was extremely low, and duties were arduous. As many as eighty pupils would be crowded into a single classroom, and ages varied greatly.

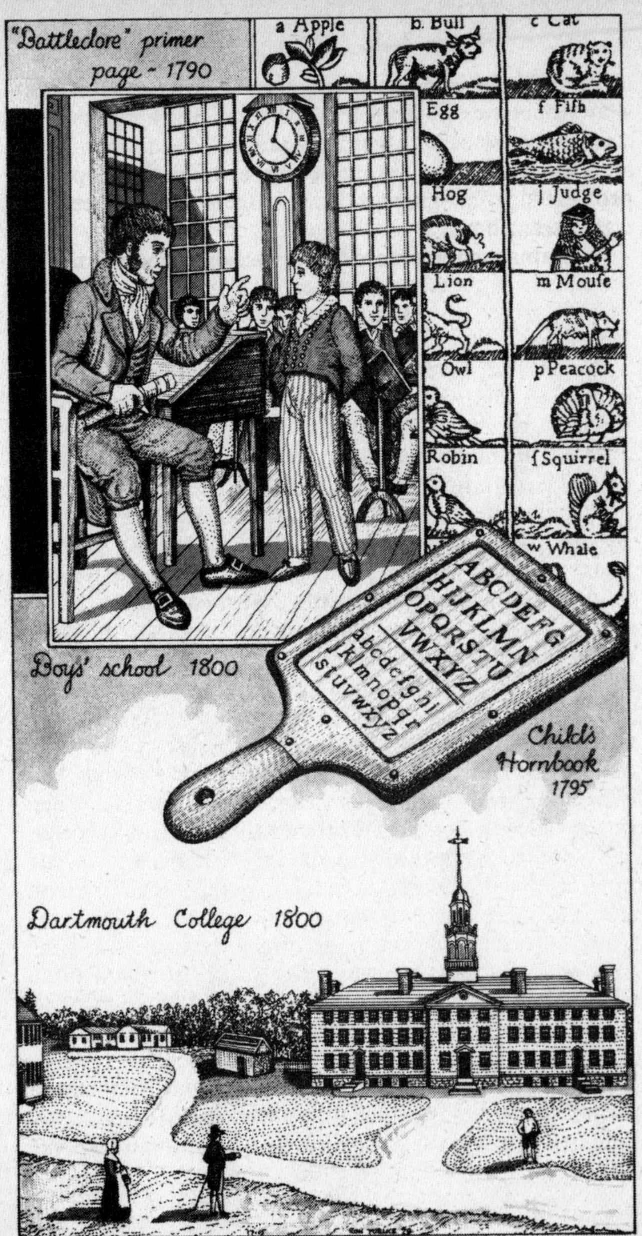
"Battledore" primer page - 1790
a Apple
b. Bull
c Cat
Egg
f Fifh
Hog
j Judge
Lion
m Moufe
Owl
p Peacock
Robin
ſ Squirrel
w Whale
ABCDEFG
HIJKLMN
OPQRSTU
VWXYZ
abcdefghi
jklmnopqr
stuvwxyz
Boys' school 1800
Child's Hornbook 1795
Dartmouth College 1800

Needless to say, none of these conditions was attractive to superior types; schoolmasters were often drunkards, thieves, or just plain ignoramuses.

There were some good teachers, dedicated men and later women, who performed miracles of teaching under the most adverse conditions. There were even some advantages to teaching then: a teacher had few administrators to contend with, hardly any reports to make or records to keep, and a surprising amount of academic freedom.

Prominent Americans gave a good deal of attention to education immediately after the Revolution. Numerous plans for federally controlled systems sprang up, all based on the principle that education is a public responsibility of federal government. Ironically, the liberal faction in their antifederalism provided the most vehement opposition. At the same time religious and other conservative interests were unwilling to relinquish control of the schools. In the opinion of many the arm of education was moral and theological and government should have nothing to do with it. Others feared putting schools in the hands of dangerous liberals like Thomas Jefferson.

Latin America had twelve universities before the first was founded in the North American English colonies. By the time of the Revolution, there were nine and only two of these were nondenominational—Columbia, then called Queens, founded 1754; and Pennsylvania, originally named College of Philadelphia, 1740. The others were Harvard, the first, 1636, Congregational; William and Mary, 1693, the Church of England; Yale, 1701, Congregational; Princeton, originally the College of New Jersey, 1746, Presbyterian; Brown, formerly Rhode Island College, 1764, Baptist; Rutgers, originally called Queens, 1766, Reformed; Dartmouth, 1769, Congregational. In the postwar years many new colleges appeared.

Life at college was strictly regimented, with fixed periods for rising, prayers, study, bed. At many colleges students were specifically enjoined from dancing, drinking, racing horses, swearing, dueling, and breaking furniture. Many colleges carried rules on their books having to do with smashing doors, ringing bells without permission, defacing walls, striking teachers, and locking instructors in their rooms. Punishment ranged from fines, both large and small, to rustication (a euphemism for a temporary suspension) or expulsion.

Then as now, routine practical jokes were a favorite pastime of university students. Putting a cow in the chapel headed the list. Occasionally these pranks turned into something more serious, and student rioting was not uncommon. In 1807 at Princeton, 125 of the total enrollment of 200 were expelled for rioting.

Despite a rigid daily schedule, there was little organized student life. Sports were what one chose to do to keep fit—informal games and boxing, fencing, or swimming. Some students also formed debating societies or literary discussion groups.

The university curriculum for the first two or three decades reflected a tradition inherited from England and the Continent. With a core of the classics, logic, philosophy, and theology, the course of study in the early eighteenth century was intended to provide knowledge that would assure the young gentleman of his place among educated men. This body of knowledge was relatively fixed. Any acquaintance with the arts was considered ornamental, not essential. This academic training represented a system that grew out of the rediscovery of classical civilization during the Renaissance.

Shortly before the Revolution, a quiet reaction to the traditional curriculum set in. Widening horizons in both science and the humanities demanded broader education in a growing urban society enjoying the benefits of expanding trade.

Discussions of free will and predestination gradually gave way to debates on taxation and theories of government. The great new burst of scientific knowledge forced more and more American colleges by the last decade of the eighteenth century to support professors of mathematics, astronomy, and physics, or of "natural philosophy" as well as teachers of logic, philosophy, and the classics. History, up to then merely a corollary of classical studies, began to appear as a separate study.

In 1800 the average college student in his first year pursued a course that included the Greek and Latin writers (he knew their grammar better than his own), rhetoric, something called universal history, arithmetic, English grammar, Hebrew, logic, and geography.

In his second year he continued much the same course, but added to it algebra, mensuration (geometry), and philosophy. The student's only relief was that he dropped his course in logic. In the third year he added the writing of English essays and forensic disputation—a kind of public speaking. In his final year the curriculum was much the same, with the addition of a course in theology.

The new Americans were by no means indifferent to science, in spite of the fact that native geniuses in the field like Benjamin Franklin and Thomas Jefferson had turned their energies more and more to diplomatic and governmental duties, and had left the American scientific world without distinguished leadership.

Because agriculture was the cornerstone of the new nation's economy, most active scientific research naturally had to do with farming. Shortly after the war, experimenters attempted to introduce silkworms into the country, as well as new crops such as hemp and mangelwurzel, a coarse beet intended for cattle food. Research centered on crop yield, pest and disease control, fertilizers, and harvesting methods. Americans soon learned that farming was a science in every way amenable to an experimental approach.

Mathematics as a separate scientific study was not well developed in the early days of the United States, but its practical applications in surveying, engineering, and navigation soon became apparent.

The leading practical mathematician was a self-taught New England genius, Nathaniel Bowditch, whose experience as a seaman led him to correct errors in navigation guides then in use and in 1802 to write his own book, *The New American Practical Navigator*. The book soon became the standard work for all navigation in the Western world and went into fifty-six editions. Bowditch also developed actuarial tables for insurance companies as well as publishing papers on astronomy and meteorology.

At the beginning of the nineteenth century earth scientists were engaged in the gargantuan task of describing, gathering, and classifying materials. Botanists had the chore of classifying the flora of a continent, which was not only of primary importance to basic research, but of practical value to agriculture and medicine.

At the same time, American zoologists were concerned with classifying and naming a bewildering variety of fauna. Alexander Wilson, a Scotsman, came to America at the age of twenty-eight, in 1794, the year Abraham Kent fought under General Wayne in the Maumee Valley. In 1804 Wilson set about collecting and drawing all the bird specimens of North America. He did not live to complete his task, dying in 1813 just after the appearance of his eighth volume. Wilson's pioneering efforts paved the way for America's most important ornithologist, John James Audubon, at whose store in Louisville Jared found temporary work before he and Amanda set off for the Cumberland Trail.

Of all the scientific interests of this period, none received more attention than that given to geography. After all, they had an entire continent to explore and map. More than any other science geography was of utilitarian value because of its importance to land settlement. The government sponsored several expeditions that not only advanced geographical science, but added greatly to botanical, zoological, meteorological, ethnological, and agricultural knowledge.

Of these scientific expeditions none was more important than the one Abraham Kent refused to join—that of Meriwether Lewis and William Clark, the brother of George Clark, Judson Fletcher's friend. Both Lewis and Clark were Virginians, Lewis being a near neighbor of Thomas Jefferson. After serving in the Indian Wars, Lewis, who was well educated in science, language, and mathematics, became personal secretary to President Jefferson. In 1803 Jefferson squeezed twenty-five hundred dollars from a tight-fisted Congress to finance an expedition to the Pacific.

Lewis accepted the post of joint leader with Clark, who by this time had become a Kentuckian. Both men studied astronomy, botany, mineralogy, cartography, zoology, and what history there was of the American Indian. Jefferson himself, a scientist in his own right, spent weeks with Lewis and Clark preparing them for their expedition.

In 1804 the group left St. Louis to pursue the Missouri to its source. The men were charged with making detailed reports of flora and fauna, minerals, weather, rainfall, rivers, and fossils. They were to make maps, observe Indian society, and collect scientific specimens. After reaching the headwaters of the Missouri, the group followed the Columbia to the Pacific. When they returned in 1806, Lewis and Clark had made one of the most important scientific surveys in American history.

We should not leave Lewis and Clark without recalling the role played by an Indian woman in the Lewis and Clark expeditions.

A Shoshone woman named Sacajawea ("Bird Woman") and her Canadian husband, Toussaint Charbonneau, accompanied Lewis and Clark as interpreter-guides. Sacajawea was immeasurably helpful in guiding

Lewis and Clark with Sacajawea July 1805

the expedition over the Great Divide and in gaining the friendship of the Shoshone for the explorers.

As America took on shape and character as a nation, the desire for a distinctly American culture grew. In 1783 Noah Webster wrote in the preface to his speller—a book found in almost every classroom, and in some the only one—"America must be as independent in literature as she is in politics." He was not, of course, advocating cultural isolation. Americans continued to be proud that they were part of the British tradition, and there was greater interest than ever before in continental Europe. French influence was considerable, especially since America had discovered in the French *philosophes* and the encyclopedists of the eighteenth century substantiation of principles on which their new nation was founded. Subsequently, Americans became interested in Germany too.

How did Americans go about creating a distinctively national literature? It was the consensus that American authors should studiously avoid imitating foreign models and reject any that were subversive of American principles. But in addition to being native and original, American writers strove to meet universal standards of taste and beauty.

American literature had the Indian and the frontier—both native and original themes. James Fenimore Cooper seized upon that material, and by 1821 had written *The Spy.* Henry Wadsworth Longfellow, somewhat later, in 1855, attempted an American epic with his *Hiawatha.* William Cullen Bryant took the land itself, fresh, unspoiled, and vast, and extolled its beauty in such poems as "To a Waterfowl" and "To the Fringed Gentian."

Despite demands for a fresh, new literature, readers felt secure with time-tested models. It was more comfortable to admire Scott, who was deemed to be the greatest novelist of all time, than to offer an opinion about an unknown. In order to get a hearing, Cooper encouraged the rumor that his first novel was really written by a prominent Englishman.

In 1800 there were more than one hundred fifty newspapers in the United States; by 1810 that number was doubled. Almost every one of them had its essayist who was more or less successful in creating a style that could be said to be "American." It was not, however, until Washington Irving's *Sketch Book* appeared in 1820 that the country had a writer who was truly American in style, content, and spirit. That was the first literary work by an American to receive international acclaim.

Washington Irving must be singled out because it was he of all American writers who, in the early years of the Republic, helped American literature emerge from its colonial dependency. Born into a rich New York City family, he casually studied law, traveled widely in Europe, and hobnobbed with the fashionable. Occasionally he tried his hand at the family hardware business. He also served as American ambassador to Spain for four years, but most of his adult life was spent writing.

No one has ever accredited Irving with intellectualism. There is little action or plot in his stories. His charm and effectiveness lie in his ability to create mood and color, his ability to describe and to characterize. His writing is a mix of wonderful humor, urbanity, and sentiment. His interest in nature and humanity, seasoned by good sense and good taste, places him in an exalted position among American writers of any period.

The early American novel did not fare as well as the essay. In the first place, the religious atmosphere of the times did not encourage a form which many considered corrupt. Those novels that were written were imitations either of Samuel Richardson, sentimental and didactic, or of Walter Scott, historical and romantic.

The Richardson imitations were numerous and were written according to the accepted formula—seduction (attempted or realized) and duels or suicide or both. If the protagonists survived the vicissitudes of their harrowing

Benjamin West R.A. 1795
Concert Violinist 1812
Washington Irving 1809
James Fenimore Cooper 1822
The Painter at Work 1812
17-17
RON TOELKE 79

existence, they usually married. Whatever their fate, there was a moral to be derived from these novels with the assistance of subtitles like "Female Frailty," "Delicate Embarrassment," or "Venial Trespasses."

Two spectacular examples of this genre of early American novels were *The Power of Sympathy* (1784) by William Hill Brown and *Charlotte Temple* (1791) by Susanna Rowson. The Brown opus was, according to its moralizing preface, intended to "expose the dangerous consequences of seduction and to set forth the advantages of female education." It attempted to do so by way of a plot that included seduction, a near miss on incest, kidnapping, attempted rape, and suicide. Mrs. Rowson's book, built along the same lurid lines, went into two hundred editions. Its sequel, *Lucy Temple*, the trials and tribulations of Charlotte's illegitimate daughter, went through thirty-one editions.

The Gothic novels of Mrs. Radcliffe, Monk Lewis, Charles Maturin, and William Godwin, which captivated England with their tales of terror, suspense, and mystery, had a competent emulator in Charles Brockden Brown. *Wieland*, his first and best novel, brought praise from such English notables as John Keats and William Hazlitt.

Sir Walter Scott's popularity in America was immense. By 1823 Americans had bought a half million of his novels of legend and history, adventure and folklore, love and scenery. American imitations of Scott were legion, but except for the works of Cooper, few bear reading today. When Natty Bumppo, Cooper's archetypal hero, walked across the pages of *The Pioneers*, the first of *The Leatherstocking Tales*, the American novel was born.

If first attempts at an American novel were feeble, those at poetry were more so. Only one name stands out—Philip Freneau. He was a Princeton graduate who had served a sentence on a British prison ship and then enlisted in the Revolutionary army. He sailed as a sea captain and spent several years as a journalist. He wrote a certain amount of political verse which was violently anti-Federalist. His lyric poetry was, however, delicate and skillful. He also produced a number of rough, realistic poems that fall somewhere between Robert Burns and Robert Service.

The first American settlers held strong religious objections to drama, which was then experiencing its golden age in England. By the beginning of the eighteenth century itinerant players were found in the southern and middle colonies, but they were not welcome in New England. The first theaters were ballrooms, barns, and taverns. By 1735, there were real theaters in Williamsburg, New York, and Charleston. By midcentury theaters were springing up all over the colonies, except in New England.

London provided the plays and most of the players well on through the century, except for the plays of Royall Tyler (1757–1826) and William Dunlap (1766–1839). Tyler, a Boston lawyer who later became chief justice of the Vermont Supreme Court, wrote a comedy of manners, *The Contrast*, that was first performed in 1787. It is the account of Colonel Manly, a stalwart American, and his encounters with Billy Dimple, an Anglicized fop. Another character in the comedy is Jonathan, a Yankee farmer, who became the prototype of the lovable American comic rustic. Dunlap was even more important than Tyler. He wrote at least sixty-five original plays as well as adapting a number of French and German dramas.

An amazing number of plays were written by Americans between 1800 and 1830, and while most of them were undistinguished, their themes and characters were resoundingly American—Rip Van Winkle, Pocahontas, Indians and white men, the frontiersman, the city dude, and many others.

The early Americans loved music, especially those in the South. Ladies and gentlemen played musical instruments as a matter of course—flute, violin, harpsichord, guitar, and harp. Jefferson was a tolerable violinist, and Washington played the flute. Benjamin Franklin was proficient at the harp, guitar, and violin and even composed a string quartet. Charleston's St. Cecilia Society, which was organized in 1737, supported a large orchestra and sponsored concerts. The Moravians in Bethlehem, Pennsylvania, founded a musical college in 1745. Their choir and other choral groups were excellent.

The French refugees who arrived after 1790 exerted a strong influence on American musical taste. Other immigrants from Europe also brought scores of talented musicians. Cities like New York and Philadelphia supported orchestras composed almost wholly of foreign musicians, who played Scarlatti, Haydn, Vivaldi, Mozart, Corelli, Gluck, Purcell, and Handel. Bach had been forgotten, if ever known, and his genius would not be appreciated until the third decade of the nineteenth century, when Felix Mendelssohn would be instrumental in reviving interest in him.

Despite the inundation from Europe, a small group of native American musicians continued to compose. Francis Hopkinson of Philadelphia, an organist and chamber music director, composed a large number of songs and instrumental pieces. William Billings, who lived from 1746 to 1800, was probably the first native musician of any importance. His *New England Psalm Singer* was published in 1770. Justin Morgan, famous more for the breed of horse he developed in Vermont than for his artistic endeavor, was a singer and composer who was able to support his family by his music.

Of all the arts, painting received the least attention in the new nation, probably because from the start, New England Puritans suspected pictorial arts. There was, however, no prejudice against portraits, and the limner, as he was called, was in great demand.

Other kinds of paintings were regarded as frivolous by Americans, who were busy with (in their opinion) the more serious business of building a nation. Even John Adams, a man of taste and education, once remarked, "I would not give sixpence for a picture of Raphael or a statue of Phidias."

Despite Adams's remark and the prevailing lack of interest in painting, there were nevertheless American painters of renown. Almost all of these were portraitists or painters of historical scenes, for the solid reason that such works were commissioned. The public was conscious of its recent heroic past, and families wanted family likenesses.

One native painter of the time, Benjamin West (1738–1820), a poor Pennsylvania Quaker, was sent to Europe by rich Philadelphians. His visit to Italy, and Italy's influence on him, precluded any possibility of his becoming an "American" painter. As a matter of fact, he settled down in England, achieved great success there, and did not return to his native country.

John Singleton Copley (1738–1815) was the most sought-after portrait painter in America before the Revolution. Caught in the Tory-patriot conflict in Boston, he went to Rome in 1774 and thence to London, and never returned.

Charles Willson Peale (1741–1827) found time during his command of troops at Valley Forge to paint forty portraits. An ardent patriot, he also founded the first museum in the United States, organized the first public art exhibition—held in Philadelphia in 1794—and helped establish the Pennsylvania Academy of Fine Arts in 1805.

Gilbert Stuart (1755–1828) went to England for his early training but returned to the United States in 1792, where he dominated American portrait painting until his death. During his career he painted more than 1,150 portraits, including those of the first five presidents of the country.

In the early years of the Republic Americans built for a shifting and expanding population with the result that few buildings were regarded as permanent. Until well into the nineteenth century there was not an identifiable American style of building. Even the frame cottage, often quickly built of necessity, was a composite of English, Dutch, and Swedish influences. The typical eighteenth-century architecture in America was Georgian. There were no professional architects in America until very late in the eighteenth century, but working from British books and drawings, amateur architects produced some creditable edifices, such as Independence Hall in Philadelphia, the (Truro) synagogue in Newport, Christ Church in Philadelphia, and King's Chapel in Boston.

By 1800 there were two distinct architectural styles evident in America—"federal," a modified British style, popular in New England and in some of the middle states, and the "classical" style popular in the South. The two greatest practitioners of these styles were, respectively, Charles Bulfinch of Boston and Thomas Jefferson of Virginia.

Bulfinch was much impressed during his travels in England by the work of the brothers Adam and believed its elegance suited his native New England. Like the Adam brothers, Bulfinch modified the heavy forms of the Georgian (or, in America, "colonial") style to achieve a new gracefulness. But he also added his own touches and created in the process the beginnings of an indigenous American architecture. He designed many houses in Boston and enlarged Faneuil Hall. He also designed capitols at Boston, Hartford, and Augusta, Maine; Boston's New South Church, India Wharf, and Massachusetts General Hospital. Bulfinch's style, augmented by the work of Samuel McIntire and Asher Benjamin, can still be found throughout New England, and copies of it exist in communities in Ohio, Michigan, Illinois, and Iowa.

Most United States government buildings constructed after 1790 were in the classical tradition favored by Jefferson and other builders in the South. Refusing to copy things British, these Americans turned to Greece and Rome for architectural inspiration. The classical style

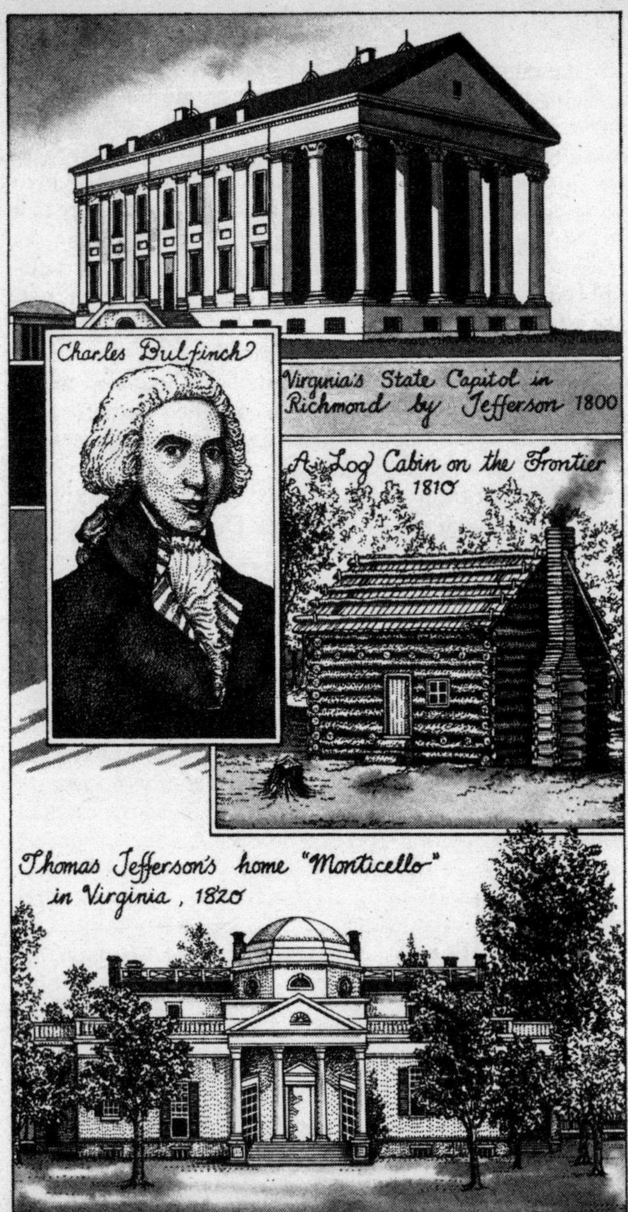
Charles Bulfinch
Virginia's State Capitol in Richmond by Jefferson 1800
A Log Cabin on the Frontier 1810
Thomas Jefferson's home "Monticello" in Virginia, 1820

gave the impression of logic, order, and stability—virtues much admired by the beneficiaries of the Enlightenment, that extraordinary intellectual fomentation of the eighteenth century that in a large part fostered the American Revolution. In addition Americans were infected with the classical craze that a few years earlier had swept Europe, so not only did they erect buildings after Greek and Roman models, but they gave new American cities classical names—Troy, Rome, Syracuse, Athens, Memphis, and Cairo, to name a few.

By 1815, America had thus begun to express itself artistically and architecturally. But an even more important endeavor for the new, sprawling nation was the establishment of communications and improved transportation. For while travel by water was comparatively easy, overland travel was another matter.

Roads in the long-settled areas of the East had been made passable by use; they were free of stumps, and some were even graveled. Turnpikes, which were privately owned, were even better, and better conveyances could travel on them.

One such vehicle was the Concord coach, named after the New Hampshire town where it was developed. It was high-slung on wide-tired wheels. It carried from six to twelve passengers, depending on its length. The commonest model carried nine passengers—three on a front seat, three on a rear seat, and three athwart the carriage supported by a leather backstrap. To absorb the unremitting road shock the rocker-bottomed body was hung on wide multi-ply leather straps—less likely to break than steel springs, but causing a motion like that of the pitching of a boat. Motion sickness was not uncommon. To compensate for such discomfort, these carriages were elegantly appointed and beautifully paneled.

Coaches were drawn by four or six horses. Their average speed was six miles an hour; eight was possible only under the best road and weather conditions.

Backwoods roads consisted of twelve-foot logs laid across the roadbed to keep coach wheels from sinking into the ground. Such roads were extremely bumpy, especially if conveyances were not carefully suspended above excellent springs; and few were. Later the round logs were replaced by heavy planks secured to parallel stringers. When the wood was new, these carriageways were passable enough; but once they began to rot, they were no better than the mud holes they were meant to cover.

In the eighteenth century, bridges, although not unknown, were few. Rivers were forded whenever possible. The alternative was a crude ferry. Then early in the nineteenth century, Americans began constructing covered bridges, many of which survive to this day. The covering was not designed to provide protection from the elements, but as an extension of the trusses holding the bridge together. Although light, these bridges were firm and durable. Floods that destroy modern concrete and steel structures merely floated these covered spans downstream, where they were put back into service with new approaches.

There was great interest in canals in the mid-eighteenth century, but the Revolution prevented construction of any. After the war, a few canals were built, but only to bypass falls or rapids or to connect immediate backcountry with seaports. With the completion of the Erie Canal in 1825—from the upper reaches of the Hudson River to Lake Erie—America achieved the longest canal in the world.

The Germans in Philadelphia not only gave the Kentucky rifle to frontiersmen, they developed the Conestoga wagon, named after the lower Susquehanna village where it was perfected. Originally intended to carry heavy freight to Philadelphia markets, this conveyance became the chief overland means to the West. It had heavy wheels and tires and a body shaped like a whaleboat to keep the load from sliding out on steep grades. The top was made of white canvas stretched over bows. Along the sides hung buckets of grease for lubricating the axles and boxes of tools for making frequent roadside repairs. These wagons were drawn by teams of four or six horses.

Most settlers could not afford such wagons. They either hired them, as Abraham and Elizabeth did, or they traveled in smaller wagons or carts. Oxen were commoner than horses, because they were cheaper and sturdier, but they were also much slower.

Waterways provided the most comfortable means of transportation, and fortunately, rivers ran the way the westward movers were going. So settlers traveled by water as soon as they could—on the Monongahela or the Allegheny or where the two joined at Pittsburgh to form the Ohio.

The workhorse of the rivers before steam was the keelboat. Seventy feet long and ten or twelve feet wide, it made good time downstream under six pairs of oars with a crew of twenty-odd. By 1794 packet keelboats were running regularly from Pittsburgh to Cincinnati. Since Indians were still troublesome, these boats carried small arms for crew and passengers as well as six-pound cannons.

Boat builders met the needs of westward travelers by creating large, clumsy craft never meant to come back upstream. Their owners broke them up downriver and sold the timber or used it to build their dwellings. One such boat was the broadhorn barge, so called because of its two huge sweeps forward; it carried up to one hundred tons. The flatboat, an immense, oblong, watertight open box, had room for the livestock and wagons of several families. The ark was a flatboat with a shelter amidships and accommodations for cooking.

During these years of American history, the westward movement was becoming paramount. The exciting search for new frontiers in a new world ruled the American course and formed the American character.

A Conestoga Wagon carrying freight
1805
A Keelboat on the Missouri River
1820
"Diligence" type
public coach,
1810
RON TOELKE 79

The Furies

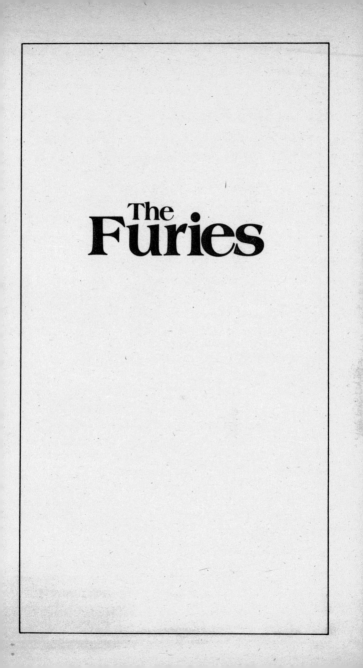

A CONDENSATION OF

The Furies

1836–1852

BOOK 1

Sunday, March 6, 1836, marked the thirteenth day of the siege of the Alamo. Amanda Kent de la Gura was afraid.

"I don't want to die here," she said to herself. "But if this is the end, I ought to face it the way my own grandfather, Philip Kent, did when he fought against the British. I wouldn't want him to be ashamed of how I die."

Only the most foolishly optimistic of the hundred and eighty-odd men walled up in the mission of San Antonio de Valero believed there was a chance of escape. Amanda had come into the mission to nurse her dying friend, Jim Bowie, and had not left when the last possibility was open to her.

As she sat by his side, Bowie turned to her, saying, "You've been a good friend, Mandy."

"Your family were always good friends to me—even when most respectable citizens wouldn't deign to speak to me."

"Well, you weren't in the most respectable of professions. To most people Gura's Hotel was a whorehouse—nothing more."

Amanda looked crestfallen. "I don't claim I've lived a perfect life. Sometimes just to survive I've done things I'm not proud of. But I have only one regret at thirty-three—that none of my children survived. The boy was stillborn. The girl lived six weeks. When she died, it broke Jaimie's spirit."

Bowie had dozed off. In the ensuing silence Amanda's mind drifted to the past. She thought fondly of her late husband, Jaimie de la Gura, a struggling farmer.

A year before the birth of their daughter, Jaimie had thought about planting cotton; but cotton required plenty of laborers, and in principle he was against owning slaves. So they had sold their land and bought a house in Bexar, Texas. Amanda had been thankful for the decision.

Soon afterwards, Jaimie had left for his native New Orleans to buy merchandise for a store he intended to open. While there he was struck down by cholera.

After her husband's death, Amanda wanted nothing to do with storekeeping. Instead, she sold her house in 1832 and decided to open a decent hotel—something Bexar lacked.

Then, when the sons of the town's better families began complaining about the lack of feminine companionship in Bexar, Amanda converted part of Gura's Hotel into a brothel. She had spent her adolescence and young womanhood among the Teton Sioux, and had come to regard sex as they did—not as a sin, but as a celebration, a wondrous and necessary part of life.

Amanda had prospered, but she was only tolerated—never accepted—by Bexar's reigning families.

The Alamo plaza fell first and then rooms where defenders had barricaded themselves. The chapel, into which women and children had been herded, was the last bastion to fall to the attacking Mexicans.

As soldiers converged on the sacristy door, Amanda watched a soldier deliberately aim and shoot a young boy through the stomach. Enraged, she shouted, "God damn you for a pack of animals!"

Another soldier slammed the butt of his musket

against Amanda's forehead. She sprawled, hitting hard. She expected a bayonet stroke, but none came. Instead, an officer was flailing her attacker with the flat of his saber.

"His Excellency gave no orders for slaughtering women! Get out!"

As the soldiers went scurrying, Amanda got a look at the officer, a swarthy, stout man in his thirties. His round face showed surprise as she spat on his boots.

"I will overlook your disrespect; I am Major Cordoba. I am here to escort you to His Excellency General Antonio López de Santa Anna. The Mexican women and children will be set free."

Standing before Santa Anna, Amanda showed a defiance that angered the Mexican general. "You will regret your insolence," he said. "By God, you will!"

Suddenly, she was struck viciously by Cordoba's fist. Then Cordoba hit her in the stomach and flung her to the floor.

Amanda tried to rise, tried to comprehend the change that had come over this man who had treated her and the other women so humanely, almost gallantly, only a few hours earlier.

"Let me take her, Excellency. I've lost my serving woman. If you'll put her in my keeping, I'll teach her respect."

"Very well, Major. She will not go free now or ever. If she finds the work of a camp woman too difficult . . . if she should sicken and die—that's your affair."

Amanda opened her eyes and saw Cordoba. "You stupid, intemperate woman!" Rage colored his cheeks, but it was a puzzling, different kind of rage than he'd displayed in front of the general. "You know you nearly got yourself sentenced to a firing squad—or worse. I had to mistreat you, don't you understand? I knew of no other way to get you out. Señora, if you stay with me, I'll treat you decently. I'll make few demands—clean clothes and a hot meal at night."

Thus Amanda Kent in yet another struggle for survival became a *soldadera*, a woman attached to an officer to look after his needs and to provide comfort. After a short time an affection that turned to love grew up between the two. Amanda was pregnant with Luis Cordoba's child when the major was killed in a charge led by General Sam Houston in the Battle of San Jacinto.

In January of 1837 Louis Kent was born.

From the Journal of Jephtha Kent

In April of 1844 the Reverend Jephtha Kent, as recorded in his journal, arrived in New York City. He had come from Lexington, Virginia, where he had held the Methodist itinerancy for two years. In New York, he was attending the general conference of his church, at which opinions on slavery were causing sharp differences among Methodists. There was in Jephtha's own heart uncertainty about the whole issue of slavery.

Jephtha was the twenty-four-year-old son of Jared Kent and his wife, Singing Grass, who had now been dead for three years. The young man had the blue eyes of the Kents and the dark hair of the Shoshone. He was married and had a son of his own, named Gideon.

In 1837, Jared Kent with Singing Grass and Jephtha had traveled to Oregon, where he still worked at wheat farming but did not fare well. He lived alone in the Willamette River valley.

BOOK 2

In April, 1848, the clipper *Manifest Destiny* sailed into the California settlement of Yerba Buena, later called San Francisco. As her captain, Barton McGill, stepped ashore, he fixed his eyes on Amanda and her eleven-year-old son, Louis. With them was Israel, an ex-slave, who was Amanda's devoted employee. Everyone knew that Amanda, the proprietor of Kent's Tavern, was Captain McGill's woman. Forty-four years old, she looked ten years younger.

She eyed the parcel McGill was carrying, knowing it contained Kent editions. She had told Bart about her past, but she had no idea her father's firm was still in existence until she ran across a book carrying the words *Kent and Son* and a design respresenting a bottle of tea on its title page. Now she asked Bart to bring her Kent books whenever he could and whatever news he found. He had been disturbed by the expression on her face when she spoke of the man who had won the family firm from her stepfather in a dice game.

"Is Stovall still running Kent and Son?"

"Yes, but through underlings. He's the third biggest steelmaker in the United States and living in New York. He's opening up a new steel mill in Pittsburgh."

"He's treating Kent and Son like a stepchild?"

"Not exactly. Kent's is still a popular and successful imprint. It's being run by a man named Walpole. Old man almost ready to retire. He was shot by one of the Kents back in '14 or '15."

"Then Stovall let Jared think..."

"Think what?"

"He let Jared think he had done murder. By God, I'm going back there!"

As Amanda and Bart talked about Kent and Son, there was a shout in the street: "Gold!" Within seconds a half dozen voices began to bawl the word through the fog. And soon, like everyone else in Yerba Buena, Amanda caught gold fever.

"Bart," she said a day or so later, "I've decided to stay. I won't go back without money, and there's money to be made here."

In the whole noisy, smoky place Amanda was the only person distinctive this Christmas Eve, 1849. She was alert, brisk, energetic, looking handsome too. She had prospered mightily since the first cry of "Gold" had been heard a year ago. She had realized four hundred percent on her first investment in a quantity of pickaxes and pans. Then she had switched to lumber. Amanda's behavior worried Israel; she no longer had time for anything except business.

Amanda Kent was one of the few human beings who had ever treated Israel as a person. She was kind, thoughtful of others; at least she had been until the craziness had struck the whole town.

Israel warily approached Felker, the bartender at the Exchange. He was sure the man would recognize him. Amanda had once used her Colt to back down Felker and a bunch of hooligans who had tried to come into Kent's for a meal. Felker was now standing at the bar telling an obscene story to a group of miners. One of them stood apart, his blue eyes registering his dislike of the story.

"I know the rules round town say a nigger is entitled to one drink in any public place. But the rules are suspended when I'm tending the store."

"I came to buy whiskey for Kent's; we're out."

"So am I."

"All right," Israel said, "but I'll have a drink."

"No, you won't," said Felker, and he grabbed a knotted rope kept behind the bar to subdue rowdy patrons and lashed at Israel's face.

Blinded and enraged, Israel fastened his hands around Felker's neck. Felker tried one more slash, and as he did so, he hit a hanging lantern. It fell to the floor and broke, spilling oil that ignited in a second.

Israel was still holding Felker's throat as flames engulfed the room. Then the canvas ceiling collapsed and enveloped Felker.

Israel felt hands pulling him to safety. They belonged to the solitary miner.

From a distance Amanda came running. She knelt down and began ministering to Israel's burned legs. She stroked the side of his face; and numb though he was, Israel could feel the old, worn rope bracelet that never left Amanda's wrist.

The miner grabbed her arm. "Where'd you get this piece of rope, woman? What's your name?"

"My name's Amanda Kent. I don't see why you—"

"I'm Jared. *Jared Kent*."

Jared Kent couldn't remember when he had spent a more joyous Christmas day. After Israel had been seen by a doctor, who assured Amanda that her assistant would suffer no permanent damage, the two cousins talked through the night, building a bridge across the thirty-five years of their separation.

Jared's mind could scarcely hold all that Amanda told him—her abduction in Tennessee, her life with the Teton Sioux Plenty Coups, her marriage to a Spanish trapper, her experiences in Texas with Cordoba, and Louis's birth; then her migration to California, and now prosperity brought on by the discovery of gold.

In turn Jared told Amanda about his life as a trapper and about his unsuccessful years as a wheat farmer. He told about his son Jephtha, who had remained with the Southern side when the Methodist Church split over the slavery issue. He described Jephtha's wife, Fan, and their three sons, Gideon, Matthew, and Jeremiah.

Amanda allowed that she longed to go back East. "I want to see our old home; that's one of the reasons I am working so hard to make money."

A sadness touched Jared. His memory showed him dim pictures of the house on Beacon Street. He recalled Stovall's advances, Kent and Son in flames, his shooting of Walpole. He could look back on all that without anger.

Once he had harbored hopes of revenge, but they had been burned out of him by distance and time and his acceptance of the life he had made for himself in a land he found beautiful.

Aware that Amanda and Louis were watching him, he resumed the saga of his life since 1814. "I sold the farm when Oregon got news of the gold and tramped down the coast. I've done pretty well—that is, the Ophir Mineralogical Combine's done well. There are three of us. One of my partners is an Englishman; the other a Baptist from Georgia. At the rate the Ophir is producing now, it won't make me rich by the time I die. But at least I'll be comfortable."

"Comfortable enough to go East to see Jephtha?" Amanda began. "Louis and I could go with you. We could visit your son and then Boston."

"Talking about Boston is pointless, Amanda. I have no desire to go there."

It was well after dark. A lamp glowed on the small table next to Jared's chair by the window. Amanda moved to a shelf of books. She drew one down and handed it to Jared. "Look at the title page."

"My God! Kent and Son!"

Amanda took hold of his shoulder. "Stovall rebuilt the company. He's ruined the firm. It publishes outdated reprints and scurrilous books. I've got to bring Kent and Son back into the hands of its rightful owners."

"Not for my sake. I don't care anymore."

"You don't care that Stovall let you believe you were a murderer all these years?"

"Let me believe . . . What do you mean?"

"That you killed Walpole. He's alive today—just as Stovall is!"

Jared saw the face of Hamilton Stovall on the day the printing house burned and remembered his own rage. But trying to undo a wrong committed more than thirty years ago was futile and destructive.

"Don't do it, Amanda." Gently he touched his cousin's

forehead. "Trying to hurt Stovall, you'll only hurt yourself—and your son."

"God, you've turned spineless!" She stopped and glanced at the window beyond the lamp. "There's someone out th— Jared, move away from the window!"

Her rush to push him came too late. Two pistols exploded, and Jared dropped to his knees. The skin beneath his shirt was warm and sticky.

Amanda knelt and rested her cheek against his. How warm her lips felt against the tangle of his beard.

"Don't take—the Ophir gold."

"No, that belongs to your son."

"He's not worldly, probably won't want..."

"If Jephtha will permit me, I'll be the steward of it..."

Pain shot into his head. A haze obscured his sight. Amanda was on her knees asking a question.

"Jared, tell me the name of the family attorney."

His lips jerked; a whisper: "Ben—"

"What? Jared, try. Try!"

"Ben. Bow. Benbow—yes, oh, God, that's it!"

"Jared, oh, Jared, don't die. We're all that's left to bring the Kents into the world again."

The two mounted figures were dwarfed by the dripping pines and spruces. The reluctant mules struggled over the rocky terrain.

"Israel, how much farther? I'm worn out."

Amanda would be thankful when they reached their destination. Winter dampness penetrated to the bone. Since Christmas night a kind of daze had enveloped her. Now, three weeks into 1850, she was not entirely free of her despondency. To find Jared with such abruptness and to lose him just as abruptly had been a profound shock.

After trying and failing to track down Jared's killers, Amanda had realized that she should also look after his interests up in the diggings. She and Israel set out on a gloomy morning. To add to the somber mood, there was

Amanda's concern about Bart. The morning she and Israel set out, his ship was seven days overdue.

How ridiculous for a woman almost forty-seven years old to go traipsing into the gold country like the very fools she had once condemned.

"Guess we've arrived safe and sound," Israel called. "There's civilization!"

Amanda kept her hat pulled down as she and Israel rode along the main street. She had seldom seen such a confusion of humanity—but no women anywhere. She was so intent on watching a merchant who was hawking boots that she failed to see a drunk come lurching toward her. He stumbled against her mule. The animal bucked, and Amanda went toppling off. Her hat rolled off.

"God bless us all, a woman! Madam, Otto Plankveld, late of Albany, New York. Allow me to assist you," said the tipsy gentleman.

"No, thanks; I'm all right," Amanda said, jamming her hat back on her head. Too late.

"A woman! The Dutchman's got a woman."

Instantly men rushed toward Amanda from both sides. One particularly foul-smelling fellow whom the others called the Pike grabbed her arm, and when the German ran to her assistance, the Pike drove his knee into his groin and flung him into the mud. The Pike then raised his right foot and brought his boot down on Plankveld's temple.

Israel had remained mounted as the men surrounded Amanda. Now Amanda shot her hand toward him, snatched a whip he was holding, and laid it across the Pike's neck.

The Pike faced Amanda. "Well, ain't the little bee got a sting. I got me a sting too, woman." He drew a cheap pocket pistol out of his coat and pointed the stubby muzzle at her eyes. Amanda freed the revolver from her holster while the Pike, whose hand shook because he had been drinking, tried to correct his aim.

Amanda extended the revolver to the full length of her arm and fired.

The pistol slipped from the Pike's hands as he fell face down in the mud.

Someone exclaimed, "She killed him outright!"

Amanda whirled. "He was going to shoot me."

Men surged around her. Some claimed Amanda had committed cold-blooded murder; others said she had only defended herself. Someone demanded she attend miners' court at five.

"I'll be there," Amanda said.

Francis Pelham, an Englishman, and Joseph Nichols, a rotund Baptist from Georgia, welcomed Amanda into the tent and listened to her story.

"I came here principally because my cousin has a son in Virginia."

"Do you wish Joseph and me to buy out his interest?"

"No, I intend to take over Jared's third."

Pelham frowned. "Absentee ownership is not practical. Every partner must share in the work."

"Israel has agreed to act as my representative."

After some discussion of arrangements, Amanda decided she liked the cut of Jared's partners.

Pelham said, "We shall do our best to shower you with gold, dear lady."

"My cousin's son is a preacher. I don't think he'll have much use for it. But I do, believe me."

The miners' court brought no charges against Amanda, so she returned to San Francisco, leaving Israel behind to manage the share of the mine belonging to Jephtha. Her determination to return to the East was firm. Before she went, she sold Kent's Tavern for ninety thousand dollars. Then, with regret, she refused Bart McGill's proposal of marriage.

From the Journal of Jephtha Kent

Jephtha Kent's journal of 1850 tells of his concern about slavery and the division in his family caused by the issue. His uncertainty about slavery had resolved itself into a firm disavowal of it, and he had spoken out against bondage from his pulpit. Fan, Jephtha's wife, a strong supporter of the "peculiar institution" of slavery, no longer shared his bed. In addition, she was alienating Jephtha's sons from him.

Amanda's unexpected arrival in Lexington, Virginia, with Louis further confused the household. Fan tried to conceal from her the tensions that had divided the family, but Fan's father, Captain Tunworth, was not so courteous. When Amanda happened to mention that she had employed a runaway slave, the captain launched a diatribe against those who harbor slaves. Amanda's caustic retorts caused the captain to depart in foul humor and Fan to dislike her husband's relative.

The next morning Amanda revealed Jephtha's share in the gold mine and urged him to let her manage it. Jephtha readily agreed, but Fan suspected some scheme on Amanda's part to deprive their sons of what was theirs. Then Amanda spoke explicitly of her determination to see Kent and Son restored to the hands of the founding family. In this pursuit, she said, she would require the use of the California gold. Again to Fan this seemed a glib fraud.

Before Amanda left, another reason for disagreement between Fan and Jephtha arose. Matthew, their middle son, owned a pet toad, which he refused to let Louis examine. Amanda's son snatched the toad out of Matthew's hand, only to have the creature hop into the shrubbery, never to be seen again. When Jephtha wanted to console his son, the boy would not admit him to his room.

To make matters worse, Jephtha was removed from his itinerancy because of his outspokenness on the slavery issue. This gave rise to further arguments, and finally Fan declared that there was no place within her house for a traitor.

Reduced to penury, Jephtha became a stable hand at the Military Institute in Lexington. When Fan and their sons saw him, Fan would not permit the boys to speak to him.

The Furies

At the end of the summer Jephtha resolved to seek out a Yankee grain merchant in Lexington who provided a station in the Underground Railroad for fugitive slaves.

BOOK 3

Amanda and Louis sailed from Norfolk to Boston. On board they met Frederick Douglass, the most famous runaway slave in America and publisher of *The North Star*. Only Amanda and Louis would sit with him at meals, and when Louis asked why this was so, Amanda answered, "Because he's a black man."

"But he's very nice," Louis scowled. "People should be whipped for treating him that way."

Amanda said nothing, but the remark about whipping disturbed her. Louis was beginning to display an aggressive attitude. He was also a very private person, and Amanda wondered how a new life in the East would affect him.

Less than an hour after Amanda landed in Boston, she was in a private office of Benbow and Benbow.

"Incredible," William Benbow said at the end of Amanda's rapid summary of her history. "You do resemble your father. Do you plan to stay in the East permanently?"

"That depends on a number of factors. Are you familiar with the house my father owned on Beacon Street?"

"Yes, a handsome residence."

"Who lives in the house now?"

"Mr. and Mrs. Charles Wheeler. They've owned it for nearly twenty years."

"I'm asking because my father once kept certain family mementos in the house. There's a slim chance they weren't discarded. Would you imagine the Wheelers would let me inspect the attic and the cellar?"

"I doubt it."

"Would you guess the items that might have been stored in the house would still be there?"

"I'm told they've packed the place with art objects, but I don't know the answer to your question."

"Then the only way to answer it is to buy the house. How much is it worth?"

"In that area of town, forty to fifty thousand."

"I'm prepared to pay seventy, though if you can get it for less, so much the better. You must stipulate that nothing stored in the house when the Wheelers purchased it is to be removed. I'll call on you tomorrow to learn whether you've been successful."

Amanda showed Benbow the draft for ninety thousand which she had received for the sale of Kent's in San Francisco. The lawyer was reluctant to hold such a large sum and suggested she deposit it with the Rothman Bank on State Street. "Ask for the president, Mr. Joshua Rothman. I think you'll find he has some important information for you."

Mr. Rothman received Amanda in his opulent office.

"I'd like your opinion on something, Mr. Rothman. What are the chances of my purchasing Kent and Son?"

"I would say excellent. Mr. Stovall devotes little time to the publishing operation. I should imagine he'd be happy to dispose of it if he could realize a profit. Moreover, you needn't delay making an offer to Mr. Stovall. Our bank has been the steward of certain assets of which you are probably unaware. Your father invested one hundred thousand dollars in 1803 in the Black Stone Company. It's still operating. You are the recipient of your father's legacy—conservatively six million dollars."

Slowly Amanda started toward the third floor of the Beacon Street house. Her affairs were prospering, but she was depressed. Louis wasn't behaving well.

With a sigh she climbed to the attic, where she glanced at the old crates of Kent possessions. Behind one of the crates was a large painting, from which Philip Kent's eyes stared at her.

She wept with happiness. "Louis, I found them!" she called. "Your great-grandfather Kent's portrait—the sword, the rifle, the bottle of tea. Come see!"

Kent and Son had been relocated in a dingy district of warehouses. The building was layered with grime. As Amanda opened the door, five decrepit men—not one under fifty—watched her from their desks.

"Who's in charge here?" Amanda asked one of them.

"Mr. Payne. But he's busy."

As Amanda headed toward the offices, the man snorted, "See here! You've no right—"

"I certainly do. I'm trying to buy this company."

At the door of Mr. Theo Payne's office, she paused. From within came deep masculine tones belonging, surprisingly, to a woman.

"Theo, I frankly get sick of your Harvard snobbery."

"The title makes me ill."

"What's wrong with *Convicted by Love*?"

"If you don't understand . . . Will you stop puffing that disgusting weed in my face!"

"Indulge me, Theo. You have your habit; I have mine."

Amanda knocked and opened the door. "Excuse me . . ."

The small man behind the desk was in his mid-thirties. His neckcloth and shirt had seen better days, and he smelled of whiskey. The woman with him was exceptionally robust; she was about Amanda's age.

"This is a private conference, madam!" said the little man.

"My name is Mrs. de la Gura. I hope to purchase Kent and Son."

"Oh, excuse me. This is Kent's romantic novelist, Rose Ludwig of New York City."

"Down in New York nobody knows I'm Mrs. A. Penn.

Being an authoress isn't an occupation my late husband would have considered proper."

The woman intimidated Amanda a little at first, but in a short time they found they were kindred spirits and even arranged to dine together that evening. During their meal, Amanda discovered that the deep-voiced woman was outgoing, opinionated, and occasionally profane. They got along famously.

Two mornings later, Joshua Rothman called at Amanda's suite. He was distressed that Amanda had been so outspoken at Kent and Son. Payne, who was given to drink and had a loose tongue, had revealed Amanda's intention to buy the firm. As soon as the word reached Stovall, he refused all negotiations permanently.

"If we can't buy the firm straightforwardly, we'll have to get control some other way."

"I can see no open, legal means of—"

"Then we'll do it illegally! *I'm going to own Kent and Son.*"

Sixteen months later, in February, 1852, Amanda and Rose sat among the three thousand who packed the Bowery Theater in New York to hear William Cullen Bryant, editor of the New York *Post* and one of the most outstanding foes of slavery in the city, introduce the speaker of the evening, Frederick Douglass, whom Amanda had met aboard ship on her way to Boston.

"And thus," Bryant said, "in our distinguished guest's own words, 'a slave was made a man'."

Applause. Then, as the clapping died away, hissing came from a front box. And all during Douglass's impassioned speech, after each burst of applause, the hissing sound was heard. The source was the brothers Wood, close friends of the Tammany politician Isaiah Rynders, who bossed the sixth ward and was notorious for his hatred of blacks and foreigners—his Irish constituents excepted. The Woods were also members of the Order of the Star Spangled Banner, a faction within the American party referred to as Know Nothings by their adversaries.

As the two women left the theater, Rose turned on a man behind her. "Damn it! You're stepping on my skirt!"

The man was slender and erect despite his age. He had a white scarf tied around his head, and as it fluttered in the wind, Amanda glimpsed a bit of ugly, discolored scar tissue. The man's left eye, brown and amused, glowed like a dark gem.

"My sincere apologies, Mrs. Ludwig," said Hamilton Stovall. "May I present my secretary, Mr. Jones? Jones, this is Mrs. Ludwig. I'm afraid I'm not acquainted with your companion, Mrs. Ludwig."

"Amanda, let me introduce Mr. Hamilton Stovall. This is Mrs. de la Gura."

"Indeed! So you're the lady who tried to buy Kent and Son. Why would anyone in the world with substantial mining and textile holdings abruptly decide to venture into book publishing?" Obviously Stovall had checked into her background.

"I was searching for a way to diversify. A publishing house seemed a sound investment."

"I really wish we had been able to reach an agreement. I have very little interest in the firm. I never wanted the company except as a means to an end. I assumed ownership as a result of a sporting wager and a desire to see the founders, a clan of wild-eyed mobocrats, put out of business. The heirs of a Mr. Gilbert Kent. Despicable people."

On the drive home, Amanda asked Rose, "When did Stovall's wife die?"

"Early in '50, I believe," Rose replied. "I heard a whisper or two that it was suicide."

"Perhaps she found out Stovall wasn't quite as respectable as he pretended to be."

"Well, he does admit to a few vices. He drinks a good deal. He's a heavy gambler. But aside from that, I have a peculiar feeling about that Mr. Jones we just met. I wonder if he's something more than a secretary."

"Stovall's lover?"

"That was exactly my suspicion."

"There's evidence to support it."

"What evidence?"

"Michael Boyle, my clerk, goes back to the Five Points now and again. There's a story circulating that Stovall occasionally takes a little holiday under another name with a young whore and her brother, twins named Joseph and Aggie; they're part of a triangular relationship."

Rose shuddered. "I don't care to learn any more details. If he prefers male companionship to female . . . well, you can be sure he'll be careful no one can prove it—any more than people can prove your relationship with Michael Boyle's something other than business."

Aghast, Amanda said, "Do they accuse me of having Michael for a lover?"

"Well, my God, he *is* good-looking. He *is* your private clerk. And you did give him a room as well as a position."

Not much more than an hour left. All evening Louis had thought about her. He had struggled to convince himself that what he wanted to do was perfectly proper. Some of his classmates at Professor Pemberton's Day School boasted of their affairs with household girls.

Kathleen was seventeen, on the plump side, but pretty. She came from a tenement somewhere in the Five Points.

Louis's mother had left earlier to dine with Mrs. Ludwig and attend an abolitionist lecture.

"I must do it," he said silently. "Tonight while it's quiet and Ma's away."

What would his ma do in a comparable situation? He thought he knew. She did whatever she wanted, went where she pleased, and brooked no interference. All right. What he wanted, he would take. That was the privilege of rich people, wasn't it?

Michael Boyle was a head taller than Louis. He was handsome and well and powerfully built. Both of his parents had died when he was very young. He was self-educated and a voracious reader. Amanda was well pleased with her choice of confidential clerk.

Amanda let herself into the house. She would be forty-nine before the year was out, and she felt every one of those years tonight. Feeling incredibly weary, she opened the library doors and gasped at the heat. She was always amused by Michael's passion for food and warmth, but she understood the reason for both cravings.

Six months earlier, when Amanda decided she could trust Michael Boyle, she had revealed to him her plans to regain control of Kent and Son. She suspected he didn't approve, but he kept his personal views to himself. Tonight she asked, "You think I should drop the campaign to take back the firm, don't you?"

"It's not for me to say. I am, after all, just your employee."

"Nonsense, Michael. You know you're closer to me in some ways than my own son. Where is he, by the way?"

"Popped off to sleep, I think."

For months Amanda had been engaged in a covert plan to accumulate stock in the Stovall works. When she had acquired a controlling interest, she intended to present Stovall's attorneys with a demand that Kent and Son be sold to her in exchange for the number of shares that would return Stovall to the position of majority stockholder. Amanda's great concern was that Stovall would discover that it was she, a Kent, who was attempting to corner the stock before her goal was accomplished.

To add to her worries was a letter from her cousin Jephtha. In previous letters he had alluded to mysterious activities which led her to believe he had involved himself in the work of what was popularly called the Underground Railroad. A sentence in this letter read, "We grow desperate for safe destinations for certain freight and may be forced to call upon some we would otherwise not burden or endanger." The word *freight* had been heavily underscored.

In addition, a letter had come from Professor Pemberton complaining of Louis's performance at school. She decided not to wait until morning to have it out with Louis. She went up to his room and knocked.

"Louis?"

No answer.

"Louis, this is your mother. Please open the door at once!"

"I'm here, Mother," he said with the sound of a yawn too exaggerated to be genuine. "What do you want?"

"Louis, let me in!"

The door opened, but not far.

"Mother, you woke me out of a sound sleep."

"The deuce I did!" She rushed past him.

Louis started to speak, but Kathleen was quicker.

"Ma'am, please, believe me. He forced me."

"Every bit of it's a lie. She practically begged me."

"As God is my witness," Kathleen said, "he locked the door—"

"Shut your mouth!" Louis cried, running at her with hand upraised.

Amanda put her arm around Kathleen. "Don't be afraid to speak. If Louis abused you, he'll be punished."

"He said that he wanted me in his bed; if I wouldn't, he'd say he caught me trying to steal something."

"Louis, do you deny what Kathleen's saying?"

"Yes. She flaunted herself!"

"I didn't!" the girl burst out. "I'd never do such a thing. I'd never risk losing this job."

Amanda ordered Louis to remain in his room. She put her arm around Kathleen again and led her to her own quarters.

Amanda pitied the young girl. But she also knew what

had to be done. Louis must be dealt with firmly at once. Turning to the girl, she said, "I think you can realize it would only make things more difficult if you were to remain in the house."

"You're going to turn me out?"

"I don't want to, but—"

"Think for God's sake how much I need this position."

"I've considered that. I'm asking you to leave for your own sake. Tonight. Tell Michael to write you a draft for eight weeks' wages."

"I won't be treated this way. You'd better not do this to me. If you force me to leave, I have friends who'll take my part. My uncle's a pal of Mr. Rynders."

With a hateful glance at Amanda, the girl rushed from the room.

Amanda sat motionless for a full five minutes and then walked down to Louis's room. "I'll be back to speak with you as soon as I have talked to Michael."

Amanda learned from Michael that there wasn't a major gang in New York with which Rynders didn't have connections. If Rynders could do Kathleen's uncle a favor—or rather, have some of his thugs do it—he would. Such little acts of kindness insured loyalty to the Society of Saint Tammany at election time. He described their tactics.

"Well," Amanda said, "I suppose it's time for me to resurrect my old revolver and keep it handy."

"Not a bad notion," he agreed.

"As for Louis, I intend to punish him personally. Then I'm going to withdraw him from school for a while. Put him to work around the house. Any sort of project that needs doing—or can be invented. I want you to take charge of that phase. Work him to exhaustion. Be sure Louis is awake at six. I'll inform him before I go to bed that you'll be—"

A commotion at the rear of the house whirled them both toward the doors. The butler rushed in. "Mrs. de la Gura, two deliverymen are bringing in a large crate."

"At this hour? Oh, my God," Amanda exclaimed as an incredible suspicion formed in her mind. "Jephtha's letter . . ."

The freight was human. Huddled inside the crate in a tangle of cheap blankets was a light-skinned colored girl named Mary, who had belonged to Captain Tunworth, Jephtha's father-in-law. The Underground Railroad had used this ruse several times before.

"We'll put her in the bedroom next to yours, Michael," Amanda said, "until I decide what we can do with—" She froze. At the door stood Kathleen.

That Jephtha Kent had relied on her willingness to harbor a runaway—a clear violation of the Fugitive Slave Act—was upsetting enough. That Kathleen had seen the runaway was an absolute disaster.

At breakfast the next morning Amanda said to Louis, "When we finish breakfast, I'm going to punish you for what you did last night. I don't hate you, Louis. I love you, but I can't forgive or excuse what you did."

In the stable she took down a stiff-handled whip.

"Louis, take off your robe and put your hands on the post, over your head."

She ached at the thought of what she had to do. Yet it had to be done. Louis took off the robe.

"Now," she said, "you remember this moment. You'll never treat another person the way you treated Kathleen. I want the memory of this to keep you from hurting any other blameless person again."

The whip flicked up and forward. The top struck between Louis's shoulder blades with a sharp, smacking sound.

Again.

Six strokes . . . seven . . .

Louis screamed, and started to slide down the post. White-faced, Amanda hissed, "Stand up! Stand up and feel it!"

He screamed when the whip flayed him.

"All right," Amanda said, ashen. "Come here."

She caught him in both arms. "Cry if you want. No one will hear you."

He did, letting the long sobs free him of some of his pain.

On Sunday evening Amanda received a visit from Captain Tunworth. He had discovered Mary's whereabouts by torturing one of his other slaves, who knew the plans of her flight. He demanded that Amanda turn the girl over at once, but Amanda denied knowing anything about the matter.

Michael too felt Amanda should give the girl up, for he feared news of the affair would reach the newspapers. Such stories made very good copy. Jephtha's role in the escape was known, so the name Kent would very probably be smeared all over the press along with Amanda's. If Stovall saw the stories, he would make a connection at once.

Through a desperate plan, Mary was spirited from the house despite the vigilance of men Tunworth had hired to guard the place. She was taken to the White Star Pier on North River.

The story did reach the *Journal of Commerce*, which was pro-South. Headlines read:

FUGITIVE SLAVE IN MADISON SQUARE
Virginian lodges accusation
against textile heiress
Seeks warrant

Tunworth returned the next day with a United States marshal, who searched the house thoroughly but could find no traces of Mary.

In the late afternoon Amanda was informed that someone had taken action to prevent her from gaining controlling shares of the Stovall works and thus had deprived her of her last chance to run Kent and Son. But she had more immediate concerns. Michael had heard that hoodlums in the Five Points, where Kathleen lived, under the pretext of searching for a fugitive slave planned to attack Amanda's house in order to avenge Kathleen.

Michael and Louis were in the dining room eating a late supper. Amanda was sitting alone in the library when the maid announced a visitor—Mr. Hamilton Stovall.

"Mrs. de la Gura—or should I say Kent?—I drove here to satisfy my curiosity. Who are you?"

"The cousin of Jared Kent, who served with you aboard *Constitution*."

"The boy who attacked me?"

"Wasn't it the other way around? Once in your cabin? Once on deck?"

After an interchange that grew increasingly acrimonious, Amanda breathed, "Get out. Get out before—"

"Before what, Mrs. Kent? You've no trump cards to play. They're all mine. You have a son, do you not?"

"I—"

"I know you do, and I'll do everything in my power to make his life difficult. I'm going to see that your boy will never—" The rest of his sentence was blurred by the explosive sound of glass shattering in a nearby window.

Hamilton Stovall leaped to his feet as another window broke. He was two steps from the door when Louis broke in. "Ma, there are men out front—twenty or thirty!"

Rynders's thugs had struck.

Realizing the danger, Stovall bolted for the door. He slashed his cane wildly to clear the way, and the gold knob struck Louis's head. The boy fell sideways.

He's killed him! Amanda thought. *He's killed Louis*.

She wasn't even conscious of tearing open the drawer of her desk and pulling out the old Colt and firing. Hamilton Stovall pitched forward and fell at the feet of Michael Boyle.

"There she is!" someone outside yelled. "That's the one who hid the nigger."

The whole house thundered as the men overran the hall: heavy thumps and thuds and splintering sounds. The library door opened, and just as Amanda started to duck behind a chair, something struck her below her left breast.

She gasped, staggered, but stood despite the pain. She glanced at the wall clock.

Fifteen until ten.

Fifteen minutes more and the steamer with Mary aboard would put out from North River bound for Canada.

She fell, unconscious before she struck the carpet.

Stovall's estate was willing to sell Kent and Son to Amanda. She summoned Payne from Boston and entrusted him with teaching Louis the printing business. A few days later Benbow arrived from Boston with a document transferring legal guardianship of Louis Kent to Michael Boyle. Amanda also asked Michael to see that Jephtha received all that was rightfully his from the California mine.

Then, seventeen days after Rynders's thugs had shot her, Amanda Kent died.

Jackson's America

Background to THE FURIES

If the War of 1812 divided American opinion, the coming of peace in 1815 brought on a period of national unity and prosperity, commonly called the era of good feeling. In spite of postwar expansion and optimism, however, sectional conflicts remained, and they reemerged with renewed vigor in the late 1820s. By then, old parties were beginning to break up and new alliances were forming. At the center of this activity stood the man who gave his name to the age—Jackson.

Andrew Jackson was elected president in 1828, the first man from the western part of the country to be so honored. Born in a settlement on Waxhaw Creek in western South Carolina, he had moved to Tennessee when he was twenty. A man with a fiery temperament, a clear sense of justice, and strong moral and political convictions, Jackson was both loved and hated. Former President John Quincy Adams, for example, refused to attend the ceremony at Harvard when Jackson was to be awarded an honorary degree. Adams would not attend because he did not wish to see his college being disgraced by conferring a degree "upon a barbarian and savage who could scarcely spell his own name." In fact, Jackson's enemies threatened him with assassination at least a hundred times.

Present-day historians agree that his presidency was one of the most important in our history because of the way in which it strengthened the executive office. There was a strong element of authoritarianism in Jackson's administration, and his "kitchen cabinet"—an unofficial group of advisers—was powerful. Party loyalty was intense, and favored members were rewarded with government posts in what has come to be known as the spoils system.

Although Jackson's rages against bullies and self-seekers are legendary, they were more theatrical than real. Contemporaries described him as a man of great tenderness, especially with children. He had faith in democracy and a hatred of privilege that was consistent with the principles of the Constitution if not with the interpretation of it evinced by many other politicians of the day.

Though we sometimes think of Jackson's America as charming and rural, it was in fact not unlike modern America. The East in particular was already experiencing urban crowding, crime, poverty, and juvenile delinquency. Of course, much remained that was archaic; lawbreakers were still lashed, and in Boston in 1831 more than fifteen hundred people were in debtors' prisons, some for less than twenty dollars. Even so, modern industrial America with all its problems was emerging in the Jacksonian era.

Once steamboats began to move on American waters, a mania hit the country to link all the rivers by means of canals. The greatest of these was the Erie Canal, the longest in the world; it linked New York City with the new states to the west. Railroads were also being built, despite farmers' protests that they endangered any and all livestock near the right-of-way.

By the 1830s, hordes of immigrants were arriving. America's population rose by one-third every ten years. Ireland in a few decades virtually emptied itself into the United States. Although unskilled labor was sorely needed in the developing West, many of the new arrivals preferred to remain in the coastal cities. The depression of the mid and late 1830s left untold thousands of them starving and bewildered.

Economic hardships led inevitably to bigotry. In Philadelphia, men out of work purportedly because of competition from blacks stormed the Negro section of the city, destroying houses and a church. In Massachusetts an anti-Catholic mob burned a convent in 1834.

Young people presented a special problem. There were no jobs in the city, and public schools were still rare. It would be some time before Horace Mann in Massachusetts could rally the Congregationalists and Unitarians to urge the establishment of tax-supported schools. In the meantime, unschooled, uncontrolled young people loitered in the streets, attacked and insulted passersby, robbed and indulged in all kinds of vandalism.

In 1837, Jackson completed his second term and was succeeded by another Democrat, Martin Van Buren of Kinderhook, New York, the first president to be born an American citizen.

Van Buren came to office with uncertain popular support—he received only 1.8 percent more of the popular vote than the opposing Whigs—and before long was beset by a myriad of troubles. Jackson's financial reforms had been shortsighted, and Van Buren found himself with a severe depression on his hands.

What kind of president was Van Buren? Probably better than many historians have made him out to be. He was under the shadow of his predecessor, who had become a revered symbol of the democratic sentiments of the time. Van Buren was accused of stubbornness, superficiality, and inability to handle subordinates, but no one ever impugned his honesty or humility.

During his entire one-term presidency, Van Buren was faced with catastrophic economic conditions that had sprung from a number of sources, with "overbanking and overtrading" said to be chief among them. Banks had multiplied; loans and note issues had expanded. Borrowing rates went as high as 30 percent. Land speculators were making as much as 75 percent on their transactions. Certain real estate values increased 400 percent. Then within a year after Van Buren's election, deflation set in. Businesses failed by the hundreds in New York alone. Plantations in the South were selling at a tenth their real value, and banks were failing everywhere.

In an attempt to combat the panic of 1837, Van Buren called a special session of the Congress and asked for the establishment of an independent treasury system so that the government could control tax receipts rather than deposit them in private banks. He also proposed that the government issue paper money in the form of treasury notes. Not until 1840, however, did a foot-dragging Congress pass the Independent Treasury Act.

Van Buren's reluctance to interfere with slavery in states where it existed outraged the growing number of abolitionists. At the same time he refused to push for the annexation of Texas because he feared it would mean the extension of slavery. This latter stance probably cost him reelection.

In 1840, the Whigs presented their candidate, William Henry Harrison, as a homespun, hardworking farmer of log-cabin birth. Actually Harrison's birthplace was Berkeley, his distinguished family's seat in Virginia. His father was a rich Virginia planter who had signed the Declaration of Independence. In this election Harrison received 234 electoral votes to Van Buren's 60. What kind of president Harrison would have made will never be known. He died on April 4, 1841, a month to the day of his inauguration, the first United States president to die in office.

Amanda Kent's misfortune—or was it her genius?—was to be at the wrong place at the wrong time. But the immediate woes of the depression passed her by. She wasn't even in the country that had elected Van Buren to office. In 1836, she was in Texas at the Alamo.

In the early 1800s the northern boundaries of Texas were not precisely drawn; the area called Texas included the present-day states of New Mexico, Colorado, Wyoming, Kansas, and Oklahoma. Other boundaries were more clearly defined: the southwest and western borders followed the Rio Grande to its headwaters in Colorado and beyond in Wyoming. The eastern boundary was the Sabine River, flowing south between Texas and the United States into the Gulf of Mexico.

Though part of the Spanish colony of Mexico, Texas was miles away from the government in Mexico City. A few indigenous Indians lived within its vast southern and western reaches. Across the northern boundaries, however, there were many Americans for whom the rich, empty land was an irresistible temptation. In the early years of the century, while Mexico was breaking away from Spain, countless restless Yankees left for this new country. By the 1830s, Americans outnumbered the Mexican settlers and were talking about independence.

The early stages of the struggle for independence occurred in San Antonio, one of the few scattered oases of Spanish civilization in Texas. It had been a settlement long before the first English colonists arrived in America and was the capital of the territory and home of the Spanish governor's sophisticated and elegant court. The elite of the town lived according to the fashionable Spanish mode; and long after Texans had become Americans, San Antonio continued in customs and appearance to be a Spanish city.

In the 1830s, Mexico took steps to regain control over its unruly northern province. The government banned

General Sam Houston
at San Jacinto
April, 1836
Santa
Anna
A Mexican
Soldier
1836
The Church at the Alamo
March 5, 1836
17-20
RON TOELKE 79

immigration and dispatched troops to collect heavy taxes. In 1835, the American settlers rebelled.

The Texas revolution, which lasted only six months, was badly handled by both sides. There were three major battles. The first two were won by the numerically superior Mexicans, who lost the third—and the war—to a small band led by a former governor of Tennessee, Sam Houston.

The expeditionary force that entered Texas in the early spring of 1836 was called the Mexican army. Many of the troops were, however, European and American mercenaries. The commander was General Don Antonio López de Santa Anna. His soldiers, like his political supporters, were known as Santanistas.

In 1833, Santa Anna, who called himself the Napoleon of the West, became president of Mexico and placed the country under a military dictatorship. He was a man of many contradictions. Perhaps the radical changes in his attitudes and behavior were the result of his unconcealed addiction to opium. Some well-documented stories attest to his bravery; others to a ludicrous cowardice. His word was worthless, yet he theatrically maintained an exaggerated code of honor. Although he surrounded himself with effeminate luxuries, he was passionately fond of the most cruel of blood sports. And though his hobby was women, beautiful women, his wife was of particularly ugly mien.

Such was the man who led seven thousand troops into Texas in February of 1836. Santa Anna was furious that a short time before four hundred Texas militia had stormed San Antonio and secured the surrender of twelve hundred federal troops under the command of his brother-in-law. The Texans had barricaded themselves in the church-fortress called the Alamo.

The events of the siege are too well known to need recounting here; equally familiar is General Sam Houston's brilliant charge at Jacinto which avenged the Alamo and won Texas its independence.

Border incidents plagued the region even after Texas

had won its independence from Mexico and continued long after the Republic of Texas was annexed to the United States in 1845.

The annexation of Texas was made possible against strong opposition from the antislavery bloc in the Senate through the efforts of John Tyler—and that was about his only noteworthy accomplishment. Tyler was the first vice president to succeed to the office of chief executive because of the death of the incumbent. An ex-Democrat from Virginia, he had been persuaded to run on Harrison's Whig ticket to attract Southern votes. It soon became evident that all he had in common with the Whigs was a dislike of Andrew Jackson.

By September of 1841, five months after taking office, Tyler had twice trumped his partner's ace. The Whigs had come to office on the promise of reestablishing the national bank, which had ceased to exist during Jackson's administration; Tyler twice vetoed the measure. As a result, his entire cabinet resigned, with the exception of his secretary of state, Daniel Webster, who remained out of loyalty, not to Tyler, but to the office of the presidency. Denounced by the Whigs and with few friends among the Democrats, Tyler was a president without a party.

Tyler fathered fifteen children by two wives. All but one lived to maturity, and the last died in 1947, one hundred fifty-seven years after her father's birth.

James Knox Polk, supported by Andrew Jackson, became the eleventh president of the United States in 1845. He was an avowed expansionist in the age of manifest destiny—a phrase made popular by one J. L. O'Sullivan, editor of a political periodical called *The United States Magazine: A Democratic Review*. Polk managed to defeat Henry Clay, one of the most famous statesmen of the day.

Once in the White House, Polk pushed through the annexation of Texas. He sent a personal emissary to Mexico, whom the Mexican government refused to receive. Polk then sent troops under General Zachary

Taylor into the disputed area. Naturally, the Mexican troops attacked them, and Polk could conveniently aver that war had been begun by an act of Mexico.

By and large the war was a squalid, one-sided affair. The enthusiastic recruits who rushed to fill Polk's call for fifty thousand men soon grew to be tough and skillful in combat that was chiefly hand-to-hand. It is estimated that 1,700 Americans fell on the battlefield; another 11,300 died of wounds and disease—measles, fever, and dysentery; but the American slogan remained: "We may be killed, but we can't be whipped!"

The war ended with the Treaty of Guadalupe Hidalgo, signed February 2, 1848. Mexico accepted the boundary claims of Texas and for $15 million ceded to the United States the area that was to become California, New Mexico, Arizona, Nevada, Utah, and parts of Colorado and Wyoming.

This war, besides resulting in the largest accession of territory to the United States since the Louisiana Purchase, brought together on one side officers who in a few years would become famous enemies—Grant, Lee, Sherman, Pickett, Hooker, and Longstreet, among others. The most popular officer of all was Zachary Taylor, who succeeded Polk in 1849 and spent one brief year in the White House.

Before leaving office, Polk had negotiated an Oregon border agreement with Great Britain, whose intervention in the Mexican War he feared. The rich wilderness of a half-million square miles known as Oregon had long been disputed territory, at various times claimed not only by the United States and Britain, but by Spain and Russia. By 1818 the only two serious contenders for the region were the United States and Great Britain, who agreed to occupy the land jointly. In 1827 the arrangement was renewed for an indefinite period subject to cancelation on a year's notice. The powerful Hudson's Bay Company established a string of trading posts along the north bank of the Columbia River, but Americans, deterred by the isolation and sheer distance of Oregon from the rest of the country, did not arrive in large numbers. By 1839 there were fewer than one hundred Americans in Oregon.

But the stage was being set. Trails across the Great Plains had been explored, and the South Pass through the Rockies was open. Word slowly reached the East, but by 1843 hundreds of Americans were succumbing to "Oregon fever."

The Oregon Trail began at Independence, Missouri, and followed the Missouri, the Platte, and the Sweetwater rivers for almost a thousand miles through the Great Plains to the mountains. The route cut through the Rockies at the South Pass, then followed the Snake River into the area that is now Idaho, then climbed over the dangerous and difficult Blue Mountains. Fort Vancouver, the western terminus, was over two thousand miles from Independence. The trip, which took six months, exposed the traveler to extremes of heat and cold.

In 1843, when there were about 1,500 Americans in Oregon, a small group decided to create a government. They drew up a provisional constitution for self-protection until the United States saw fit to establish its sovereignty over the area. Although the United States had tried to settle the boundary at the forty-ninth parallel, now there were demands for the entire Oregon territory, all the way to 54° 40′. Americans took up the cry "54-40 or fight!" and in 1844 elected Polk to achieve the demand. Polk, however, ignored his campaign slogan and accepted the forty-ninth parallel—which he himself had advocated earlier—as the permanent boundary.

Long before gold was discovered in California, many Americans believed it was manifest destiny that the United States should one day include California. This was militarily important, for if the United States failed to acquire it from Mexico, perhaps Britain or France would.

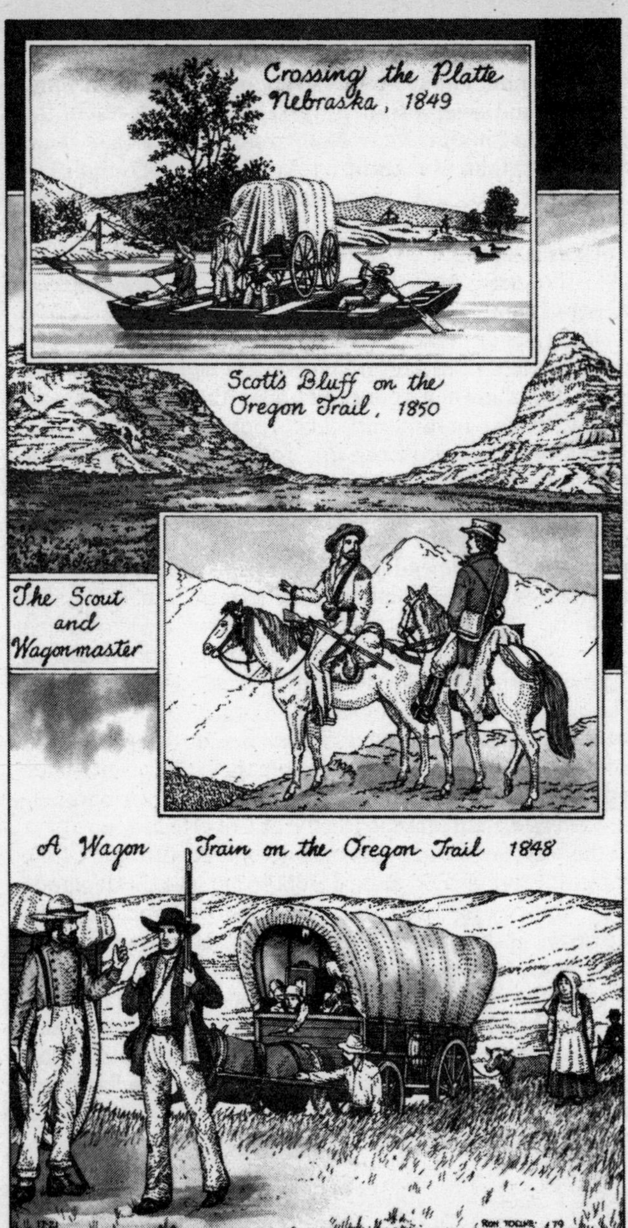
Crossing the Platte
Nebraska, 1849
Scott's Bluff on the
Oregon Trail, 1850
The Scout
and
Wagonmaster
A Wagon Train on the Oregon Trail 1848

Furthermore, Yankee traders were making a good thing out of California, and if England bought or seized the country, this rich trade would come to an end.

Descriptions of California varied tremendously: barren desert, mountainous country, great valleys flowing with milk and honey. In 1821, Mexico had gained California along with its independence from Spain, but was almost as indifferent to this languid, dreamy province as Spain had been . There were no courts, police, postal facilities, or schools. The heart of Spanish rule had been the Franciscan mission, but under loose Mexican rule the missions began to disappear, and their vast landholdings were seized and sold.

When the Americans began arriving in the 1840s, they found a small and scattered population living a leisurely life. These were the *caballeros*, whose ranches were often forty miles square. Their existence was the stuff of which romances are spun. But such idyllic life could not remain undisturbed. The hardworking, ambitious Yankee was arriving, and President Polk was determined to annex California to the United States by hook or by crook.

It was mostly by crook. Polk was a straitlaced Methodist in his personal habits, and his wife was a strict Presbyterian. They banned card playing, dancing, and alcoholic beverages from the White House. During the negotiations that led to Texas's becoming the twenty-eighth state, Sam Houston remarked that the trouble with Polk was that he drank too much water. But behind all this austerity was a ruthless, determined man not above very shrewd conniving.

In the late spring of 1845, Polk sent Captain John Charles Frémont of the Army Topography Corps to "visit" the area. Frémont had already earned the sobriquet of Pathfinder for previous western exploits. An extraordinarily handsome and suave man, he was the illegitimate son of a French Royalist refugee and a young lady from a distinguished Virginia family. His wife, Jessie, was a vivacious, beautiful young woman, the daughter of Senator Benton, called the Thunderer, who had cried out for years in Congress for the opening of the West. Jessie turned her husband's reports into works of literary distinction that were widely published.

The thirty-two-year-old Pathfinder traveled west under secret orders. Once in Monterey, he convinced the Mexican authorities that his mission was purely scientific; his goal was to make a geographic survey from the Atlantic to the Pacific. But when Frémont headed for the Southwest rather than for Oregon, the Mexicans asked him to leave California at once. At first he defied them by building fortifications and raising the American flag, but then he withdrew toward Oregon—for a time.

Frémont saw Polk's dilemma. The President wanted California but would not commit the act of aggression necessary to secure it. If Frémont resigned from the army, he could take California as a private citizen, without official authorization, and no one could accuse Polk of imperialism.

In May of 1846, Frémont left Oregon for California, where he incited American settlers to capture the settlement of Sonoma north of San Francisco and to proclaim the Bear Flag Republic. On June 14, they hoisted their homemade ensign, consisting of a star and a bear and painted with pokeberry juice, it is said, by William Todd, a nephew of Abraham Lincoln's wife. The Mexicans sneered and said the bear had the lineaments of a pig.

A few days later, Frémont entered Sonoma at the head of his troops. Although some blood was shed, there was little resistance from the Californians. By the time news of the outbreak of the Mexican War arrived, the American flag was flying over all important California settlements.

Los Angeles drove out the Americans, but was retaken by Commodore Robert Stockton and General Stephen Kearny. Two days later the "civilian" Frémont arrived with newly recruited troops and negotiated a surrender, calmly going over the heads of both the commodore and the general. Then Frémont chose to recognize Stockton as the officer in command. Enraged, Kearny invoked his absolute authority under fresh orders from Washington and, without permitting Frémont to join his regiment in Mexico, as Polk had suggested, or even to take with him the scientific data and specimens he had collected, ordered the Pathfinder to accompany him to Fort Leavenworth, where he was arrested and sent to Washington.

Frémont's court-martial in the capital in 1847 accused him of doing precisely what he had been secretly ordered to do. He was found guilty, but the verdict was rescinded by order of President Polk.

Then, on January 24, 1848, before the signing of the peace treaty with Mexico, gold was discovered at Sutter's Mill.

Overnight the state was transformed; Latin California ceased to exist. Gold fever had struck.

Men came from all over the world, but at least three-quarters were American. They arrived by ship—an eight-month journey around Cape Horn or a much more perilous two months across the pestilential isthmus of Panama. They also came by wagon; over forty-five thousand crossed the Sierra Nevada in 1849 alone. Most of them were young; some were well educated and of good family. Very few women came.

In 1848, California had fewer than 15,000 white inhabitants. Most of them lived along the coastal road, El Camino Real; in the tiny settlements of San Diego, Los Angeles, and San Francisco; or at missions, such as San Luis Obispo and Santa Barbara. Ten years later, the population was half a million. In 1864 alone, sixty thousand settlers arrived. Most people lived in filthy mining camps with names like Scratch Gulch, Grizzly Flat, Fiddle Town, Whiskey Slide, Rattlesnake Diggings, and Flea Town—all too indicative of the changes that had taken place in the area since the days of the *caballeros*.

Miners flooded into San Francisco, and suddenly the

Gold Miner's tools 1849

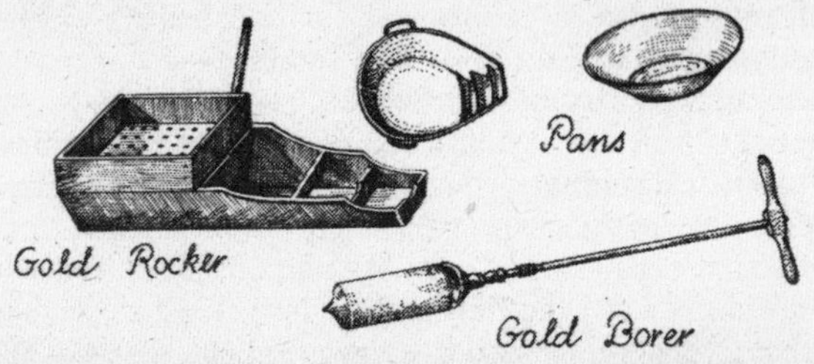

Placer Mining in California - 1851

peaceful, beautiful little town became a metropolis hideous beyond belief. Crime and disease flourished. Records show that in the early 1850s there were a thousand murders with only one conviction, although justice was frequently meted out in lynchings.

Despite battles and depressions, Americans in the first half of the nineteenth century believed—and not without justification—that they lived in the best of all possible worlds. If a man failed at something in one place, he could try something different elsewhere. Almost every visitor to America at the time remarked on how ready people were to cast off community ties. To be sure, reasons other than failure at home prompted the westward movement; there were probably as many different motives as there were travelers. And there were so many travelers that by midcentury moving westward was comparatively easy. Handbooks for overland expeditions were available. Their contents not only indicated routes, but gave such practical information as the organization of companies—only the most foolhardy tried it alone—and the election of leaders. One of the more widely used of these manuals was written by Randolph Marcy, a captain in the United States Army. His *Prairie Traveler: Handbook for Overland Expeditions*, was authorized by the War Department. Detailed among its 350 pages are such topics as "Relative Merits of Mules and Oxen," "Dessicated and Canned Vegetables," "Sanitary Conditions," "Storms," "Stampedes," "Rattlesnake Bites," and "Similarity of Prairie Tribes to the Arabs." Marcy's book was a reliable volume, full of useful and accurate information; but many such volumes were more imaginative than factual. Their authors were men without experience, anxious to capitalize on a growing market.

The history of all the trails west is rich and deep. To examine the story of perhaps the oldest of them, the Santa Fe, it is necessary to go back to the early years of the seventeenth century in the Southwest. The Spanish province of New Mexico was ignored until word came that the Indians were embracing Christianity. Next to the Spaniard's desire to find gold was his determination to spread his religion. So by royal order a capital city, Santa Fe, was established in 1609, and soon farmers settled around Taos and other tiny settlements. Once a year a fair was held in Taos, which attracted local Indians as well as Comanches and tribes from the plains. The only link at the time with Mexico, the parent province, was the January fair at Chihuahua, five hundred miles to the south along a well-defined caravan route.

In 1789, Fernando de la Concha became governor of New Mexico. He decided that the north-south commerce of his province was insufficient and that there should be east-west routes through Indian country to the Missouri. Abortive attempts were made to establish such a route, but interference from Spain prompted by a jealous dislike of enterprising Americans resulted in little being accomplished.

American traders who ventured into Santa Fe were regarded as alien smugglers, and their goods were confiscated; but when Mexico threw off Spanish rule in 1821, American trade began in earnest.

That same year, William Becknell traced the trail that would become the standard one from the Missouri River to Santa Fe. Not that there was one clearly defined trail; that would have to wait for the coming of stagecoaches. Rather, on level grassy grounds ruts and paths spread and diverged, but they came together where there was only one passable point. By 1830, the Santa Fe Trail began in Independence, Missouri, and proceeded west and south across Kansas to the Arkansas River. After following the river, the trail divided, one fork proceeding west to Bent's Fort and south to Santa Fe, the other fork heading southwest to the Cimarron River and thence to Santa Fe.

For ten years, beginning in 1849, the boats of the Pacific Mail Steamship Company carried mail around the long water route between the Pacific and the Atlantic coasts, but this service was painfully slow and infrequent. The Westerners pushed for more direct communication, and in 1857, the government passed the Post Appropriation Act, authorizing an overland mail service to California. For some time stagecoaches had been carrying mail from Independence, Missouri, to western settlements, but the service was unreliable and stopped altogether in the winter.

The government asked for bids for the new service and laid out a general route. It was to begin at either St. Louis or Memphis, touch at Fort Smith, Arkansas, and then go through Texas to the best point of crossing the Rio Grande above El Paso. It was then to continue along a new road being built by the government, through New Mexico Territory to Yuma, California. The concluding specifications were vague at best: "through the best passes and along the best valleys for staging to San Francisco." The ultimate route in fact touched at Los Angeles, then went north to San Jose and San Francisco.

On September 15, 1858, one of the coaches of John Butterfield, who had been awarded the six-year contract, left St. Louis as another set out from San Francisco. Both coaches made their destinations a day earlier than had been anticipated.

Until the Civil War, Butterfield's coaches provided dependable service to California, even though passengers often complained about the circuitous, 2,800-mile trip which they dubbed the ox-bow route. The coaches were known as Concord coaches, because they were made in Concord, New Hampshire.

Mail rates on the coach were ten cents for each half ounce; passenger fares were one hundred dollars in gold. The first coaches carried four passengers and their baggage in addition to five or six hundred pounds of mail. Later stages held six to nine passengers and even more for those intrepid enough to sit on the roof. Travelers were usually provided with inflated rubber pillows to absorb the bumps of the rough roadbeds.

The stages provided food, but the cautious travelers carried their own nonperishable provisions with them; and although this diet was monotonous, it was usually more appetizing than the greasy fare dispensed by filthy cooks along the way.

For sixteen months, beginning in 1860, the Pony Express competed with Butterfield's Overland Mail Company and provided a romantic and efficient interlude in the history of mail service. The Pony Express route extended from St. Joseph, Missouri, to Salt Lake City and Sacramento, California. It took seventy-five ponies to make the trip from Missouri to California; a time of ten days, promised at the outset, was occasionally achieved.

The service was not cheap, even by today's standards. Letters sent by Pony Express from San Francisco to Salt Lake City cost three dollars a half ounce; to points beyond Salt Lake, five dollars a half ounce. But it was an expensive operation, with station houses every fifteen miles along the trail and two men at each station to look after the horses. These were the best California mustangs, and the well-paid riders were all young men selected for nerve, jockey weight, and courage. Pony Express riders rode alone.

Overland mail service to California was short-lived. Its doom was sealed with the opening of the first transcontinental telegraph lines in October, 1861.

Jephtha Kent was a special kind of American, but by no means unusual. He was by his vocation the conspicuous product of a unique religious environment, the result of the decision made at the Constitutional Convention that no agency of government, federal or state, could assume responsibility for the religious life of the citizen. It naturally followed that a church was an association of individuals who joined it by choice, that it was responsible to no civil authority and equal to all other churches. American churches were denominational—that is, organized according to belief in particular doctrines. New denominations could be formed or old ones discarded by consent of their members. American Protestantism of the period was missionary. The evangelical mood was activist: once saved, one's duty was to save others and to win converts.

Americans in 1850 were predominantly Protestant, although the largest single denomination was Roman Catholic, followed in order by Methodist, Baptist, Presbyterian, Congregationalist, Lutheran, Christian Disciples, Episcopal, and Latter-Day Saints.

The most important fact about American Protestantism during the first half of the nineteenth century was that it was evangelical, revivalist Christianity. Evangelism was generally understood to encompass beliefs and practices that resulted in instantaneous, conscious conversion, preceded by an overwhelming sense of personal guilt and followed by a joyous assurance of acceptance. A revival was a religious service at which attempts were made to convince the unconverted of their need for regeneration.

Evangelism cut across sectarian lines, but occurred most often in nonliturgical churches, that is, those which emphasized the role of the individual in seeking salvation and were not very ritualistic. Of these Jephtha's church, the Methodist Episcopal (episcopal to indicate its government), increased its membership sevenfold. And no small amount of that increase was the result of missionary societies established among Negroes in both the North and South. Of the half million blacks who were church members by 1850, two hundred thousand were Methodists. In 1850, the Methodists had over one hundred full-time missionary workers in the slave states, most of them Negroes themselves.

Until the second decade of the nineteenth century, American churches were nearly unanimous in their opposition to slavery. Much of the support for abolition in its early phases came from evangelical leaders. Within the churches controversy was, however, arising; and it centered on two related issues—whether the Bible sanctioned slavery, and whether or not slavery was morally justifiable in nineteenth-century America. Southern clergymen, and some Northern ones too, argued that the Old Testament sanctioned slavery and that nothing in the New Testament denied it. Northern clergymen and a few Southern ones claimed the opposite.

But the specific point of conflict between pro and antislavery was not theological, but practical: what should the relationship between the churches and the abolitionist movement be? To what degree and in what manner should churches become involved in the struggle for or against the system?

The Baptists were the first to divide. As early as 1843, the Southern churches withdrew. The Methodists came next. Many Methodists had begun organizing antislavery societies in the thirties; at their annual general conferences contests had developed over whether or not the church should adopt an official position on slavery. Then in 1844, after eleven days of the debate detailed in Jephtha's journals, the Southern delegates withdrew; a year later they formed the Methodist Episcopal Church South. The Presbyterians managed to stay together until 1857.

Jephtha's association with the Underground Railway and his subsequent involvement of Amanda in the transportation of a fugitive slave were logical steps in his abolitionist activities. Despite the name, there was no established system or association for helping runaway slaves to reach Canada or some other place in the North where they could be free. The "stations" were usually homes of Northern abolitionists. The routes followed were more or less fixed, and "conductors" took the slaves, usually at night, from one station to another in a hit-or-miss fashion.

Although there were stringent fugitive slave laws forbidding the harboring of runaway slaves, many idealists risked prosecution. They felt they were aiding

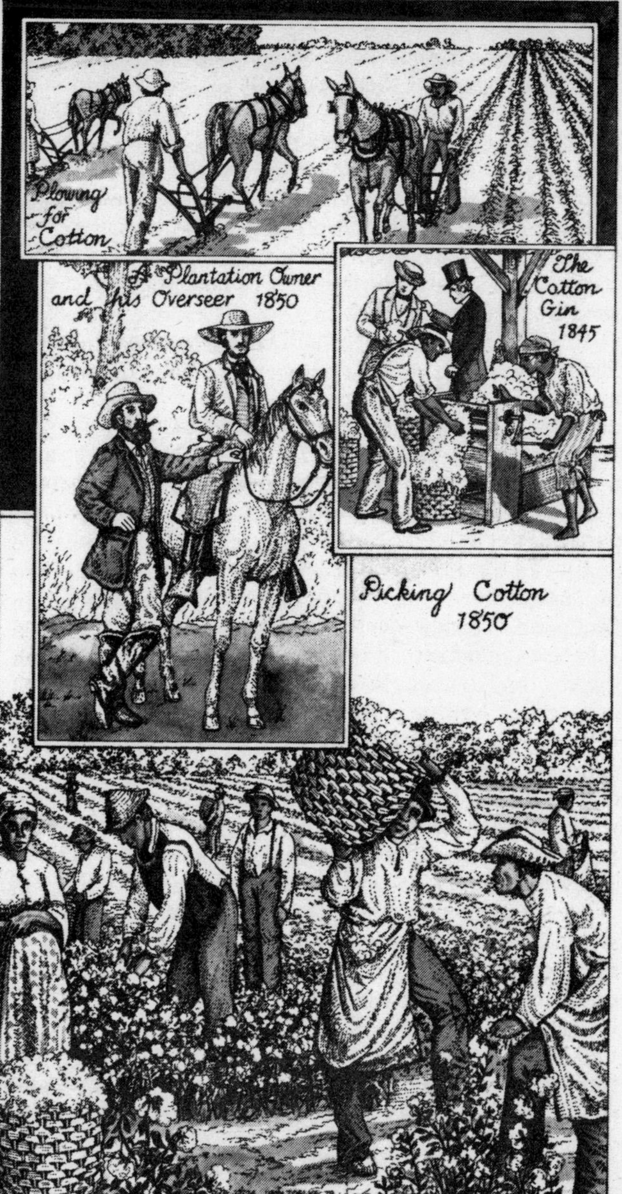
Plowing for Cotton
A Plantation Owner and his Overseer 1850
The Cotton Gin 1845
Picking Cotton 1850

humanity, even though they were illegally depriving Southern owners of their property.

At about the time Amanda and Louis took up residence in New York, a new word was coined—*millionaire*. Of course, Amanda qualified handsomely. She had chosen residence in the city the better to watch the comings and goings of Hamilton Stovall, but the atmosphere of this metropolis suited her spirit in a way staid Boston never could have.

In 1830, New York was still largely contained within the southern tip of Manhattan, but rapid growth was under way. In 1830, Broadway from City Hall Park northward was residential; by 1850, scarcely a private house remained below Bleecker Street. The new houses that were going up were being built chiefly of a brown stone that was soon to give the residential sections their particular character.

By midcentury, Fifth Avenue from Washington Square to Madison Square (Twenty-third Street) was becoming the new center of fashion and wealth. The avenue extended north of Twenty-third Street, but above there it had the appearance of a country lane passing between vacant lots and fields. By the time one reached what is now Fortieth Street, one was well into the country. That is where the Croton Reservoir stood. Its high stone walls provided an excellent promenade from which to view the rolling country that stretched north toward the smart residential communities of Yorkville and Harlem.

New York was beginning to support elegant hotels, for which the rest of America was hardly noted. The day of the opulent had not yet reached its zenith, but it was well on its way. Delmonico's was costly and exclusive to a degree that was scarcely American in principle. Much more in keeping with the tastes of the New Yorker of the time was the Astor House. It was built by John Jacob Astor in the 1830s, when a room and full board cost three dollars a week. Now prices were considerably higher, but this vast hotel still boasted the longest bar in the city and was famous for the bounty of its free lunch—a generous custom that did not wholly disappear until Prohibition. These hors d'oeuvres, free for the taking to drinking customers, provided a meal for the price of a nickel glass of beer.

The Astor House was by 1850 chiefly the hangout of politicians and journalists; and its former glories had been eclipsed by the magnificence of two newer establishments farther uptown. The St. Nicholas Hotel, built of white marble, cost more than one million dollars to build and accommodated nearly eight hundred guests. Besides being elegantly furnished, it boasted the comfortable novelty of central heating. Just north of the St. Nicholas was the Metropolitan, equally costly and luxurious. It contained one hundred suites, called family apartments, and could accommodate six hundred. Both hotels were conducted on the "American plan," termed by the less pretentious as "board and room." A family of four or five could reside at these hotels for about one hundred dollars a week.

Surpassing all in splendor was the Fifth Avenue Hotel, built at Madison Square in 1859. It not only contained an elevator, but provided private bathrooms. The dining room seated guests at tables accommodating twenty or thirty people. The Fifth Avenue Hotel also offered a fourth meal daily, a late supper; it was included in the daily rate of two and one half dollars a day.

Hotel living was something new in America, and there were those who disapproved strongly. They were certain hotel living could lead only to immorality, since it encouraged herd behavior.

On Broadway and Franklin Street, a dazzling new ice cream parlor daringly opened its door to unescorted women. Such gestures toward feminine freedom worried conservative New Yorkers, who were appalled in 1853 when a Woman's Rights Convention was held in the

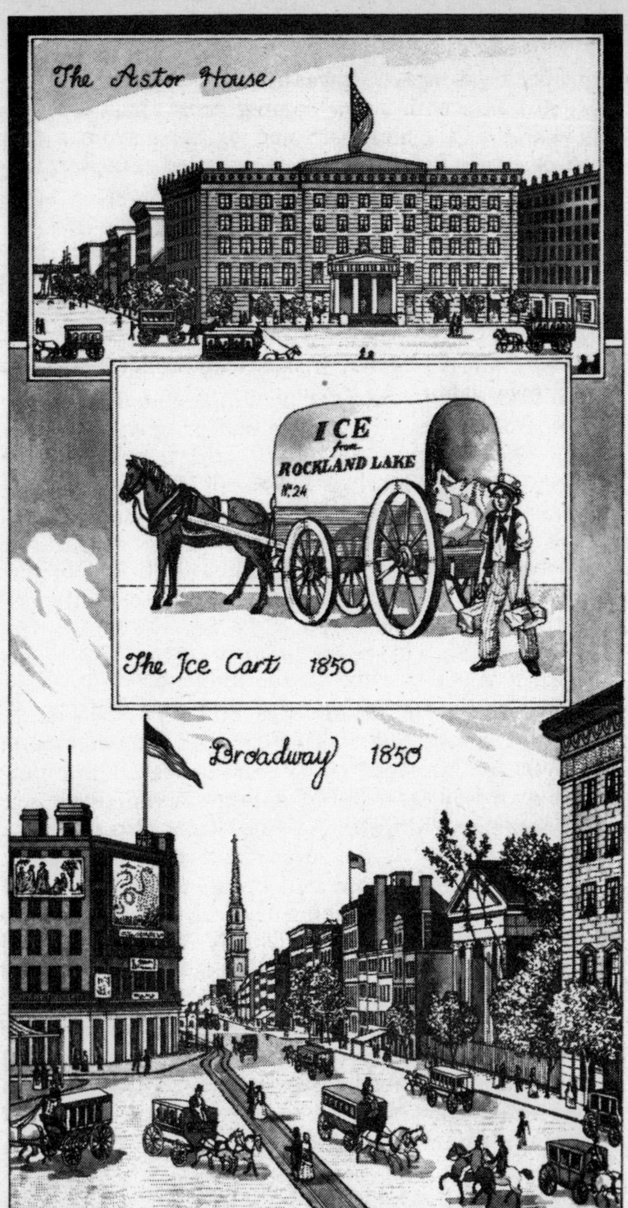
The Astor House
ICE
from
ROCKLAND LAKE
No. 24
The Ice Cart 1850
Broadway 1850
17-22

Broadway Tabernacle. It was attended by delegates from eastern cities, with a few coming from as far away as Cleveland and Chicago. Some of these women had already earned the reputation of being radical agitators—Susan B. Anthony, Lucretia Mott, Elizabeth Cady Stanton, and Lucy Stone. They wanted the vote; they demanded full equality with men. Women, they proclaimed, must no longer be confined to the home; they must be allowed to enter public life, engage in any profession or business they chose, manage their own property, and do as they wished with money earned by their own labor. At their convention, Miss Stone defiantly wore the new costume of the suffragists—bloomers named after their innovator, Amelia Bloomer—clothing which Rose Ludwig found to her taste.

An era of splendor had set in, and Mrs. William Clifford Schermerhorn decided to give a costume ball in keeping with the new extravagance. Her guests were commanded to appear in costumes like those of the court of Louis XV. The Schermerhorn mansion was refurnished and decorated in the authentic style of the period. At this party New York society became acquainted with the cotillion, a dance introduced to society by the Empress Eugenie, wife of Napoleon III. The cotillion, which lasted two hours, eventually became a New York rite, lasting well into this century.

Not all was opulence and party giving. Only a stone's throw from Broadway was the Five Points, the most dangerous and depraved quarter of Manhattan—a district well known to Michael Boyle and Kathleen McCreery. Its narrow, crooked streets and dismal courts bore such names as Murderer's Alley and Cow Bay. At its center was a triangular open space of about an acre, known grotesquely as Paradise Square. It was the retreat of a gang of criminal hoodlums who called themselves the

Dead Rabbits; it was the haunt of murderers, thieves, prostitutes, and contrabandists.

The squalor was beyond belief; the filth lay deep. There were numerous pawn shops trafficking in stolen goods and saloons that sold to children as well as adults. At night these places turned into dance halls patronized by prostitutes, thieves, and hoodlums. The area teemed with vagrant children, half-naked in winter and always shoeless. The Five Points was where "Captain" Isaiah Rynders recruited the thugs who vandalized Amanda's house and shot her.

Rynders for a time occupied the office of United States Marshal in New York. He was a former New Orleans gambler who owned a saloon. He had gained control over the immigrant Irish vote in Five Points and held command over the dreaded Dead Rabbits gang. He was, of course, very useful to Tammany Hall. By sending his gang to terrorize polling places during elections, Rynders helped Tammany to maintain its domination. In return, Rynders was granted legal immunity for the operations of his henchmen—houses of prostitution, gambling establishments, and other illicit businesses in which he had a large financial interest.

This arrangement for mutual benefits extended to all the slum wards of the city, of which the Five Points was the foulest. The arrangement was benevolently fostered by Fernando Wood, the city's mayor. During Wood's administration, factional strife broke out among Tammany leaders and split them into two hostile camps. The war for political supremacy that ensued broke out in a wave of crime and disorder that went unchecked by Mayor Wood's police force. As a result, in 1857, the state legislature abolished New York's municipal police force and set up a Metropolitan Police District under a board of commissioners appointed by the governor which deprived Wood of control over the new police force. The Mayor refused, however, to disband his municipal police, and a bloody confrontation between the two forces occurred. For several months two antagonistic police forces battled for authority in the streets of the city. This situation was ideal for gangsters and other criminals to do their worst.

Matters continued this way until the beginning of the Civil War when energies had to be directed to more important concerns.

In response to a Methodist bishop's assertion that there were as many prostitutes as Methodists in New York City—some twenty thousand—the outraged superintendent of police, in order to prove the bishop wrong, undertook a census which was intended to vindicate the city against such charges. New York had only 621 houses of prostitution, 99 houses of assignation, and 75 saloons of ill repute. The number of public prostitutes was a mere thirty-three hundred—many fewer than the good bishop's estimation. The superintendent of police acknowledged that there were, of course, "other women," but he had no way of determining their number.

New York's underworld never slept; it did business around the clock in every quarter of the city. Day and night and in all seasons of the year, women of the street paraded up and down Broadway from Canal Street to Madison Square.

For the hurried businessman, New York had developed a unique institution of pleasure—the cigar store battery. To the unknowing, these places had the appearance of bona fide cigar stores; their windows were full of cigar boxes, and there were even a few cigars on sale inside; but the chief merchandise was the girls who maintained private rooms in the back or above the store where liquor was dispensed and other services rendered. Girls would line up behind the counters and solicit passersby during the lengthy noon meal hour or in the early evening when businessmen were homeward bound.

Greene Street was the most notorious thoroughfare in the United States; nearly every other house was a brothel.

But as one traveled northward along Greene Street, the quality of the brothels improved; there, proprietoresses maintained discreet establishments where decorum was the word.

Not all entertainment in midcentury New York was illicit. The first of the great American impresarios, P. T. Barnum, was hard at work, providing the American stage with the great artists of the day. Among them none was more famous than Jenny Lind—the Swedish nightingale—the first European singer of renown to come to America. Perhaps it was not Lind's desire to bring her act to America so much as the extraordinary fee Barnum promised her—more money than any other singer had ever been paid anywhere else.

Barnum's advance publicity brought public curiosity to a high pitch. According to Barnum, the singer embodied every noble virtue, and her piety and good works were endless. She had given up opera singing because operatic heroines were usually abandoned women and she could not bear to enact such degradation. A fabulously rich woman, she had in two months given sixty thousand dollars to charity.

By the night of her first concert, Barnum had whipped up such excitement that seats were sold at auction. The first ticket went for $225. Sixty policemen were required to keep order in the immense mob that had gathered in Battery Park at the foot of Manhattan. Hundreds of New Yorkers were bobbing about in small boats on the water surrounding Castle Garden, where six thousand waited in the vast auditorium to hear the Swedish Nightingale.

Although critics found her vocal purity extraordinary, they wished for a bit more flesh and blood; but the public paid no attention to the critics and continued to pay twenty or thirty dollars for a seat. And when Jenny Lind donated all of the $12,600 she received for her first performance to New York philanthropic and cultural institutions, New York and the rest of America were hers to command.

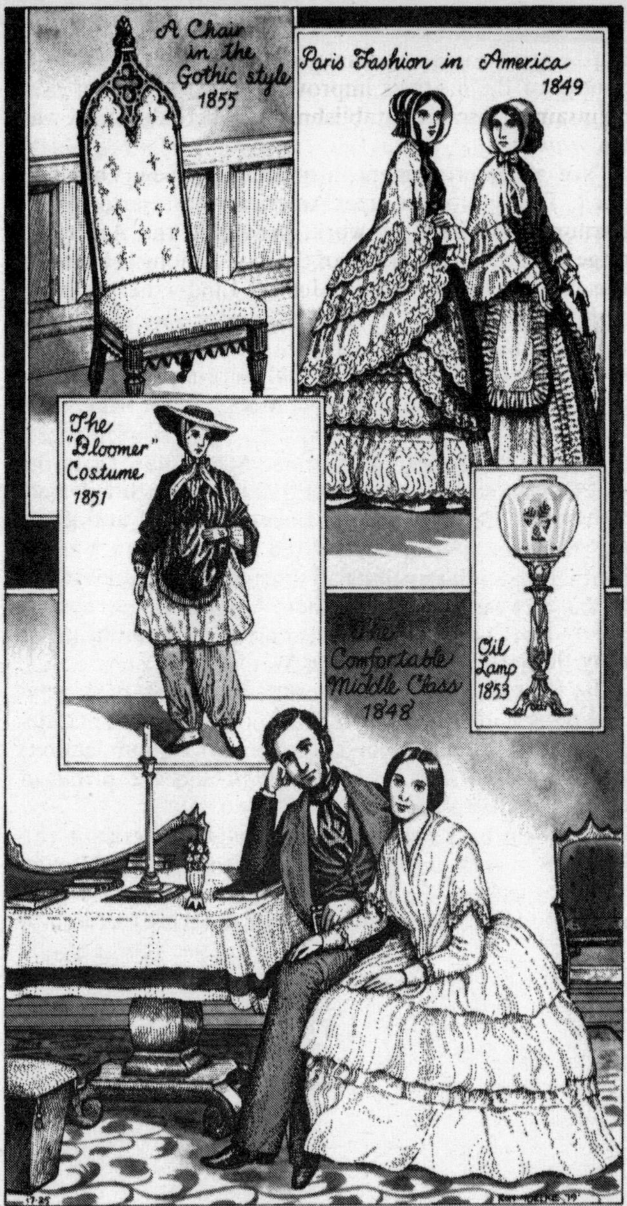
A Chair
in the
Gothic style
1855
Paris Fashion in America
1849
The
"Bloomer"
Costume
1851
The
Comfortable
Middle Class
1848
Oil
Lamp
1853

But New York with its abundance of life, its millionaires and its squalor, was far from the sum of life in America, and the impression should not be the last we have of America in the 1840s and 1850s. A more widely accepted notion, even at the time, was that America during these years was consummately a nation of the middle class, that class that was held in such contempt among both European aristocrats and the rising bands of radical proletarians. For even as millions of Irish and other Europeans were crowding to American shores, making America grow faster than at any other time since the Revolution, the prevailing view was that America was safely middle-class. Certainly it was true that Americans in these years had more comforts, more conveniences, than they had ever had before. More than that, the middle-class values of home and hearth reigned supreme. Those who defended these values—essentially values of the status quo—said they derived from the same Yankee courage and industry that had spurred the earliest settlers. Detractors were quick to point to Americans' narrowness of mind and heart and their ever present concern with the dollar. Articles and sermons by the score debated the point, whenever, that is, the issue was not that of slavery. The reflection of the state of mind of this well-off, middle-class America can be found in contemporary publications as diverse as *Godey's Lady's Book* and the prints of Currier and Ives.

Looking back, who could begrudge Americans this moment of tranquillity? For already, amidst all the calm and prosperity of the 1850s, the clouds were gathering for a mighty battle that would change America forever.

The Titans

A CONDENSATION OF

The Titans

1860-1862

PROLOGUE

New York, election night, 1860. As Michael Boyle's carriage neared the corner of Forty-third Street, someone yelled, "Pull up! There's a man hurt yonder!"

Suspecting a trick, Michael hammered his fist on the ceiling. "Joel, don't stop!" he called to his black driver.

The order came too late. Joel had already jerked the reins and booted the brake.

"They got guns, Mr. Michael," he said from the driver's seat.

"And if we weren't so damned full of Christian virtue, we would, too!"

"Shut your face and get down, lad," one of the men said to Joel.

Michael detected a familiar lilt in the robber's speech. "Is this any way for one Irishman to treat another?"

"Irishman, hell," the man said. "You're not a good one if you got a nigger driving for you. A Black Republican's what you are! That'll make emptying your pockets twice the pleasure."

Michael understood the hatred in the man's voice. He had once harbored such hatred himself. When he first went to work for Amanda Kent, he had hated Negroes and resented that they were entitled to the same rights as white men. Thousands of freed Negroes suddenly added to the labor market would only increase the competition.

Amanda had talked to him about that and had finally convinced him that if the principles of liberty for which her grandfather, Philip Kent, had fought meant anything at all, those principles had to apply to all Americans. Now he thought as she had. He thought as a Kent. And Kents always objected to intrusion such as robbery. Objected strongly.

Michael was able to overcome his assailant, but not without a struggle in which he was cut. The assault itself hadn't been half so unnerving as the viciousness in the robber's voice.

Hate, Michael thought to himself. *That's all there is in the country anymore. And how much worse will it be tomorrow? You can take part of the blame. You voted for Mr. Abraham Lincoln.*

Michael headed for the office of the *Union*, the New York newspaper owned by Kent and Son. It was empty, save for Theo Payne, the editor. On her deathbed eight years earlier, Amanda had charged Theo with establishing a Kent family newspaper opposed to slavery but firm in its support of any reasonable compromise to maintain national union. At the same time, she had asked Michael to look after Jephtha Kent, her cousin Jared's son. Jephtha had been a minister in the Methodist Episcopal Church South until his antislavery views caused him to be defrocked. Seeing this as a disgrace, his wife had taken their three sons and left him. Shortly after Amanda's death, Jephtha had fled to New York, where with Michael's help he had rebuilt his life. For the past three years, he had been the *Union*'s reporter in the nation's capital. An innocent where money was concerned, he was content to let Michael and Louis, Amanda's son, administer the money that flowed from the California gold mines he had inherited from his father.

Jephtha had just wired from Washington:

SECESSION OF ONE OR MORE SOUTHERN STATES SEEN HERE AS CERTAIN CONSEQUENCE OF LINCOLN ELECTION. PRAY IT WILL NOT LEAD TO WAR.

"Y'see, Michael?" Theo asked. "Jephtha knows what's coming."

"And just what is my cousin's prediction? Biblical apocalypse?"

The man who had spoken was Louis Kent.

Michael gave him the telegram and nodded to Louis's wife. "Good evening, Julia."

"Good evening, Mi—heaven above! You're cut and covered with dust!"

"You didn't get that pounding from the Stovall board, I hope. How did the meeting go?" Louis asked.

"Miserably."

Louis scowled. He was slender and strongly built. Although only twenty-three, he possessed a confidence and maturity that turned feminine heads. More and more of late, friction was developing between him and Michael.

Julia Kent was small, with glossy dark brown hair and blue eyes. "I'm sorry you got hurt. You could have avoided it if you'd joined us. I was looking forward to your company."

Julia's remark was coupled with a glance other men might have interpreted as sexual. Michael didn't, because he knew such glances were automatic and impersonal. Through polite but unmistakable rebuffs, Michael had long ago made it clear he didn't want to play Julia's little game. It was the ability to attract men that excited her. Any idiot rash enough to make an overture would probably be stunned by a scathing rebuff.

Julia and Louis had married a year and a half after the conclusion of his last term at Harvard. Louis had never received his degree. Not that he wasn't intelligent. He quickly absorbed the training Michael had given him and grew into a shrewd and capable administrator who weighed every decision in terms of profit and loss.

A year after his marriage, Louis succumbed to Julia's wish to have a second residence. He presented his wife with a country house more opulent than their Madison Square mansion. At Michael's suggestion they named their country place Kentland after the English home of Philip Kent's father, James Amberly.

As was his right, Louis gradually assumed control of the family enterprises—the Boston publishing house, the *Union*, the Kent interests in the textile mill in Rhode Island, the gold mines, and the Stovall steelworks, in which Amanda had acquired a substantial interest during her lifetime. The more Louis learned, the more he changed; and Julia's presence only accelerated the change.

While Michael saw Amanda Kent in her son, it was a subtly warped reflection. Louis possessed much of his mother's strength, but without the innate decency and compassion that tempered her occasionally ruthless use of that strength. One day—perhaps quite soon—his differences with Louis would no longer be contained.

BOOK 1

Jephtha Kent was a tall, stern-looking man of forty-one. From time to time he completely forgot that he was heir to his father's considerable fortune. Young Louis found his forgetfulness puzzling. Fan, who had divorced him and had since married an actor, Edward Lamont, found it unbelievable.

Jephtha's thoughts often turned to his three sons. Gideon, the eldest, would be eighteen in June. Matthew was but a year younger. Jeremiah, thank heaven, was not yet fifteen. He wished he knew where they were. He also wished he and Fan had not parted so bitterly. He always thought of his sons with longing and of his former wife with anger. Her behavior the past nine years often sent him into violent rages that upset his relationship with Molly, the woman with whom he had been living for over a year.

Jephtha had just come from an interview with President Lincoln at the executive mansion. He had nothing solid to send to the *Union*, and his lack of copy would infuriate Payne. But what the hell could he send? Then he remembered a note he had jotted down while with the President: "R. Lee. Arlington."

Jephtha hired a mare and started for Virginia. He was detained briefly near the Virginia end of Long Bridge by a Pinkerton man, a fellow named Dorn, with whom he had tangled earlier while working on a story on Lincoln. Jephtha had a healthy fear of a brute like Dorn, but he stood his ground, and Dorn ultimately let him pass into Virginia.

Lee granted Jephtha an interview on the condition that he would not print a word until Lee made public whether or not he would accept the command of the United States Army. Again, no story for the *Union*, but this time Jephtha was overcome with gloom. For after his two interviews, he began to see the essence of the tragedy that was breaking like a torrential storm.

Upon his return to Washington Jephtha was totally unprepared for the advertisement he found in the day's edition.

Dramatic Presentations
in Prose and Poesy
by the Noted Tragedian
MR. EDWARD LAMONT

If Lamont was in the city, had Fan and the boys come with him? Could he find the courage to face them? To face

Fan? The thought of her started his heart beating faster. The hatred in him was beyond control.

Molly Emerson knew her weariness came less from her day's work in her boardinghouse than from worrying about Jephtha.

Now and then Molly felt embarrassed by her feelings for Jephtha. Thirty-eight and a widow, she was too old for the sort of vaporish thrills young women experienced in the name of love. Yet Jephtha could make her feel sentimental, even romantic.

Her husband had died four years ago; and with the money he left her she had set up a boardinghouse in a respectable section in Washington. Soon after Jephtha moved in their friendship had developed into something more intimate—akin to marriage—though he had insisted on maintaining the fiction of separate quarters. He worked in his room but slept with her.

As she climbed into bed, she said, "Jephtha, you've shared this bed long enough for me to know when something's bothering you."

Finally, with her innate sense of timing, she was able to draw from Jephtha his anxiety about his sons and his uncontrollable hatred of their mother. He said he planned to attend Lamont's performance in order to ask his former wife the whereabouts of their sons.

"Fan's the only one who can tell me. That's why I am frightened. I'm frightened that if she won't tell me, I'll hit her. Throttle her. God Himself only knows. I *hate* the bitch!"

When Molly went to tidy up their room in the morning, she found a drawer of her bureau slightly open, the one in which she kept her four-barrel pepperbox, .22 caliber, with ivory grips. She pulled the drawer out; the gun was gone.

Fan Lamont woke at ten. Edward was already up. Since her second marriage she had gradually accustomed herself to the peculiar hours kept by actors. She hoped Jeremiah was busy with his studies in his room. All at once she remembered what day it was. Edward and his strange friend Josiah Cheever had predicted that a new flag would wave beside the Potomac by the first of May, and Edward wanted to help bring it about. He had turned down a six week engagement playing the title role in *Macbeth* so that he could be in Washington on this particular day.

She wished Gideon could have been here to attend the theater tonight. But he had gone to Richmond, hoping to join a military unit that would be mobilized the moment Virginia seceded.

She thought of Matthew. He wouldn't know for weeks, or perhaps months, about his stepfather's high-principled action. Fan and Edward two years before had given up prodding Matthew into further schooling. Grudgingly, they had permitted him to take a mess boy's berth on a cotton packet traveling out of Charleston.

But Gideon would be back soon. Of all her sons, Gideon would have the greatest appreciation for Edward's bravery. Of the three, he believed most strongly that Jephtha's fanaticism was responsible for the dissolution of the family.

Fan lay thinking about her children. Matthew was introspective, almost uncommunicative. He would not do his lessons. Only two things interested him—ungentlemanly games and drawing. He'd sketch anything that caught his interest. His latest letter contained a portrait of his skipper. The picture was called "Captain McGill, 1861."

She thanked God that the independence the boys displayed was her responsibility alone to control. Her efforts weren't perfect, but at least she was spared Jephtha's damaging influence. She thanked God too that her husband directed his stepsons' political thinking properly. Edward treated the boys well. If they felt no love for him, at least they were respectful.

Edward's family was opposed to abolitionism—and with reason. A favorite aunt had been brutally murdered by a crazed houseboy. From that time on the Lamonts worshiped at the altar of an impassioned hatred for the black who had taken the aunt's life. The hatred soon expanded to include any whites who believed such monsters should be allowed freedom. Sometimes Fan was actually fearful of where Edward's hatred of the Negroes, the abolitionists, and the Republicans might carry him.

As the turmoil in the nation moved steadily toward armed conflict, Edward's acting career had become almost a sideline. He spoke more and more of politics, less and less of roles and bookings.

Edward was meeting Josiah Cheever, who was a ringleader of Southern sympathizers in Washington. Cheever wasn't a free agent in the sense that Edward was. He still worked for the War Department; and now that Lincoln had declared the existence of an "insurrection," Cheever was technically a traitor. Edward and Josiah didn't care for one another; only their politics united them.

As Edward was leaving for his appointment with Cheever, he said to Fan, "I wonder if your former husband is in the city. If he is, it might be wise to look him up and get him to promise in writing that no matter what the boys do in the war, he'll honor their claim to the inheritance."

"Edward, I honestly don't think it's necessary. Jephtha may be a Northerner now, but he cares for his sons."

After Edward left, Fan thought, "What *is* he involved in? Much more than he's telling me, I'm certain."

A gold piece slipped to the clerk at the National Hotel provided Jephtha with the information that Mr. and Mrs. Edward Lamont and family were registered there.

Jephtha's spirits soared. He hadn't seen his sons in

almost nine years. He had to see Fan! What if Fan denied him admittance? He had to approach her properly.

Canterbury Hall, where Lamont was to perform, usually attracted mechanics and day laborers poorly dressed and working big wads of tobacco in their jaws. Tonight, however, tobacco chewers were in the minority. Young dandies instead clustered in small groups. Almost all of them displayed the rosette of rebellion on their hats or lapels.

As Jephtha approached the hall, he noticed a short, heavily bearded man in civilian dress.

"Hello, Pinkerton."

"You've made a mistake. My name's Allen. Major E. J. Allen."

"Allen, is it? I realize not many people in the capital know what you look like. But you won't get away with that name for long. Especially if I say your real one a little louder."

"Don't cause trouble for me, Kent. Take a word of advice. Don't go into the bar. Dorn's there. He doesn't like you. I can't say I do either."

"Why are you here? At whose request?"

"Kent, don't you understand? Washington could go up like powder. The government needs to identify potentially dangerous agitators."

"You are making lists, I assume?"

"Mental ones."

"I call that assigning guilt without proof. I have doubts that the President would like it."

"There's no way the President will find out—unless someone talks too freely. You will keep quiet, won't you?"

"It depends on what happens tonight. We'll see if you can control the men you've posted in the hall."

"They're under orders to watch—nothing more," Pinkerton retorted.

"I'm not sure Mr. Dorn has the mental capacity to

understand orders in English or any other language."

"He'll obey orders! But I can't be responsible for what happens between the two of you."

After two dreary acts—a gallopade performed by superannuated "girls" and a banal acrobatic turn—Edward Lamont appeared on the stage. In his sonorous voice he reviled with innuendo President Lincoln and with outright statement the North. He concluded his harangue by asking the audience to sing "Dixie," which had become the unofficial national anthem of the Confederacy.

"No! No!" men howled, leaping over benches, pushing forward. But over their protests and cursing, the lyric Lamont had begun was picked up by a dozen voices, then two dozen, then a hundred, until the song began to swell, proud and defiant.

Presently, pandemonium broke loose: rocks, rotten fruit, even a bowie knife were thrown at Lamont. A pistol went off.

Bedlam.

Lamont still hadn't left the stage. Eight Southerners formed a chain in front of the shallow orchestra pit. Suddenly, Dorn and another Pinkerton man charged the line.

Five of the men started to go to Lamont's assistance. Dorn brandished his gun.

"Stay away! We're friends. We'll protect him."

By outwitting Miller, Dorn's assistant, Jephtha gained access to the room where Lamont was being beaten by the murderous Dorn. When Jephtha attempted to stop Dorn, the detective came at him with a knife and brass knuckles. Jephtha, knowing the detective wanted to kill him, shot him with Molly's pepperbox. The wound was, however, not fatal.

Jephtha helped Lamont into a hackney and accompanied him back to his hotel. The prospect of seeing Fan made Jephtha increasingly nervous.

"Feeling any better, Lamont?"

"Some. You have me at a disadvantage. I don't know who you are."

"My name is Kent. Jephtha Kent."

"Not Fan's—?"

"Yes, but I couldn't stand by and see you killed for speaking your mind."

"Well, I owe you a great many thanks. All differences aside, let me offer them sincerely."

Lamont, supported by Jephtha, climbed to his suite. Fan came to the door. "Oh, dear God! Edward—"

"He's all right. Help me get him inside."

Fan's eyes grew ugly. "Who hurt him. You?"

Except for the burden of Lamont, Jephtha would have struck her.

"Don't be a damned fool," he said. "If you aren't going to help, at least move out of the way."

Jephtha hauled Lamont, nearly unconscious again, to his bed and lowered him onto it.

"Fetch some whiskey if you have any," he said to Fan.

She disappeared into the parlor. The anger that had burst loose when she accused him was gone. He was able to face her calmly.

Lamont was soon asleep. "I think he looks worse than he feels," Jephtha said as he followed Fan into the parlor.

"I am really grateful to you, Jephtha, more grateful than I can say. What you did this evening brings back memories that make me feel extremely guilty. I was cruel in the things I said about you and your cousin Amanda, accusing you two of trying to cheat the boys."

"You know I would never deny my sons what's theirs. I've written a will to insure that each of them will get a substantial inheritance when I die. I haven't touched a penny of the income from California nor the profits from its investment. Fan, are the boys well? Are they here?"

Fan reported that Jeremiah was asleep in an adjoining room and that Gideon was in Richmond but would soon be in Washington. She produced Matthew's latest letter, written in New Orleans, and promised she would notify

Jephtha the minute Gideon returned. Before leaving, Jephtha was able to look in on the sleeping Jeremiah, who stirred, turned his head on the pillow, and spoke a few muffled syllables. When he was quiet again, Jephtha touched his hand and cried silently, without shame.

Jephtha left Fan's suite happy beyond belief.

The next afternoon he received a note:

> My dear Kent,
>
> I am moved to thank you again for your brave action on my behalf. I have been wishing I could express my gratitude in a more tangible manner. Now perhaps I can. I understand when Union troops bound for this city attempt to pass through Baltimore, certain combinations of men will make the passage difficult, if not impossible. Utilize this information as you see fit.
>
> Yours obediently,
> Edw. Lamont

In an untidy boardinghouse room off Seventh Street, Josiah Cheever's pen rasped across a sheet of paper:

> . . . his performance at C. H. conclusively demonstrated the depth of his loyalty. I was also advised that the object of our common interest was in the audience. . . . Our mutual friend insists upon superintending all arrangements and proceeding at his own pace so as not to arouse unduly his wife's suspicions. . . . With my assistance and encouragement he will make certain that Parson K. departs this earth. . . .

Jephtha's black suit was unbearably hot. His skin felt gritty from the soot that had accumulated during the early morning ride up to Baltimore. The loaded pepperbox was in his pocket.

He began to scrutinize the crowds jamming both sides of President Street, watching the passage of the slow-moving railway car. Jephtha was startled at seeing Josiah Cheever. What the hell was a War Department clerk doing in Baltimore? Jephtha nodded. Cheever stared but gave no sign of recognition. He merely turned to speak to a man beside him—a huge fellow with a red beard. Jephtha had the uneasy feeling they were talking about him.

Jephtha moved on with the hostile crowd that was taunting the Sixth Massachusetts Regiment. The soldiers had to walk from one depot to the next because sand had been dumped on the tracks to prevent passage of the train.

A man hurrying into the street shoved him. Something tore the skirt of his black coat. Astonished, Jephtha saw a length of metal tangled in the fabric. Only the accidental jostling had saved him. Spinning around, he saw the red-bearded man, stunned because he had failed. But he held the bowie, ready to use it again. After a scuffle—which no one seemed to notice—Jephtha subdued the man. To escape the dozen or so who had gathered around him, Jephtha backed away and began running. A panicky glance backward showed no pursuit. There was too much confusion for one fight to attract great attention.

On a train chugging through the Maryland countryside later, questions came quickly to Jephtha. Why was Cheever in Baltimore? Why?

All at once Jephtha knew the answers. Cheever had been at Canterbury Hall to support Edward Lamont. And Lamont had written him saying he might find it worthwhile to be in Baltimore when the troops came through.

My God, was I gulled by Lamont? thought Jephtha. *If I was, did Fan know*?

"Jephtha!"

"How the devil—?" Fan and the boys didn't see the color drain from Edward's cheeks. They were staring at the wild-eyed man who was storming into the room. His suit was filthy and torn. And his face was terrifying.

"Gideon—Jeremiah—I am sorry to meet you again under such circumstances. I think it would be better if you both went into the next room."

"See here, Kent!" Edward said. "This is the most—"

Jephtha whirled on him. "Is it, now? I don't doubt you're surprised I'm here at all."

"Jephtha—" Fan rushed toward him. "Why are you so furious?"

"Don't tell me you don't know. Don't lie to me one more time!"

"Damn you!" Gideon shouted. "Don't say such things about—"

Edward broke in. "Let him rave until we find out what this is all about."

"It's about my trip to Baltimore today. In the mob I saw a clerk named Josiah Cheever, who had a red-bearded roughneck with him."

"My dear, I think your former husband is suffering from some sort of persecution mania."

Jephtha whipped the four-barrel pepperbox from his pocket. "Shut your mouth and listen! The red-bearded man tried to put a knife in my back. I was a fool to swallow the note you wrote—the suggestion that I might find it worthwhile to go to Baltimore when the troops came through."

"Of course I wrote him a note," Edward said to the others, "to express my thanks, but the rest is a complete fabrication! I said nothing about Baltimore, absolutely nothing."

"I'd show it to you if I could. The note disappeared from my desk. Evidently it fell on the floor and was swept up," Jephtha retorted. "He's lying. You both know that."

"No, I don't!" Fan burst into tears. "Dear God, I can't comprehend what's caused all this!"

"Your hatred," Jephtha whispered, "and the money. The mining money the boys will inherit after my death. You told me your husband was worried about the money. To make sure I didn't change my mind about the money you would try to have me killed. Or perhaps you two want the money for yourselves. It's you who disappoint me the most, Fan. I just wouldn't have thought you could sink so low. *You deceiving slut!*" He took one swift step and slapped her face.

Gideon leaped for his father's throat. "A crazy man, that's what you are! A crazy goddamned Yankee fanatic!" He snatched Edward's cane and struck Jephtha's neck with a whipping sound.

Whip. Jephtha cried aloud, his cheek laid open. Gideon had his fist tangled in his father's hair.

Edward stepped toward him. "You've done enough. Just get him out of here!"

INTERLUDE

Michael Boyle was baffled as to why Louis had summoned him up to the country. He didn't believe the pretext given in the invitation—a dinner party honoring the Kents' western manager, Israel Hope, whose book *West to Freedom* had been one of the books responsible for the resurgence of Kent and Son after its purchase from the Stovall estate. Joshua Rothman, the Kents' banker, would be there too. And Michael felt guilty. The Seventh New York militia had left for Washington earlier in the month. He had wanted to join them, but he remembered thinking, "I'm staying because there's a gentleman named Louis Kent who needs to be watched."

And Louis indeed needed to be watched, as Michael found out in the library all too clearly after dinner. To the utter dismay of his guests, Louis announced plans for trading with both the North and the South, for prolonging the war, if possible, and profiteering from it. The sole source of his risk capital would come from the Ophir mine profits, which, if not legally, he was morally enjoined from touching by his mother's wish.

An acrimonious interchange followed, which resulted in Israel Hope's resigning his managership of the mines. When he left the library, Louis said, "He'll change his mind after he's calmed down."

"No, Louis," Michael said, "not every man in the world is for sale."

Joshua Rothman excused himself in barely audible words, "I'm going to bed."

"And I'm going to have a drink," Michael said, "in my room." Then he added, "I stand with Joshua. I'll have no part in profiteering at the expense of human lives."

"Then you're not for sale either?"

"Not to you. Good night, Louis."

The whiskey sent to his room did not help. Michael drank, paced, drank, swore, and kept drinking an hour or more.

What could he do to stop Louis? Nothing.

Finally, sick of the house and aware that he was not only drunk but wide awake, he prowled through the darkness and went outside. He had gone only a few steps from the house when he thought he heard a sound. And another sound. He peered through the trees. Someone was moving on the lawn. It was Julia.

"Bit late for a stroll, isn't it?"

"How could I possibly sleep? Louis stormed into his bedroom swearing. He wouldn't answer my knocks. Why is he so upset?"

"Ask him."

All at once a tiny suspicion stole into his thoughts. Had she left the house solely to find out what had taken place in the library?

"Julia, I believe you had better go back."

"My bed clothes are thin, but my cloak's very warm."

Game playing again, he thought. *Damn you, Michael Boyle, you know what she's doing. Are you so weak that you'll stand and permit it?*

"I need you to be my friend. I have no one else. I don't need anyone else."

Be careful!

Gently she kissed him. His self-control shattered, he pulled her against him and kissed her as she was begging to be kissed. She opened her mouth; their tongues touched.

"Michael, we mustn't.... We've gone too far already.... I didn't intend to lead you on."

"Of course you did, and you're getting a bit more than you bargained for!"

Later Michael was vaguely ashamed of what he had done. But mingled with the shame there was pleasure.

An hour before dawn Michael left Kentland. As the carriage bounced, he stared at the woods slipping by. Self-deception wasn't possible any longer. She was beautiful, and he had envied Louis for possessing her.

Added to the rupture that had taken place in the library, their encounter on the lawn had produced an impossible situation. So he was fleeing back to New York. But what peace could he find there?

None.

The next day Michael Boyle joined the Irish Zouaves, a company of one hundred men attached to the Sixty-ninth New York Regiment.

BOOK 2

Eighteen-year-old Margaret Marble was of slender build. She had a generous mouth, brown hair that matched her lively eyes, and a stubby nose she had always hated because it made her look too boyish. Gideon Kent had charmed her on sight when he walked into West and Johnston's, a bookshop where she worked part time. The rest of the week she worked for her aunt, Eliza Marble, who owned La Mode, a dress shop which enjoyed the patronage of a few of Richmond's well-to-do ladies.

Margaret had seen Gideon almost daily for the past month. She had frequently asked herself if it was possible to care for a man and at the same time despise him for the abandon with which he was plunging into preparations for war.

She had never known a boy who affected her as deeply as Gideon did. She had had only two beaux who could be classed as serious. Both came from good families. Margaret had finally allowed each to call on her at the poor flat she and her father shared in Rockett's. Neither boy had ever come back.

Margaret had been born in Kentucky. Her father had gone to Mexico to fight, leaving an ailing wife who died of influenza while he was away. When he came home, he was incapable of running the farm. Ever since, he and his daughter had survived on the charity of Eliza Marble.

Margaret did not want Gideon to see the terrible place where she lived, or her father, who gloried in being called sergeant and whose sole friend was a man he hadn't seen for years, one whom military service had left totally unfit for civilian life. He, too, had a drinking problem.

The sounds of hatred were being heard in Richmond. On once drowsy streets Margaret had seen savage mobs hang straw men from the stanchions of gas lamps. And she had heard the voices of false prophets saying the South's cause was just and the North would be defeated in a swift, relatively bloodless war.

Was she the only person in the city who saw the insanity of it? Who understood it took only one bullet to destroy a man forever? As always these days, her thoughts turned to Gideon.

If I can't make him understand what war really means, I could lose him.

I mustn't lose him.

Because I—I love him.

Margaret spun around at the sound of her name. There he was, running recklessly.

"Margaret! Margaret! I've got the grandest news! Miss Marble, I have the honor of introducing the new second lieutenant of Macomb's Hussars. Sunday we're going up to Harpers Ferry."

Her thoughts sped ahead to what she would say later. Not to persuade Gideon to resign from the troop; he would never do that. But she had to counteract the fatal bravado that could lead him straight to the grave—or to the kind of living death her father suffered.

That evening, after they confessed their love for each other, Margaret took Gideon to meet her father.

Three rickety frame buildings formed a U at the end of the cul-de-sac.

Without looking around, Margaret said, "I didn't want to bring you here. I've always been ashamed of it."

"There's nothing shameful about being poor."

"Oh, yes, there is. Especially when the thing that brought us here is the very thing you're so eager to experience. Come inside. I'll show you how splendid it is to be a soldier."

A grotesque figure popped into sight at the end of the hall. It was a man—or half of one—on a small wood platform with rollers affixed to the bottom. Glasses and a bottle gleamed in the man's lap as he propelled himself along the corridor. He pushed against the floor with his palms—strong, vigorous pushes. The odor of whiskey sat on him.

"This is really quite unlike you, Papa. I mean drinking before Aunt Eliza or I get home."

"Had to celebrate. Heard from Uncle Sam today. He's in the army again. It's the wrong army, but at least he's back where he belongs. We'll hear plenty about him—Uncle Sam. Grant. You remember his name and see if I ain't right."

Margaret's father continued to drink while telling Gideon about his war experiences. Finally, his head flopped over and he dozed.

Gideon started out, with Margaret after him. She slammed the door and faced him on the landing. "Do you still want to be what he was? Papa was just like you before he went to Mexico! I want you to be realistic about what can happen to you."

"What am I supposed to do? Put in a request for duty behind the lines? I want a chance at the Yanks."

"I'll have nothing to do with this war—or any man who involves himself in it." Margaret closed her eyes and spoke from pain.

"Then you'll have nothing to do with me, goddamn it!"

She flung an arm around his neck and pressed her wet cheek against his. "Good-bye, Gideon."

Before he could think what to say, she rushed back into the flat. He heard the bolt slide home.

"Margaret," he roared. "Open up!"

Within a little more than a month, Gideon Kent's life had changed to such a remarkable degree that his parting with Margaret seemed unreal. He thought of her with regret; but he didn't write her, or she him.

The only letters he received were from his mother—cheerful and chatty. In one she wrote, "Edward works long hours. Perhaps fatigue explains a curious incident. After church recently we encountered an old acquaintance, Mr. Cheever. But neither he nor Edward acknowledged the other. When I mentioned it later, Edward grew quite sharp and refused to discuss it."

Gideon remembered the name. That night at the National Hotel, his father had mentioned someone named Cheever being involved in that imaginary murder plot. Edward had admitted knowing Cheever while denying everything else.

Gideon's first real battle experience came at Manassas in July. It was ugly and frightening as hell; that was the truth Gideon Kent saw in those moments when he headed into action. All during that incredible afternoon, the First Virginia Cavalry crashed against the Union ranks, horses rearing, sabers rattling. Gideon's men chased the Yanks until they broke and ran. Although Gideon was unscathed in the rout, his close friend Rodney Arbuckle was killed.

Against all her scruples, Margaret had allowed herself to be shamed into assisting those wounded at Manassas as they arrived at the depot in Richmond.

Coffins were unloaded from the head end of the train, stretcher cases from the middle. The walking wounded were climbing down at the rear. She thought she spied a familiar face in the press of soldiers limping up the platform.

"Gideon—here! *Here I am!*"

A strange, hesitant smile lifted his mouth. She ran frantically around the coffins. They crashed into one another. He flung his arms around her waist, hugging her so hard that she felt her spine would break. She didn't care.

"Margaret, *Margaret.*" It sounded like a sob and a laugh in one. "Hearing you call to me was like a miracle. One thing would make it a devil of a lot easier to go back."

"What?"

"Knowing that when it's all over, you'll marry me."

She shook her head. "I love you, Gideon. I want to marry you now. *Before* you go back."

"By God," Edward Lamont smiled, "that crazy Jephtha Kent's in Richmond."

"Until I'd read we had captured civilians along with soldiers, I couldn't believe it myself," Josiah Cheever said. "Sounds like he's half dead, too."

A rear corner table in Mrs. Muller's Saloon provided

the two men with the privacy they desired.

"Makes the task that much easier, Josiah."

"You have no reservations about going through with it?"

"Not for gain. I didn't give a damn about the money that belongs to her sons until the political situation made it important. Yes, it's finally going to happen. Let's drink to the most important performance of my career."

Gideon had just returned to the Lamonts' flat about two after seeing Margaret home. Edward sat opposite him, having just finished his night's work at the Treasury. For patriotic reasons he had given up his lucrative acting career to take on a clerk's position.

Edward was in unusually high spirits, and Gideon found that peculiar in someone forced to work until after two in the morning.

Gideon stretched and yawned. "I may sleep for two days, but I also have to hunt up a horse to replace the one I lost at Manassas and send that flag there to Miss Wonderly."

Miss Wonderly was the fiancée of Rodney Arbuckle, who had fallen at Manassas. Rodney had made Gideon promise to return the flag to his beloved in the event of his death. She had made it, and Rodney had been carrying it inside his coat when he was struck by a Yankee bullet. The blood-marked Stars and Bars now lay folded beside the clock on the mantel.

"I nearly forgot," Edward said, "a piece of news I read." He then told them about Jephtha, that he had received a bad concussion and was now imprisoned in the Richmond Almshouse. "They'll give him medical attention, but I'm certainly not going to fret about his welfare."

That angered Gideon. Ever since Fan had written about the street encounter with Cheever, Gideon had had doubts about Edward's honesty. Also, he had smelled the odor of beer on Edward's breath. "I can't imagine the Treasury serves beer to clerks who stay late. And he said he had come straight home."

A few days later Margaret suggested to Gideon that he inquire at the Almshouse about his father. Fan urged him to do the same. Gideon had come close to attempting to see his father several times. In spite of the violence in the National Hotel, or perhaps because of it, he felt guilty about ignoring the man who had given him life.

With Josiah Cheever's help, Edward Lamont disguised himself as Artemus McAfee, a backwoods farmer from Mechanicsville, Hanover County, and set out with a forged pass and a basket of gifts for his wife's cousin, Mr. Jephtha Kent. Everything was planned. After "Mr. McAfee" had accomplished his mission at the Almshouse, he would disappear from Richmond forever, having given a single flawless performance.

That same evening Gideon sat alone with his mother and told her he planned to go to the Almshouse to inquire about his father. He said, "I hesitated to bring it up because I thought Edward would object. Where is he, by the way?"

"Working late at the Treasury."

"Mama, Margaret and I passed the Treasury. There wasn't a light burning in the place. Sometimes I ask myself whether Edward's always truthful. I've thought about Papa's accusations in Washington. I was convinced he was out of his head until Cheever's name cropped up in your letter."

"I must confess to you that I've been suspicious of Edward myself. Why he should see fit to deny knowing Mr. Cheever..."

Gideon had to get out of the flat to think things through. As he prepared to leave, his eye came level with the mantel. The flag for Miss Wonderly was gone.

"Mama, did you move the flag?"

"It was there before Edward left."

"What the hell is Edward up to? No one else could have taken the flag."

"Certainly not. But why on earth would he?"

"I don't know, but I'm going to the Almshouse right now. Maybe he does want us to get control of the California money—not for himself, not for us—but for the government."

Gideon ran out. *Perhaps*, he thought, *Edward, the patriot, the actor, was planning to play one more role—murderer.*

Edward's disguise and falsified papers got him to Jephtha's room with no trouble. He pulled out the missing Stars and Bars from his bag of gifts and relished the poetic justice of strangling with the flag of the Confederacy the semicomatose Yankee who lay before him. He would be finished and gone in less than half an hour. The guards probably wouldn't even detect the death until morning.

"Listen!" the sergeant said. "There's no visiting without a pass. Sorry, sir. You say this Kent's your pa?"

"That's right. I want to know how he's getting along."

"Sure's a popular fellow, that Kent. He's already got one visitor. Some old farmer—relative of his wife from Hanover County."

Gideon yanked the revolver from his sash. "He's got no relatives in Hanover County. You take me up there. If we meet any guards, you tell them to stay away or I'll blow your head off."

Lamont pressed the folded flag over Jephtha's face. When the feeble man struggled, Lamont pressed harder.

"You murdering son of a bitch!"

With a scream, Lamont tumbled over on his side as Gideon's boots smashed into his ribs a second time.

"Gideon, please! After he's gone, the money will be yours. For you. For your brothers." He dove for his satchel and swung it at Gideon with all his strength, but Gideon managed to pound his fist into the man's stomach. Off balance, Edward reeled and floundered backward. His spine struck the window. Glass shattered. His nails scratched for a hold on the frame; he found none.

Edward fell to the ground three floors below.

The circumstances of Edward's death brought a reconciliation between Gideon and Jephtha, and it was the father's great pleasure to be at his son's wedding. Later, Jephtha was given safe conduct to the border, and there he parted from Gideon.

Jephtha had tears in his eyes. So did Gideon.

"I don't want this war to destroy you."

"I'll come through just fine, Papa."

"I pray so because I love you."

The quiet words faded quickly. Something drove Gideon forward—a bursting relief, a draining of old pain. He took his father in his arms and held him close.

When they drew apart, Jephtha said, "One way or another I am going to see that you receive five thousand in gold from the Ophir money to buy horses. It's the only gift I can give you besides a father's love and a prayer for your forgiveness."

Michael Boyle's regiment had been badly beaten at Bull Run, and he now found himself in Washington awaiting further duty. He accepted an invitation from Joshua Rothman, but he had no stomach for the elegant supper Rothman had arranged for him.

"What brings you here, Joshua?"

"Louis. His plans will make a mockery of the Kent name. The only way to stop him is to threaten to expose him in the papers."

"Who'd write such an article?"

"I think Jephtha would. I think he'd do it even though it would cost him his job."

"It will cost us all something," Michael said.

EPILOGUE

On Saturday, May 31, 1862, Margaret Marble Kent was delivered of a daughter.

On Wednesday, June 11, Gideon was assigned to a special cavalry detachment of twelve hundred troopers. He was in a good mood as the detachment rode completely around McClellan's army.

Three days later the regimental roster listed Captain Gideon Kent as missing in action.

Prelude to War

Background to THE TITANS

The decade before the Civil War was a generally prosperous one in America; and if Americans were not then a consumer society in today's understanding of the term, they nonetheless used the dollar to enjoy a level of comfort and pleasure that belied the austerity of their puritanical past. For the first time, great numbers of them gladly paid for recreation. In the cities, they filled amusement parks, theaters, and music halls; in the country, they flocked to circuses and fairs, which featured balloon ascensions, tightrope walkers, and horse races. Everywhere Americans took to sports, especially the newfangled baseball. (Fan Lamont was an exception; she thought it uncouth.)

If baseball was uncouth, boxing as practiced in the mid-1800s was barbaric. The "sport" was performed by teams, who squared off in a kind of battle royal in which uninjured barefisted boxers substituted for their damaged teammates until only one side was left standing. Boxing was unlawful almost everywhere until the turn of the century. Enthusiasts were, however, able to circumvent the law by holding the sport in places which by accident or design were immune from the constabulary. One such was the hamlet of Boston Corners, which was claimed simultaneously by New York, Massachusetts, and Connecticut. In its uncertain alignment, it was conveniently deemed extra-legal and became famous for its bouts of bare fisticuffs until New York proved its claim and asserted its authority.

City audiences supported innumerable music halls like the Canterbury Theater in Washington, where Edward Lamont delivered his incendiary speech and sang "Dixie." They also thronged to legitimate theaters to see Edwin Forrest, the Booths, and Fanny Kemble in Shakespearean productions.

Nowhere were midcentury prosperity and confidence more beautifully in evidence than in the many public buildings and private homes that were dotted throughout the cities and countryside of all but the newest states.

The classical revival so gloriously begun by Jefferson and others before 1800 was carried to a peak of perfection in the first decades of the nineteenth century, particularly in Washington, where the dignified simplicity and grandness of buildings based on Roman models did so much to suggest the ideals of the Republic.

With the competition in 1792 for a national capitol, the profession of architecture was established in the United States, even though the winner was an amateur, William Thornton. He was succeeded by Stephen Hallet, a thoroughly trained designer. Later, an Englishman, George Hadfield, took charge of the construction and also designed the first buildings for the executive department in Washington. But the man who did most was the Yorkshireman, Benjamin Henry Latrobe, an architect of imagination and taste and an engineer of great skill. He designed the south wing of the Capitol, made alterations in the White House, and remodeled the Patent Office. After the destruction of the Capitol by the British in 1814, Latrobe was engaged to rebuild it.

During this time, even New England's famous architect

Charles Bulfinch was not indifferent to the classical revival, although his buildings were usually in the Robert Adam style, called "federal" over here. The Massachusetts General Hospital, for example, which he designed in 1817, was certainly based in part on the popular Roman models of the day. That is probably why he was asked to complete the Capitol when Latrobe resigned.

The Greek revival, as distinct from the more eclectic classical revival, began in 1818 with the competition for the design of the Second Bank of the United States in Philadelphia. Specifications called for a faithful imitation of Greek design—no domes or other Roman adulterations. The winning architect was William Strickland, a pupil of Latrobe. For the porticoes, Strickland followed the Doric order of the Parthenon; his entire building was contained under a single temple roof of low pitch, and the doors and windows were trabeated—that is, constructed of horizontal lintels—since the arch held no place in Greek temple architecture. With this building Strickland put himself at the head of a growing number who believed in the absolute superiority of Greek architecture.

Not all Greek Revivalists were as "pure" as Strickland. Some used domes here and there to good effect, or omitted fluting from Doric columns, or substituted square pillars for columns. Gradually, buildings in the Greek style, pure and impure, spread from Maine to Georgia and westward into New York State and beyond. The most extravagant examples appeared on the rich cotton plantations of the South.

Another style, the pseudo-Gothic, which had gained popularity in England in the eighteenth century in such masterpieces as Horace Walpole's Strawberry Hill at Twickenham, finally reached America in midcentury. Since construction in wood, which was abundant, cost about half that of the same design in stone, American architects translated Gothic detail into wood in dwellings as well as in churches, banks, railroad stations, even in warehouses. The fashion imposed itself on everything,

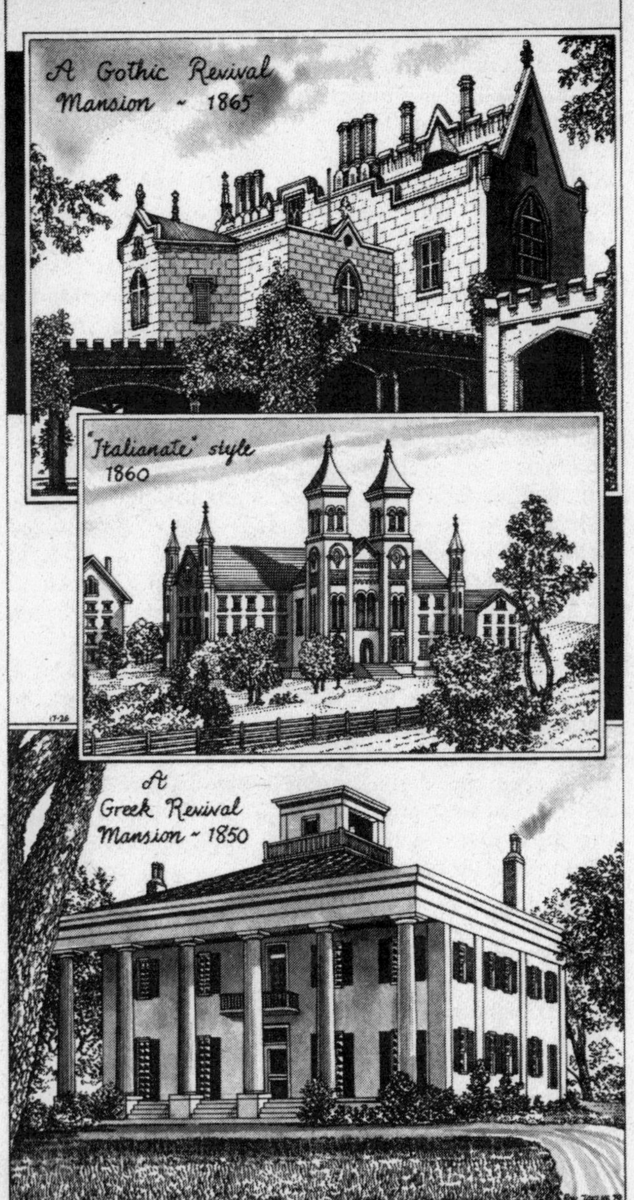

A Gothic Revival
Mansion ~ 1865
"Italianate" style
1860
A
Greek Revival
Mansion ~ 1850

including the passenger cars of the Erie and Kalamazoo Railroad, which were a story and a half, replete with ogival arches.

Today, surviving "carpenter Gothic," as it is now called, often appears in bright colors, which give it a cheerful look. The original architects of this uniquely American design would have deplored such frivolity. They used dark grays and browns, and even darker trim to create the Gothic mood. These romantics criticized the white paint favored by the Greek revivalists as too glaring in sunshine and making buildings too prominent on the landscape.

The pile built by Louis for Julia was in the Gothic style, but in stone; it also had much of the Italian villa style that was making its appearance in the American countryside. Such buildings were fussy, not greatly unlike the high Gothic of the cathedral in Milan; but they were twice removed from the source of their inspiration—American adaptations of English modifications of tall Italian country houses.

Eaves were wide, and moldings were exaggerated. Square towers rising high above the main block were a significant feature. Ornate brackets supporting the eaves were also a requirement.

These houses, in spite of their ostentation, were not uncomfortable. Massive walls, high ceilings, and central stairwells meant coolness in summer, and the tall windows lighted the large rooms gracefully.

One drawback to the Italianate style was that it inspired overornamentation within as well as without. Interior furnishings in fashionable houses, which up to this time had reflected the chaste elegance of the Regency and the Empire, was now giving way to massive fake Jacobean or rococo designs.

Louis's Kentland no doubt was equipped with the newest domestic innovations, especially in the kitchens, where coal ranges had taken the place of fireplaces. These new stoves were not readily accepted, however, by all cooks. They not only felt that the ancient hearth cookery produced better food, but provided a healthier atmosphere than that found in newfangled kitchens where redhot stoves gave the air a close and disagreeable smell.

Central heating of a sort had appeared early in the century, and by the 1850s had replaced—in elegant homes, at least—stoves and fireplaces as the chief sources of heat. This source of heat, too, had its opponents, not always reactionaries ready to condemn anything new. Some feared—quite rightly—that the dehydration caused by central heating was inimical to good health. The role of oxygen in metabolism had recently been discovered, and the dangers of carbon dioxide were well advertised. Some timid beneficiaries of central heating were vitiating its effects by ventilating rooms so thoroughly with open windows that they were colder than when they relied on fireplaces for warmth.

With more and more central heating being introduced, the hearth was no longer the focus of the room. Instead, the large table in the middle of the evenly heated room was, as we can see in thousands upon thousands of nineteenth-century lithographs and family photographs. The lamp hanging over the table, usually round, illuminated father's paper, mother's sewing, sister's fancy work and brother's schoolbooks. The all-important lamp was as much improved as household heating; the astral lamp, for example, cut out downward shadows. Until 1860, the best light was produced by a dangerously combustible combination of alcohol and turpentine, but the introduction of kerosine in that year removed the fire hazard.

Michael Boyle had a keen sense of failure and foreboding during the election of 1860. In view of its momentous consequences, he was entirely justified.

It was at best a confused election. When the Democrats gathered for their convention in Charleston, South

Carolina, in April, the Southerners were determined to adopt a platform for federal protection of slavery in the territories, an area that comprised what is now the Dakotas, the Rocky Mountain States, and much of the Southwest. The Western Democrats were angered by the Southern attitude, but they were willing to negotiate a compromise in order to hold the party together. They endorsed without great enthusiasm popular sovereignty and proposed that all questions concerning slavery in the territories be left up to the Supreme Court.

When the convention adopted the Western platform, the delegations from eight of the lower Southern states withdrew; those remaining attempted to select a candidate. Stephen Douglas of Illinois led on every ballot, but he could not muster the two-thirds majority of the original number of delegates required by party rules.

Finally, the managers adjourned the convention to reconvene in Baltimore in June. The states that had walked out of the Charleston convention proceeded to hold a rival convention in Richmond. The "official" Baltimore gathering nominated Douglas, while the men in Richmond nominated John C. Breckinridge of Kentucky, with the result that there were two Democratic candidates in 1860.

The Republicans, who were no longer a one-idea party composed of crusaders against slavery, met in Chicago in May. They were determined to appear to the electorate as representing conservatism, stability, and moderation, and they hoped to appeal to major groups in the North who believed that the South was blocking their economic progress.

The Republican platform called for a high tariff (to protect the industrial Northeast, which was developing a flourishing trade with the West), a homestead bill, and an east-west railroad to be built with federal financial aid. On the issue of slavery, the Republicans were not quite so progressive. They affirmed the right of each state to control its own institutions; at the same time, they denied the authority of Congress or a territorial legislature to legalize slavery in the territories.

The Republicans chose Abraham Lincoln over the better-known William Seward. Lincoln was obscure enough to have only a few enemies. His antislavery stance pleased the liberals in the party, but he was conservative enough to appeal to the former Whigs who now called themselves Republicans.

To add to the turmoil of this election was a fourth party. Although calling itself new, the Constitutional Union party was the last remnant of the oldest conservative tradition in the country, composed of elder statesmen who stood for the Constitution, the Union, and law and order.

In the November election, Lincoln received 180 electoral votes but only 39.8 percent of the popular vote; Breckinridge, the Southern Democrat, received 72 electoral votes and 18.1 percent of the popular vote; Douglas, the Northern Democrat, 12 and 27.5 percent; and Bell, the Constitutional Unionist, 30 and 12.6 percent. The Republicans had a president, but they had failed to secure a majority in Congress.

Southerners had threatened secession for some time, but nothing had happened; so when they threatened during the campaign to secede from the Union if the Republicans won the election, Northerners did not take them seriously.

There was no doubt among some Southerners that secession was legal. Sovereign states could leave the Union, but the process had to be a solemn one. Voters elected a convention, which then took the state out of the Union by due process of law.

South Carolina, the state with the longest history of strong separatist leaning, was the first to secede by unanimous vote of its legislature on December 20, 1860, a little more than a month after Lincoln's election. Six other states followed in rapid succession—Mississippi, Florida, Alabama, Georgia, Louisiana, and Texas. By

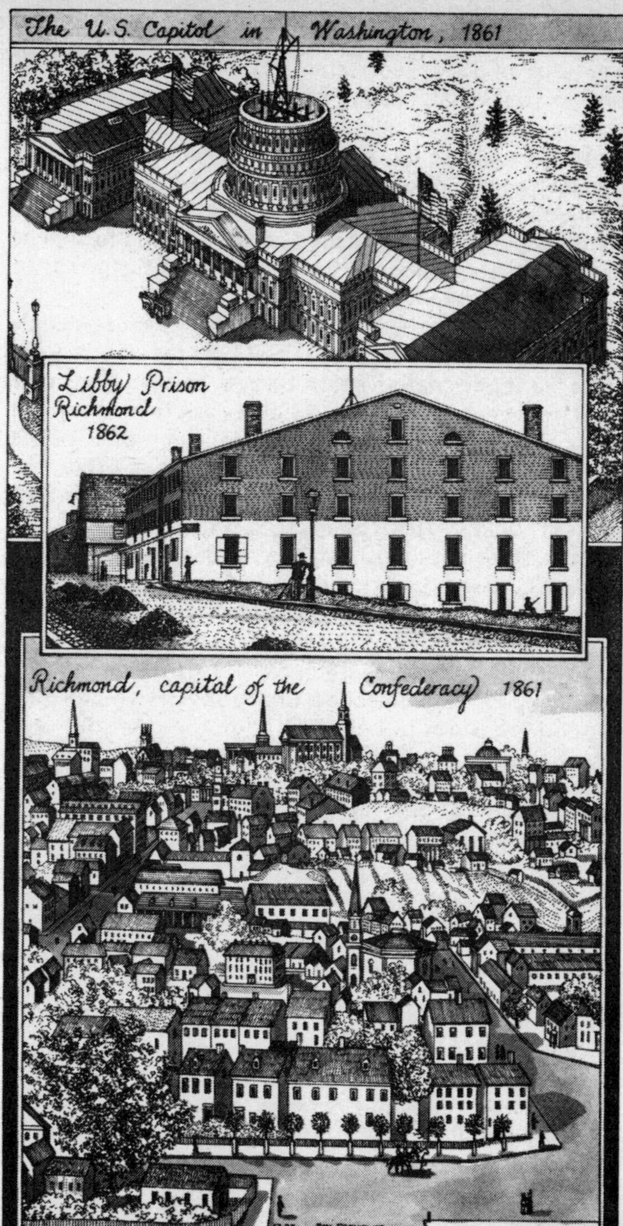
The U.S. Capitol in Washington, 1861
Libby Prison
Richmond
1862
Richmond, capital of the Confederacy 1861

February of 1861, representatives of the seceded states had met in Montgomery, Alabama, and formed a new nation, the Confederate States of America.

Lincoln would not be inaugurated until March 4. In the meantime, President Buchanan in his message to Congress in December of 1860 denied the right of a state to secede, but he reflected his indecision by adding that he did not think the federal government had the power to demand that a state reenter the Union.

Buchanan had been elected mainly because people thought he would compromise and keep the slavery issue from tearing the nation apart. Clearly, his intention in the final weeks of his one-term presidency was to avoid armed collision and to maintain the symbolic authority of the national government until his successor took office.

As the states seceded, they took possession of federal property within their boundaries, but they lacked the force to seize certain offshore forts, such as Fort Sumter in the Charleston harbor and Fort Pickens off Pensacola, Florida. South Carolina demanded that Washington surrender Sumter, but Buchanan, despite his fear of provoking an armed conflict, refused to yield the fort.

Buchanan recommended that Congress frame compromise measures to hold the Union together. But each time it appeared that there might be some agreement, the question of slavery in the territories split Congress apart.

By March 4, 1861, when Lincoln took office, nothing had been resolved. The President's inaugural address laid down some basic principles: the Union was older than the Constitution and therefore no state could of its own volition leave the Union; the ordinances of secession were illegal; and acts to support secession were insurrectionary. He further declared that he meant to execute the laws in all the states and to lay claim to all federal property in seceded states.

Before long, Lincoln's policy concerning federal property was put to the test at Fort Sumter. The garrison was manned by a small force under the command of

Major Robert Anderson; and unless fresh supplies were received, the post would have to be abandoned. Lincoln decided to dispatch a relief expedition to the fort. By so doing he placed the Confederates in a dilemma. If they permitted the relief force to land, they would be acknowledging federal authority. Their only chance, therefore, was to seize the fort before aid arrived. General P. G. T. Beauregard demanded Anderson's surrender, but Anderson refused. The Confederates then bombarded the fort for two days, and on April 14, Anderson surrendered.

War had come. President Lincoln increased the army and called on the states to furnish troops to restore the Union.

Four more slave states seceded and joined the Confederacy: Virginia on April 17, Arkansas on May 6, Tennessee on May 7, and North Carolina on May 20. The mountain counties in northwestern Virginia refused to join their state. In 1863, they entered the Union as the new state of West Virginia. The four remaining slave states—Maryland, Delaware, Kentucky, and Missouri—remained within the Union.

The North, or the United States, comprised twenty-three states with a population of approximately twenty-two million. The eleven Confederate States had a population of nine million, of whom almost three and a half million were slaves.

Because Congress was not in session when hostilities began, Lincoln called for 42,000 volunteers and authorized an increase of 23,000 in the regular army. When Congress convened in July of 1861, it legalized the President's bold measures and provided for enlisting a half million volunteers for three years.

At first, the volunteer system brought in enough men, but after the initial enthusiasm waned, even the cash bounties offered by both the federal government and the states proved inadequate lures. Finally, in March of 1863, Congress passed the first national draft law in American history. (The Confederate States had enacted a similar law almost a year earlier.) The only exemptions were high national and state officials, clergymen, and men who were the sole support of a family. But a drafted man could escape service by hiring a substitute or by paying a fee of three hundred dollars. Eventually, the cash commutation was repealed.

The draft law was designed to spur enlistments by threatening to invoke conscription. Each state was divided into districts and assigned a quota of men. If a state, by bounties or other means, could fill the quota, it escaped the draft completely. Although the draft actually inducted only a relatively few men, it stimulated enlistments enormously. The federal forces reached their maximum in 1865. Accurate statistics are not available, but it would appear that about a million and a half Northerners served for three years, as contrasted with nine hundred thousand Confederate forces.

The casualty rate in the Civil War was appalling for two reasons—one military and the other medical. The new weapons employed were much more effective than those used in previous wars, so in many battles the proportion of men killed was as high as thirty percent. Furthermore, although medical knowledge in 1861 was extensive, there was much yet to be discovered concerning the care of wounds, diet, and sanitation. As a result, more men died of disease in the Civil War than from bullets.

So much has been written about Abraham Lincoln that it is scarcely possible to separate the man from the legend.

When Lincoln first went to Washington in 1846, as a Whig congressman, he was considered an ungainly, small-time prairie politician, hardly fit for his job. But despite popular opinion and his unpretentious airs, he was a man of great self-confidence, which he demonstrated eminently in 1860 by his choice of a cabinet. Representing every faction of the Republican party and every segment of Northern opinion, his cabinet was an extraordinary assemblage of talents and temperaments. Three of his most capable secretaries—William H. Seward (State), Salmon P. Chase (Treasury), and Edwin M. Stanton (War)—were all disappointed in their opinion that they could dominate Lincoln. The President dominated them.

Lincoln's confidence in his own strength was revealed by his bold, if not ruthless, exercise of the war powers of his office. In order to accomplish a goal, he was prepared to violate parts of the Constitution. He explained that he would not lose the whole by being afraid to disregard a part. And so he called for troops to repress the rebellion, which was tantamount to a declaration of war; illegally increased the size of the regular army; and proclaimed a naval blockade of the South.

There was not a wholehearted support of the war in the North. Opposition came from two fronts—Southern sympathizers in the Union slave states and from the peace wing, the doves, of the Democratic party. War Democrats, the hawks, not only supported the war but were even willing to accept offices from the Republican administration. Peace Democrats, or copperheads, as their enemies called them, feared that agriculture and the West were being subordinated to industry and the East and that states' rights were being sacrificed to nationalism. The peace Democrats wanted to call a truce and invite the South to attend a national convention in order to amend the Constitution and preserve states' rights.

To deal with opponents of the war, Lincoln resorted to military arrests. He suspended the right of habeas corpus so that an alleged offender could be arrested and held without trial or, if tried, be forced to appear before a military court. In 1862, he proclaimed that all persons who discouraged enlistments or engaged in other disloyal practices would come under martial law. Over thirteen thousand Northerners were arrested and imprisoned for varying periods.

There were factions within Lincoln's own party—the radicals and the conservatives. On economic matters they were in fundamental agreement, but they differed on the slavery issue. The radicals wanted to seize the opportunity of the war to put an abrupt end to slavery. The conservatives were just as antislavery, but they wanted to put an end to the institution easily and gradually. Lincoln, whose leanings were conservative, tried unsuccessfully to persuade the Union slave states to agree to a program of compensated gradual emancipation.

As the war demanded more sacrifices of the North, public opinion became increasingly antislavery. In July of 1862, Congress enacted the second Confiscation Act, which was an attempt to bring about emancipation by legislative action. It declared the property of persons supporting the rebellion subject to forfeiture to the United States. It proclaimed free the slaves of persons aiding and supporting the insurrection, and it authorized the President to employ Negroes, including freed slaves, as soldiers. The act marked a turning point in the war. The country had come to accept emancipation as an aim of the conflict.

Lincoln was an astute politician and saw that in order to achieve his larger purpose of saving the Union he would have to sacrifice his desire to prevent the sudden destruction of slavery. In order to accomplish his goals, he of course needed the support of his party—particularly that of the radicals. If a majority of Northerners wanted slavery destroyed, he could not afford to oppose their will.

On September 22, 1862, after the Battle of Antietam, Lincoln issued his preliminary Emancipation Proclamation, and on January 1, 1863, a final Emancipation Proclamation. Few slaves were freed immediately, but eventually, as Union armies occupied large areas of the South, the proclamation became a practical reality and hundreds of thousands of slaves became free. Of great military importance in the process of emancipation was

Robert Toombs
Judah P. Benjamin
Confederate
Secretary of
State 1861
Confederate
Secretary of War
& Attorney General
1862
Jefferson Davis,
President of
the Confederacy
1861
President Lincoln
meeting with his Cabinet
1862

the induction of many former slaves into the armed forces.

Although the first seven Southern states to secede left the Union as individual sovereignties, they at no time intended to maintain separate political existences. It was understood from the beginning that they would come together in a common federation to which, they hoped, the states of the upper South would eventually adhere. To create a Southern nation, representatives of the seceding states convened early in February, 1861, in Montgomery, Alabama, which served as the capital of the new nation until Virginia seceded. The capital then moved to Richmond, one of the few southern cities large enough to house the government.

The name Confederate States was significant. The new nation was a confederation of sovereign states, not a federation of united ones. In the constitution, the sovereignty of the states was expressly recognized; but proposals for the right of a state to secede were not adopted. The structure of the Confederate government, interestingly enough, was an almost exact duplicate of the model Southerners had just rejected.

The Montgomery Convention elected Jefferson Davis of Mississippi president of the Confederacy; the vice-president was Alexander Stephens of Georgia. Davis had been a dedicated, but not fanatical, advocate of Southern rights in the former Union; he was a moderate, not an extreme secessionist. Stephens had been chief among those who believed that secession was unnecessary.

Davis was intelligent and honest, but lacked the ability to be a wartime leader. He tended to waste time on routine details and so lost sight of the essential fact that the Confederacy was not an established, recognized nation, but a revolutionary government. Circumstances demanded that the South act with ruthless efficiency, as Lincoln was doing in the North; instead Davis was punctilious to a fault.

The Confederate cabinet contained none of the brilliant, though exasperating, talent characteristic of Lincoln's best advisers. They were a pedestrian lot who were selected on a geographical basis, not according to ability or fitness for a particular post.

The personnel of the cabinet changed rapidly and often. In its brief existence, the Confederacy had three secretaries of state, two of the treasury, four attorney generals, and five secretaries of war. Not a man in the cabinet dared oppose Davis's will.

The year 1861 saw several minor battles that were significant and one large encounter that proved very little. The minor engagements took place in Missouri and in western Virginia, the mountainous area that in a short time would become the Union state of West Virginia. In Missouri, which was divided over the issue of slavery, Union forces were able to hold most of the state. In western Virginia, a Northern force, chiefly Ohioans, was under the command of George B. McClellan. By the end of 1861, the West Virginians were freed of Confederate control.

The one big battle of the year was fought in Virginia in the area between Washington, D.C., and Richmond, Virginia, the two capitals. A Federal army of over thirty thousand under the command of General Irvin McDowell opposed a Confederate army of twenty thousand under General P. G. T. Beauregard. This battle gave Gideon Kent his first real taste of war and also made him understand Margaret's feelings about war.

In mid-July, McDowell marched his inexperienced troops toward Manassas, a small settlement. His movement was no surprise, having been well advertised to the Confederates by Northern newspapers and Southern spies. Beauregard retired behind Bull Run, a small stream north of Manassas, and asked Jefferson Davis to order General Joseph Johnston to join him. When Johnston's troops arrived, they swelled Beauregard's forces to approximately the size of McDowell's army.

The Battle of Bull Run, or Manassas, took place on July 21. Beauregard did not get his offenses into motion, so McDowell's attack almost succeeded. The Confederates, however, stopped a last strong Union assault and then made a counterattack. As the Southern troops surged forward, the Union troops panicked. They crossed Bull Run in a rout. Unable to reorganize his men, McDowell ordered a retreat to Washington.

The Confederates were as disorganized in victory as the Federal troops were in defeat; and lacking supplies and transport, they were unable to undertake a forward movement toward Washington.

Lincoln promptly replaced McDowell with General McClellan, the victor of the fighting in western Virginia, and took immediate steps to increase the size of the army. At this point both sides dug in for a real war.

Hard facts faced the Southerners who sought to devise means for financing the war. Banking houses, except those in New Orleans, were smaller and fewer than the Northern establishments. Liquid assets were few, and the only specie possessed by the government was that seized in United States mints located in the South.

The Confederate Congress, like the Northern body, was not anxious to impose rigorous wartime taxes. In 1861, the legislators provided for a direct tax on property to be levied through the medium of the states. Most of the states, instead of taxing their people, assumed the tax themselves by issuing bonds or their own notes. This measure produced a disappointing return of only $18 million. The Confederate Congress then, in a bolder move, passed a bill licensing levies and another providing for an income tax. There was also a "tax in kind"; that is, every farmer and planter had to contribute one-tenth of his produce to the government. Later, the Confederate Congress raised the rates of their internal revenue measure and imposed other taxes, but the money realized

Stuart's Virginia Cavalry charge at Bull Run
Centreville, Virginia the Union objective, July, 1861
Union Infantry Advancing to the Attack at Bull Run

was relatively small. The Confederacy raised only a little over one percent of its total income in taxes.

The bond record of the Confederacy was little better than its tax program. The Confederate Congress authorized a $100 million loan to be paid in specie, paper money, or produce. The loan was subscribed partly in paper currency but mostly in produce or pledges of produce. Many of the pledges were not redeemed, and often the promised products were destroyed by the enemy. The Confederacy also attempted to borrow money in Europe by pledging cotton stored in the South for future delivery, but it secured little from European sources.

Since ready revenue was needed and currency was scarce, the government resorted to issuing paper money and treasury notes. Once this expedient was employed, it could not be stopped. By 1864, $1 billion had been issued by the Confederacy in addition to the notes issued by the states and by cities. Inevitably, the value of the money depreciated, and prices were at astronomical heights. Flour was three hundred dollars a barrel, chickens were thirty-five dollars a pair, and clothing was out of reach. Obviously, few could pay these prices, so morale among the citizens was soon very low.

Like the United States, the Confederate States first raised troops by calling for volunteers, but by the latter part of 1861, volunteering had dropped off badly. By the beginning of 1862, the Confederacy was short of manpower. The situation was met head on by enacting in April of that year a conscription act which declared all able-bodied white males between eighteen and thirty-five liable to military service for three years. As in the North, a draftee could evade his summons if he furnished a substitute. The intention of this arrangement was to exempt key men in agriculture and industry; but to those who could not afford substitutes, it seemed like a special privilege for the rich. After arousing bitter class discontent, the law was repealed late in 1863.

The first draft act and later measures provided other exemptions, chiefly on an occupational basis. A provision that was bitterly criticized exempted one white man on each plantation with twenty or more slaves. It gave rise to the saying "It's a rich man's war, but a poor man's fight."

In September of 1862, a second conscription measure raised the age limit to forty-five. By the end of that year, there were an estimated half million soldiers in the armies of the Confederacy. Thereafter, conscription provided fewer and fewer men, and the Southern forces steadily decreased in size.

By 1864, the situation was desperate. The Confederate Congress lowered the draft age to seventeen and raised it to fifty. But few men were obtained. War weariness and the certainty of defeat were making their influence felt. The last year of the war saw one hundred thousand desertions. The army rolls in 1865 carried two hundred thousand names, but fewer than half of these were in service. In a frantic final attempt to raise men, the Confederate Congress authorized in 1865 the drafting of three hundred thousand slaves. The war ended, however, before this grotesquely incongruous measure could be put into effect.

Most Southerners were united in support of the war, but they soon became bitterly divided over how it should be conducted. Ironically, the divisive force was the principle of states' rights, which had become a cult with Southerners to the degree that they reacted against the central controls necessary to win the war. If there was an organized opposition to the government, it was those who regarded Vice President Stephens as their leader. They believed first in state sovereignty and then in the Confederacy. They wanted the Confederacy to win its independence, but if victory had to be gained at the expense of states' rights, they preferred defeat.

The Civil War had more in common with World War I, fifty-some years in the future, than it did with the

Napoleonic conflicts that had occurred half a century before. New techniques were coming into play that completely changed the way wars were waged. First of all, before the war was a year old, nearly every infantryman carried a rifle. They were still muzzleloaders, but entirely different from the Brown Bess, on which tactics and combat formations were still based.

Although the Pennsylvania (Kentucky) rifle had been used occasionally as a combat piece some years before the Civil War, it was not until that conflict that the rifle became a major weapon of war. As a matter of fact, in the Civil War it was *the* tactical weapon, and both sides used the same rifles—the American Springfield and the British Enfield.

A rifle could fire a bullet with deadly accuracy over eight hundred yards, much farther than the range of the smoothbore musket. Yet the battles of the war were fought for the most part with tactics adapted to musketry engagement. And that accounts to a great extent for the Civil War's being the bloodiest conflict of modern times. A decisive engagement could have taken place with opposing lines more than a quarter of a mile apart. Obviously, the older manner of attack no longer worked. To form an assaulting column, as Philip Kent did in the Revolutionary War, was to ask for annihilation.

Artillery tactics changed too. If artillery was amassed in a defensive line along with the infantry, it was subjected to killing fire by sharpshooters. Some soldiers showed amazing skill in using their guns at close range, but by and large artillery suffered from the infantry's expanded range of fire.

If things were bad for the artillery, they were worse for the cavalry. It was suicide for cavalry to attack formed infantry or artillery with infantry support. Cavalry became less and less a combat arm, but it remained extremely important as a means of scouting and screening an army's movement.

Generals on both sides were slow to adjust to the

changes that were occurring while the war was going on. The repeated disastrous frontal assaults with their frightful toll of casualties were the result of the generals' not taking into account the modernization of their weapons; they had been trained to tactics that were outmoded.

The Battle of Fredericksburg, Virginia (December 11 through 15, 1862), proves the case all too savagely. In General Burnside's assault on the high ground beyond Fredericksburg, Union troops with bayonets charged a fortified position occupied by six thousand Confederate troops and twenty guns. While some troops, notably the Irish brigade commanded by Michael Boyle's friend, Thomas Francis Meagher, reached the stone wall at the base of the hill, they were cut to pieces by rifle fire on the way. Meanwhile, their supporting columns had also been exposed to the rifle fire of Confederate artillery batteries. Then the whirling balls delivered in a cannon burst at a thousand yards cut the troops down. The stone wall became a sheet of flame, and men fell so rapidly that orders could not be passed. Officers with sabers and enlisted men with rifles and bayonets charged on the run, employing tactics that were devised for Brown Bess warfare of one hundred years earlier. It was only the weight of numbers that allowed part of the Union lines to reach the entrenched Confederates, and even then the assault ultimately failed.

Technology altered not only combat tactics in the Civil War but also uniforms. As firearms improved in range, neutral-colored uniforms became a safeguard against enemy marksmanship. Gone, except for the most ceremonious occasions, were cocked hats, brightly colored coats with facings of contrasting colors, and white trousers.

The machine-made shoe was becoming common at the outbreak of the Civil War. Army brogans, or "fade-aways," as the troops called them, proved extraordinarily

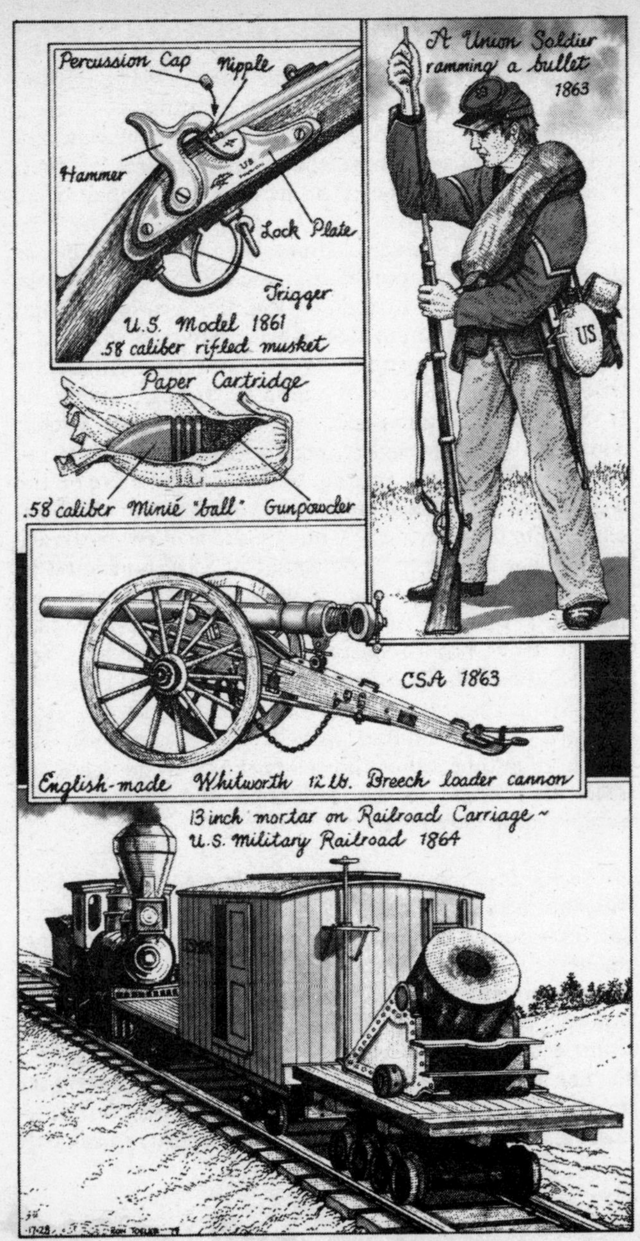

Percussion Cap
Nipple
Hammer
Lock Plate
Trigger
U.S. Model 1861
.58 caliber rifled musket
A Union Soldier ramming a bullet 1863
US
Paper Cartridge
.58 caliber Minié "ball"
Gunpowder
CSA 1863
English-made Whitworth 12 lb. Breech loader cannon
13 inch mortar on Railroad Carriage ~
U.S. military Railroad 1864

durable. Straights—shoes that were the same shape for both feet—disappeared from the feet of Northern troops. "Crooked shoes"—rights and lefts—were enthusiastically adopted by civilians, even though only two widths were available.

The sewing machine, patented in 1851, was a crude mechanism, but it made a tremendous difference in the manufacture of clothing. The governments of both North and South purchased hand-cranked or treadle machines and lent them free of charge to sewing groups or to anyone willing to put together some of the thousands upon thousands of uniforms needed.

The Northern armies were clothed in blue—dark blue coats, gray-blue trousers, and dark blue kepis. The Confederates wore a uniform entirely of gray—trousers, double-breasted tunic, and felt hat.

The Northern cavalry private's jacket was blue with gilt buttons and black leather belts. His breeches were light blue, and his boots were black. He wore a blue forage cap. Buckskin gauntlets, a leather pouch, and a saber completed his outfit. His officer's dress was not significantly different from his except for insignia and a slouch hat. In the decade after the Civil War, the cavalry officer's campaign dress in the West consisted of a fringed buckskin tunic, gauntlets, light blue breeches, black boots and belts, and a neckerchief for use in heavy dust. He also wore a cartridge belt and carried a rifle.

A corporal in the United States infantry wore a blue cloth sack coat or a tunic; both had a turned-down collar. His light blue trousers had welting of dark blue. His forage cap was blue, while his waist and cross belts were black leather. He carried a canvas pouch, knapsack, and canteen in addition to a blanket roll and a rifle with a bayonet. His commanding officer wore a dark blue uniform with gilt trim and a standing white collar. Light blue was the color of his shoulder straps and trouser welts. His black leather belt with a gilt eagle buckle supported a sword chain and was worn over a red fringed sash. His black felt hat was cocked, with a gilt eagle and ostrich plumes.

Confederate officers wore a somewhat fuller uniform than their Union counterparts. A lieutenant colonel wore a gray frock coat with a buff collar and cuffs with gilt buttons. His trousers were light blue, and his kepi was black and gray. He carried a saber. A colonel in charge of a band of raiders usually wore a short gray jacket decorated with gray braid looped in Austrian knots. He tucked his long trousers in black boots and covered his head with a felt hat adorned with a silk band and a small bit of ostrich feather. A brigadier commander's gray frock coat was trimmed with gilt Austrian knots to indicate superior rank. His light blue trousers were worn over leather boots. He also carried a saber.

The men of the Confederate army wore uniforms that varied in detail according to company. Basically, the uniform was gray trimmed with red. The kepi was red, too. The belts were white.

If, in general, the men and officers on both sides of the conflict were soberly uniformed, the Northern and Southern Zouaves made up for any absence of color and panache. The Confederate Zouave's short, well-frogged jacket was brown trimmed with red. His shirt was red, as was his blue-tasseled cap. His pantaloons were of wide blue and white striped ticking. He wore a wide black leather belt over a wrapped red sash. Leather garters, a blanket roll, knapsack, canteen, rifle, and hunting knife completed his outfit.

Equally attired for the light opera stage was the Union Zouave. If anything, he outdid his Confederate counterpart in the romantic character of his uniform. His blue bolero with red applique and his blue girdle and sash edged with lighter blue topped red bloomers. His red fez carried a blue tassel. His garters were white, and so were the leather pouch and knapsack he carried.

The Confederate sailor's winter uniform was gray flannel with black pie hat, neckerchief, and shoes. He

Infantry
Artillery
New York Volunteers 1861
New York
"Fire Zouave"
1861
Virginia Cavalry CSA
1861
Confederate
Horse
Artillery
1861
17-29
RON TOELKE '79

wore a middy blouse or a black and white shirt with a black neckerchief. His summer uniform was all white. Captain was the highest rank in the Confederate navy. A captain's uniform consisted of a gray frock coat over a short jacket and trousers, a gray forage cap trimmed in black and black shoes.

The Union seaman's uniform was navy blue with white braid on the square collar. The trousers had a fall front with thirteen buttons; at the back was a laced gusset. He wore a pie cap and a black silk neckerchief. The rank of admiral was introduced into the Union navy during the Civil War. The admiral's uniform was a navy blue with gilt adorning the double-breasted frock coat. The kepi was blue with gilt.

The Union marine officer also wore a navy blue double-breasted frock coat, with a blue velvet standing collar. His epaulets were blue and white. His trousers were light blue, and his black shako was decorated with a gilt and red pom-pom. He carried a saber and a sword.

It was fortunate that Jephtha Kent was in excellent physical shape. The highly competitive new field of war reporting required unusual stamina. A correspondent had to bear all the hardship, except for actual armed conflict, that the men he was writing about endured. He wrote all night, galloped off at daybreak to the nearest telegraph or rail post to lodge his copy, and then raced back to witness the day's events. No wonder very few correspondents lasted the entire war.

Prior to the mid-1800s; war news was haphazardly reported by junior officers hired to send letters from the battlegrounds. These men were rarely qualified journalists; they were soldiers who incidentally were correspondents.

The demand for news of the Civil War was great, a demand no doubt created by the newspapers themselves. As newspaper circulations soared and profits increased, managers used much of their newfound wealth to send more and more correspondents into the field to provide wider coverage of the conflict. It is estimated that there were at least five hundred reporting for the North. The New York *Herald* alone put sixty-three men into the field and spent nearly a million dollars in covering the war. The New York *Tribune* and the New York *Times* each had at least twenty correspondents. Newspapers of smaller cities also had men in the field. Even foreign correspondents were there, including William Howard Russell of the London *Times*, whose accounts from the Crimean front remain to this day a monument of war reporting.

Technology was not far enough advanced for newspapers to reprint the photographs that Matthew Brady took as he followed the Northern armies into battle, but war artists abounded to sketch the battle scenes as the correspondents wrote about them.

For the first time in history the telegraph was available for large-scale use. Even though rates were high—companies often demanded cash in advance before they would transmit stories—more and more frequently as the war progressed the by-line "By Telegraph" appeared. This new technology provided readers with the news in a day instead of a week.

Of the many legends that have grown out of the Civil War perhaps none has been more hallowed by time than that to do with the courage and resourcefulness of the war correspondents. In reality, the majority appear to have been unethical to an extraordinary degree. Among them, Jephtha would have been conspicuous for his integrity. They would go to any length to prevent rivals from completing their assignments. For example, Joseph Howard of the New York *Times* telegraphed to his paper the genealogy of Jesus just to keep a competitor from using the wire. Their dispatches were frequently inaccurate, often invented, partisan, and inflammatory. But it must be remembered, too, that it was an era of journalism in which objectivity was not sought.

These correspondents assumed propagandistic as well

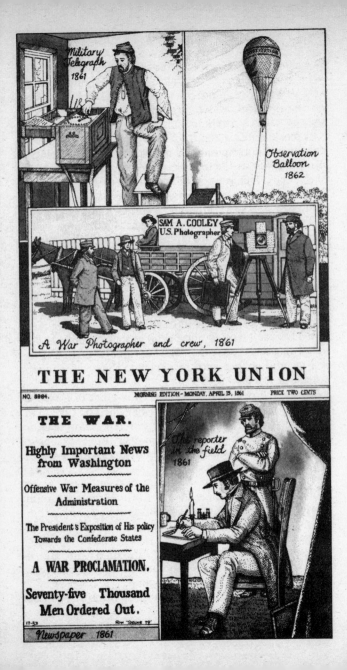

Military Telegraph 1861

Observation Balloon 1862

SAM A. COOLEY
U.S. Photographer

A War Photographer and crew, 1861

THE NEW YORK UNION

NO. 8884. MORNING EDITION - MONDAY, APRIL 15, 1861 PRICE TWO CENTS

THE WAR.

Highly Important News from Washington

Offensive War Measures of the Administration

The President's Exposition of His policy Towards the Confederate States

A WAR PROCLAMATION.

Seventy-five Thousand Men Ordered Out.

17-32

Newspaper 1861

as journalistic responsibility in their reporting. They saw sustaining civilian and army morale as part of their task. Their writing was therefore lurid in detail and frequently incendiary in intent. Obviously, in this kind of reporting, accuracy was at best secondary in importance.

These correspondents whom legend has romanticized usually failed to envisage their real mission. Why they did not recognize that they were privileged to be present at and to report moments millions would later want to study is not hard to understand. The most obvious reason was that the American correspondent had had no previous experience to prepare him for such reporting. Most correspondents were chosen because of their ability to use a telegraph key; journalistic talent was secondary. Correspondents were usually young—another instance of Jephtha's being atypical—inexperienced reporters. Pay was minimal; twenty-five dollars a week was maximum until late in the war.

At the same time that editors and publishers were unwilling to pay higher wages, they were becoming unreasonably demanding. They had created a market for war news and they had to supply it. New York papers could sell five times their normal edition when they ran details of a significant battle. The Philadelphia *Inquirer*, nearer the front than any other large Northern publication, could sell twenty-five thousand copies of a single edition to troops alone. When no news was available, editors pressed their reporters to work harder than ever. Soon, getting a scoop was more important than being accurate. Pressure was such that a correspondent was more likely to be fired for sending no news than for sending an interesting but completely fabricated story.

In the South at the outbreak of the war, journalism was behind the times. Most papers were weeklies. Even a daily like the New Orleans *Picayune* had a circulation of less than six thousand. There was little attempt at objective reporting, and news columns were full of political propaganda. Correspondents were generally officers who would send a telegram or letter if circumstances permitted. There were never more than one hundred bona fide Confederate war correspondents.

As the war progressed, journalism in the South suffered. When Federal forces moved into the Confederate States, they shut down many newspapers. For the rest, there was a constant struggle to get papers out because of the shortage of workers. And as supplies of newsprint and ink dried up, most papers were cut down to a single sheet. Some Southern papers were actually printed on paper bags and the blank side of wallpaper.

Producing an accurate record of the war would have been difficult enough under these circumstances, but the attitude of most Confederate correspondents made it impossible. Loyalty to the cause came before truth and objectivity. In addition, Southern writers maintained an entirely unrealistic optimism even as the Confederacy was collapsing at their feet. They exaggerated Northern losses while minimizing their own; they reported the capture of Northern towns that had never been attacked and refused to admit that Confederate armies ever retreated.

On both sides accuracy became a minor consideration, and the reportage that resulted became a kind of parody of itself. But the Civil War did have the effect of making war correspondence a separate function in the practice of journalism. For better or worse, it created a new kind of reporter—and also a new kind of reader.

In the years immediately following the Civil War, Americans from both North and South set about preserving the multitudinous songs that had sprung up during the conflict. Over ten thousand of these works are extant, many of them set to the same tunes. No other war in which the United States has been involved has inspired so many songs of such quality, and there are a number of reasons for this.

At the very time the Union was falling apart, American musicians were struggling to shed their European heritage and write "American" music. The Civil War with its military and political urgencies, with its need for songs of inspiration and sorrow, hastened, as war always does, those changes that were already in the wind. Literature had recently become recognizably American. And now the war liberated American music as surely as it liberated the slave.

The black man's music began to penetrate the national awareness. Stephen Foster and Daniel Decatur Emmett had already begun to fashion the rich melodies and rhythms of the Southern Negro into songs. During the war, this music emerged as a distinctively American musical idiom.

Patriotic songs are propaganda, and for that reason many lose their appeal as soon as the cause they support no longer exists. Yet a number of the Civil War songs, such as "The Battle Cry of Freedom," "John Brown's Body," "The Battle Hymn of the Republic," and "Marching through Georgia," have become engrained in our national consciousness.

George F. Root probably wrote more Civil War songs than any other composer. Three days after the attack on Sumter, his song "The First Gun Is Fired" was in print. Root's "Battle Cry of Freedom" appeared a year after Sumter, and by the end of the war, it was being sung from New York to California; numerous Confederate versions also existed. More than 350,000 copies were sold during the war, but that figure doesn't begin to indicate the popularity of the song. The catchy tune and the simple words passed easily from mouth to mouth without printed copies.

Julia Ward Howe's "Battle Hymn of the Republic," based on a well-known tune, was the first great inspirational song of the Union. The origins of the tune are obscure, but the story behind the words is well documented. Mrs. Howe, a prominent Bostonian, was in Washington in the late autumn of 1861 with her husband, Dr. Samuel Gridley Howe, a member of President

Lincoln's Military Sanitary Commission. One day, while visiting an army encampment, she and others began singing some of the more popular war songs, including "John Brown's Body." One member of the group suggested that Mrs. Howe write new words to the John Brown tune. Inspiration came to her in the first gray of dawn the next day. In February of 1862, the song appeared on the first page of the *Atlantic Monthly*. Mrs. Howe was paid five dollars for her efforts.

Curiously enough, the John Brown of the tune was not the John Brown of Harpers Ferry fame, but a Sergeant Brown of Boston, a member of the Second Battalion, Boston Light Infantry, Massachusetts Volunteer Militia. In time, of course, the song attained its popularity because it did become associated with the fervent abolitionist.

Stephen Foster died in New York City before the war was over. He tried his hand at war songs, but he was past his prime; and his war songs are among his minor works. The words of his "For the Dear Old Flag I Die" are typical.

"For the dear old flag I die,"
Said the wounded drummer boy;
"Mother, press your lips to mine,
Oh, they bring me peace and joy.
'Tis the last time on earth
I shall ever see your face.
Mother, take me to your heart,
Let me die in your embrace."

CHORUS:
For the dear old flag I die.
Mother, dry your weeping eye.
For the honor of our land
And the dear old flag I die.

Mothers and drummer boys were favorite subjects of many Civil War songwriters, for example, "Just Before the Battle, Mother," "Farewell, Mother, Who Will Care for Mother Now?," and "The Drummer Boy of Shiloh."

Southern composers, for reasons of class, history, and attitude, failed to tap the great riches of Negro music which was springing up around them. Northern composers, on the other hand, had no such compunctions, and their works benefited from Negro influences. The only inspirational Confederate song to draw upon the Negro idiom was "Dixie," which ironically was the work of a Northerner, Daniel Decatur Emmett. The other two great songs of the South, "The Bonnie Blue Flag" and "Maryland, My Maryland," were based on European tunes.

As with supplies, ammunition, and troops, in songs, the North had more than the South. The musical output of the Union during the war was about ten times that of the Confederacy. But those differ from their Northern counterparts only in partisan outlook, and in no other way.

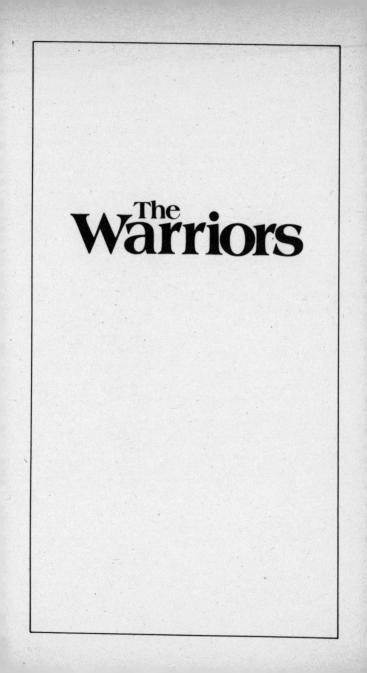

The Warriors

A CONDENSATION OF

The Warriors

1864–1868

PROLOGUE

Major Gideon Kent was worn out. About six that afternoon he had witnessed more than the beginning of a battle. He had seen the start of a slaughter. By now the sun had set. It was Saturday, the second day of May, 1863.

A year earlier, when he had been chosen as one of the twelve hundred men to ride with Jeb Stuart to scout McClellan's Peninsular army, he had nearly lost his life at Tunstall's Station. That sort of brush with death—the first had come at Manassas in 1861—had relieved him of all conviction that this war was glorious.

After two years of fighting, Gideon had changed from a cheerful, contentious young man eager to see battle to a weary professional who knew the dreadful cost of the South's principles.

BOOK 1

November 20, 1864. Jeremiah Kent, eighteen years old, pondered a question he had asked himself many times before: what had become of the brave, honorable war he had gone to fight?

At Jonesboro, a Yankee ball would have killed him if Lieutenant Colonel Rose had not lunged and knocked him out of the Yankee's line of fire. Then just a few hours later Rose, the honorable soldier whom Jeremiah so wanted to be like, had been mortally wounded. As he lay dying, he had charged Jeremiah with carrying a letter he had written ten days earlier to his wife and daughter—even if it meant deserting. Jeremiah's promise to do so had become an obsession.

His opportunity to set out for Rose's plantation in Jefferson County, Georgia, came after a siege of recurring dysentery, when he was too weak to keep up with his unit and was left behind. He was free.

His first sensation was heat. Panicky, he tried to recall where he was. Yesterday was Tuesday. He remembered trying to follow directions given him by a farm boy, but somehow he had taken a wrong turn. Still sick, he had blundered ahead. Then he had lain down to rest only ten minutes. That was all he remembered until now.

He grew alarmed by a weightlessness in two places where there should have been weight. His precious Enfield rifle no longer pressed against his shoulder, and his cartridge box was missing. The oilskin pouch with Rose's letter in it was still there, thank God.

Then he heard a voice, neither friendly nor hostile. "You 'wake, mister soldier?" the superbly built black man asked.

"Who are you? Where am I?"

"Rosewood."

"Colonel Henry Rose's place?"

"Reckon there ain't another Rosewood in the county."

"Then you're from the plantation? What's your name?" Jeremiah asked.

"Price."

Price led Jeremiah up to the house and into a cluttered

office, where the black stood between Jeremiah and the woman at the desk. Jeremiah couldn't see much of her, but he noted objects on the desk—open ledgers, keys, and a goblet half full of wine. Near the ledgers, he glimpsed a small frame with a curling lock of bright red hair sealed under the glass; a card under it read, "Serena, 1846."

Serena was Rose's daughter by his first wife. Jeremiah had the impression that Serena's mother must have been the wrong sort, since Rose was closemouthed about her, in contrast to his constant praise of Catherine, the woman whom he had married after his first wife's death and before whom Jeremiah now stood.

Jeremiah unburdened himself of the letter he had traveled so far to deliver.

Catherine guessed the reason for Jeremiah's being at Rosewood before he could tell her.

"Oh, dear Lord in heaven. He's dead. That's why you're here. . . ."

All of a sudden the ringing in Jeremiah's ears turned to a high, windy whine. Without warning, he began to tumble forward. Price could have caught him, but he did not move.

Jeremiah fell to the oak floor.

He woke at twilight in a bedroom on the second floor. His filthy uniform had disappeared, and he wore a man's flannel nightshirt.

A knock on the door was followed by a respectful "Sir?"

"I'm awake. Come in."

A small black woman appeared. "I'm Maum Isabella. I've brought you one of my toddies. If it sets well, I've got ham and hominy in the kitchen." Jeremiah found the beverage delicious.

There was nothing servile in the diminutive woman's speech or demeanor, none of Price's pretenses, which disguised a simmering hostility. Maum Isabella obviously occupied a position of importance in the house and knew it. As she left, she said, "Well, I got things to do. We'll have dinner tomorrow afternoon, late. In the morning there's to be a memorial service in the parlor for the colonel."

Soon Catherine Rose looked in on Jeremiah. Her eyes looked puffy, but otherwise she was in perfect control. Then Serena appeared. She was twenty, two years older than Jeremiah. The difference seemed an abyss to him. Even before he had a chance to answer her perfunctory question about his health, she had glided to a wall mirror to study her hair. Somehow that angered him.

Serena was hard to read. Her every move was studied. While Catherine's politeness masked feelings she felt it might be unseemly to reveal, Serena's behavior apparently concealed a lack of any feeling whatever. She seemed to regard Jeremiah as a mere boy.

"Where do you come from, Mr. Kent?" Serena asked.

"Virginia."

"Virginia," Serena repeated. "That's a mighty long way from Georgia."

Jeremiah told them a little about his family—that his mother was still in the endangered Shenandoah; that his brother Gideon had been captured in the fire fight that slew Jeb Stuart at Yellow Tavern and was presumed in a Northern prison; that no word had come from his brother Matt in months, but that he was still thought to be on a blockade runner. He mentioned his father briefly, telling how he had returned to preaching after working on the New York *Union*. He also revealed that his grandfather had struck it rich in California in the goldfields and that one day he and his brothers would come into a considerable sum of money.

"There's at least one more in the family up north. He has a wife and a son, and he's a rich man."

Serena's blue eyes showed interest.

"I think we've taxed Jeremiah long enough," Catherine

said. "I hate to tire you further. But you mentioned something about a musket when you came in."

"Yes, I slept all night on the creek bank, where Price found me. When I woke, my musket and cartridge box were both gone. Your nigra claimed someone else must have come along and taken them, but I'm certain he took them. I think that buck should be questioned until he admits the theft."

"So do I!" Serena exclaimed.

With a shake of her head, Catherine negated the idea. "At this difficult time, I won't have the nigras losing their trust in me because of Price."

Serena refused to surrender. "We should force Price to admit he's lying. *Whip* him!"

During the memorial service for Colonel Rose held Thanksgiving morning at Rosewood, word came that the Yankees were nearby. The service came to an abrupt end, and the participants began returning at once to their homes.

Thanksgiving dinner was a tense, joyless affair. Unpleasant questions seemed to come up almost at once. Catherine inquired about Jeremiah's initiation into the war. He told them how he had shot his first Yankee, but he didn't mention the disturbing feelings he had experienced as he watched the young man fall. It had been a kind of cold joy.

During the next two days, Jeremiah helped with the heavy work of hiding possessions and stores. Sherman's army was coming, and the general's permission for his soldiers to forage liberally was being interpreted as permission to steal anything the invaders pleased.

Jeremiah worked with a companionable black named Leon. Although they kept an eye out for Price whenever they drove a wagonload of goods to hide among the trees, they never saw him; but they were sure he was well aware of their activities.

BOOK 2

"Would you fetch a couple of chairs out here, Jeremiah?" Catherine asked. "We might as well be comfortable while we wait."

Jeremiah carried the chairs out to the veranda and lined them up a yard to the right of the open windows of the sitting room.

Catherine gazed at the oaks tinged with the fires the Yankees had set. "I've noticed a change in Serena's attitude toward you. Surely you've noticed it as well?"

Jeremiah nodded.

"She's discovered you're not a poor boy. I suspect you've better prospects for the future than the half dozen beaux Serena's had since leaving school. Oh, she's charming to the eye. But those same young men—there wasn't one among them who called more than three or four times. Her behavior shocked them. Serena is—not possessed of a stable temperament. She's greedy: she's lewd. *Not a moral person.* Leave her alone, Jeremiah, for your own sake."

"I can't do that, ma'am."

"Why not?"

He was saved from answering because just then Catherine jerked around in her chair to face the highway. There was the muffled, unmistakable ragged rhythm of marching.

"If it's the Yanks, they aren't going to set foot on this property!" All at once she was dashing wildly down the lane. Jeremiah ran after her.

By the time he reached the closed white gate, he saw two companies of scruffy, bearded Union soldiers halted on the highway that separated Rosewood from a neighboring farm, which was now aflame. There were two officers. The senior was a square-faced, middle-aged man with mild blue eyes. Near him was a young, nervous lieutenant.

The older man addressed Catherine in heavily accented English. "Captain Franz Poppel, madam. I give you my word no incidents will take place here if you cooperate."

"What choice do we have?" Catherine responded in a bitter voice.

Poppel, following orders, searched Rosewood with one of his sergeants and Jeremiah in attendance. The Union captain examined everything, but he replaced each article carefully. He then dismissed the sergeant and confessed to a thirst for coffee.

In the kitchen they found Maum Isabella and Serena, who abruptly excused herself and left.

"I wonder if Mr. Kent and I might have a word in private?" Poppel asked the black woman.

Expressionless, Maum Isabella walked out.

"That red-haired girl, she's quite handsome. Lovely. There are undisciplined men in the army. Permit me to make you an offer, Mr. Kent. In the morning I will go up to the attic for one more search. There I can hand you a spare revolver I happen to have in my kit. You should keep it hidden because of that girl."

The next morning in the attic Poppel slipped Jeremiah a .44-caliber Kerr with four shots left. Poppel had no spare ammunition. Jeremiah placed the revolver under a floorboard.

For two hours after Poppel's men had left, Rosewood was quiet. Then down at the gate the bell began clanging.

By the time Jeremiah reached the piazza, Catherine was at the foot of the staircase. As she joined him outside, blue-coated cavalrymen came thundering up the lane. They looked more like riffraff than soldiers.

Their commander, a man in his late thirties, greeted Jeremiah and Catherine with a mocking touch of his hat brim.

"Your servant. Major Ambrose Grace of the Eighth Indiana, General Kilpatrick's Third Cavalry Division."

"The Kill-cavalry," Jeremiah said.

"Sometimes we're complimented with that term, yes."

Suddenly, laughing men pulled their mounts aside as a black on a mule jogged out of the dust cloud. Catherine drew a breath, loud and sharp.

Price tugged the mule to a stop beside the commanding officer.

"This here's the place I was tellin' you about. Plenty of good things on this place. I'll help you get 'em all," he said, reaching down to grasp the Enfield musket lying across his thigh.

"Damn you," Jeremiah said. "You had it after all."

"Did you really think I didn't, mister soldier? Or that I wouldn't come back and use it?"

Major Grace, preceded by Price and followed by Jeremiah, escorted Catherine with mock gallantry into the sitting room. Price plumped himself down in a wing chair, drew up an ottoman, and put his right foot on it. Tiny bits of mud fell on the embroidered fabric.

"Now, ma'am," Grace said, "we'll be requisitioning supplies and equipment from you."

Boots thudded in the hall, and a man stomped in—the most appallingly filthy human being Jeremiah had ever seen or smelled. "General Skimmerhorn reportin' for duty, Major." Jeremiah couldn't take his eyes off the hulking creature Grace characterized as his forager-in-chief.

All at once the house was overrun by marauding, looting soldiers. Within minutes, furniture was smashed, books were strewn everywhere, and glass was broken.

In the melee that ensued, Skimmerhorn dragged Catherine out of the house and Price knocked Jeremiah unconscious. When he awoke two hours later, Serena was standing over him. His first thoughts were of Catherine.

"Where is your stepmother?"

"I don't know." Her voice was curiously flat. "That filthy man dragged her out. I tried to stop him."

"Then by now she's been—"

"I expect she'll live through it."

"My God, Serena, is that all you can say—*she'll live through it*?"

"Jeremiah, they've *got* her. We can't do anything about what's happened. Let's worry about what might happen. I can talk to Major Grace. I think I can handle that roughneck."

Catherine did not live through it. She had been brutally assaulted. Her half-clad body had been dragged two or three hundred yards through the red clay of Rosewood. But Serena—although Jeremiah had yet to learn the fact—by offering her body to Major Grace, had exacted a promise from the Union officer to save the house at Rosewood. She had even managed to get Jeremiah released from the sitting room, where he had been imprisoned for twenty-four hours. "I love you, Jeremiah," Serena said.

Once released, Jeremiah stole up to the attic to recover the revolver he had hidden. By promising Skimmerhorn that he would lead him to Catherine's buried jewels in exchange for food, Jeremiah took the man into the woods. While Skimmerhorn was being led into Jeremiah's trap, he disclosed how Grace had boasted of his dealings with Serena—how she had willingly given herself to the Yankee major. As Skimmerhorn began to dig for the bogus treasure, Jeremiah shot him. Sourness climbed in Jeremiah's throat as he pulled the Colt from the dead man's grip. He straightened up and turned away, his face a study in confusion and pain.

I love you. She had said that after she had whored all night.

Jeremiah didn't want to go back to Rosewood, but since the house was his dead colonel's only monument, he couldn't stand by and let it burn. He had an obligation to the man who had saved his life.

When he reached the edge of the woods, he broke open the Colt. There was no ammunition in it. Then he felt the Kerr under his shirt. Three bullets left.

As he stole forward through high weeds, the sky was bright red and there was the roar of conflagration. At the head of the lane he saw men and women silhouetted against the blaze. Among them, standing at full height on the rim of the stone well, was Price. He had the stolen Enfield in his hands and was preventing the slaves from carrying water to protect the house. Jeremiah stole around the burning outbuildings and onto the piazza. He positioned himself so that he had a clear target and aimed carefully. The bullet took Price in the left arm, and he fell sideways. His hands gripped the well, and he tried to pull himself up.

"Mister Jeremiah? You hit me bad. Leave me be now. *Please*!"

All at once Jeremiah seemed to see Serena in place of Price. He and the Kerr were welded into one—and there was joy in the thin curve of his mouth. He fired. The bullet blew a black and red hole in Price's shirt. He fell.

Serena rushed to Jeremiah and flung herself into his arms. He seized her wrist, his fingers biting so hard she winced. He dragged her toward the piazza and into the larder.

"Jeremiah, let go! What's wrong with you? Why are you treating me this way?"

"You whored for him. Grace. You whored for him." He called her the foulest name he knew.

"Jeremiah, I had to."

"You said you cared about me. You don't. I was taken in for a while, but now I know it's just the money you want. Whore!"

"Jeremiah, I *had* to do what Grace asked."

"He didn't ask. You *begged.* Skimmerhorn told me."

Caught, she started to say something else. But he saw the truth on her face.

"Admit you begged him, Serena."

"Yes. Yes! He was good, too. Almost as good as a lot of the others. Better than you'd ever be! You're just a boy!"

Jeremiah started toward the dining room. He heard Serena's breathing and a sound he didn't recognize until she came rushing toward him. The sound had been a drawer sliding. Then he saw a butcher knife raised in her fist. She stabbed downward. As he jerked his head to the side, the blade raked his cheek and snapped in half when it struck the door beside his head.

He caught her wrist with his left hand as she tried to cut him with the broken blade.

"Take your damned money. I'll find someone else. Someone who's rich . . . and . . . and a man! Not a boy! Not a baby! *Baby! Baby! Baby!*"

As she screamed, he pulled out the Kerr with his right hand and fired the last bullet into her stomach.

He had to flee. Never tell Fan what he had done. Never give her the slightest hint. To keep from hurting her. And to keep from being found. Westward. That was the best direction.

Jeremiah Kent. He didn't dare use that name any longer. What would he call himself?

On the Monday morning following Thanksgiving, as Jeremiah was leaving ravaged Rosewood, Gideon Kent sat in Fort Delaware, the Union prison where he had been for six months. He had been captured at Yellow Tavern in the fire fight that slew Jeb Stuart.

The wind speared through dozens of ill-fitting joints in the boards of the shedlike structure. The aging sergeant in charge of this particular pen was temperamental, given to violent outbursts of temper. It was inevitable that he and Gideon would one day come to a showdown. His vicious, sadistic nature was in direct contrast to Gideon's altruistic and dignified character. The sergeant in his hatred of Southern officers—Gideon in particular—finally so provoked Gideon that the young man attacked him. In retaliation, the sergeant put out one of Gideon's eyes.

Thanks to the prompt and expert action of the prison doctor, the evisceration did not disfigure Gideon's handsome face. The eyepatch he would wear the rest of his life would, in the words of Dr. Lemon, give him "a certain air of dash and mystery."

The doctor was a man of bristly good cheer that was infectious, and Gideon soon stopped thinking how unfortunate he was and became thankful that he had pulled through. His spirits improved even more when he learned that the sergeant had been transferred to the most squalid and dangerous shed in the prison, the one housing the criminals from the Union Army.

Most of all, he was impatient to return home to Margaret and Eleanor and to begin piecing his life back together. Grant had met Lee at Appomattox, and Gideon was returning to Richmond. He had telegraphed Margaret and received a four-word reply. "All well. Hurry home."

BOOK 3

Someone jabbed his hip.

Michael Boyle's eyes popped open. He lay on his side in the cramped top bunk in the railroad car. As he rolled over to face the aisle, his eyes met Sean Murphy's. Murphy occupied the bunk below Michael's.

"You must have had some night, Michael me boy. You been tossin' and babblin'."

"I was back in the wilderness the afternoon I got hit." A Confederate ball had buzzed in over the barricades and slammed him out of action—and out of the war.

Michael was a thirty-six-year-old Irishman. Tall with fair hair already showing gray, he had no flab on him. He was spare and hard after eleven weeks as a rust-eater on the Union Pacific.

After being discharged from the army, Michael Boyle had spent a season in Ohio while Lee gave up to Grant at Appomattox. He had then moved on to Chicago, where he met Sean Murphy. He decided to join Murphy and a few other Paddies heading for the prairie to build a mile of track daily. General Jack Casement's army of rust-eaters was growing week by week. Over four hundred men worked at the railhead now.

Michael and Sean found work in the same gang. Their boss, Leonidas Worthing, was an unreconstructed Virginian with whom Michael was a bit too willing to bump heads on the subject of the war, among other things. Twice he had protested when the Virginian badgered members of Michael's gang. One argument had nearly reached the point of violence. Worthing warned, "Before we finish, I'm going to break your back."

Among Michael's gang was a young man who called himself Christian. He was lean and dark with high cheekbones and straight black hair that reminded Michael of Jephtha. Christian said that he was a Delaware Indian from Ohio. His startling blue eyes suggested at least one white parent or grandparent. Christian was soft-spoken, well-mannered, and mule-strong.

An ordinary mule-drawn wagon creaked along beside the advancing rails six days a week. It stopped where the crews stopped. Two large barrels were lashed on the side, and a dipper hung from each. One barrel bore the name *Dorn*, the other said *Whiskey*. Gustav Dorn, the bearded Dutchman who sold the whiskey, had a fondness for his own product. With him was a fourteen-year-old son and a daughter, seldom seen, but reported to be young and pretty and of a religious turn. She read the Bible a good deal.

Without having met the girl, Michael admired her pluck. It took nerve to come to the railhead, even protected as she was by her father and brother. Dorn felt she was safer with him than she would have been alone in Grand Island. Michael suspected the girl wasn't as pretty as described. Being the only female for a hundred miles could elevate plainness to stunning beauty in the eye of the lustful beholder.

The labor of the crews was monotonous, mindless, but the five men on Michael's gang worked well together and took pride in their efficiency. No one broke the rhythm of the work. This Saturday, however, there were shouts when an emigrant wagon passed by. Worthing objected because he considered any deviation from routine a violation of his authority. When he overheard Christian's caustic remarks about him, he struck the young man's cheek and drew blood. As a means of getting at Boyle, who among all the men was the chief target of his hatred, Worthing told Christian to rest a minute. "Paddy Boyle's strong enough for a bit of double duty."

"Hold on, Captain!" Murphy exclaimed. "One man can't haul the front of a rail all by—"

"Quiet!" Worthing snapped. "Paddy Boyle can. Can't you?"

Worthing was relentless. He forced Michael to do the work of two men for the remainder of the morning by refusing to let Christian return to the gang. Michael resolved to suffer Worthing's punishment until he dropped. Worthing, he knew, planned to keep him working until a mishap occurred. And one did occur involving a drayman's horse and a brief work stoppage.

"You've cost us time, Boyle. You'll be docked two weeks' pay."

Before Michael could say a word, Christian shouldered past him. "No one caused the accident but you, Captain. That's what we'll tell General Jack when he's back from Kearney."

"You think Casement'll believe an Injun over a white man."

"You don't qualify as a white man or any other kind of man. The most appropriate word for you is *animal*."

Worthing's right hand reached for his four-barrel derringer. Exhausted and dizzy as he was, Michael lunged forward and knocked Christian aside as the revolver exploded. Worthing's ball hit Christian's right calf.

Michael's restraint collapsed. Head down and fists up, he went for Leonidas Worthing.

"That's all?" The very brevity of the question indicated Casement's anger.

"Yes, that's how it happened."

"I don't like it one blasted bit—even though I know you're telling the truth."

"How is Christian?"

"Flesh wound. Nothing serious. I asked Dorn's daughter to look after him. He's on a pallet in her tent."

"Where's Worthing now, General?"

"Confined to his bunk. From now on, stay out of his way. If he comes after you, I'll deal with him. If he starts, you walk away."

As Michael turned to leave, Casement said, "You tell another man this, and I'll deny it to the gates of paradise, but I wish you had broken the back of that son of a bitch. Now get out of here, find yourself a replacement, and take charge of Worthing's gang."

"Take charge?"

"Someone's got to fill the man's spot. You're diligent. You're promoted."

Normally, Michael Boyle loved the calm of the prairie evenings, but the Nebraska sunset held little attraction for him tonight. He was tormented by pain; he was ashamed of having lost control and of having turned on Worthing. Worthing would soon be plotting retaliation, if he wasn't already.

After supper, Michael planned to visit Christian, if Dorn's daughter would allow him in the tent. But first he went to see if the weekly commissary train had brought him any mail. There were two letters from Jephtha. Both contained news of his sons, and one contained a sketch Matthew Kent had made of a Cuban milk vendor while he was in Havana. Jephtha feared that Jeremiah had been killed in battle, since nothing had been heard from him since the autumn of 1864. Matthew, who had been on a blockade runner during the war, had unexpectedly turned up, announcing his intention to marry an English girl he had met in Liverpool. Jephtha also mentioned his hope of purchasing Kent and Son, the Boston publishing firm founded by his great-grandfather, from Louis Kent, who had no interest in the business and had allowed it to slip. If Jephtha managed to buy the company, it was his intention to divide the ownership equally among Gideon, Matthew, and Michael.

As Michael strode toward Dorn's tent, he felt he was being observed.

Once inside, Michael discovered that Dorn's daughter was lively and well-spoken. After some conversation, he decided the girl was fascinating.

As Michael crawled into his bunk that night, he found that his blanket had been hacked to pieces and a butcher knife had been driven into the mattress where he usually rested his head. Jephtha's letters had been chopped to bits, but Matthew's sketch had not been touched. He called himself a fool for thinking that Worthing's enmity would confine itself to threats.

The next morning being Sunday, Michael walked away from the railhead to bathe in the river. Shortly after entering the water he saw a band of Cheyenne. They had captured a member of the gang who had wandered away in search of prairie chickens.

So, thought Michael, *it seems I've found another enemy.*

And another war.

BOOK 4

Michael felt more fear than he had ever felt in his life, but the Indians promised not to harm him if he would lead them to the camp and give them sugared coffee, a drink highly esteemed by them.

Michael did as they requested, and all went well

enough until the Indians espied Dorn's whiskey barrels. The Dutchman attempted to prevent them from taking the drink, and in the melee that ensued, one of the Cheyenne killed him. Then Worthing shot into the Indians, and pandemonium was unleashed. When Casement tried to ward off Worthing, the Virginian turned on him.

Michael and the other men rushed to help Casement, but they were not quick enough. Worthing's third blow knocked Casement to the ground.

Michael ran faster, and Worthing saw him coming. The Cheyenne were now out of range, but the Virginian wanted a target. As he aimed his Spencer at Michael, his eyes glowed with perverse joy. Michael flung himself forward as the rifle thundered. Worthing aimed for Michael again, but couldn't get a clear shot. On his knees, Casement groped for Worthing's leg. The Virginian turned and bashed him on the head with the stock of his rifle. Then once again Worthing leveled the rifle at Michael. With his gun hand extended and his view unimpeded, Michael pulled the trigger and caught Worthing squarely in the chest.

The canvas-wrapped bodies of Dorn and Worthing were buried at sunset. Immediately following the brief ceremony, Hannah Dorn and her brother Klaus, accompanied by Michael, began the trip back to Grand Island.

As the three made camp that night, a wagon drawn by mules rolled through the purple shadows. A Sioux Indian clad in a hide shirt drove the mule tream, and beside the lead wheel rode a lean white man. The contents of their wagon showed they were buffalo hunters. Wagon and rider soon passed close enough for Michael to note the white man's face. He was sure he had seen it before.

"Sure don't look friendly," Klaus murmured just as the white man jerked two fingers to his hat brim to acknowledge their presence. Then he booted his mount.

Michael still felt he had seen the white man before.

"Will you and Klaus be staying in Grand Island?" Michael asked Hannah.

"Yes, I'll take over the store and run it as well as I can."

They started east at sunup. Around eight they spied two dilapidated phaetons coming toward them. The first was piled high with bags, crates, and a folded canvas. The driver was a bearded, vacant-eyed young man with a shotgun resting across his lap.

The second carriage was driven by a heavyset, red-faced man of about forty. Beside him sat a pale, coarsely attractive girl. In the second seat were two other women of about thirty or thirty-five.

Again Michael was encountering someone he thought he had seen before.

After an exchange of only a few words, Michael recognized the man. His name was Adolphus Brown. Michael had seen him in a gambling house in Omaha, where he was caught cheating at poker. Brown had all but killed the man who exposed him. Before Michael left Omaha, he had heard that Brown had killed at least four men. Now Brown said he was going to set up business at the railhead, and he would see Michael there.

When Michael and the Dorns reached Grand Island, Hannah surprised Michael by saying, "Come back this winter and help me build a good store. The territory will soon be ready for civilized things."

"No, Hannah."

"Why not? Am I unattractive?"

"You're very attractive. But—"

"You don't think you could ever love me?"

"Hannah, I like you too much to pretend I feel anything more."

"Love will come. Give it a chance."

Brown had set up Brown's Paradise—whiskey,

women, and cards—immediately upon reaching the railhead. Besides the three women there was his half-witted young helper, Toby Harkness, whose devotion to Brown was expressed in his willingness to "fix" anyone who interfered with his boss.

Early on, Michael had a run-in with Harkness, who caught him alone on a September evening and demanded that he stop talking about Brown's habit of winning against all opponents.

As Harkness left muttering threats, Michael remembered the vow he had taken while riding back after leaving Hannah. Sickened by the corpses of four whites mutilated by Indians, but aware of the Indians' justified frustration, Michael had sworn, "Never again, while I breathe, will I lift my hand against another human being, no matter what the provocation. Never."

That same night Michael spied the white hunter and the Indian, whom he had seen in August. The white man tipped his hat to one of Brown's girls. Even at a distance a white streak in the man's fair hair stood out clearly. Michael was convinced he had met the man during the war. He made up his mind to find out.

Brown was in a vile temper. Business was not good, although his competitors had more than they could handle. Furthermore, that hunter named Kingston had stayed with Nancy longer than he had paid for.

Brown knew that his loss in business had come from Michael's warning new workers that his establishment was dishonest. "Toby, we can't fool with the mick any longer. Watch the Irishman till he's alone."

Brown inveigled Jeremiah, whose alias was now Joseph Kingston, out of Nancy's tent by assuring him he was unarmed. Then Brown went for him with his head and fists. The younger man's superior strength eventually overcame the middle-aged Brown. Jeremiah laughed at the sudden and pathetic fright in the saloon keeper's eyes as he shoved his rifle down like a bar across Brown's throat. His body arched three times, each spasm less violent than the one before. Then it was over.

For a moment, Jeremiah felt sick at his stomach. But it always ended the same way. *You enjoy doing a man to death. Don't deny it. You started to enjoy it the moment you pulled the trigger on Serena Rose.*

A few minutes earlier, Michael had decided to satisfy his curiosity about the white hunter. As he turned to retrace his steps, his eye caught a shambling figure rounding the corner. He recognized Brown's helper, who was carrying some kind of club. "Hello there, mick. Hear you're still spoutin' off about my boss."

"The way I answer questions about your boss is my affair. Good night."

Michael heard the hiss of air as the maul handle came down and slammed his right shoulder.

"Plan to give you a few more like that. Then maybe you'll plug your mouth!"

Quietly Michael said, "I'm not going to fight you."

"Yellow bastard!" Toby Harkness hissed as he continued jabbing Michael with the handle.

A pitiless inner voice spoke the truth of it to Michael. *There is no way out of this unless you go after him.*

Growing incoherent, Toby rammed the handle into Michael's belly. "Act like a man!" He spat on Michael.

Michael surprised Harkness by fastening both hands on the maul handle and wresting it from him. Then he flung it away. He turned his back on Toby and started to walk away.

He heard Toby run for him.

Just then the white man with the streaked hair lurched out of the dark and asked, "Where's Kola? Where's the Indian?"

"You," Toby sounded less confident as he began edging toward his fallen club, "you fold your hand, mister. My confab with this mick is private."

"And one-sided from the look of it. I'd suggest you

light out of here, boy. You've lost your number one backer."

"Did you do somethin' to Brown?"

"Just shut up and *move*."

As the hunter walked away, Toby dashed for the maul handle and swung it with his full force. It landed athwart Jeremiah's temple and knocked him backward. He floundered against the wagon, stabbing the split stock of his rifle into the dirt to prop himself up. Toby kicked the stock. Jeremiah crashed to his knees, hurt but refusing to quit. Then Toby reached for the hunter's hair. With an almost regretful expression, Jeremiah fired the rifle from his hip.

Instantly, men were shouting and clamoring around Michael, who barely saw the hunter collapse. Just then the Sioux ran in. He saw his fallen friend, ran to him, knelt, then glanced up with furious eyes.

"Who did this?"

The Sioux cradled the white man's head in his lap.

"Joseph, Joseph, do you hear?"

Michael walked to the Sioux, "Your friend's hurt. He needs attention. You want to pick him up, or shall I? I think he'd better rest on the train. Did you say your partner's name was Joseph?"

"Yes, Joseph Kingston. He is my *Kola*. My sworn friend."

The name meant nothing. Undoubtedly, Michael had been wrong about having seen the white man before.

"Well, he's mine too. Pick him up and bring him along to the train. We'll put him in my bunk."

Jeremiah came fully awake at the top of a tier of three beds. His eyes focused on the man who had almost taken a beating at the wagon.

"Easy now. You're safe," the man said.

"Where's my rifle?"

"The Indian has it; he's down here. No harm will come

to him. By the way, my name is Boyle. I've learned yours is Kingston."

"I want out of here!" Jeremiah sat up too quickly and knocked his head on the plank ceiling. He lay down again, breathing hard.

He fell asleep once more, and when he awoke, his aches were not quite so painful. Wriggling into position to drop to the floor, he glimpsed Kola with his rifle—a reassuring sight.

He saw a paper tacked to the wall at the head of the bunk—a drawing of a vendor carrying milk. Two words below the caption tore him like a bullet.

M. Kent.

Michael helped Kingston and the Sioux hitch the mules.

As soon as the wagon was ready, Kingston ordered Kola to drive to the end of the tract and wait.

"I have a question for you," he said to Michael. "Where did you get the drawing in your bunk? Do you know the artist's father?"

"Yes, I know him."

"He's my father too."

Jeremiah refused to answer Michael's questions about the past, although he eagerly sought news of his family.

"Is my mother well?"

"She died this past summer."

Jeremiah bent his head but made no sound. "I'm happy to hear my father's alive."

"He'll be happy to learn you are, too."

"You're not going to tell him."

"Of course I am. As soon as possible."

"You won't tell him a thing unless you want to hurt him."

"You expect me to keep it from Jephtha forever? I can't do it."

"To convince you my father musn't know, I'll tell you

this much. There's a bounty on my head. Now do I have your promise you'll keep silent?"

"All right. For his sake. I promise."

"Good-bye, Mr. Boyle."

"Would you have shot me if I hadn't given my word?"

"Yes."

Michael hoped to God he would never reach the point Jeremiah had. Yet between the young man and him there remained a fearful bond. Both were rootless; both were running. Jeremiah had little choice; he did. It was time to seek a hope of peace, however tenuous, some other way.

Michael arrived in Grand Island close to midnight. He found Hannah still up. "I imagine you're surprised to see me."

"No, I've been expecting you, though I wasn't certain when." She put her arms around his neck and kissed him.

BOOK 5

At thirty, Louis Kent, who had recently been divorced from his wife, was trim, handsome, urbane, and in the midst of business machinations that he hoped would increase his already enormous holdings. He had become allied with two of the shrewdest and most powerful men on Wall Street—Jim Fisk and Jay Gould. Those business connections should have meant almost unbelievable profits and prestige and would have except for Louis's family connections. A certain Gideon Kent was emerging as a champion of exploited workers.

Gideon's campaign for decent and humane treatment of the families of men killed or maimed while working for Gould's Erie Railroad led him to a confrontation in Louis's presence with the sanctimonious Gould, whose private life was thought to be without reproach. Gideon, by sheer strength of determination, managed his way into Mrs. Bell's elegant brothel in New York City, which was frequented by moguls of the day. There he found Gould and asked him for money for the needy families of two Erie employees. One had been killed on duty; the other had lost both legs.

When the financier refused, Gideon said, "I thank you for listening to me anyway. Your decision will be announced Sunday, along with an account of when and where you made it. Your comments will be repeated from my father's pulpit in St. Mark's Church on Orange Street."

Gould then acceded to Gideon's demands; but from that time on, Louis's favor with him and Fisk began to wane. Louis was excluded from one of the financiers' biggest coups because Gould blamed Louis for Gideon's blackmail.

"You led that cousin of yours to Mrs. Bell's."

"How many times must I tell you, Jay, that I had no idea he was following me."

"Carelessness is not a virtue in business. Some of the people I use remain my friends. Some don't. You fall into the latter group. You can't be trusted."

A few night later Louis was stabbed in the back by an unknown assailant. Paralyzed from the waist down, he was confined to St. Luke's Hospital. There he decided to divest himself of several properties.

EPILOGUE

Spring weather usually banished the worst of Jephtha's pessimism, and the spring of 1868 proved no exception. But when he heard an item of gossip from an attorney friend, his spirits positively soared. He had resigned himself about not being able to purchase Kent and Son; it must remain an unattainable goal. But something else he coveted just as shamelessly might not be unattainable. The Monday morning he heard that, he set out for Tarrytown.

The agent cast a dubious eye at Jephtha's rumpled black suit. "It's quite expensive."

"But is it for sale, and does your price include the furnishings?"

"It does."

"Everything? Every last book? Every item of bric-a-brac?"

"May I ask why that is so important, Mister—?"

"Kent, the same as the owner's, but I don't want my name mentioned. That's a condition of my offer. I'll meet the price, whatever it is—but only if the furnishings are left intact."

"Of course. I'm sure everything can be arranged to your satisfaction."

Jephtha took from Kentland all the cherished Kent mementos. Then he ordered the house torn down—every last stone of it.

Terrible Swift Swords

Background to THE WARRIORS

By 1862, when the Civil War was a year old, it was clear to all observers that it was sure to be an extended conflict. Analysts on both sides looked carefully and soberly at the relative strengths of the contenders.

Northern industrial production, as Louis Kent was quick to observe, was vastly greater than that of the South; eighty percent of the country's factories were located in the Northern states. The North could produce all the goods needed by both its military and civilian populations. The South, although its industrial system was expanding during the war, was unable to meet its military needs, to say nothing of civilian necessities. This in no small way accounted for the serious lessening of Southern morale after the early stages of the war.

Another major difference between the two sections was in transportation. By 1860, the North had more and better inland water transport, more surfaced roads, and a greater number of draft animals and conveyances. The North could boast of twenty thousand miles of railroads; for a comparable land area, the South had half that amount, and there were significant gaps between key points, which meant that goods had to be detoured long distances or carried between depots by wagons.

These material conditions would seem to indicate that the South had no chance to win the war from the outset, but there were compensating factors. First of all, the South for the most part fought on the defensive within its own area. The Northerners had to command long lines of communication where transportation was defective. In addition, the North had to do more than defeat enemy armies; it often had to fight and seize the holdings of private Southern civilians, many of whom would have died rather than yield on the issues at stake.

As Louis Kent judged only too well, the war years were a period of prosperity and expansion. Both industry and agriculture increased in productivity. Cyrus McCormick's invention of the reaper enabled the North to raise bumper crops. In Wilmington, Delaware, Henry du Pont, the largest supplier of explosives to the Union forces, was able through his paternalistic methods to encourage his workers to triple their output. But much of the economic stimulus was provided by legislation enacted by the Republican party, which represented the North. And since the war had removed Southern opposition, the Republicans put into effect the kind of program their supporters expected.

It was the responsibility of the President—both Lincoln and Davis—as commander in chief of the army and navy to see to the making and carrying out of a strategy for winning the war. Lincoln had no military education or experience except for a brief period in the Illinois militia. Yet he became a great war president and a great commander in chief, much superior to Davis, who was graduated from West Point in 1828. Lincoln made himself a fine strategist, often evincing keener insight than his generals. He knew that numbers and supplies were the long suit of the North and immediately moved to take advantage of the fact. He urged his generals to keep constant pressure on the whole defensive line of the

Confederacy until a breakthrough could be realized. He knew early on that the objective of his armies should be the destruction of the Confederate armies, not the occupation of Southern territory.

During the first three years of the war, Lincoln performed many of the duties that today would be the functions of the chief of the general staff or the joint chiefs of staff: he formulated policy, devised strategic plans, and even directed tactical movements. Not all of his decisions were right; but in the long run his "interference," as his generals regarded it, was fortunate for the North.

In the command system that was devised in 1864, Ulysses S. Grant was named general in chief, charged with directing the movements of all Union armies. Although it is fashionable to regard Grant as an alcoholic misfit, he was the man for whom Lincoln had been searching. He had an extraordinary capacity for thinking of the war in its overall terms and devising appropriate strategy. Lincoln trusted the man and gave him a relatively free hand.

The Confederacy never had a modern command system. Almost everything remained in the hands of President Davis, who early in 1862 assigned General Robert E. Lee to duty "under the direction of the President" and "charged" him with the conduct of the Confederate armies. What these words meant was that Lee, who had a brilliant military mind, was nothing more than Davis's adviser, who could furnish counsel only when called upon.

Lincoln made the most of the North's sea power, which was much greater than the South's. He used it to enforce the blockade of the Confederate coast and to serve in combined land and water operations.

In the Western theater, the vast tract between the Appalachian Mountains and the Mississippi River, the largest rivers were navigable by vessels of considerable size. The Union navy helped the Union armies to conquer this area by transporting troops and supplies and by attacking Confederate encampments. The Southerners' only means of defense against Union gunboats was land fortifications, no match against the Union's land and water mobility.

The blockade proclaimed by President Lincoln at the very start of the war, April 16, 1861, was a task too large for the Union navy. Even after it had grown to its maximum size, the navy was unable to seal off completely the very long shoreline of the Confederacy. Even though oceangoing ships were kept away, small blockade runners continued to carry goods into and out of some of the Southern ports (the kind of operation Matthew Kent was involved in). As the war continued, the Federal blockade became tighter, and fewer and fewer blockade runners got through; this increasingly hurt the South.

The Confederates, in an attempt to break the blockade, introduced an ironclad warship by plating with iron a former United States frigate, the *Merrimack*, which was scuttled in Norfolk Harbor by Yankees when Virginia seceded. The *Merrimack* steamed out of the harbor on March 8, 1862, to attack the blockading squadron of wooden ships in Hampton Roads. Two of the ships were destroyed, and the rest were scattered. Of course, the South was jubilant, and Washington was concerned, but not greatly, because the Union had already placed orders for several ironclads to add to the one it already owned, the *Monitor*. As a matter of fact, the very evening of the *Merrimack*'s first successes, the *Monitor* arrived in Hampton Roads and engaged the Southern ship. Neither vessel was able to penetrate the other's armor, but the *Monitor* put an end to the depredations of the *Merrimack*.

In an effort to pierce the blockade, the Confederates introduced other new kinds of craft. One of these, more ingenious than efficacious, was a torpedo boat which carried a mine on a long pole projecting from the prow. Another was the first submarine in the history of warfare to make a successful strike.

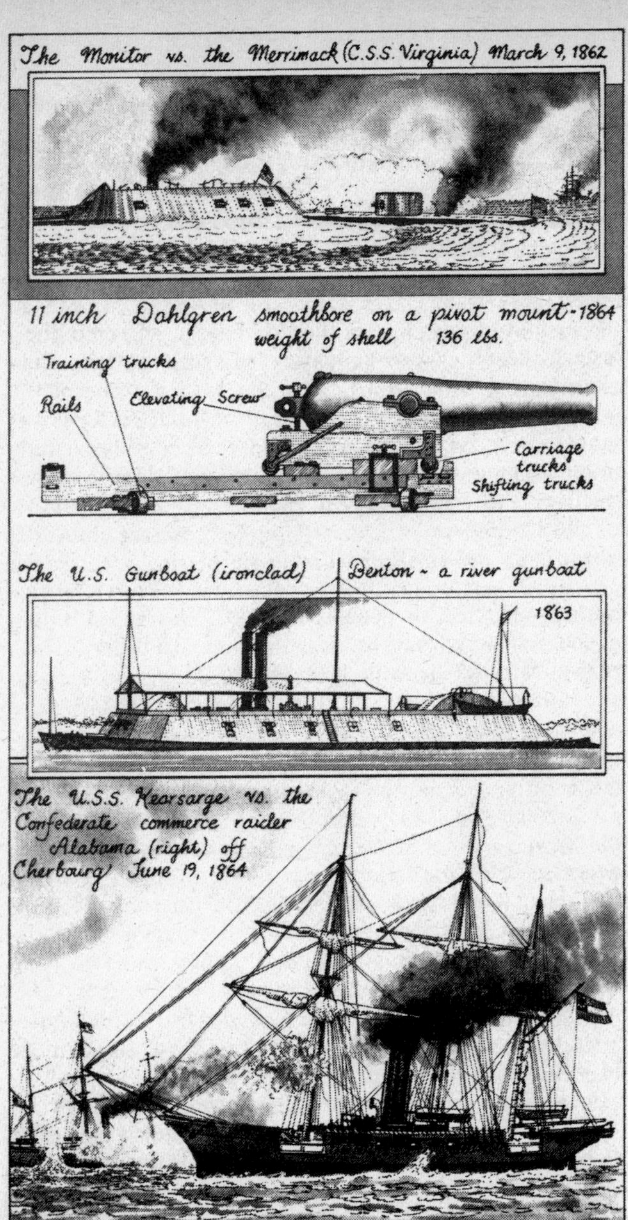

The Monitor vs. the Merrimack (C.S.S. Virginia) March 9, 1862
11 inch Dahlgren smoothbore on a pivot mount - 1864
weight of shell 136 lbs.
Training trucks
Rails
Elevating Screw
Carriage trucks
Shifting trucks
The U.S. Gunboat (ironclad) Benton - a river gunboat
1863
The U.S.S. Kearsarge vs. the Confederate commerce raider Alabama (right) off Cherbourg June 19, 1864

In Charleston Harbor in 1864, a small cigar-shaped, hand-powered submarine pulling a mine behind it on a cable dived under a blockading vessel and exploded the mine against the hull, but the contraption itself was dragged to the bottom by the sinking ship.

These and other imaginative efforts failed, however, even to weaken the blockade.

The first decisive operations in 1862 were in the Western theater, which encompassed areas in Missouri, Arkansas, Kentucky, Tennessee, and, to a lesser extent, Louisiana and Mississippi. Here, Federal troops were trying to secure control of the Mississippi by means of combined land and naval offensives. To achieve their objective, Federal troops advanced on the Mississippi from both north and south, moving down from Kentucky and up from the Gulf of Mexico.

In April, a Union squadron of ironclads and wooden vessels forced the civil authorities of New Orleans to surrender the city, and for the remainder of the war the North controlled the southern region of Louisiana. In this one operation, they had closed off the mouth of the river to Confederate trade, seized the largest city in the South and its banking center, and secured a base for future operations.

A serious weakness marked the Confederate line in Kentucky. The center, through which flowed the Tennessee and Cumberland rivers, was defended by two forts, Henry on the Tennessee and Donelson on the Cumberland. The forts had been built when Kentucky was trying to maintain a position of neutrality and were located just over the Tennessee lines. If the Union forces with the aid of naval power could break through the center, they would be between the two Confederate flanks and in position to destroy either.

In February, that is just what happened. Grant attacked Fort Henry, whose defenders struggled without much resistance, apparently overawed by the ironclad river boats accompanying the Union army. Grant then proceeded toward Fort Donelson while his naval auxiliary moved to the Cumberland River.

The Confederates put up a good fight at Donelson, but by February 16, the Union forces had captured the garrison of twenty thousand. This was a serious blow for the Confederacy; their troops were forced out of Kentucky, and they had to yield half of Tennessee.

Grant, with close to forty thousand troops, was advancing southward along the Tennessee River. His objective was to destroy Confederate railroad communications in Corinth, Mississippi. He disembarked with his army about thirty miles from Corinth, and on April 6 and 7 fought the Battle of Shiloh. The Confederates surprised Grant, and by the end of the first day had driven him back to the river. But the next day Grant, with a reinforcement of twenty-five thousand fresh troops, assumed the offensive and regained his original lines. The result was a narrow Union victory. Federal troops eventually seized Corinth and the rail lines that converged there, and by early June had occupied territory as far away as Memphis.

The Confederates held the eastern half of Tennessee and hoped to recover the rest of the state and, if possible, carry the war back to Kentucky. When Confederate General Braxton Bragg moved from Tennessee into Kentucky, Union General Don Carlos Buell followed him. On October 8, the two armies fought the indecisive Battle of Perryville, and Bragg returned to Tennessee. Buell was relieved of his command for not pursuing him.

Union operations in 1862 in the Eastern theater were directed by General George B. McClellan, the commander of the Army of the Potomac and one of the most controversial figures of the whole war. He knew how to train men and organize troops, but he was diffident about committing his men to decisive battle.

During the winter of 1861–1862, McClellan remained inactive, training 150,000 men near Washington. He finally settled on a plan for a spring campaign. Instead of driving toward Richmond by moving southward from Washington, he would have the navy transport his army to the Peninsula, the land lying between two rivers, the York and the James.

The Confederate high command, Davis and Lee, were uneasy about General Joseph E. Johnston's strategy of drawing McClellan closer to Richmond before fighting; they were afraid that reinforcements might join McClellan. To prevent this, the commander of the Confederate forces in the Shenandoah Valley, Thomas J. "Stonewall" Jackson—he was Jephtha's friend in Lexington, Virginia—moved northward to give the impression that he meant to cross the Potomac. To defend the approaches to Washington and to trap Jackson, Lincoln rushed forces to the Shenandoah Valley. Jackson, however, slipped back to safety before the Union forces could converge on him.

While these events were unfolding, Johnston attacked McClellan at Fair Oaks (the battle is also called Seven Pines) just east of Richmond. The attack not only failed to budge McClellan, but it also saw Johnston so seriously wounded that he had to give up his command. In his place, Davis named General Robert E. Lee, who led the Army of Northern Virginia for the remainder of the war.

Lee knew that the Confederacy could not win merely by repelling offensives. He decided to call Jackson from the Shenandoah Valley—which brought his army to eighty-five thousand as compared with McClellan's one hundred and ten thousand—and to attack. The engagements that followed are known as the Battles of Seven Days, June 25 through July 1. Things did not go as Lee had envisaged them. He drove McClellan southward and pursued him in a desperate attempt to destroy the Federal troops, but McClellan extricated his army and repulsed Lee in a bloody conflict at Malvern Hill. McClellan then drove on to Harrison's Landing on the James, where, with

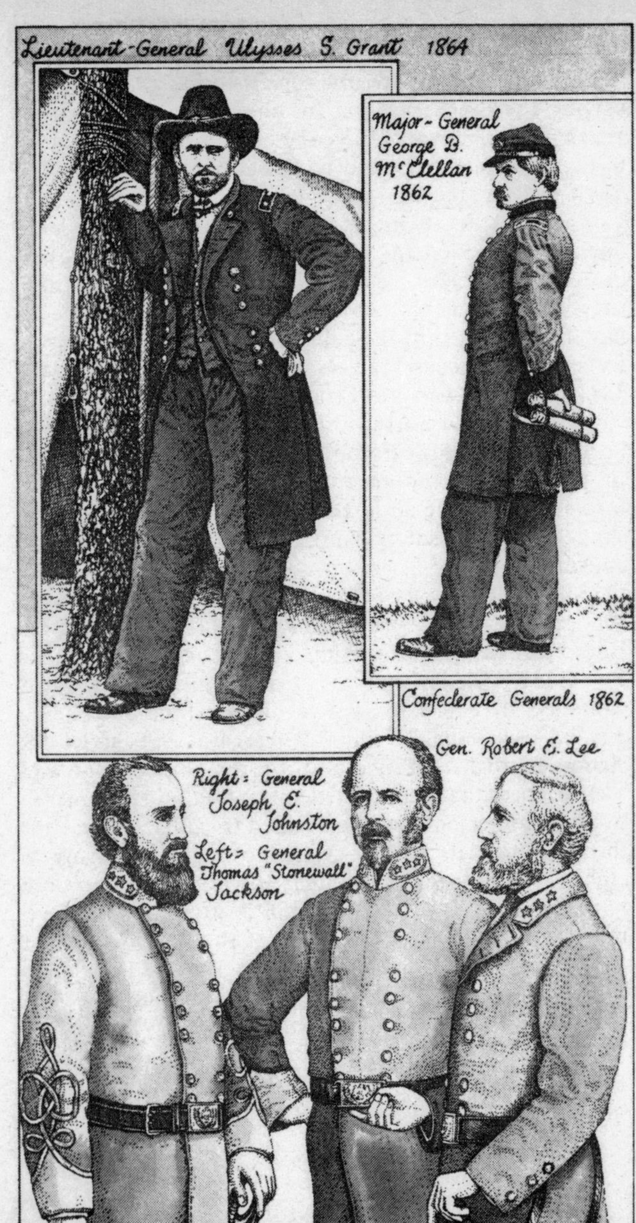
Lieutenant-General Ulysses S. Grant 1864
Major-General George B. McClellan 1862
Confederate Generals 1862
Gen. Robert E. Lee
Right = General Joseph E. Johnston
Left = General Thomas "Stonewall" Jackson

naval support, he was safe from any attack Lee could make.

At Harrison's Landing, the Union army was only twenty-five miles from Richmond, and it had a secure line of water communication. But Lincoln, instead of replacing McClellan with a more aggressive commander, decided to evacuate the army to northern Virginia, where it would be combined with a smaller force under John Pope to begin a new operation on the land route from Washington to Richmond.

As the Army of the Potomac left the Peninsula by water, Lee moved his army northward with the intention of striking Pope before he could be joined by McClellan.

Pope, who was as rash as McClellan was timid, attacked the Confederates in the Second Battle of Manassas, or Bull Run, in the last days of August. Lee stopped him handily with a counterstroke that swept him from the field. The Union troops then retreated to Washington, where Lincoln relieved Pope of his command and placed all the troops in the city under McClellan's command.

Lee's military brilliance was beginning to be felt, and he gave the Federal forces no respite. In September he assumed the offensive and invaded western Maryland. McClellan went to meet him, but by this time Lee had pulled most of his army together behind Antietam Creek near the tiny village of Sharpsburg, Maryland. There on September 17, 1862, McClellan with eighty-seven thousand men threw a series of powerful attacks at Lee's fifty thousand. With one more assault McClellan might have gained the day, but with characteristic caution he withdrew. The long-suffering Lincoln then relieved McClellan of his command and replaced him with Ambrose E. Burnside. (More famous for his whiskers than his military genius, this general gave his name, now corrupted to "sideburns," to a facial hair fashion, still in vogue, which he is said to have made popular.)

Burnside planned to drive at Richmond by crossing the Rappahannock at Fredericksburg, Virginia. On December 13, he attacked Lee's defenses. It was a bloody, hopeless failure, resulting in twelve thousand casualties. Burnside then withdrew and returned to Washington, where he was relieved of his command at his own request.

Burnside's successor was General Joseph Hooker, known as Fighting Joe. His army of one hundred twenty thousand took a defensive position in an area of Virginia known as the Wilderness.

It was here near Chancellorsville during the first five days of May, 1863—Gideon fought in this battle—that one of Lee's most brilliant exploits occurred. Dividing an army half the size of Hooker's, he sent Jackson to hit the Union's right flank, which was exposed, while he struck from in front. Although the victory was Lee's, he lost Jackson, who was accidentally wounded by fire from his own troops and died on May 10.

The Union troops may have been failing badly in the East, but it was a different story in the West. Grant was driving towards Vicksburg, Mississippi, the most strongly fortified Confederate post on the Mississippi River. Although Grant failed to storm the Confederate bastion, he began a siege which lasted six weeks, until Vicksburg capitulated on July 4, 1863.

The Union troops had achieved one of their principal strategic aims—gaining control of the Mississippi and thereby splitting the Confederacy into two parts, each isolated from the other. This marked an important turning point in the war.

When the siege of Vicksburg began, the high command in Richmond was dismayed by the prospect of losing their greatest river fortress. The Confederacy considered sending Lee with part of his army to Tennessee to launch an offensive. But Lee proposed a counterscheme—an invasion of Pennsylvania. If the South could win a victory on Northern soil, Lee felt that great changes of fortune would follow. Perhaps England and France—up until now effectually indifferent to the American conflict—might be persuaded to intervene, and the pressure on Vicksburg and other fronts would be stopped. Accordingly, in June, 1863, Lee began his movement west toward the Shenandoah Valley and then north through Maryland into Pennsylvania.

As Lee advanced, Hooker moved back to confront him, marching parallel to the line of Lee's route. But long before any engagement, Hooker asked to be relieved of his post. He was replaced by George G. Meade, who followed Lee, driving toward the strategic rear of the Confederate army in southern Pennsylvania.

Lee apparently had not expected the Union troops to move so rapidly. With his army marching in three columns, he was in a dangerous position and hurriedly had to concentrate his forces. Meanwhile, Meade selected a strong defensive site at the small town of Gettysburg, Pennsylvania, a road hub in the region; and Lee, seeking a confrontation with the Union forces, moved toward the same spot. There on the first three days of July, 1863, the most celebrated battle of the war was fought.

As Lee finally withdrew his shattered forces to Virginia, Meade made but a feeble pursuit. He had thrown away an opportunity to end the war, but Gettysburg was another turning point. The Confederates lost almost twenty-five thousand men. Never again would Lee feel strong enough to fight offensively.

A third turning point against the Confederacy occurred in Tennessee. In the autumn, as Union General William S. Rosecrans moved toward Chattanooga, the Confederate commander, Braxton Bragg, evacuated the town. Rosecrans went in pursuit and plunged over the Georgia line, where Bragg, with reinforcements from Lee's army, was lying in wait. Bragg delivered a crushing assault at Chickamauga on September 19, 1863, and the Union forces had to retreat to their Chattanooga defenses.

Bragg was eventually able to occupy the heights south

of Chattanooga. By mounting batteries on these points, he commanded all roads leading into the city and thereby shut off supplies. By this time, Grant had been named departmental commander of the West. He came at once with part of his own army to the relief of the beleaguered city. At the Battle of Chattanooga late in November, the Union troops hurled Bragg from his lines on Missionary Ridge and Lookout Mountain back into northern Georgia and then went on to occupy most of the eastern half of Tennessee.

From their base in Chattanooga, the Federal troops were in a position to split what was left of the Confederacy. The Battle of Chattanooga, like Vicksburg and Gettysburg, was a decisive victory for the Union. The only hope left for the Confederacy was to exhaust the Northerners' will to fight.

Grant's plans for 1864 called for two great offensives. The Army of the Potomac, commanded ostensibly by Meade but in reality directed by Grant, was to try to bring Lee to a decisive showdown in northern Virginia while the Western army, under the command of William T. Sherman, would advance into northern Georgia, destroy General Joseph E. Johnston's army, and wreck the economic resources of Atlanta.

From its position in northern Virginia, the Army of the Potomac, 115,000 troops, crossed the Rappahannock and Rapidan and plunged into the Wilderness area. Grant's intention was to envelop Lee's right and force him to a showdown. Lee, whose army numbered about seventy-five thousand at the onset of the campaign, wanted to avoid a showdown unless he saw a chance to deal a decisive blow. In the battles at Wilderness (May 5–7), Spotsylvania Court House (May 8–19), and Cold Harbor (June 1–3), Grant pressed relentlessly on toward Richmond, regardless of the human cost. In one month of fighting he lost fifty-five thousand men—killed, wounded, and captured—to Lee's thirty-one thousand.

Union Infantryman
on campaign, 1864
Union Brigadier
General
1864
Infantry
Lieutenant
on Staff
1864
Confederate Infantryman
1864
Union Cavalryman
with repeating
Carbine, 1864
RON TOELKE 79

Grant now had to alter his strategy. If he remained where he was, Lee would naturally retire to Richmond to withstand a siege. Grant wanted to avoid that because of the time and manpower it would require, so masking his movement from Lee, he moved southward across the James and headed for Petersburg, immediately south of Richmond, the hub of all railroads feeding into the Confederate capital. If Grant could secure Petersburg, he could force Lee to come into the open to fight. Grant almost succeeded, but he ultimately resorted to a siege. The trench lines—trench warfare came in with the Civil War—of the two armies extended for miles on either side of Petersburg. Grant strove to extend his left around Lee's right in order to get at the railroads, which were the lifeline of the Confederate armies; it took him almost nine months before he reached his objective.

Meanwhile, General Sherman with an army of over ninety thousand was moving against Johnston, whose forces were at the beginning thirty thousand fewer. Johnston hoped to retard Sherman's advance, to stall, and not to commit his forces until conditions were propitious. As Sherman drew near Atlanta, Jefferson Davis, perhaps capriciously, replaced Johnston with John B. Hood, who threw two attacks, both failures, at Sherman. On September 2, 1864, Sherman's Union army occupied Atlanta.

Even so, Sherman had not destroyed the Confederate army. But eager to strike deeper into Georgia, Sherman deployed thirty thousand of his men to Tennessee under the command of George Thomas and at the same time prepared to move to the coast, to Savannah. Concurrently, Hood decided to invade Tennessee, hoping to force Sherman to follow him.

Hood sustained disastrous losses at Franklin, Tennessee, on November 30, but even so he moved northward and took up a position near Nashville. In the Battle of Nashville (December 15 and 16), Thomas drove Hood from the field. As the Confederates retreated toward Mississippi, they were harried by the most merciless Northern cavalry pursuit in the war. Very few units reached Mississippi intact. The Confederate Army of Tennessee had, in effect, ceased to exist.

In the meantime, Sherman was marching virtually unopposed across Georgia, inaugurating a new kind of warfare, total warfare, in which there really are no civilians, a war intended, by attacking everybody and everything, to break the enemy's will to resist. Sherman's army marched along a sixty-mile front, destroying property and supplies that might be useful to the Confederates. In addition, they committed individual depredations that today are commonplace in war, but in 1864 were atrocities. Jeremiah's experiences at the Rose plantation were, alas, typical.

By December 20, Sherman had reached Savannah. He then turned into South Carolina and continued to destroy enemy property. When he advanced into North Carolina, a Confederate army of thirty thousand commanded by Johnston was there to oppose him, but this small force could do no more than delay his march.

In April, Grant passed a part of his army around Lee's right to the railroads.

The Confederates evacuated Petersburg and then Richmond. Lee marched toward the west with his now tragically reduced army, about twenty-five thousand. His desperate hope was to reach a rail line to North Carolina and unite with Johnston, but the pursuing Federals barred his escape route.

Lee knew that further fighting was pointless, and on April 9—five days short of four years after the Confederates had seized Fort Sumter—he surrendered the Army of Northern Virginia to Grant at Appomattox. Meanwhile, in North Carolina, Johnston too realized the war was hopeless; on April 18 he surrendered to Sherman near Durham. Jefferson Davis, defiant to the end, refused

In the rear of Sherman's army ~ Georgia, 1864
The Savannah Waterfront ~ 1864
William T. Sherman
Sherman's troops destroying
Georgia railroads ~ October, 1864
F17-36
RON TOELKE 79

to accept defeat. Fleeing southward, the Confederate President was captured in Georgia. The war was over.

In the North, the prosperity of the war years continued on into the postwar years. In the South, there was only devastation—gutted towns, wrecked plantations, neglected fields, collapsed bridges, ruined railroads. Much of the personal property of Southerners had been lost; Confederate bonds and currency were worthless. There was little except loved ones to cheer the thousands of soldiers who drifted back to their homes, and 258,000 never returned; other thousands went back maimed or sick.

Conditions were bad for Southern whites, but they were generally worse for the four million blacks who were emerging from the bondage that had held them and their ancestors for over two hundred and fifty years. Many of these people had seen service as servants for Confederate officers or as laborers for the Confederate armies. Many thousands fought on the Northern side, and more than thirty-eight thousand died for the Union cause.

The Thirteenth Amendment, which would outlaw slavery, had yet to be ratified. On many plantations, the blacks were being detained and forced to work. Others were leaving their old masters. They trudged to the nearest town, or they roamed the countryside, sleeping on the bare ground. Few had any possessions except the rags on their backs, but they managed to survive.

The Negroes wanted to feel their freedom and to exercise it, but first of all they needed relief from the threat of starvation. Beyond that they needed farms of their own and economic independence. A few of the freed slaves had already settled on abandoned plantations, notably on islands along the South Carolina coast and on land in Mississippi that had belonged to the Davis family. The Negroes also wanted education for their children and themselves. In some places, especially in New Orleans, there were well-educated blacks who had been free for generations. But to the newly freed, education was rare and precious; most of them were illiterate, as the slave code intended they should be.

The federal government, besides keeping troops (many of them black) in the South to preserve order and protect the Negroes, helped them in making the transition from slavery to freedom. In March of 1865, Congress set up the Bureau of Freemen, Refugees, and Abandoned Lands as an agency of the army. The bureau was empowered to provide food, transporation, and assistance in getting jobs and fair wages, and to set up schools for former slaves. Cooperating with the bureau, particularly in educational work, were missionaries and teachers who had been sent to the South by the Freedmen's Aid Societies and other private and church groups in the North. While these Northern "do-gooders" performed a valuable and necessary service, their presence was keenly resented by Southern whites and helped delay the cooperation at a personal level necessary for a speedy reconstruction.

Reconstruction was the word used at the time for the process of bringing the Confederate states back into the Union. A quick restoration would have been to the advantage of the former Confederates and both the Northern and Southern Democrats. The Democrats could then rejoin and seize control of both the Congress and the presidency. The consequences of a quick peace could, on the other hand, have been disastrous for Northern businessmen, who during the war had obtained favor from the government—a high tariff, railroad subsidies, a national banking system—which would have come to an end if the Democrats had regained power. For the Negroes, a quick restoration of the Southern states would not have been good either. The master class, which had dominated state politics before the war, would have continued to do so, and the Negroes would have found themselves somewhere between slavery and freedom.

The Radical Republicans, directed by men like Thaddeus Stevens of Pennsylvania and Charles Sumner of Massachusetts, stood for a retributive peace. They wanted the civil and military leaders of the late Confederacy to be severely disciplined, large numbers of Southerners to be disenfranchised, and the property of rich Southerners to be confiscated and distributed among the freedmen.

Democrats and Conservative Republicans claimed that secession was illegal in the first place; therefore, the Confederate States had never really been out of the Union, were still in it, and had all the rights of any Northern state. On the other hand, Southerners who had fought to uphold the right of secession now demanded all the privileges in the Union they had tried to dissolve.

During his entire presidency, Lincoln was concerned with principle as well as politics. The principle was the inviolability of the Union. He regarded the question of whether or not the Confederate states were in the Union as irrelevant. As far as Lincoln was concerned, they were out of their proper relationship to the Union and should be restored to the right relationship as soon as possible.

Lincoln's program for effecting a restoration of the former Confederate states was mild and benign. It simply offered a general amnesty to all who would take an oath of loyalty to the government. Temporarily excluded from the right to swear the oath were high Confederate civil and military officials. In any state where ten percent of the number of voters in 1860 took the oath, that state would be allowed to set up a government.

The Radical Republicans did not approve of Lincoln's generosity of spirit. In 1864, they passed the Wade-Davis Bill, which was far more severe than Lincoln's plan, requiring among other stringent measures a majority, instead of Lincoln's ten percent, to take an oath of future loyalty. Since the bill was passed only a few days before Congress adjourned, Lincoln disposed of it with a pocket veto.

Displaced ex-slaves 1865
A Street scene in occupied Richmond 1866
Confederate Soldiers returning home, 1865
A Ruined Southern City - 1865
RON TOELKE '79

This action enraged the authors of the measure, who warned the President not to interfere with the powers of Congress to control Reconstruction. An astute politician as well as a practical man, Lincoln did not ignore the bitterness and strength of the Radical opposition; he realized he would have to accept some of the Radicals' objections. He was beginning to move toward a new approach to Reconstruction when, on April 14, 1865, five days after Lee's surrender at Appomattox, a crazed actor, John Wilkes Booth, under the delusion that he was helping the South, shot the President as he was watching a performance of *Our American Cousin* in Ford's Theater in Washington. Lincoln died early the following morning. Because of the circumstances of his death, he achieved immediate martyrdom. In the excitement of the hour, it was widely assumed that Booth's mad act had been instigated by Southern leaders. The Radicals capitalized on this assumption and implicated important Confederate officials.

Louis Kent's pre-Civil War machinations and training put him in good stead for the sensational economic expansion experienced in America between 1865 and 1900. In those years, the United States became the foremost manufacturing nation of the world. This rise to eminence rested on firm bases: the inventive and organizational skills of Americans, seemingly limitless natural resources, and an ever growing labor force.

Business developed new and larger forms of organization. Before the Civil War business had been content with single proprietorship, partnership, and the corporation, which was owned by a limited number of shareholders. After the war the corporation came into increasing favor and became larger in every way, but exceeding the corporation in size were forms combining a number of corporations—pools, trusts, and holding companies. A pool was an informal organization of several corporations manufacturing the same goods. A trust came into being when the stockholders of a number of corporations transferred their stock to a directing board of trustees. A holding company came into being when the directing company actually bought the stock of competing corporations.

Powerful economic forces were behind the movement toward concentration. The growing number of businesses intensified competition and the scramble for profits. Also, a steady decline in prices between 1865 and 1897 forced businessmen to consider every means of cutting cost. Organization into larger units eliminated competition, lowered costs, and increased profits.

Thus, American industry moved unconsciously toward monopoly, with fewer and fewer companies producing more and more of the nation's goods. By 1900, fewer than two percent of the manufacturing establishments were turning out almost fifty percent of all the manufactured goods in the United States.

The first large American industry was the railroads, and after the Civil War they continued to expand. Their trackage figure doubled every decade, and by 1900, the United States had the most extensive transporation system in the world.

Perhaps no technological achievement has inspired as much romantic lore as the railroad. But the facts themselves are romantic enough in that empire that attracted Louis Kent at the top level and Michael Boyle at the other extreme.

Before the Civil War, railroad construction had been confined to the eastern half of the country in an east-west network that connected terminals on the Atlantic coast with points along the Mississippi River, but in the years immediately following the war, important developments occurred.

To begin with, the railroads of the Northeast were consolidated into four major roads—the New York Central, the Pennsylvania, the Erie, and the Baltimore and Ohio. These lines then established connections with Chicago and the Western market. In the meantime, railroads in the South that had been damaged during the war were repaired, and there was an outburst of new construction; the area had three major lines—the South, the Atlantic Coast, and the Illinois Central. Somewhat later, lines in the Mississippi Valley, such as the Chicago and Northwestern, the Missouri Pacific, and the Kansas Pacific, began pushing toward the Great Plains.

But the development that caught the popular imagination was the building of the great transcontinental lines. During the Civil War, Congress acted to bring about a road from the Mississippi Valley to the Pacific by chartering two railroad corporations, the Union Pacific and the Central Pacific. The Union Pacific was to build westward from Omaha, Nebraska, and the Central Pacific eastward from Sacramento, California, until they met.

To provide the necessary financial aid, Congress donated a right-of-way across the public domain and offered the companies special benefits. For each mile of track a company laid, it would receive twenty square miles of land in alternate sections along the right-of-way and a thirty-year loan of $16,000, $32,000, or $48,000, depending on where the construction was—in plains, foothills, or mountains. The government also accepted a second mortgage on the loans, and permitted the companies to issue first mortgage bonds up to the amount of the official loan. By the terms of the legislation, the Union Pacific and the Central Pacific stood to receive almost twenty million acres of land and $60 million in loans.

Work began in 1865, and overwhelming obstacles faced the workers—mountains, deserts, hostile Indians. In addition, supplies and labor had to be brought in from distant points. The Central Pacific imported Chinese laborers, while the Union Pacific hired thousands of Irish immigrants. Even so, the work went ahead, and in the

A Steam Locomotive 1870
Right - The elegant facilities of the Dining Saloon - Central Pacific Railroad, 1870
Below - A Refrigerator car for shipping beef - 1871
RANKIN'S
REFRIGERATOR & CONDENCER.
Building the Central Pacific 1868
RON TOELKE 79

spring of 1869—four years after it was begun—the West was linked to the East by rail. This achievement gave cause for a national celebration.

Promoters came forward with proposals for other transcontinental lines, but this time congressional largess was limited to land grants. By the end of the century, five continental systems were in operation, and all except one—the Great Northern—had been built with some form of aid from either the federal government or the states.

As a network of rails covered the country, it was obvious that the industry was becoming overextended. Many railroad corporations, including some of the largest ones, were burdened with impossible debts. Many roads were looted and wrecked by their own directors, or they were subject to harassing competition by speculators like Jay Gould. In some sections of the country, railroads enjoyed monopolies; but wherever competition existed, it was cutthroat and persistent. Competing roads fought savage rate wars and sought business by offering rebates to big shippers. The inevitable results of overexpansion, fraudulent management, and fierce competition occurred. In the depression of the seventies, 450 railroads went into bankruptcy; twenty years later in another depression, 318 other companies with sixty-seven thousand miles of tracks fell into the hands of receivers.

During the years of reconstruction and the American industrial revolution, a dramatic transformation was occurring west of the Mississippi. In this vast area, which consisted of the Great Plains, the Rockies, and the plateau between the Rockies and the Sierra Nevada, a propulsive movement of population was gradually settling what was the last frontier in America.

During the war, Congress had aided in this migration by passing the Homestead Act and the Morrill Land Grant Act of 1862. The former provided that any citizen (or alien who had declared his intention of becoming a citizen) could register claim to a quarter-section of land (a section was 640 acres, or one square mile). After having given proof that he had lived on the land for five years, he would receive title to it upon payment of a minimal fee. The Morrill Law provided that each state was to receive thirty thousand acres for each of its congressional representatives, the proceeds of which were to be used in providing education in agriculture, engineering, and the military sciences. At least twenty-six state universities, as well as a number of other institutions, are the direct result of the Morrill Act.

But at first it was mineral wealth that drew settlers to the last frontier. This frontier—the mining camps of Colorado, Nevada, and South Dakota—flourished brilliantly, if briefly, from about 1860 to 1880. And at about the same time, another colorful economic province took shape—the cattle kingdom of the Great Plains. It too had a brief and brilliant existence. The rise of the cattlemen on the Great Plains was directly related to the developing industrial society of urban America; the concentration of population in cities created a new market for meat and other foods. Open range, the unclaimed grasslands of the public domain, provided a vast area where cattlemen could graze their herds free of charge. The ever expanding railroads gave cattlemen access to Eastern markets. These two factors accounted for the spreading of the industry over the Great Plains.

The profits to be made in the cattle industry were tremendous; more and more investors were, therefore, tempted into it, with the result that the ranges became overstocked and prices fell drastically. So as abruptly as it had risen, the cattle kingdom fell. Cattlemen turned to more modest operations; they acquired title to their lands and fenced them in. They became settled ranchers.

In the decades following the Civil War, the north central plains gradually yielded to farmers, the "sodbusters" of legend. By the end of the century, practically every part of the region—and indeed the whole of the "last

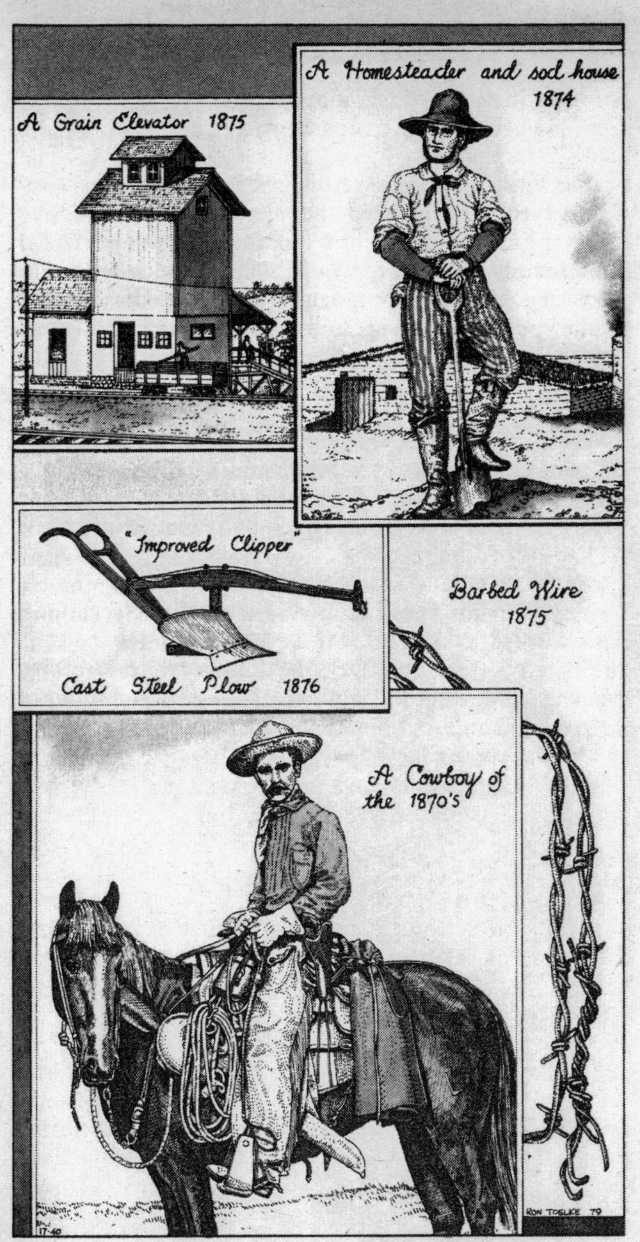
A Homesteader and sod house
1874
A Grain Elevator 1875
"Improved Clipper"
Barbed Wire
1875
Cast Steel Plow 1876
A Cowboy of
the 1870's
RON TOELKE '79
17-40

frontier" from the Mississippi to the Sierra Nevada—had been organized into territories or states.

The settlers of the last frontier had to advance against determined and sustained Indian resistance. There were about a quarter of a million Indians in the area, divided into numerous tribes, of whom the two principal nations were the Dakotas of the northern plains and the Apaches of the southwestern highlands. Mounted on their small, powerful horses—descendants of the horses of the conquistadors—these Indians had mobility, and they were superb warriors.

From the sixties through the eighties, there were incessant Indian wars. The white man's fighting was done for him by the cavalry of the regular army, of which two regiments were Negroes. Eventually, superior white technology triumphed.

As the Indians were suppressed, the government moved them into specified areas, now called reservations. This worked to break down the basis of Indian culture, the tribal system. In effect, the Indians were forced to become white men. But not until 1924 were full rights of citizenship conferred on all Indians.

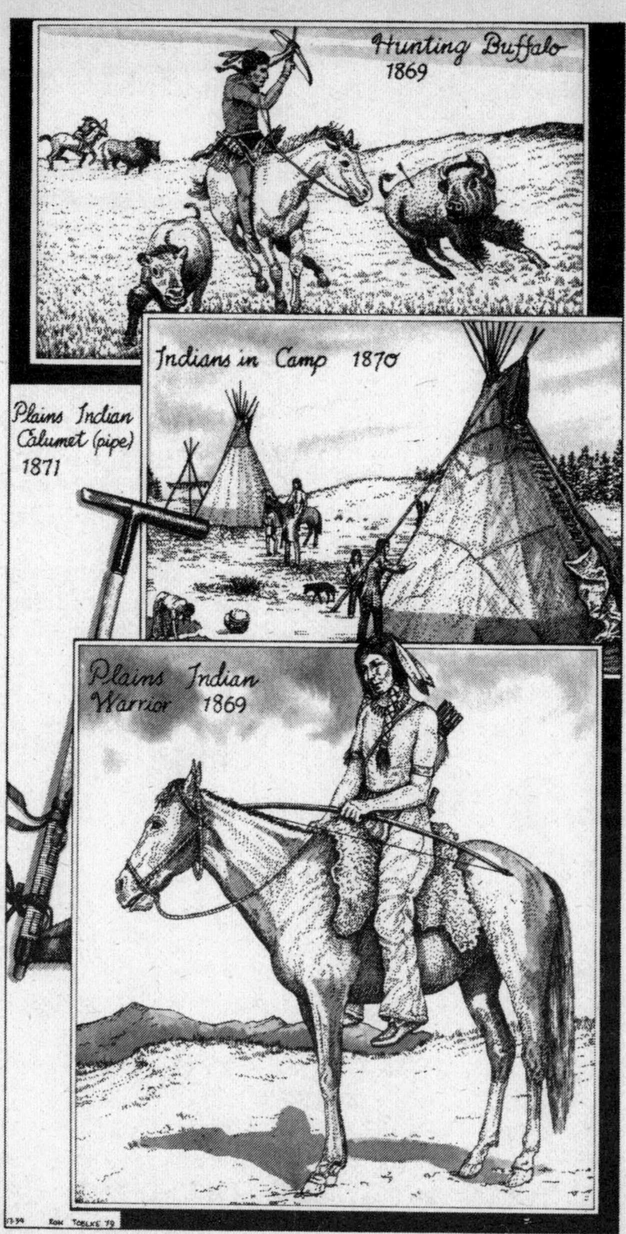
Hunting Buffalo
1869
Indians in Camp 1870
Plains Indian
Calumet (pipe)
1871
Plains Indian
Warrior 1869

The Lawless

A CONDENSATION OF

The Lawless

(1869-1877)

PROLOGUE

They hunted buffalo and lived in the open. But sometimes even the most robust constitutions cannot withstand foul weather. So it proved with Jeremiah Kent, who surrendered to fever in April of 1869. Kola, the Oglala Sioux with whom he had traveled since '66 kept watch.

Kola was three years older than Jeremiah, who had found the Indian nearly beaten to death by his own tribe for adultery. Jeremiah had cared for him until he recovered, and they had become sworn lifetime friends.

Looking at Jeremiah with eyes that brimmed with misery, Kola said, "While I slept, a vision came." The Sioux put great stock in visions. "I dreamed I saw you with your guns again."

"It must be a false vision. I packed them away last winter."

I killed eight men and one woman before I came to see that always settling things with guns was a sickness that would whip me one day if I didn't whip it first.

"In the dream I also heard a voice," the Sioux continued. "The holy voice said to me, once you take up the guns again, you will never put them down. There will be no end to the killing. The guns will bring great luster to your name for a while, but it will vanish; and you will be killed by one of your own."

Jeremiah wiped his perspiring forehead. "It couldn't happen. The only person who knows Jeremiah Kent is still alive is my father's friend Boyle, and he swore never to say a word about meeting me."

When Jeremiah's fever still lay on him after another twenty-four hours, Kola announced he was going to seek help. Knowing that it would be dangerous for one Indian to ride into a white settlement, Jeremiah protested, but Kola insisted. With apprehension, Jeremiah watched the Indian ride into the blurred dusk.

He never came back.

On the following Tuesday, Jeremiah rode toward the settlement of Ellsworth, still suffering from a slight fever. Although the evening was cool, perspiration gathered under his hatband. He wanted to take the hat off, but he didn't, for it concealed the one mark that made him easy to identify—a streak of white hair caused by a Minié ball that had grazed his scalp at Chickamauga.

Light streaking from a cottage to a line of trees showed him a still form turning slowly in the wind. He rode close enough to be sure. "Jesus," he said under his breath. "Oh, dear Jesus."

In the settlement, after some discreet questioning, he found out what had happened and who had been responsible for Kola's hanging.

He found the man, Graves by name, in the town's sleazy bar. Jeremiah shot both him and the foolish bartender, who, at the moment Graves fell, stabbed his hands beneath the bar. What weapon he concealed, no one saw. Jeremiah merely shifted slightly and fired.

One long stride and Jeremiah was outside. He reached his horse with no difficulty and galloped out of Ellsworth.

BOOK 1

For Matthew Kent, Paris in June, 1870, was the ideal place to pursue his two loves—painting and a young woman named Dolly Stubbs, who at the moment was in England visiting her parents. Furthermore, Matthew had turned his back on America. It had become for him a country of parvenus and social climbers. Money was all that mattered there. He hated the very idea of the war in which a half million men had lost their lives while a few profiteers made fortunes.

Matt and Dolly had arrived in Paris in 1866, wickedly in love with the notion of living together without benefit of clergy. They rented two rooms from the Widow Rochambeau, who was militantly moral. They fibbed to her—and to Dolly's parents—about their marital status. But when Dolly found herself pregnant, her attitude changed.

"I do want the baby to be reared properly. I know," Dolly said, "that may pose some problems in connection with your work. But when a man and woman love each other and they have a child, that changes things."

Not for me, he thought. Much as he loved her, he couldn't sacrifice his time and concentration on the altar of parenthood.

Matt was well known in the artistic world of Paris; he counted among his friends Édouard Manet, the shockingly realistic painter, and Paul Cézanne, who the critics said "painted with a pistol." Matt's teacher was the irascible Fochet, whose highest praise was a few grunts. Matt was a part of the café group that acknowledged Manet as their leader. Besides Matt and Paul, there were Renoir, Degas, Fantin-Latour, Monet, and Pissarro.

The group usually gathered at the Café Guerbois late

on Fridays. The proprietress was the earthy Lisa, who liked to tease Matt.

"Believe me, if that English girl ever turns her back on you, I'll snatch you away."

"You'll be too busy avoiding all your other suitors. I saw one of them yesterday. That Prussian, Lepp."

"Oh, God. Spare me!"

"He asked me to tell you that he still thought of you. And even though you had refused him twice, he did not consider himself refused permanently."

"Let's hope not. I've made a few inquiries. He keeps a *pied-à-terre* on the Left Bank where prostitutes and impoverished students satisfy his peculiar needs."

Matt and Dolly's neighbors were a young Russian couple named Leah and Sime Strelnik. Sime, who had been born in Russian Georgia, had come to Paris via Berlin, the home of his only living relative, a brother. Both Strelnik brothers were active in the workingman's movement. Sime spent half the day sleeping, the other half reading or writing pamphlets, and most of the night attending meetings with people Madame Rochambeau characterized as "atheistic, unwashed, and sinister."

One day Sime left home, but he would tell no one where he was going. "It will be safer that way" was his only explanation.

As the weeks passed, Dolly's temper grew short. All Matt wanted to do when he returned from Fochet's studio was to eat and then fall asleep. He wasn't eager to hear about Dolly's day at the English school where she taught or even about her visits to her physician.

"I should think you'd be interested in the welfare of your own child."

"I am, Dolly. But your sawbones hasn't told me anything we didn't already know."

"I suppose you don't worry about poor Sime either."

"Of course I worry." But that was only partially true. In

the studio, thoughts of the child or his vanished neighbor never entered his mind.

On Saturday Matt decided to take Dolly out in order to make her feel better. They waltzed under lanterns. At the end of one number, they walked back to their table to find that Auguste Renoir had just completed a cartoon of them pressed close together.

As they returned home that night, they discovered a man watching their house.

A few days later, upon returning to his apartment, Matt found the Prussian officer Lepp with a grotesque gnome who appeared to be the German's aide. They had come to talk with Leah Strelnik.

"If you're looking for my husband, he isn't here."

"We're aware of that. We have him. Show them, Josef."

The gnome took from his pocket the cap Sime was wearing when he had left home a few days earlier. Now, however, there was a huge blackish stain of dried blood on the crown.

"If you'll just give us what we came for, we'll be pleased to leave you alone. We want the correspondence from your husband's brother."

"It isn't here!" Leah screamed. "I don't even know whether it exists."

Lepp bobbed his head at the helpers he had with him. "Get on with the search."

Within minutes, the contents of the entire house had been upturned, broken, or demolished. When nothing was found, Lepp pronounced, "At the end of forty-eight hours, if you do not give us the documents, your husband will be killed."

Just as the men turned to go, Dolly returned home from school. As she opened the door, the gnome whipped out a revolver and pointed it.

Dolly stared at the gun in disbelief while Matt watched the gnome's finger apply pressure on the trigger. Matt couldn't move fast enough to stop him, but Lepp did. He jabbed his cane into the gnome's shoulder, and the revolver exploded. Dolly fell sideways.

Matt dropped to his knees beside her. She was breathing in a loud, uneven way.

Then he knew he had been wrong. She hadn't been hit. The deflected bullet had lodged above the door. He slipped his hands under Dolly's neck and shoulders. "I love you, Dolly" was all he could say. "I never knew how much. We'll get married as soon as you want."

Matt knew he had to find Sime. With help from Lisa, he was able to find Lepp's rooms in the Latin Quarter.

"Heaven knows how you found me," Lepp said. "It was rash and stupid of you to come here."

Matt scanned the room. *Strelnik wasn't here*!

Then the Prussian lunged and rammed his knee into Matt's groin. He uttered a short, self-satisfied laugh as Matt reeled backward. Then he seized Matt's gun and tossed it across the room. "I don't need that to deal with a foolish person like you, Herr Kent. First, however, I'll show you something."

He paced swiftly to a corner and pushed aside a framed paper screen. Behind it, Strelnik lay motionless.

"Don't worry. He's breathing. We've pacified him with a special draught."

The Prussian still had one hand on the frame of the screen. Without warning he threw the screen at Matt.

In the scuffle that ensued, Matt was finally able to reach his revolver. He fired three times. The first bullet pierced Lepp's left ribs. The second missed. The third tore into his groin.

Matt hid his head, fighting sickness. He had never killed before. God almighty, that was a vile thing, no matter what the justification.

Voices in the corridor and hammering at the door started Matt into action. He lifted Strelnik to his feet. Fortunately, the man didn't weigh much. He slipped an arm around Strelnik's waist, looped the Russian's arm over his neck, and half carried and half dragged him out a back entrance.

Matt knew he could not remain in France. That very night he and Dolly and the Strelniks left for England.

On July 22, 1870, Matt and Dolly were married in London. The second week in August, with money advanced by Matt, the Strelniks sailed for the United States. That same day Dolly told Matt that she was leaving him.

"It's goddamned insanity!" Matt cried. "I married you because I loved you."

"And I love you. I'll never love any man so much. But I also know how you feel about domesticity. I'm going to have the baby at my new place of employment. I'm leaving England."

"To go where?"

"The Empire is very large, you know. I've secured a position in a rather remote part of it."

"Do you want a divorce?"

"I don't want that unless you do," she said.

"No. Why the hell won't you tell me where you're going? Why do you have to leave at all?"

"The truth is, you don't need anyone or anything except your work."

Some months later word arrived from Lahore in India announcing the birth of Thomas Matthew Kent on Christmas Day, 1870.

INTERLUDE

The first warm weekend in June of 1871, Jephtha Kent relinquished his pulpit to his assistant and traveled down to the Jersey shore to open the summer house. His second wife, Molly, was recovering from a spring cold and decided not to accompany him. She made him promise he would secure local laborers to do any hard work, because Jephtha had been having chest pains for the past couple of years and his doctor had warned him to avoid undue exertion. But Jephtha did not heed their advice. That weekend he worked too hard, and on his way home he suffered a fatal heart attack.

BOOK 2

Gideon Kent had the ability to guide either or both of the family businesses that had been purchased from Louis Kent's estate after his death in 1868, but in fact he wasn't interested in the daily paper or in the publishing house. All he cared about was the cause of the workingman.

At twenty-eight, Gideon still had the soft accent of Virginia and walked with the unconscious swagger of the cavalryman he was during the war. Sometimes it astonished him that he could love New York with such fervor. He even loved the racket of lower Third Avenue, where he and Sime Strelnik, his assistant, labored to produce a bimonthly newspaper called *Labor's Beacon*, which few people read.

For the past months, Gideon hadn't been going home to his wife with the joy he had once experienced. Ever since he had started *Labor's Beacon*, Margaret had grown more and more critical of his interest in the cause.

Lately, Gideon had begun to see certain disturbing signs in her behavior. He had also detected the smell of wine on her breath.

He knew she was upset by his work and by the modest surroundings in which he insisted they live. She found their circumstances particularly galling because she knew there was so much money available. Gideon had inherited four and a half million dollars in addition to a quarter interest in Kent and Son and the New York *Union*. Jephtha's estate had been divided equally among his widow, Molly, his sons Gideon and Matthew, and the Irishman Michael Boyle.

Molly Kent nominally operated both the newspaper and the book company, though each firm was actually run by professional managers. Gideon had a standing offer from his stepmother to move into the management of the *Union*, but he had never even considered it. That upset Margaret, as did the inevitable danger in his work. Gideon had received threats against his life for exposing unfair practices of the railroads, but he was not much concerned.

Margaret's displeasure had made their household very tense recently. He and Margaret had not made love in five or six weeks. The thought of sex produced in Gideon's mind a slightly embarrassing image—Julia Sedgwick, the late Louis Kent's former wife.

Gideon had met Julia when she had come to Louis's funeral with her son, Carter Kent.

Julia lived in Chicago. Rich in her own right, she used her money to finance her work as a lecturer for the American Woman Suffrage Association. She had impressed Gideon greatly, both by her intellect and by her physical attractiveness.

One night when Gideon was working alone at the *Beacon*, three men arrived who warned him against writing further articles about the Washington railroad lobby. Then they beat him unconscious and wrecked the office.

When Gideon arrived home late that night, he found his nine-year-old daughter, Eleanor, still up downstairs. She said her mother was upstairs with Will, her two-year-old brother, who had a stomach ache. When

Margaret came down, she was in a terrible mood. Clearly she had been drinking. Her apparent indifference to his cause and her insistence on their living more comfortably led to a confrontation that marked the real trouble between them. When Gideon said he was planning a trip to Chicago to attend a labor organization meeting, Margaret laid down an ultimatum: "Your work or this family. Chicago or this family."

Julia Sedgwick popped into Gideon's mind as his train pulled into the La Salle Street Station. It struck him that if any human being would understand why he had to continue his work, it would be a suffragist. They were nearly as unpopular as trade unionists. He resolved to call on her.

Gideon checked in at a modest hotel and found a caller waiting for him, one Sidney Florian, an agent for Thomas Courtleigh, owner of the Wisconsin and Prairie, an immensely profitable trunk line which was one of the most repressively managed roads in the entire country. Florian warned Gideon that any publicity about the meeting he was holding with Nils Ericsson, the Chicago labor organizer, would only result in danger for Ericsson's family.

Ericsson had an almost messianic belief in the need for organizing the working force. When Gideon reported Florian's threats to him, he didn't take them lightly, but neither was he cowed by them.

Julia Sedgwick and her nine-year-old son, Carter, received Gideon hospitably in their splendid mansion at State and Twenty-first streets in the fashionable part of Chicago. Julia's house was next to Thomas Courtleigh's, but she had never been received there. Her stand on women's rights made her unwelcome.

Gideon dined with Julia that evening, and she expressed a desire to attend the meeting he had come to Chicago to address. By the end of the meal she had so charmed him that against his better judgment he agreed to take her to Ericsson's.

Chicago had been suffering a serious drought; and since most of its buildings were made of wood, now completely dried out, fires occurred regularly. As Gideon left Julia's house that evening, he saw the beginning of a fire that razed a four-block area before it finally burned out. As a waiter in Gideon's hotel commented, "One spark in the wrong place at the wrong time, this town would burn like a caldron of kerosine."

It was dark by the time Gideon and Julia reached Ericsson's barn. They were met by ten-year-old Torvald Ericsson. Only about a dozen men were gathered.

Just as the meeting began, an express wagon drew up. At once Gideon perceived its contents. He drew out his LeMat and ordered, "Douse those lanterns. Courtleigh's sent us a few visitors."

Only one man succeeded in extinguishing a lamp before Florian swaggered in. "Toss that gun to me, Kent. No? Then I'll take it."

Gideon raised the LeMat in a swift, smooth motion and shot at the lantern. Kerosine and glass cascaded on Florian, who screamed like a woman.

"Run!" Gideon yelled.

"Kent, we're not going to run from a bunch of—"

"They *want* you to fight. If one or two get hurt, the rest will never organize."

Most of the labor group scrambled out of the window, leaving Julia, Gideon, Ericsson, and Torvald to face Florian and his burly bodyguards. The two thugs came at Gideon, but they were too slow for him. Gideon managed to recover the LeMat. His bullet got one of the men in the arm, but the other managed to throw Ericsson down. Then Gideon fired the LeMat again. This time he caught Florian's right shoulder. The man tried to crawl away toward the door. All the while the thug who had downed

Ericsson was slashing at his face with a knife. Torvald rushed to help his father by grabbing the thug's left shoulder. The man plunged his blade into the boy's ribs and then jumped up and fled outside. Gideon whirled toward the barn door.

A bright, ruddy light was shimmering on the walls of the cottages facing the barn. Voices yelled that DeKoven Street was burning.

"Where's that?" Gideon asked.

His eyes wild, Ericsson said, "Only one block south."

It was the beginning of the great Chicago fire. Gideon and Julia escaped, but Ericsson didn't. He was trapped as he attempted to bring a picture of his late wife out of his burning home. Nor did Torvald. They took the boy to Julia's home, and Gideon went to find a doctor; but three hooligans knocked him out and stole his landau and horses. When he returned to Julia's house for another horse, he learned that Ericsson's boy had died a few minutes before.

Out of Gideon's sense of failure came a searing determination. He would settle with Mr. Thomas Courtleigh, who had caused all this grief.

Then weariness sapped his anger, and he was barely aware of Julia's taking his hand and leading him across the kitchen.

When he was himself again, he found he was sprawled on a lounge in Julia's bedroom. Soon she came to him, and that night they became lovers.

They buried Torvald in Julia's garden. His body was dressed in one of Carter's suits, because Gideon wanted the boy's blood-covered shirt to present to Courtleigh. How and when he would deliver it, Gideon was not certain.

On the Friday following the fire, Thomas Courtleigh gave a party in honor of his fiancée, Miss Gwendolyn Strother. Gideon invaded the affair and denounced

Courtleigh as a murderer before the entire company. To provide a climax for his speech, he drew out Torvald's shirt.

"You're a murderer, Courtleigh!" Gideon flung the shirt, which fluttered down to the hem of Miss Strother's ball gown. The sight of it completely deranged the young woman. "Get him out of here!"

Two stable hands rushed up behind Gideon and grabbed him. They hauled him to the front steps and booted him down them.

Gideon decided, with Julia's encouragement, to take over the management of the *Union*; it would be far more effective than *Labor's Beacon* could ever be. He and Julia were discussing the matter when a visitor was announced. It was Thomas Courtleigh.

"Kent, you hurt the young woman I intend to marry. I pray to God the damage you did to her frail nature is not permanent. I am going to crush your family and your slut here, and I am going to crush you. Before God, I will do it all. That I swear."

INTERLUDE

On the night the Chicago fire began, Jeremiah Kent was in Abilene, Kansas, where he had turned his favorite pastime into a successful profession. He dealt poker, monte, and other games of chance.

The odds favored the dealer, and his customers were usually besotted when they played, which further heightened the dealer's advantage. Jeremiah drank too, at least a pint of gin a day, but he took care never to be as drunk as his customers.

He was now known as Jason Kane, and he had gained a

certain notoriety. Since Ellsworth, he hadn't put the guns away. Kola had told him the killing would never stop, and that too was turning out to be correct.

His latest victim was a young Texan, Timothy Stirling, whose uncle Jeremiah had killed when the man had tried to steal a load of freshly shot buffalo. He had foolishly spared the boy. The young man had sought Jeremiah ever since that time to avenge his uncle's death, only to be brought down by the man he had wanted to kill.

This time Jeremiah was ordered out of town by the marshal of Abilene, Wild Bill Hickok.

BOOK 3

Gideon's relations with Margaret did not improve upon his return from Chicago. He thought his taking a position on the *Union* would please her, but it did not. Matters between them simply grew worse, and they no longer shared a bedroom.

One night in November, the office of *Labor's Beacon* was burned out. In December, a fire at the printer's destroyed the completed press run of an issue attacking Courtleigh. Letters from Julia reported a pattern of increased harassment at her lectures. Surely, Courtleigh was behind it all.

Not quite two years later, Julia and Carter moved from their Chicago mansion. The panic of 1873 had sharply reduced her income. Gideon's money was safe, and he offered Julia whatever help she needed, but characteristically, she refused his offer.

Gideon had been doing well. He had been trying his hand at editorials and devoting himself to the business side of the enterprise. He had raised salaries and shortened working hours, thereby attracting better writing talent.

Julia's and Gideon's roles had reversed. When they first came together, she had been living affluently, and he and his family modestly. Now she had the bare essentials, while the publisher of the New York *Union* occupied a splendid new mansion on upper Fifth Avenue—a move undertaken to placate his wife, but one which had not fulfilled its purpose. Margaret's behavior was growing more erratic and hostile because of heavy drinking, which she now hardly bothered to conceal.

On a bright April afternoon in 1876, Julia rode into Deadwood Gulch on a Concord stage. A party of outriders accompanied the coach. Among them was a slender chap named Jason Kane, about thirty, who had the complexion of a heavy drinker. His manners were, however, excellent, and his smile was engaging. Julia had never met the man before, but there was something familiar about him.

Deadwood City was a hodgepodge of lean-tos and tents with a few pine buildings mixed in. Upon arriving, Julia was met with the news that her lecture had been canceled because a vile-tempered man named Lute Sims had promised to break it up. Back in Ohio, Sims's wife had become interested in the suffragist movement and had left him. Sims had never forgiven the organization that had prompted her behavior.

But Julia was determined to give her lecture, and things actually went well until Sims arrived. He held a shotgun in hands that were none too steady. He interrupted her speaking again and again with mounting invective, until finally he screamed, "You're a whore preaching a whore's doctrine!" and leveled his gun at her stomach.

"Shut up and turn around, you son of a bitch," said a voice from the dark behind Sims. Jason Kane stepped into the light. Julia was immensely thankful, but she was also disturbed by the amusement in Kane's eyes.

"Who the hell are you?"

"Name's Jason Kane. I want you to remember the name when they ask who sent you to hell." His revolver was out, and he aimed from the hip. The shot missed.

Sims yelped and dropped his gun as he ran. Kane shot. Shot again. Again. Until Sims dropped with four bullets in his back.

Gideon continued to live at Sixty-first Street and Fifth Avenue only because his children lived there. Will was now a stocky boy of seven. He struck Gideon as timid, unwilling to try anything new for fear he would upset his mother. Eleanor was his pride. She was going on fourteen and had taken a fancy to things theatrical, to which Margaret objected strongly.

Gideon and Margaret hadn't done more than touch in a perfunctory way for nearly five years. Lately, he had even started to think Will and Eleanor were growing less fond of him. He wondered whether Margaret had a hand in that.

Margaret hardly resembled the girl he had married in Richmond. She had put on thirty pounds, wore only the plainest of dresses, left the house only when absolutely necessary, and had no friends. Drinking had become an integral part of her life. Furthermore, her mind showed alarming symptoms of failing.

Gideon met Julia and Carter in Philadelphia for the opening of the Centennial Exhibition. Gideon had gone to the exhibition for the *Union* and was busy making notes about Alexander Bell's new invention, the telephone, when he had the sensation of being watched. He looked up to see Thomas Courtleigh staring at him.

Five years, Gideon thought. It had been that long since he had stormed into Courtleigh's mansion. And that act of bravado had accomplished nothing.

He hadn't thought of Courtleigh's threats for months. He had assumed the railroad president had forgotten them. Yet now, Courtleigh was staring at him with a fury as great as that he had demonstrated after the fire.

Gideon could verify the fact that newsmen got some of their best ideas at unexpected moments. While he was in Philadelphia, he passed a book shop in which were displayed commemorative volumes. He wished Kent and Son were represented, but the firm had produced no book in honor of the hundred years of . . . Instantly the whole idea was there. A book called *100 Years*. An expensive book produced with the finest typography, paper, and binding. One hundred engravings done by Matt, whose etchings were now highly esteemed and commanded high prices.

Since Gideon's return from the opening of the Centennial Exhibition, things had taken a new turn at home, Eleanor thought. He seemed to be making a special effort to be kind to Margaret. To all of them, in fact. But nothing really changed in his relationship with his wife. Margaret's periods of forgetfulness were recurring with greater regularity, and Will was becoming more withdrawn every day.

The only bright spot in Eleanor's life was what she called her Tuesday scheme. She always said that she was going to Charlie Whittaker's for tutoring in Latin. Actually, the two young people were attending meetings of the Booth Association, an acting society that met every Tuesday night. Among the young people was a handsome young man with a beautiful speaking voice whose confidence and determination attracted Eleanor to him. His name was Leo Goldman.

Gideon wanted a special present for his daughter's fourteenth birthday. He happened on the idea of elegantly binding the script of George Aiken's dramatization of *Uncle Tom's Cabin*. The popularity of the play had not diminished since its first performance in 1853.

Silver candelabra the length of the table lent the dining room a festive air on Eleanor's birthday, yet somehow Gideon knew the evening was foredoomed. Margaret was in a bad mood. Mercifully, the meal was quickly eaten.

Matters came to a climax when Gideon gave Eleanor his gift.

"It's a deluxe edition of *Uncle Tom's Cabin*," Eleanor cried out in delight.

Margaret bent forward. "The Stowe woman's novel? Let me see that." She grabbed the book and tore it open. "It's the play version."

Silence. A small log broke in the grate. Rain pelted the window.

"I saw no harm—" Gideon began.

"You did this to defy me. You know I won't permit this kind of thing in my home, this kind of filth. Anything connected with the theater is filthy!" She flung the book into the fireplace.

Gideon dismissed the children. Then an acrimonious interchange ensued, which ended with Gideon's saying, "You'll find it understandable if I'm no longer able to stay in this house with you."

From the minute Gideon moved out, Margaret became the unquestioned ruler of the household. Only a few hours after her husband's departure, she spoke to her butler. "I want to make doubly sure you bring the mail as each post arrives, Samuel. Bring it to my room. I want to see it all before anyone else does."

Margaret kept a diary, which she now began to think of as a person—an intimate and real confidante. She was given to periods of euphoria followed by depression, each calling for more and more whiskey. In addition, she began to have hallucinations along with her paranoia.

A delicate indiscretion with a peeress, which was discovered by Her Grace's husband, made it advisable for

Matt to leave England for a period. Upon the advice of friends, he returned to America and somewhat reluctantly entered into Gideon's plan for *100 Years*.

INTERLUDE

The press of business had kept Thomas Courtleigh from dealing with Gideon Kent the way he wanted to. A year or so earlier, he had sent one of his henchmen, Lorenzo Hubble, east to arrange for Gideon's murder, but Hubble had botched the attempt, and Gideon went unscathed.

Hubble was a slovenly, overweight young man. Self-educated, he was one of nine attorneys in the legal department of Courtleigh's line. He was not only ruthless; he was indiscreet.

Strikes threatened all major rail lines, and it was necessary for Courtleigh to take steps to see that his line wasn't struck. Anxious to ingratiate himself with his boss and to atone for bungling the attempt on Gideon's life, Hubble had almost four dozen blacklegs lined up.

"They're ready to go instantly if trouble spreads to Chicago. Among those I interviewed myself," Hubble told Courtleigh, "was one real find. Name's Jason Kane. He once had a big reputation out west. He's a sot, but he's tough. Killed nineteen men, they say. And I want to make a suggestion, too—that we not limit our reprisals against Mr. Kent. That we also consider his family."

BOOK 4

For his brother's sake, Matt hoped *100 Years* would be a success. He knew that Gideon was counting on the book to succeed because so much in his life was failing. Gideon's daughter refused to answer the conciliatory letters he doggedly mailed to her every four or five weeks because she felt Gideon had abandoned the family.

When the rail strike spread to Pittsburgh, Gideon went there to cover it for the *Union*. He was gunned down by men sent by Courtleigh, but he recovered from the wounds in his side.

While he was in the hospital, three men entered the house on upper Fifth Avenue and sexually assaulted Eleanor, who survived the pain and degradation. Margaret was miraculously able to send Will to a place of safety. But as she turned to face the assailants, her mind snapped, and she began screaming in a way that made the men exchange hesitant looks. As she ran away from them, she stumbled against a window at the end of the hall and fell through it. She howled and flailed as she fell, and her head rolled under her body just before the impact. Her neck broke, and she died.

When Gideon left the hospital in Pittsburgh, he went directly to the house. Eleanor was standing outside.

"Hello, Father" was all she said, but contempt animated her face when Will ran toward Gideon and threw himself into his father's arms.

Matt came down from Boston for the funeral, and Eleanor was enthralled by her uncle. Matt found her a curious girl, especially when he saw her look at her father with something close to loathing.

As the mourners were being driven back to the house

after the funeral, Gideon spoke to Eleanor. "I believe that you and I—"

"Papa," she broke in, "we have nothing to say to each other."

"Eleanor, I'm sick of your disrespectful ways and your accusing looks. There is no reason for either."

"No reason, Papa? She might be alive right now if you had behaved properly."

Gideon began to protest, but he knew he was only alienating her the more. "Will it calm things and help us start on a better footing if I admit I made many, many mistakes? If I accept my share of the blame?"

"You deserve all the blame. You never even wrote a line to find out whether we were still alive."

"But I did. I must have sent you a dozen letters. Begging you to come down to the *Union*. I was willing to meet you anywhere so that we could patch up our differences."

"That's a convenient lie now that Mama's gone."

"I swear to God I wrote you! Surely, someone in the house saw the letters."

She shook her head. "I kept asking Samuel, but there weren't any."

"Then somehow your mother must have intercepted them. It's the only explanation."

"Oh, Papa, that's cruel."

He had failed. Eleanor hated him. She always would. He could no longer put all the guilt on Margaret. He must shoulder his share, because it was deserved. The pain of it made the wound in his side a scratch, a trifle, nothing.

That evening, Gideon accompanied Margaret's casket to Boston. Margaret would be interred in the family plot in Watertown.

During his absence, Eleanor resolved to leave home. She had been offered a role in Jefferson Bascom's *Uncle Tom's* troupe. Leo Goldman would also be in the company.

"Leaving?"

Gideon's voice mingled consternation with disbelief. His ears had tricked him. She couldn't have said she was joining a theatrical troupe.

He rose so hastily from his chair that a table beside it overturned, spilling the copy of *100 Years* that Matt had just delivered. Matt was going back to England on Monday evening.

"Yes, Papa, leaving. I decided it was best for all of us."

"I don't know what you mean, best for all of us. It certainly isn't best for you. Girls your age don't just walk in and announce they're leaving home!"

She flared suddenly. "I don't want or need your permission. I could have run away without telling you."

"Eleanor, sit down. I beg you."

"I have no time to sit. I'm due at the New York Central depot in half an hour. It's a traveling troupe."

"Good Lord. Think, Eleanor. It's a wretched, disorderly life."

Very quickly, she replied, "It can't be any more wretched or disorderly than the life in this house."

Despite his pleas and arguments, Gideon could not dissuade his daughter. As she left the house, Gideon asked, "Will you write us?"

"Of course, Papa. Just as often as you wrote to me after you left."

Gideon had ordered all of Margaret's personal effects to be burned, and he had asked Julia to have nothing to do with the matter. Julia insisted, however, that the dead woman's clothes, for example, could be given to the poor. And thus it was that Julia, in going through Margaret's things, found all of Gideon's letters to his children, which Margaret had intercepted. She also discovered the diary in which Margaret revealed her hatred and deceit, and the steady deterioration of her mind.

Gideon wanted to consign the letters and the diary to the flames, but Julia convinced him to show them to

Eleanor. Perhaps this would reconcile the girl to him.

Gideon raced down to the depot and put the vindicating evidence into Eleanor's hand. As she perused the letters, her expression softened. Then with tears streaming down her face, she flung her arms around his neck and hugged him hard for one supremely joyous instant. "Papa, I love you!"

Late that afternoon, Gideon suffered violent pains in the wound he had received in Pittsburgh. The doctor ordered him to bed for four days.

Two days later, Matt came to bid his brother farewell. Although Gideon wanted to go to the dock with him, he had to be content to send Julia in his place.

As Julia was leaving the wharf to return home, a beggar came up to ask for money. When Julia started to open her reticule, a sliver of metal flashed in the sunset and the man rammed a knife through Julia's dress into her stomach.

Orderlies in white aprons moved up and down the hallway where Carter and Will waited. The boys had been sitting on the bench for nearly five hours.

A few minutes later, Gideon emerged from the nearby ward. "Any change, sir?"

"It may be hours or days before there's a change one way or another. You're too old for me to lie to you, Carter. Her condition is extremely serious. Her chances are very slim."

At sunrise, Gideon persuaded the boys to go home while he kept vigil. He then went back to Julia's bed and presently fell asleep in a chair. When the doctor awakened him, he said, "Mr. Kent, you had better go home. It may be days. There is nothing you can do."

He saw Thomas Courtleigh's face. *Yes, there is.*

"All right. I'll go home."

"Out of town at a time like this?" Theo Payne asked.

"You're going to Chicago, aren't you?"

Gideon didn't answer.

At a station in Indiana, Gideon telegraphed the *Union*. He wanted them to wire him in Chicago of Julia's condition.

In the room outside Thomas Courtleigh's office, Gideon said he wished to see the president, and was told by a clerk, "You'll have to allow Mr. Freeman to search you. It's a policy we have been forced to institute since demonstrators broke in here."

A burly man stepped to Gideon's side and patted him here and there while addressing the clerk. "When's Kane coming back? I haven't had breakfast yet. Where the hell is he? Coughing his guts out again? I don't like working around a man who's that sick."

The president's office was huge and impressive, but the furnishings were cheerless; so were the two unsmiling men staring at Gideon. One was an obese young fellow.

Thomas Courtleigh tented his fingers. "I'm genuinely astonished, Kent. I never imagined you'd have the audacity to call here. Surely you didn't travel all the way to Chicago to speak to me?"

"But I did. I'm a little surprised you'd admit me to this office, Courtleigh."

"Mr. Courtleigh thought it might be amusing," said the obese young man. Gideon looked him over. He didn't think he would cause much trouble, but he'd have to strike quickly before the guard got back.

Sure enough, what he had hoped for was right in front of him—a steel letter opener. If driven with sufficient force, Gideon was sure it could kill.

Courtleigh began to speak, but Gideon ignored him, focusing on the obese man.

"Oh, Mr. Kent, Mr. Hubble, one of our attorneys."

Gideon nodded. "I know the name. My daughter heard it the night of July 22 from one of the men who broke into the house and killed my wife."

Hubble shot a worried look at his employer and then blustered, "Do you think I'm the only man in Amcrica with that name? You said July 22. I was right here in Chicago."

"I've already checked into that story," Gideon replied, "and I don't believe it."

Then he turned to Courtleigh. "You've done what you promised six years ago. I never thought you'd carry through, but sick man that you are, you did. You've covered your tracks so you can't be touched. Unless someone's willing to settle with you on a personal basis."

"Settle?"

"Settle," Gideon said, pronouncing it very clearly. "And pay the consequences afterward. I am willing."

"Surely this is a joke!"

"After all those things you did to me and my loved ones? Hardly."

"Lorenzo, you'd better get Freeman or Kane."

"He can't be armed, Mr. Courtleigh."

Gideon continued. "I wanted to meet you face to face to see if you would deny all those things you were responsible for."

"Deny what I did—in this office? Of course not. You deserved every bit of it. And more!"

Gideon's control broke. He shot his left hand out and caught Courtleigh's throat, and with his right hand he seized the blade on the desk. Courtleigh was soft. Gideon had no trouble dragging him forward with one hand as he pressed the blade against his throat with the other.

Then Gideon saw a pistol in Hubble's hand. As Hubble aimed at point-blank range, Gideon released Courtleigh and flung himself right. He heard the office door crash open an instant before the pistol thundered.

"You stupid, stupid . . ." Courtleigh gasped. There were tears in his eyes as he fell forward. Hubble's bullet had found the wrong victim.

Hubble looked at Gideon and then flung the pistol. It hit the carpet and skidded up near Gideon's braced hand.

"Get the police. He killed Mr. Courtleigh. You all saw it, and you'll testify to it, won't you?"

"I won't testify to that, Hubble. You shot him. I saw you do it, you dishonorable son of a bitch."

Slowly, Gideon raised his head. He knew he must have gone insane—become a damned, deranged man who heard his dead brother's voice, who saw his dead brother's face.

Suddenly, Hubble went for the gun and lunged at Jeremiah. Jeremiah reached for his gun, but it was tangled in the lining of his coat. Hubble fired and hit Jeremiah in the middle. Jeremiah got his revolver loose at last and fired. Hubble stumbled back and crashed against one of the windows.

Jeremiah lay on the anteroom carpet. It was wonderful and peaceful to know it was all finished.

"Jeremiah, Jeremiah, how did you get here?" Gideon said in a hoarse voice. "We thought that after Altanta—"

"Oh," Jeremiah said, "that's a long story, as they say."

And one I'd be ashamed to have you hear.

Suddenly the pain pierced him. "Oh, Gid—hold onto me."

Gideon was too numb to feel much as they escorted him out of the building. He wasn't a prisoner. One of the officers even apologized for the shabbiness of the transportation they could provide to accompany him to the station.

He stopped first by the telegraph office. A message was there from Theo Payne. It read, "She will live."

American Empire

Background to THE LAWLESS

American tastes in the fine arts during the 1860s and '70s tended toward the explicit—paintings that told a conventional story, pointed a comfortable moral, or reproduced with photographic accuracy familiar faces and scenes. The artists who did most to set the patterns of taste were the illustrators of the popular magazines and weeklies.

But Americans were also beginning to have the opportunity to see the best paintings and sculpture of Europe's past. The newly rich business tycoons zealously patronized art and artists and made it their duty to assemble as a part of their process of acquiring culture the finest collection their money could purchase. They were convinced—or were led to believe by their agents—that the only art worthy of the name was European. These men usually displayed their acquired treasures in their homes, but occasionally they did more, such as establishing art galleries or museums of fine art. Eventually, nearly all the important collections found their way into public depositories.

At the close of the Civil War, not a single American city could boast a first-rate art gallery, but by 1900 there was at least an adequate gallery or museum in every major city.

Although Americans were getting around to having museums and giving traditional forms their due respect, they were not yet up to artistic innovation. They were just learning the rules; it was too early to break them. Paris was the place for that.

Paris was already more than two thousand years old when Matthew Kent arrived there, and for the preceding seven hundred years had enjoyed great prestige. For centuries, talented students had been flocking there—from St. Thomas Aquinas to Dante to Roger Bacon. Matthew was in the City of Light just when it was undergoing a radical change.

In the third and fourth decades of the nineteenth century Paris had suffered a crisis caused by a wave of migration that crowded the poorer areas to bursting. Just over a million in 1846, the city had a population of nearly two million twenty-five years later. This upsurge in population was in part due to the Industrial Revolution and the coming of the railroad.

The Second Empire responded to the challenge of overpopulation with an unprecedented effort at reorganization. Paris still bears the marks of this; and it is impossible not to admire its scope and efficacy while deploring its limitations and its weaknesses. Napoleon III chose the course, and it was pursued relentlessly by Baron Georges Eugène Haussmann.

Areas were "opened up"—that is, countless buildings of historical and architectural worth were razed; and the ancient character of Paris was lost forever to provide modernity, comfort, and bourgeois dignity.

Standardized architectural designs appeared at fifth- or sixth-floor level, and cast-iron balconies provided a line of ornament that replaced the cornice of earlier times. The use of iron in architecture met with great success and was regarded as a symbol of the age, reaching its apotheosis—depending one one's taste—in the erection in

1889 of the Eiffel Tower for the centenary of the French Revolution.

Haussmann's standardization was intelligently—albeit brutally—carried out, linking great new buildings to one another by straight, wide, tree-lined streets. A geometric network of thoroughfares was forcibly superimposed on the earlier irregularity of the city. In the old Paris, clearly defined formal parks and open spaces contrasted with the labyrinth of tortuous streets with their profusion of detail and character. In the new Paris, the situation was reversed: streets were built wide and straight, while gardens and parks tended towards a studied irregularity and disorder. The new open spaces were carefully laid out. The Bois de Boulogne was entirely redesigned; and for the populous areas of the eastern reaches of Paris there was the Bois de Vincennes. All across the city smaller gardens or squares were constructed.

As Paris acquired a new architectural façade, other aesthetic forces were at work, especially in the world of painters, where a certain revolution was under way for which Matthew Kent was temperamentally suited and in which he participated with characteristic intensity. Despite his avowed, but not always convincing, anti-Americanism, it was those qualities usually considered typical of Americans of the time—independence, inventiveness, even brashness—that allied Matt with such painters as Monet, Renoir, Pissarro, Sisley, Degas, Cézanne, and Berthe Morisot—the Impressionists.

The first major act of defiance of this small group was to ignore the official salon of the École des Beaux Arts in Paris and organize an exhibit of their own in 1874. That is not to say Impressionism began that year; the style took root twenty years before this exhibition, so by 1874 these painters were no longer awkward beginners. All of them were over thirty and had back of them fifteen or more years of hard work. They had studied, or attempted to do so, at the École des Beaux Arts and had sought advice from the older generation of painters.

A View along the River Seine, Paris, 1870
Edouard Manet 1869
The poor of Paris – a "rag-and bone" man, 1870
The Tuileries Palace – Parisian Residence of the Imperial Family 1869

The reaction of visitors and critics to the Impressionists' first exhibition was not friendly. They were accused of painting differently from the accepted method simply to gain attention, even to perpetrate a hoax on an innocent public. It took years before the group was able to convince the art world of their sincerity, not to mention their talent.

The word *impressionism* had been used occasionally in art criticism before Monet attached it to the style of his picture of a sunrise and made an honest word out of it. When first employed by critics, the word was derisive; it connoted incompleteness and superficiality. Ultimately, it came to be applied to paintings that were created in terms of tone rather than in terms of objects themselves.

The Impressionists did not analyze form, but only received the light reflected from that form and sought to reproduce the effect of that light rather than the form of the object reflecting it. For example, if the painter saw a tree in the distance as a green blur, he painted it as a green blur, even though he knew the tree so well he could paint it in exact detail from memory.

Impressionism as a school of painting is the climactic expression of the nineteenth century. It incorporates the conflicting schools of the first half of the century and fuses them into a way of painting from which the art of the twentieth century develops—partly as a continuation of it, partly as a reaction against it.

While the Impressionists were inspiring outrage among French traditionalists and attracting American expatriates like the obstreperous James Whistler and, a bit later, John Singer Sargent, Winslow Homer was busy at home in America being "the most intensively American painter of his time."

He never had a teacher. Boston and Cambridge, where he lived as a young man, had no academy, no museum, no school of art. His native talent led him to an apprenticeship in a lithographer's shop. From there, he went into the service of the illustrated periodicals of the day, and in 1861, *Harper's Weekly* hired him to cover Lincoln's inauguration as an artist-reporter.

During the war, he made several trips to the front, where he made sketches. After the war, he converted several of these to oil, and several received instant acclaim. Two shown at the Universal Exposition, one of the world's fairs that were the peculiar creation of the nineteenth century, in Paris in 1867 received praise from the French and English critics.

By this time, he was painting children and young people at work or play in rural settings. The realism of his Whittieresque freckled Yankee boys and healthy maidens in calico did not please everyone. One of his severest critics was Henry James, who found his works "damnably ugly," but of course James, like Matt, had a credo that required everything American to be wrong.

It is a fact of artistic discovery that identical interests often develop simultaneously, although independently, of each other, without the one ever having known the existence of the other. Many of Homer's early pictures, notably such works as *Gloucester Farm* and *Long Branch*, show the same concern with light that appears in the work of the Impressionists; yet it is doubtful that he was aware of the controversial French school at this stage of his development.

In his middle period, Homer abandoned the bucolic scenes that offended James's patrician urbanity and turned to dramatic representations of men and women confronting the elements, particularly the raging seas.

His late works were mostly watercolors, the perfect medium for his swift grasp of reality. With bold, rapid strokes of transparent color he could catch the freshness of a scene in a way he could never quite achieve in oil.

American painting of later decades tended to avail itself more and more of American materials. At a time when the Old West as Jeremiah knew it—full of cowboys and Indians, hard-bitten soldiers and free-wheeling gunfighters—was beginning to slip into history, painters like Frederic Remington were working feverishly to preserve it on canvas, in faithful but also highly romantic and evocative pictures. Though Remington worked at the end of the century, it was the reality of the 1870s and earlier that he was seeking: the final years of the open range, a period of wild expansion and exploitation, before the settled ways of farming and town life took over. His paintings are the quintessential vision of a uniquely American scene.

Another uniquely new American development was baseball. Matthew Kent was as devoted to baseball as he was to painting. The period following the Civil War found many Americans, especially those of the urban middle class and those in the professions, with both the money and the leisure time to gratify their desire for pleasure and recreation. One of the chief sources of this gratification was athletics, especially organized spectator sports for the entertainment of audiences.

The most popular of all the sports, well on its way to becoming the national game, was baseball. Tradition says it originated in 1839 in Cooperstown, New York, when Abner Doubleday, a civil engineering student, laid out a diamond-shaped field in an attempt to standardize the rules of such games as town ball and four old cat, the precursors of modern baseball. By 1865, over two hundred teams, or ball clubs, existed. Many had begun touring the country playing rivals; they were all members of a national association of players who had established a set of standard rules. These early teams were amateur or semiprofessional, but as the game increased in popularity, it offered opportunity for making money. The first professional team was the Cincinnati Red Stockings in 1869. The reader will recall Matt's interest in them.

Other cities soon supported teams, and in 1876, the present National League was organized. A rival league, the American Association, soon appeared. Competition between the two was intense, and in 1883, they played a

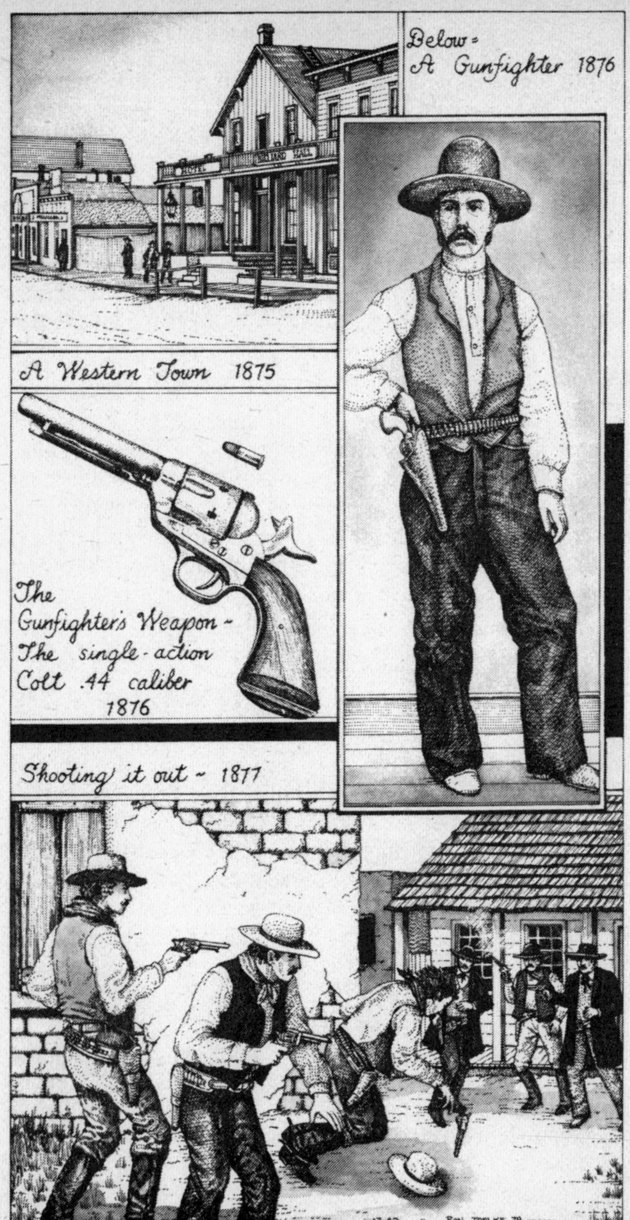
Below =
A Gunfighter 1876
A Western Town 1875
The
Gunfighter's Weapon -
The single-action
Colt .44 caliber
1876
Shooting it out ~ 1877
17-42
RON TOELKE 79

postseason game, the first World Series. The American Association eventually collapsed, but in 1900 the American League appeared.

The second most popular game, football, had its origins on university and college playing fields, and during its early years was limited to intramural competition. The first intercollegiate game in this country was between Princeton and Rutgers in 1869, when each institution sent twenty-five men onto the field. Within a short time, other colleges developed teams for intercollegiate competition. The American Intercollegiate Football Association was organized in an attempt to standardize rules.

In 1873, Julia Sedgwick lost her money in a depression caused by the overexpansion of the economy after the Civil War. The effects of this depression were not limited to urban areas; farmers suffered as severely as their city brethren. In fact, for the first time American farmers saw benefits in organization. And that organization had a profound effect on railroad owners, especially unscrupulous ones like Thomas Courtleigh.

To see how this happened, it is necessary to go back to the late 1860s, when officials of the Department of Agriculture, concerned by the isolation and drabness of farm life, founded the National Grange of the Patrons of Husbandry, now commonly called the Grange. Its purposes were social, cultural, and educational; and although it filled obvious needs, it attracted few members. Then in 1873, when the necessity for organization was felt, membership in the Grange jumped to over eight hundred thousand.

As the depression grew worse, the lodges, as the local units of the Grange were called, turned to economic issues. They stressed the necessity of eliminating the middleman through the use of cooperatives and the urgency of political action to curb the monopolistic practices of railroads like the Wisconsin and Prairie.

Grange members labored to elect to state legislatures men pledged to bringing the railroads under social control. Operating through the established political parties, they won majorities in Illinois, Iowa, Minnesota, and Wisconsin, and in these states between 1870 and 1874 enacted laws to regulate railroads and warehouse and grain elevator facilities. These "Grange laws" authorized maximum rates for freight and passenger traffic, provided rules and rates for the storing of grain, and prohibited a number of alleged discriminatory practices. They were administered and enforced by special state commissions.

The railroads contested the legality of the laws from state courts to the United States Supreme Court and eventually succeeded in destroying their effectiveness. The railroads accomplished their ends through complicated legal procedures and with the help of new justices friendly to property rights and hostile to state power.

The Civil War ushered in big business, but the laborer that made it possible shared in little of its benefits.

A dehumanization of employer-employee relations was taking place. Before the war, the worker might have toiled for very little in a small plant, but the owner at least knew him by name and might even, as he hailed him in the morning, inquire after the health of his wife. But now the factory worker was employed by an impersonal and often conscienceless corporation. The directors didn't know him. They couldn't in fairness to their stockholders engage in large-scale philanthropy, and, moreover, felt under no moral obligation to do so.

Forced in self-defense to organize and fight for their rights, workers struggled in an uphill battle. Employers had the money to retain costly lawyers, control the local press, and put pressure on politicians. More often than not they also imported strikebreakers, known as scabs, and hired armed thugs to beat up labor organizers.

Labor unions in 1861 were few and badly organized,

but the Civil War gave them a strong boost. The terrible drain on manpower in this conflict put a premium on laborers, and the high cost of living after the war provided an urgent incentive to unionize. By 1872, there were several hundred thousand organized workers and thirty-two national unions, which included such crafts as bricklaying, typesetting, and shoemaking.

The National Labor Union, organized in 1866, was a giant step forward for workingmen. It attracted well over a half million workers, including farmers. Its goal was social reform, although it agitated for an eight-hour day and the arbitration of industrial disputes and succeeded in winning a shorter working day for government workers.

The devastating depression of the 1870s dealt labor movements a deadly blow. Moreover, the public was annoyed by recurrent strikes, some of which were so violent as to verge on civil war.

A new organization replaced the defunct National Labor Union. Called the Noble Order of the Knights of Labor, it had all the trappings of a fraternal order. It began in 1869 as a secret society with a ritual, a password, and a secret handshake. The secrecy, which continued until 1881, was intended to forestall possible reprisals by employers.

The Knights of Labor zealously sought to include all workingmen in one union. They welcomed skilled and unskilled laborers, men and women, black and white, and excluded only liquor dealers, professional gamblers, lawyers, prostitutes, bankers, and stockbrokers.

Under the leadership of an Irish immigrant, Terence V. Powderly, who had remarkable powers of oratory, the Knights won a number of concessions. Soon they claimed a million members and were a force to be reckoned with.

But they were riding for a fall. They became involved in a number of May Day strikes in 1886, only about half of which succeeded. The focal point was Chicago, where there were about eighty thousand Knights. The city was also honeycombed with several hundred anarchists, most

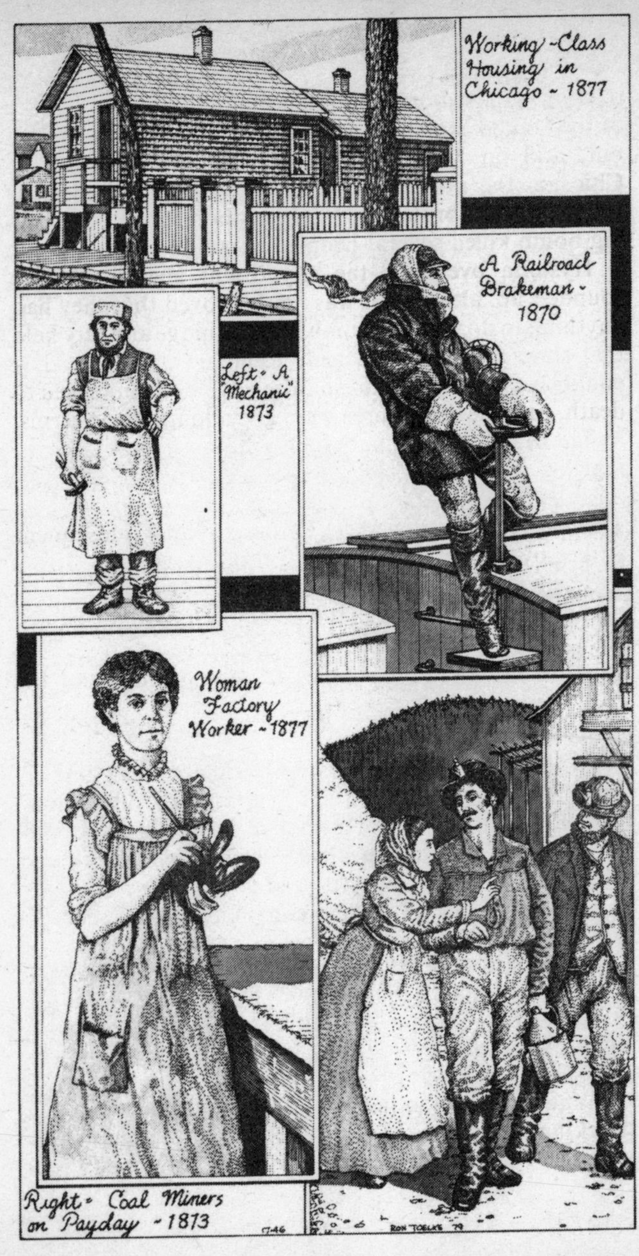
Working-Class
Housing in
Chicago ~ 1877
A Railroad
Brakeman ~
1870
Left ~ A
"Mechanic"
1873
Woman
Factory
Worker ~ 1877
Right ~ Coal Miners
on Payday ~ 1873
17-46
RON TOELKE 79

of them foreign-born, who advocated a violent overthrow of the United States government. Labor disorders broke out, and on May 4, 1886, in Haymarket Square in Chicago, the police advanced on a meeting called to protest alleged brutalities by the authorities. An exploding bomb killed several people, including a policeman.

Hysteria overcame the city. Eight anarchists were rounded up, although it was never proved that they had anything to do with the bomb. But the judge and jury held that since they had preached incendiary doctrines, they could be charged with conspiracy. Five were sentenced to death, and the other three were given long prison terms.

The Haymarket Square bomb did nothing to help the Knights of Labor. From that time on they were, albeit mistakenly, associated in the public mind with anarchy. The eight-hour movement suffered, and subsequent strikes by the Knights met with little success.

The Knights were succeeded by the American Federation of Labor, which was the creation of a London-born cigar maker, the colorful Samuel Gompers. From 1886 to 1924, except for one year, he was president of the A. F. of L.

Gompers was not a wild-eyed radical like the injudicious Sime Strelnik, but an eminently practical man who soft-pedaled attempts to engineer sweeping social reform. He was an enemy of socialism who had no quarrel with capitalism; he simply wanted labor to win its fair share.

Labor disorders continued throughout the years from 1881 to 1900, during which there was an alarming total of twenty-three thousand strikes involving over six million workers and representing to both employers and employees a loss of half a billion dollars. Strikers lost about half their strikes and won or compromised the remainder.

While workers struck for higher wages and better working conditions, management continued amassing wealth. Those who were foremost in that pursuit have

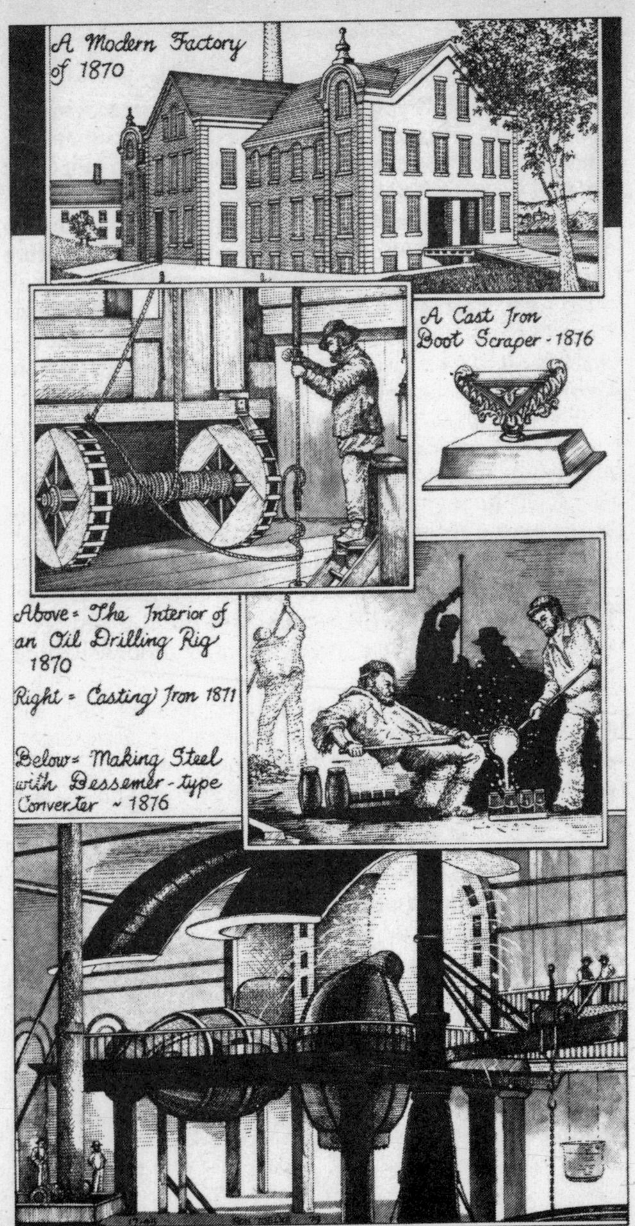
A Modern Factory of 1870
A Cast Iron Boot Scraper - 1876
Above = The Interior of an Oil Drilling Rig 1870
Right = Casting Iron 1811
Below = Making Steel with Bessemer-type Converter ~ 1876

come to be known as the robber barons, a justly fitting epithet. To treat them as a class, however, is to overlook their individualism. They differed from each other to a greater degree than the ordinary American of the time differed from his fellow citizen.

They were all acquisitive men with extraordinary energy, singleness of purpose, and audacity. A few were foreign-born; Astor came from Germany, Guggenheim from Switzerland, Du Pont from France, and Carnegie from Scotland. But for the most part they were native Americans whose forebears had come to America from Great Britain and northern Europe generations earlier.

These "rogues" comprised three categories—promoters, bankers, and industrialists, the last of which included merchants. Jay Cooke (of unhappy memory for Julia Sedgwick in 1873), J. P. Morgan, and James Stillman were bankers. The major promoters were James Fisk, Jay Gould, Daniel Drew, John Warne Gates, Thomas William Lawson, Henry H. Rogers, Henry Morrison Flagler, and Samuel Insull. Among the industrialists were Andrew Carnegie, John D. Rockefeller, Robert S. McCormick, Philip Armour, Henry Clay Frick, Henry Ford, and the Du Ponts. The Guggenheims were both promoters and industrialists, and Andrew Mellon covered the entire field. James Jerome Hill, Edward Henry Harriman, Henry Villard, George Pullman, and the first two Vanderbilts were great railroad men, virtually in a class by themselves.

As individuals, these "robber barons" defy classification. For example, Drew and Fisk were country boys, but there the comparison ends. All during his long life Drew dressed and played the part of a country bumpkin, whereas Fisk was ostentatiously a playboy. Carnegie loved publicity, while Rockefeller did not care to see his name in the papers, and Andrew Mellon, a very rich man indeed, was little known outside of his native Pittsburgh until he became Secretary of the Treasury. Henry Clay Frick was inaccessible, whereas Philip Armour was easily approached. George Pullman was notoriously arrogant, and James Hill was the most irascible of them all. He is reported to have fired an employee simply because he found his last name of Spittles offensive. Jay Cooke had a reputation for honest dealing, kindliness, and consideration.

Some of the most unsavory legends attach to the Big Four of California—Leland Stanford, Collis P. Huntington, Charles Crocker, and Mark Hopkins.

These men made deals, purchased immunity, behaved abominably. Yet during their day, they were considered "smart businessmen." Today, laws protect Americans from fellow citizens like J. P. Morgan, who, when stalled in New York traffic, commanded his chauffeur to charge ahead by way of the sidewalk.

While these robber barons fought their way to the top, their womenfolk coaxed them into erecting great houses, especially in New York City, where the *grandes dames* of high society could conduct their business with the same arrogance, determination, and ruthlessness that their menfolk conducted theirs.

The city was marching northward rapidly. Mansions were being built on Fifth Avenue as far up as Thirty-fourth Street, but to New Yorkers returning from long residences in European capitals, the city as yet seemed scarcely metropolitan. They were distressed by its architectural ugliness, untended streets, and endless blocks of identical narrow houses.

The new opulence was exemplified by fancy establishments like Delmonico's, where a typical meal usually began with oysters or cherrystone clams with a Montrachet for wine. Then there was a choice of soups, one always being terrapin. The wine with this course was a dry sherry. Next came fish and an excellent German vintage. Then appeared the first of several meat courses: filets of beef in the inevitable Madeira sauce. That required a Burgundy. The saddle of lamb—strangely, by today's tastes—was accompanied by champagne. Vegetables appeared in profusion—peas, stuffed tomatoes, potatoes in some fanciful form. The vegetable course gave way to more meat, perhaps sweetbreads: then back to something like asparagus in mayonnaise or a succulent mushroom dish. At this point appeared a *sorbet*, usually made of dry wine or fruit juices with some acidity, to "clean" the palate in preparation for game or fowl. According to the meat that was served, more wine was poured—Burgundy or claret. Salads and cheeses appeared before an onslaught of desserts and fruits. Coffee, brandy, and liqueurs brought an end to a meal that began at eight and never ended before eleven.

Fancy-dress balls occupied much of the time of the very rich. The most luxurious affair of its kind was given by Mrs. William Kissam Vanderbilt in her mansion on Fifth Avenue and Fifty-second Street, which was an ornate fusion of several incongruous architectural traditions. The costumer Lanouette made one hundred and fifty of the outfits at a cost of more than thirty thousand dollars. One hundred and forty dressmakers worked around the clock for five weeks.

Mrs. Vanderbilt invited twelve hundred guests to this particular ball, which at a cost of over one quarter of a million dollars was a monument to all that was ostentatious in an era that found nothing vulgar in being as showy as a vast fortune would allow.

A visitor to New York in the 1870s went to the theater. Certain playhouses were nationally known, and no one wanted to return home not having visited at least one or two of them. Serious drama now had the highest moral sanction. Margaret Kent's disapproval of Eleanor's theatrical interest was already decidedly old-fashioned and provincial. As someone remarked at the time, "Actresses will happen in the best regulated of families." The theatrical center of the city was the stretch of Broadway between Madison Square and Forty-second

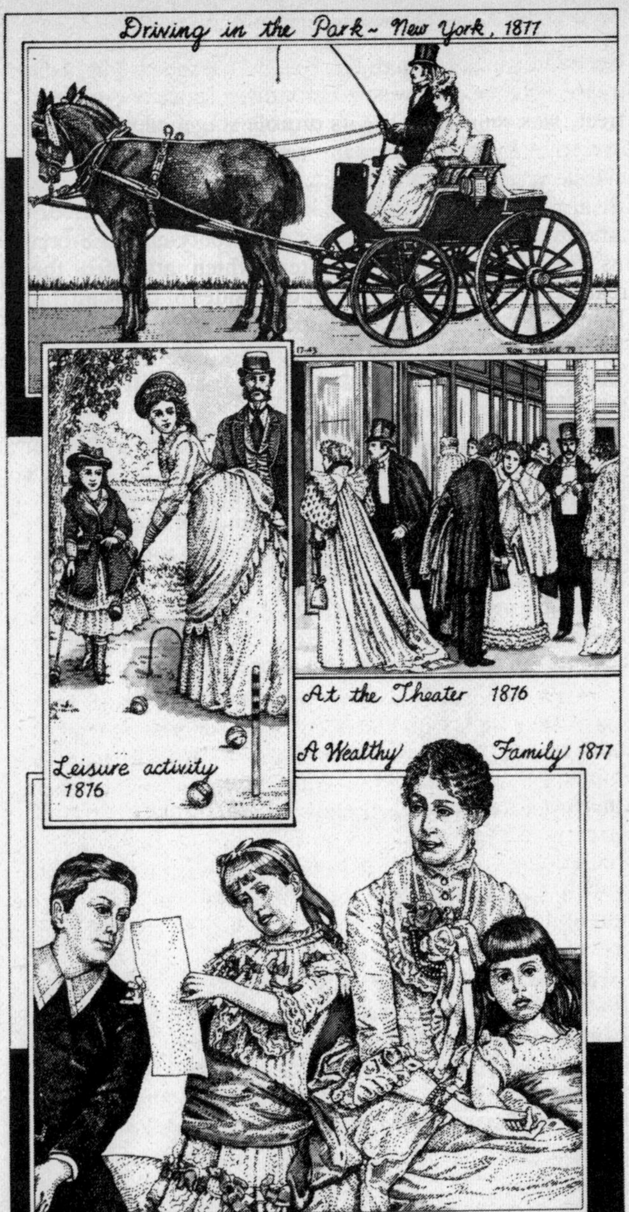

Driving in the Park ~ New York, 1877

At the Theater 1876

Leisure activity 1876

A Wealthy Family 1877

Street and was known as the Rialto. The small Madison Square Theater, just west of Broadway on Twenty-fourth Street, was renowned for its double stage, elevated and lowered by hydraulic pressure, which made scene changes possible in less than one minute. This mechanical wonder was always demonstrated to audiences after the performance. At the northwest corner of Twenty-eighth Street was the Fifth Avenue Theater, which attracted the greatest stars of the day. On opposite sides of the Rialto at Thirtieth Street were Daly's and the new Wallack's. At Thirty-third Street was the Standard, at Thirty-fifth the New Park. At Thirty-ninth was the vast Metropolitan Opera House.

Within a few years of Eleanor's joining an Uncle Tom troop for performances in the provinces, New Yorkers saw on their stages such actresses as Lillie Langtry, of unparalleled beauty from the island of Jersey; the American Mrs. James Brown Potter, who moved in the highest social circles; Mary Anderson from Kentucky, whose adoring public referred to her as "our Mary"; and the "divine Sarah Bernhardt," whom Henry James declared "too American not to succeed in America."

Gideon was in Philadelphia at the Centennial Exhibition in his professional capacity as a reporter for the *Union*. Newspapers and magazines provided most Americans' reading matter and would continue to do so at a greatly expanded rate for years to come. In 1870, the circulation of daily newspapers was about three million. By 1910, circulation had increased eightfold to twenty-four million. That was over three times as great as the increase in population.

Journalism was changing. Newspapers were becoming predominantly news organs; the editorial page and editorial opinion were declining in importance. Even the nature of news was changing. Politics received less and less attention as increased emphasis was put on what came to be known as the human-interest story. Journalism was emerging as a respected profession, resulting in the doubling of reporters' salaries and the establishment of schools of journalism in universities.

With the disappearance of personal journalism, newspapers became impersonal corporations not unlike those of industry. Their worth was often estimated to be in the millions of dollars. At the same time, newspapers were tending to become standardized, with press services furnishing the same news to all their subscribers. Syndicates came into existence to provide customers with identical feature stories, columns, editorials, and illustrations.

Overall, there was a distinct improvement in the appearance of newspapers. Pages of poorly and closely printed columns, each with its own headlines, gave way to a makeup rather like that of today's papers, with cartoons, illustrations, and imaginative advertising.

Changes were occurring in the book publishing business too, as it became more commercial and impersonal. At the time of the Civil War, book publishers sold their product by subscription only. But gradually they began selling through bookstores and reaching their buyers through advertising, until today book subscriptions are limited to the printing of very special editions.

At this point, American literature was moving toward a realistic reflection of the economic and social changes of the times. One of the outstanding novels of this kind was written by Mark Twain and Charles Dudley Warner in 1873. Called *The Gilded Age*, it satirized the men and manners of an industrial society and provided a name that is often applied to the last three decades of the nineteenth century.

Although New York City had by this time outstepped Boston as the publishing capital of the United States, there was a literary renaissance in the West and South as well as the East. Regional literature was enjoying a vogue.

Writers of the local-color schools thought of themselves as realists rebelling against the mawkish novels of such authors as Mary Jane Holmes, whose thirty-nine works sold over two million copies. The realists insisted on real people and plots and paid careful attention to details, but for all their honesty, their works were frequently superficial and often as sentimental and nonsensical as the novels they hoped to banish from contemporary bookshelves.

Chief among the popular authors of the day was Samuel Clemens, better known by his pen name Mark Twain. He began his career on a newspaper and long considered himself a journalist. The public insisted upon regarding him as a humorist, but he was primarily a novelist, probably the greatest American novelist in the years between 1864 and 1900. His first success came in 1869, *Innocents Abroad*, a scornful tale of European decay and hypocrisy and American adulation of European institutions. His greatest literary fame rests on *The Adventures of Tom Sawyer* (1876) and *The Adventures of Huckleberry Finn* (1885). These novels show not only a sympathetic understanding of life in mid-America but an insight into adolescent psychology that is unparalleled in literature.

Many writers of the day viewed with misgivings the culture of their times and deplored its materialism and economic inequalities. Had Matthew Kent's talents lain in writing instead of painting, he might well have contributed to this literature of protest. These dissenters were by and large more political than literary, and their books were mere fictionalized tracts that were unremittingly dreary.

A few novelists, such as Henry Adams in *Democracy* and John Hay in *The Bread-Winners* spoke for the old aristocracy. They deplored the crassness of the newly rich. In effect, all they were doing was expressing their resentment at having been dethroned.

No novelist of any importance concerned himself with the plight and hopes of labor until the last decade of the century, when Stephen Crane wrote *Maggie: A Girl of the Streets*, in which he described slum conditions and urban poverty with somber realism. For rural America, Hamlin Garland at the same time smashed the traditional idyllic picture of pastoral culture in *Main-Travelled Roads*, and in *The Story of a Country Town* Edgar W. Howe starkly depicted the narrow provincialism of the small American town. His was the first of a spate of such novels, culminating in Sinclair Lewis's *Main Street*, which won the Nobel Prize for Literature in 1930.

A few critics of the American scene, like Matthew Kent, retreated from its vigor and materialism and found refuge in Europe. Preeminent in this group was Henry James. Exactly like Matt, but in a different medium, he studied and described his country from abroad. In such novels as *The American* (1877), *An International Episode* (1878), and *Daisy Miller* (1879), he chronicled the impact of European culture upon visiting Americans. In these coldly realistic works, the Americans are usually frustrated or defeated by Europe; but nearly always they appear more virile and vigorous than the effete civilization they do not comprehend. A key to understanding where James stood might well be found in his confession during his later years that he wished he had remained in his native country.

Next to Mark Twain, the greatest novelist was William Dean Howells. His realism dealt with the common and the average. He was a careful historian of what was normal in America in the decades following the Civil War. In *The Rise of Silas Lapham*, published in 1885, he portrayed with shrewd insight and in not completely complimentary terms the mind and morals of the self-made businessman.

Before the Civil War, participants in the women's movement had concentrated on improving job opportunities, education, and the economic standing of women. After the war, their main efforts were addressed to securing the vote for women. It became a major goal because women saw that without the vote they had no political power, and without political power the lot of women stood no chance of improving.

After the Civil War, feminists were dismayed to see that while the Fourteenth Amendment guaranteed equal rights for black men, it appeared to deny them to black women—and all other women as well. For the first time the word *male* appeared in the Constitution, giving rise to the fear among some Americans that women were not considered citizens.

During the debate over the Fifteenth Amendment, which provides that the right to vote shall not be denied "on account of race, color, or previous condition of servitude," many feminists tried unsuccessfully to have women included in its provisions. Members of the first Equal Rights Association, the largest and most active feminist organization, were divided over this issue. Some believed that women should push as hard as they could for their rights; others felt women should be silent during the "Negro's hour."

Bitterness over this matter led to the dissolution of the Equal Rights Association. In 1868, Susan B. Anthony and Elizabeth Cady Stanton formed a new organization, the National Woman Suffrage Association. It favored pushing militantly for women's, as well as black, rights. The next year, under the leadership of Lucy Stone, less militant women formed the American Woman Suffrage Association. The main goal of both was the same, but their styles of operating were different.

The Anthony-Stanton group was involved in more than the vote for women; they fought for equality with men in jobs, education, and legal rights. They stirred up controversy and gained a reputation for radicalism. Lucy Stone's followers, on the other hand, concentrated solely on the issue of suffrage, working to encourage legislatures to pass suffrage bills. They were regarded as more respectable than the members of the National Woman

Suffrage Association. The two groups finally merged in 1890 to become the National American Woman Suffrage Association.

Three main tactics were applied to gain the vote—court actions, state laws, and a constitutional amendment.

In several elections between 1868 and 1872, women cast ballots in defiance of election laws with the intended purpose of bringing a test case before the Supreme Court to find out whether or not the provisions of the Fourteenth and Fifteenth amendments applied to women. In 1872, Miss Anthony and sixteen other women registered and voted in the presidential election. Miss Anthony was convicted of illegal voting, but before she could be tried, the court ruled in the case of Virginia Minor.

In 1873, the Supreme Court decreed that black men could not be denied the vote on account of race, because the Fourteenth Amendment had made them citizens. In Miss Minor's case, the court appeared to be reversing itself by ruling unanimously that women were citizens, but that citizenship did not give them the right of the franchise. That decision ended efforts to win the vote through court action. Feminist groups then turned toward state legislatures and the Congress for women's suffrage bills.

Some of the opposition to the vote for women centered on belief about the woman's place. Many people saw women as highly emotional, frail, childlike beings who would be corrupted by voting. Many of the polling places in nineteenth-century America bore a strong resemblance to saloons, and a number of the men who voted against women's suffrage did so because they thought women didn't belong in such places.

But such notions of propriety were hardly the compelling reasons against extending the franchise. Many opponents stood to lose power if women were allowed to vote, notably the liquor industry. The suffrage movement and the temperance movement had become linked in people's minds, if not in fact. Frances Willard, the leader of the Women's Christian Temperance Union, became an important advocate of women's suffrage. The conversion of thousands of temperance backers to the cause of suffrage aroused the fears of the liquor industry. Distillers used every means possible to defeat bills for women's suffrage.

Another group opposing women's suffrage was the factory owners in the industrial states. They were convinced women would support factory reform laws and that these would cut into profits. (It is interesting to note that the states that first gave the vote to women were not industrial—Wyoming, Utah, Colorado, and Idaho.)

The combined force of all these groups was enough to defeat most attempts at giving women the vote. Around 1900, the movement slowed down. The old leaders were dying, and the new leaders had not emerged. Activist women invested their time and energy in such social movements as trade unions and settlement houses. It would be August 26, 1920, before Julia Sedgwick's dream came true.

While this movement of great long-range significance was unfolding, there were other events of the 1870s that, in a more immediate way, seized the popular imagination. One of these was the great Chicago fire of 1871.

In the summer of 1871, less than an inch and a half of rain fell from July to October; the normal rainfall for the period was eight to ten inches. The entire city was dry as tinder—its factories, frame houses, wooden pavements, and plank sidewalks. These conditions were largely ignored, although just three years earlier a fire on Lake Street had caused millions of dollars in damage. The city had just built a new waterworks, and Chicagoans were confident that water for fire fighting would be available on a moment's notice.

Legend has it that one Mrs. Patrick O'Leary kept a

herd of five cows; and while she had gone into the house to fetch some salt for an ailing animal, one of them kicked over a lantern, setting fire to the barn.

There had been a good many relatively small fires that day which had kept fire companies hopping. Because of confusion at the central fire agency and the stubborn refusal of one of the operators to change a signal given in error, the fire that began about nine on a Saturday night in Mrs. O'Leary's barn spread unchecked.

By ten o'clock, a mass of burning material whirled four blocks through the air to the steeple of St. Paul's Roman Catholic Church. Within minutes, flames enveloped the entire church and then moved on to a neighboring factory. From there the fire leaped to a lumber mill on the banks of the Chicago River, where it was fed by a thousand cords of kindling, half a million feet of furniture lumber, and three-quarters of a million shingles.

All of a sudden, there were three separate fires. Two discrete columns of flame were moving northward to the lumber mill inferno, but before this consolidation could occur, the fire struck east of the river.

A new stable had just been completed on the southwest edge of the business district a quarter of a mile away from the holocaust on the west bank of the river. The lofts were filled with hay; fortunately, no horses had yet been moved in. In a conflagration of the magnitude of the Chicago fire, a kind of meteor display occurs, sending firebrands extraordinary distances. The new stable was hit and blazed up at once. Then the nearby gasworks were on fire.

By midnight Sunday, appeals had been made for fire-fighting equipment to be loaded on flatcars in Milwaukee, St. Louis, and Cincinnati to be rushed to Chicago. If the flames were to be stopped, a firebreak would be needed. Permission was given to blow up buildings in the path of the fire, but the operation was performed with more zeal than skill.

Meantime, the pace of the fire accelerated. The Cook County Courthouse burst into flames. As it did so, an

Fire-fighting equipment -
a Hose Cart 1871
Fashionable
Chicago - Michigan
Avenue 1871
Courthouse Square - 1:30 am
October 9th just as
the Court House
begins to burn
Below - The Chicago Riverfront
October 11th - Smoldering ruins
17-44
RON TOELKE 79

automatic mechanism set off a bell in the tower, which continued to clang monotonously until the building itself fell.

At Jackson and La Salle, the brand new Grand Pacific Hotel, made of Ohio sandstone, crashed to the ground before it had ever housed a guest, as did the equally new and opulent Bigelow Hotel. The Tremont House went up in flames for the fourth time in its history.

By this time, the flames had lighted the sky to the brilliancy of daylight, giving the entire city a lurid yellowish red color. Because of the intensity of the fire there was very little smoke, but there was a blizzard of hot cinders. Added to the terror was the danger of crazed animals dashing through the streets in a torture of pain from the hot ash that blistered even the toughest hides. In the heart of the fire, the heat was as intense as the flame of a welding torch. Iron columns two feet thick were calcined. Streetcar tracks melted into arabesques. Jets of fire bored holes through walls that were supposedly fireproof.

Crowds fled for their lives, and as they did so, looting began. Stolen beer and whiskey led to such unruliness that hoses had to be turned from the flames onto the crowds.

Later on Sunday, the fire leaped the river again and spread to a group of railway cars containing kerosine. Then a brand landed on the slate covering over the wooden roof of the waterworks. The entire building was soon on fire, and the pumps were destroyed. When the last reserve of water from the tower had been used up, the only water left for the city's fire lines was where it could be pumped from the river.

The fire continued, but with diminished force, until Monday night, more than twenty-five hours. Shortly before midnight, a light rain started to fall. Early Tuesday morning, the fire died out, but it had destroyed 2,124 acres in the central part of the city. It burned 17,450 dwellings, made 90,000 homeless, and destroyed property worth $200 million—one-third of the wealth of Chicago. Nearly three hundred people were known dead. How many others perished will never be known.

Tremendous disaster though it was, the Chicago fire did have one good effect: it gave rise to a tremendous surge of building in Chicago in the 1870s and 1880s, and it opened up opportunities for a whole generation of architects, chief of whom was Louis Sullivan. In these years, Chicago became the birthplace of modern civic architecture, a shining example of American energy and confidence.

Nowhere were American energy and ebullience more abundantly displayed, in the 1870s, than at the Philadelphia Centennial Exhibition of 1876. More than a collection of elaborate displays of art and industry, the exhibition was a symbol of the nation's pride in its past and its high expectations for the future—for a new golden age. By the time the great fair closed in November of 1876, almost ten million Americans had examined its exhibits and left with a confidence and optimism that was not totally unwarranted. The worst wounds of the Civil War had healed; even the former Confederate States were supporting the increase of federal powers. But more important, Americans had begun to manifest a certain national maturity.

The Centennial Exhibition was a wondrous display of the nation's ingenuity. Machines and inventions were by far the most popular of all the displays. Spectators marveled at the Corliss engine, which was billed as the eighth wonder of the world. The most powerful machine of its day, it generated up to 2,500 horsepower. Also among the spectacular array of machines was Alexander Graham Bell's first telephone. When the emperor of Brazil put its receiver to his ear, he exclaimed, "My God, it talks!"

Swiss chalets, minarets, and Gothic towers stood incongruously side by side. These grotesqueries of taste

A Trade Advertisement from the Centennial - 1876

The Great Corliss Engine in Machinery Hall 1876

The Torch of the Statue of Liberty on Exhibit at the Centennial Exposition 1876

Going to the Exposition 1876

The Main Exhibition Hall Fairmount Park, Philadelphia, 1876

were matched by such extraordinary displays as *Sleeping Iolanthe*—in butter. There was also the largest ceramic piece ever made, depicting America astride a bison. As a whole, the exhibition pointed out the superiority of America's machines over its art.

One great project that spanned the decade of the 1870s would ultimately be considered one of the century's finest expressions. The Brooklyn Bridge, begun in 1870 and completed in 1883, became a symbol of the new America. It was acclaimed almost at once as a triumph of modern engineering, but at first people wondered if it could be called beautiful. No effort had been made to disguise its structure, its modern materials, or its novel engineering principles. No ornament softened the strong, spare lines of the span; no sculpture or decoration relieved the severity of the towers. The Brooklyn Bridge was uncompromisingly utilitarian. Expatriates like Matt, who found their standards of beauty in the ancient cities of Europe, called the bridge arrogantly ugly, a defiant celebration of the raw, crude American civilization that they despised. They did not have the eyes to see that it was a new kind of beauty, indisputably American, and a portent of things to come in America's second hundred years.

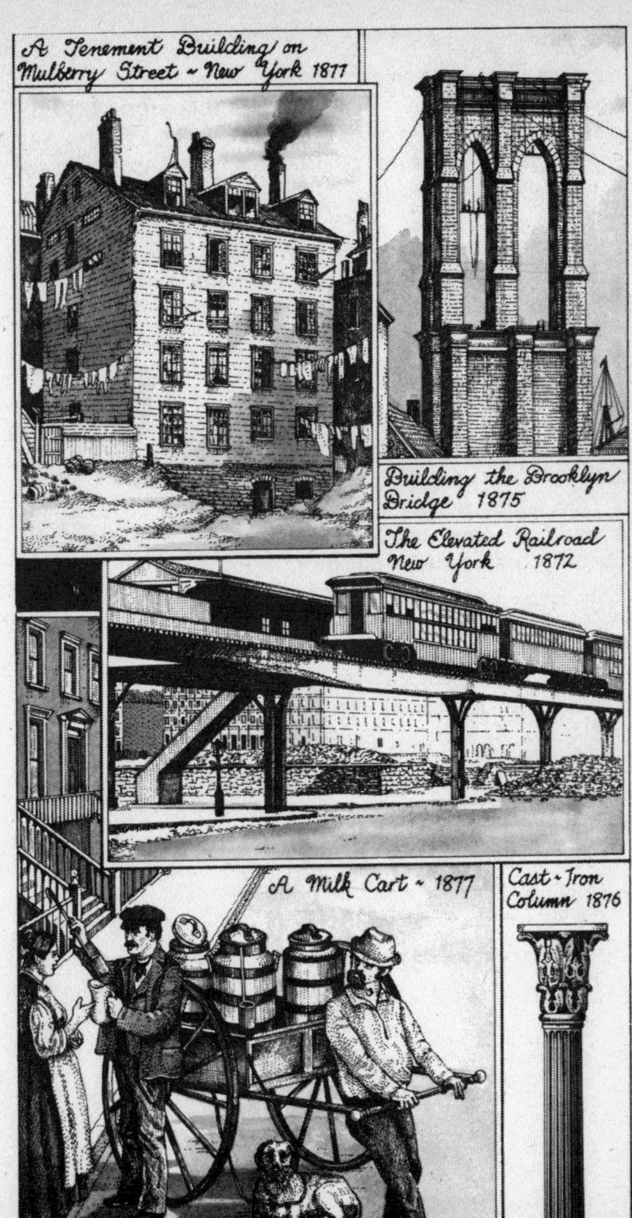

A Tenement Building on Mulberry Street ~ New York 1877
Building the Brooklyn Bridge 1875
The Elevated Railroad New York 1872
A Milk Cart ~ 1877
Cast ~ Iron Column 1876

Cast of Main Characters

Volumes of *The Kent Family Chronicles* in which each character appears are indicated thus:

B—*The Bastard*
R—*The Rebels*
S—*The Seekers*
F—*The Furies*
T—*The Titans*
W—*The Warriors*
L—*The Lawless*

Amberly, Roger. The Duke of Kentland's heir. Half brother of Philip Kent. Married to Lady Alicia Parkhurst. Died of wounds received in a struggle with Philip Kent. (B, R)

Arbuckle, Rodney. Soldier in the First Virginia Cavalry. The first of Gideon Kent's comrades to fall in battle. (T)

Bascom, Jefferson. Actor-manager of the Uncle Tom troupe with which Eleanor Kent traveled. (L)

Benbow, William, Jr. Head of Boston law firm that handled Kent family affairs. (F)

Black, Wilford. See Blackthorn, Reverend William.

Blackthorn, Reverend William (alias Wilford Black). Spurious backwoods preacher who abducted Amanda Kent in the Kentucky woods. Jared Kent killed him in a St. Louis boardinghouse. (S)

Boyle, Michael. Amanda Kent's private clerk. Born into a poor Irish immigrant family. Became Louis Kent's guardian. Married Hannah Dorn. Became owner of a prosperous chain of Midwest department stores. (F, T, W)

Brown, Adolphus (Butt). Gambler with girls for hire and whiskey for sale at the Union Pacific construction site. Strangled to death by Jeremiah Kent. (W)

Brumple, Eulalie. Neighbor of Philip and Anne Kent. After Anne's death she looked after Abraham Kent for a period. (R)

Caleb, Captain Will. American sea captain, master of the *Eclipse*, which took Phillipe to America. Caleb later entered into a business deal with Philip and Anne Kent. (B, R)

Campbell, Mr. Landlord of the Salutation, a favorite hangout of Samuel Adams's Sons of Liberty. Philip Kent's first job in America was at the Salutation. There he became acquainted with some of the foremost proponents of independence from the British crown. (B)

Charboneau, Marie. Born c. 1730. Mother of Phillipe Charboneau (Philip Kent). An actress in her youth, she formed a liaison with the English Duke of Kent and bore him Phillipe. Died 1772 at sea en route to America. (B)

Charboneau, Phillipe. See Kent, Philip.

Cheever, Josiah. Coconspirator with Edward Lamont in abortive attempts to assassinate Jephtha Kent. (T)

Christian. A Delaware Indian with some white blood who worked on Michael Boyle's gang. (W)

Clapper Family. Daniel and Edna and their two children, Daniel Junior and Danetta, befriended Abraham and Elizabeth Kent. The Kents accompanied the Clappers down the Ohio River from Pittsburgh. (S)

Courtleigh, Thomas. President of the Wisconsin and Prairie Railroad, the most repressively managed line in the country. Tried to destroy Gideon Kent and his family. Killed accidentally by his employee Lorenzo Hubble. (L)

de la Gura, Jaimie. Amanda Kent's husband, who had been a Louisiana trapper and a Texas cotton grower. He was about to open a store in Bexar, Texas, when he died of cholera in 1832. (F)

Dorn, Gustav. A provisioner along the Union Pacific line in Nebraska. Father of Hannah Dorn. (W)

Dorn, Hannah. Born 1838. Daughter of Gustav Dorn. Wife of Michael Boyle. (W)

Dorn, Klaus. Hannah Dorn's taciturn and phlegmatic younger brother. (W)

Dorn, Samuel. Pinkerton guard of a particularly brutish nature. (T)

Edes, Benjamin. Boston patriot who took Philip Kent into his printing business. (B, R)

Emerson, Molly. Proprietress of a Washington, D.C., boardinghouse where Jephtha Kent lived. She became his mistress and later his wife. (T, W, L)

Ericsson, Nils. Chicago labor organizer who lost his life during the great Chicago fire of 1871. (L)

Ericsson, Torvald. Ten-year-old son of Nils Ericsson. Killed when thugs hired by Thomas Courtleigh broke up a labor meeting in his father's barn. (L)

Fletcher, Angus. Irascible, acerbic, Bible-quoting father of Donald and Judson Fletcher. Ultraconservative Virginia planter. He and Judson were constantly at loggerheads. (R)

Fletcher, Donald. Elder of Angus Fletcher's two sons, a childless widower. A gout-ridden member of the Burgesses. He was chosen to represent Virginia at the Continental Congress. (R)

Fletcher, Elizabeth. Born 1778. Peggy Kent's daughter, born out of wedlock. Fathered by Judson Fletcher. Married Abraham Kent, her stepbrother. Mother of Jared Kent. Killed 1801 in the Northwest by a drunken Indian. (R, S)

Fletcher, Judson. Younger son of Angus Fletcher. Given to drunkenness and brawling. Fathered Philip Kent's stepdaughter, Elizabeth. Killed in Pittsburgh in the act of saving the life of his boyhood friend, George Clark. (R)

Florian, Sidney. Assistant general manager of the Wisconsin and Prairie Railroad. Ruthless henchman of the president of the line, Thomas Courtleigh. Presumed lost during Chicago fire of 1871. (L)

Goldman, Leo. Son of Jewish immigrants. Actor in the troupe Eleanor Kent traveled with. They became enamored of each other. (L)

Grace, Major Ambrose. Northern officer whose men sacked Rosewood. Serena Rose had sexual relations with him. (W)

Graves, Sergeant Amos. Man responsible for hanging Kola. Killed by Jeremiah Kent. (L)

Harkness, Toby. Adolphus Brown's devoted, dull-witted helper, who made an attempt on Michael Boyle's life because Michael had warned people about Brown's crooked gambling practices. Killed by Jeremiah Kent. (W)

Hope, Israel. Amanda's devoted mulatto servant and later her manager for the Ophir Mines. (F, T)

Hubble, Lorenzo. Member of Thomas Courtleigh's legal staff, assigned to kill Gideon Kent. Failed in each of several attempts. (L)

Hughes, Dana. Manager of Kent and Son, the Boston publishing house. (T, W, L)

Hull, Captain Isaac. Commander of the *Constitution*, the ship on which Jared Kent served. (S)

Josef. The gnome who followed von Lepp, the Prussian, about, ready to do his dirty work. (L)

Kane, Jason. See Kent, Jeremiah.

Kent, Abraham. Born 1775. Son of Philip and Anne Kent. Husband of Elizabeth Fletcher and father of Jared Adam Kent. After his wife's death he entered into a life of degradation. The circumstances and date of his death are unknown. (R, S)

Kent, Amanda. Born 1850 to Gilbert and Harriet Lebow Kent. After the death of her parents, she made her way west with Jared Kent, until separated from Jared by an abductor. Amanda lived successively on the Great Plains, in Texas, and in California. Eventually worked her way back east. Mother of Louis Kent by a Mexican army officer. Died of gunshot wounds received in New York City in 1852. (S, F, T)

Kent, Anne Ware. See Ware, Anne.

Kent, Carter. Born 1862. Son of Louis Kent and Julia Sedgwick. He lived with his mother after his parents' divorce. (L)

Kent, Eleanor. Born 1862 to Gideon Kent and his wife, Margaret Marble Kent. An aspiring actress. (W, L)

Kent, Elizabeth Fletcher. See Fletcher, Elizabeth.

Kent, Fan Tunworth. See Tunworth, Fan.

Kent, Gideon. Born 1843 to Jephtha and Fan Kent. Major in Confederate army. Married Margaret Marble in 1861. Father of Eleanor and Will Kent. Worked for the cause of labor through publications. Eventually became an editorial worker for the New York *Union*, the Kent family newspaper. (T, W, L)

Kent, Gilbert. Born 1783. The son of Philip Kent and his second wife, Peggy Ashford McLean. Half brother of Abraham Kent. Married Harriet Lebow. Father of Amanda Kent de la Gura. A successful businessman, proprietor (after Philip) of Kent and Son. Died at age 29. (S)

Kent, Harriet Lebow. Wife of Gilbert Kent and mother of Amanda Kent. Her second marriage, a disaster, was to an impostor and spendthrift, Andrew Piggott. (S)

Kent, Jared Adam. Born 1798. Son of Abraham Kent and Elizabeth Fletcher Kent. Under the mistaken notion he had killed a man, he fled from Boston with his cousin, Amanda Kent. Finally settling in Oregon, he married a Shoshone, Singing Grass. The father of Jephtha Kent, he was killed in California in 1849. (S, F)

Kent, Jephtha. Born 1821 to Jared Kent and his Shoshone wife, Singing Grass. Married twice, to Fan Tunworth and Molly Emerson. His children were all from his first marriage: Gideon, Matthew, and

Jeremiah. He left the Methodist ministry for newspaper work, but returned to the pulpit during his last years. Died 1871. (F, T, W, L)

Kent, Jeremiah (alias Jason Gray, alias Joseph Kingston, alias Jason Kane). Born 1846. Youngest son of Jephtha and Fan Kent. Fought in the Civil War. Buffalo hunter and professional gambler. Became a notorious gunman. Killed by Lorenzo Hubble in 1877 in Chicago. (T, W, L)

Kent, Louis. Born 1837 to Amanda Kent de la Gura. He was the natural child of Luis Cordoba, a Mexican army officer. Married Julia Sedgwick, from whom he was later divorced. Father of Carter Kent. Died in 1868 from complications resulting from a stab wound. (F, T, W)

Kent, Margaret Marble. See Marble, Margaret.

Kent, Matthew. Second son of Jephtha and Fan Kent. Born 1844. Seaman during the Civil War. An expatriate artist, he lived in Paris and London. Married Dolly Stubbs, an Englishwoman. Their child was Thomas Kent. (T, L)

Kent, Philip. Born 1753. The illegitimate son of the Duke of Kentland and Marie Charboneau. Emigrated to America in 1772. Anglicized his name to Philip Kent. Founder of the Kent family in America. A printer by trade. (B, R)

Kent, Will. Born 1869 to Gideon and Margaret Marble Kent. A quiet, withdrawn boy. (L)

Kentland, Duchess of (Lady Jane). Treacherous wife of the Duke of Kentland and mother of his heir, Roger Amberly. (B)

Kentland, Duke of. James Amberly, first Duke of Kentland. Father of Philip Kent and Roger Amberly. Married to Jane, Duchess of Kentland. (B, R)

Kingston, Joseph. See Kent, Jeremiah.

Kola. Teton Sioux, Jeremiah Kent's sworn life friend. He was killed when he went alone for medical help when Jeremiah was seriously ill with a fever. (W, L)

Lamont, Edward. Actor who was Fan Kent's second husband. A fanatic in the Confederate cause, he lost his life while making an abortive attempt on the life of Jephtha Kent. (T)

Lepp, Colonel. See von Lepp, Colonel.

Ludwig, Rose. Novelist and women's rights advocate. Friend of Amanda Kent. (F, T)

Lumden, Sergeant George. British soldier billeted in Abraham Ware's house. He forsook the British army and moved to Connecticut, where he became a prosperous manufacturer. Married to Daisy O'Brian. (B, R, S)

McCreery, Kathleen. Servant in Amanda Kent's New York house. Seduced by Louis Kent. Her revenge against the Kents brought certain hoodlums to Amanda's house. From them Amanda received a gun wound from which she eventually died. (F)

McGill, Barton. Sea captain and Amanda Kent's lover. They broke off their relationship at the time Amanda left California for the East. Commanded a blockade runner during the Civil War. Matthew Kent served on his ship. (F, T, W, L)

McLean, Peggy Ashford. Virginia beauty born c. 1755. Widow of Seth McLean, she bore Judson Fletcher's daughter. Her second husband was Philip Kent, by whom she had Gilbert Kent. Died in Boston in 1800. (R, S)

McLean, Seth. Respected Virginia gentleman, the husband of Peggy Ashford. He was killed during an uprising of slaves. (R)

Marble, Eliza. Margaret Marble's maiden aunt, whose profits from her Richmond dress shop went to support Margaret and her alcoholic father. (T)

Marble, Margaret. Born 1843. Daughter of a veteran of the Mexican War. Married Gideon Kent. Mother of his two children, Eleanor and Will. In her later years she gave way to excessive drinking and slow mental deterioration. Died in 1877. (T, W, L)

Marble, Willard. Alcoholic father of Margaret Marble. Widower. Lost both legs in the Mexican War. (T)

Maum Isabella. Faithful slave at Rosewood, the Georgia plantation of Colonel Henry Rose and his family. She enjoyed an exalted position in the household. (W)

Nichols, Joseph. Georgian who was a partner of Jared Kent's in the Ophir Mines in California. (F)

O'Brian, Daisy. Irish servant in the Ware household. Married Sergeant George Lumden, who deserted the British ranks. The couple moved to Connecticut. (B, R, S)

O'Brian, Mr. Concord farmer, father of Daisy O'Brian. Provided refuge for Philip Kent and Sergeant Lumden when they were fleeing from Boston. (R)

Parkhurst, Lady Alicia. Daughter of the Earl of Parkhurst. Married Roger Amberly. Committed suicide in Philadelphia in 1776. For a brief time she was Philip Kent's lover. (B, R)

Payne, Theo. Heavy-drinking manager of Kent and Son, the Boston publishing house founded by Philip Kent. Later manager of the New York *Union*, the Kent family newspaper. (F, T, W, L)

Pelham, Francis. English partner of Jared Kent in the Ophir Mines in California. (F)

Pell, Leland. Loutish teamster who attempted to rape Elizabeth Kent as he drove her and Abraham Kent to the Northwest. In rescuing Elizabeth, Abraham killed Pell. (S)

Piggott, Andrew. Urbane impostor who married Harriet Lebow Kent shortly after Harriet's first husband, Gilbert Kent, died. The marriage was brief, ending with Harriet's accidental death. (S)

Plenty Coups. Sioux warrior who bought Amanda Kent from the trapper to whom William Blackthorn had sold her. After his death, Amanda found her way to Texas. (S)

Plummer, Captain. Cutthroat hired by Jane and Roger Amberly to hunt down Phillipe Charboneau and assassinate him. He almost succeeded. (B)

Poppel, Captain Franz. Northern officer whose search of Rosewood, Colonel Henry Rose's plantation, was conducted with courtesy and respect. He gave Jeremiah a revolver with which to protect the women at Rosewood. (W)

Price. Slave at Rosewood who cooperated with General Sherman's soldiers when they sacked the plantation. Killed by Jeremiah Kent. (W)

Prouty, Oliver. Shipmate and friend of Jared Kent. Killed during the encounter of the *Guerriere* and the *Constitution.* (S)

Rackham, Captain Malachi. Lecherous partner of Will Caleb. Anne Ware Kent's abductor. Both were swept out to sea as Anne fought to protect herself from his repeated sexual assaults. (R)

Rochambeau, Madame. Owner of the house in Paris where Matthew Kent and Dolly Stubbs had rooms. (L)

Rose, Catherine. Colonel Henry Rose's second wife and Serena Rose's stepmother. Originally from Connecticut. Raped and brutally murdered by Yankee invaders of Rosewood, the plantation of which she was mistress. (W)

Rose, Lieutenant Colonel Henry. Corporal Jeremiah Kent's commanding officer, who, as he lay dying, charged Jeremiah with delivering a letter to Rosewood, his plantation, where his wife and daughter lived. (W)

Rose, Serena. Colonel Henry Rose's daughter by his first wife. She was shot and killed by Jeremiah Kent when he discovered she had spent the night with the Yankee officer who had led the invasion of Rosewood. (W)

Rothman, Joshua. Grandson of Royal Rothman and president of Rothman's Bank in Boston, which handled many of the Kent family's financial affairs. (F, T, W, L)

Rothman, Royal. Fought with Philip Kent in the Revolutionary War. Founded Rothman's Bank in Boston. Grandfather of Joshua Rothman. (R, S)

Samuel. Margaret Kent's butler, whom she threatened to discharge if he failed to intercept all mail from Gideon to Eleanor and Will. (L)

Sedgwick, Julia. Born 1840. Married Louis Kent. Mother of Carter Kent. Divorced from Louis Kent, she recovered the use of her maiden name. Was active in women's rights movement. Became Gideon Kent's mistress. (T, L)

Shaw, Lottie. Virginia slattern with whom Judson Fletcher lived after being driven by his father from the family home. (R)

Sholto Family. Solomon and Emma, London printing family, and their sons, Esau and Hosea. They befriended Marie and Phillipe Charboneau in their hour of need in London. Phillipe learned the printing trade from them. (B)

Sims, Lute. A vile-tempered man with a psychotic hatred of feminists. When he attempted to break up Julia Sedgwick's lecture in Deadwood, he was shot at an unfair advantage by Jeremiah Kent. (L)

Skimmerhorn, "General." Yankee forager who raped Catherine Rose and then handed her over to other Northerners, who killed her. He was killed by Jeremiah Kent. (W)

Stark, Captain. British officer who pursued Anne Ware and later was killed in a fight with Philip Kent on the night of the Boston Tea Party. (B)

Stirling, Timothy. Young Texan whose uncle had been killed by Jeremiah Kent. He was shot in the back by Jeremiah, who was then ordered out of Abilene, Kansas, where the killing occurred. (L)

Stovall, Lieutenant Hamilton. Incestuous issue of Abraham Kent's commanding officer, he was Jared Kent's commanding officer aboard the *Constitution*, and his resentment for Jared became a life-long obsession, which ended only when he was shot and killed by Amanda Kent. She fired believing Stovall had killed her son, Louis Kent. (S, F)

Stovall, Lieutenant. Senior officer in Abraham Kent's troop who was killed in the battle along the Maumee. Detested by his men because of his condescending manner. He was the father of Hamilton Stovall, long an enemy of the Kent family. (S)

Strelnik, Sime. Russian radical whom Matthew Kent knew in Paris. With his wife, Leah, and their young son, Anton, he went to England and then to America, where he worked on *Labor's Beacon*, Gideon Kent's paper. Killed during a labor demonstration in New York. (L)

Strother, Gwendolyn. Thomas Courtleigh's frail fiancée. She became deranged upon sight of Torvald Ericsson's bloodied shirt when Gideon Kent threw it at her feet. She died insane a few years later. Courtleigh never forgave Gideon. (L)

Stubbs, Dolly. Born 1846. English girl with whom Matthew Kent lived in Paris. After she became pregnant with their son, Thomas Kent, born in 1870, she and Matthew were married. Before the child was born, she left Matthew and went to live in India. (L)

Trumbull, Tobias. Philadelphia Tory married to Lady Alicia Parkhurst's aunt. He died from wounds received in a duel with Judson Fletcher. (R)

Tunworth, Fan. Jephtha Kent's first wife, mother of his three sons—Gideon, Matthew, and Jeremiah. Their marriage broke up because Jephtha and Fan took opposite sides in the issues leading to the Civil War. After her divorce she married Edward Lamont, an actor. (F, T)

Tunworth, Captain Virgil. Fan Tunworth's father. Firm believer in the institution of slavery. (F)

von Lepp, Colonel (alias Gruen). Prussian army officer in Paris to seek out assassination radicals like Sime Strelnik. Killed in a struggle with Matthew Kent. (L)

Walpole, Mr. Hamilton Stovall's agent, whom Jared Kent mistakenly thought he had killed when Stovall came to claim Kent and Son, which he had won in gambling from Andrew Piggott. Walpole died naturally years later. (S)

Ware, Abraham. Father of Anne Ware, Philip Kent's first wife. A Boston patriot and pamphleteer. (B, R)

Ware, Anne. Born 1753. Daughter of Abraham Ware. Married Philip Kent in 1775. Mother of Philip's son Abraham. In 1778 Anne Ware fell into the sea and drowned while attempting to fend off a sexual attack. (B, R)

Whittaker, Charlie. Eleanor Kent's youthful friend who shared her love for the theater. (L)

Worthing, Captain Leonidas. Fanatical Southerner who was boss of a Union Pacific gang of rust-eaters. Michael Boyle, who became a particular object of the man's sadistic treatment, finally shot him in self-defense. (W)

A MESSAGE TO THE READERS OF THE KENT FAMILY CHRONICLES

Ever since I created *The Kent Family Chronicles* and worked out an arrangement with John Jakes to do the writing of the series, I have wondered about producing a different series about America with the same great story values. This series would take place in an earlier America because I feel everyone who has read *The Kent Family Chronicles* will want to know what happened in America long before the signing of the Declaration of Independence.

I finally decided to go ahead with The COLONIZATION OF AMERICA Series and signed a very famous writer to do these books under the pseudonym of Donald Clayton Porter. The first book in this new series is WHITE INDIAN and it has just been published.

Bantam Books requested that they be permitted to run in this book the first chapter of WHITE INDIAN as a sample for your reading pleasure. Here, in great depth, is the wonderful story of the people and the events that gave us our great land. Here is exciting fiction that puts you right in the making of America. I know you'll like WHITE INDIAN.

Sincerely,

Lyle Kenyon Engel, Producer
THE KENT FAMILY CHRONICLES
THE COLONIZATION OF AMERICA SERIES

Chapter I

As every settler in the Connecticut Valley well knew, even in times of peace, there was no real peace. Indian nations fought each other, then banded together to attack and harass the towns and villages established along the Connecticut River by the English, French Huguenots, Dutch refugees from New York, and a few Scandinavians. From time to time columns of French troops and irregulars, often accompanied by their own Indian allies, marched south, raiding the settlements to keep the people of Massachusetts Bay off-balance and to prevent reprisals in kind. Every frontier dweller carried his flintlock into the fields by day and kept it beside him at night.

Older settlers recalled that almost four decades earlier there had been a period of genuine peace after the Pequot War of 1637, when the most populous Indian nation in the region had been virtually decimated and the colonists had moved into their territory. Lesser tribes, among them the

Agawam and Chicopee, had been subdued, too, and Fort Springfield had become the largest and most active trading post in the western part of the Massachusetts Bay Colony.

When at least one hundred members of the militia were at their posts, the log fort on the east bank of the Connecticut River was believed to be impregnable. Thick logs of oak, maple, and elm provided the defenders with ample protection from the arrows and spears of their foes, and Fort Springfield also boasted four cannon. The largest of them, a demiculverin that fired iron balls half the size of a man's head, was notoriously inaccurate, but its roar was so loud that savages who heard the sound hastily left the vicinity.

The problem, as Fort Springfield's officers well knew, was that a full complement was maintained only during bona fide publicized emergencies. The militia consisted of volunteers who were kept busy on their own farms, and most of the time no more than fifteen or twenty gunners and infantrymen were on duty.

The Mohawk, allies of the mighty Seneca nation in the powerful Iroquois League, became embroiled in a dispute with the Ottawa, their neighbors to the north. Not wanting to face the Mohawk alone, the Ottawa called their friends the Algonquian, who ruled a land that extended from the Maine District of Massachusetts Bay to the shadows of the Citadel in Quebec.

Rather than ask for aid from all four of their sister nations of the Iroquois League, the Mohawk showed their contempt for their foes by appealing only to the Seneca, whose very name struck terror in the hearts of tribes from Hudson's Bay to the Spanish Floridas.

To the consternation of his enemies, Ghonka, the Great Sachem of the Seneca nation, responded to the challenge in person. He seldom went to war, customarily going into the field only at the head of the combined columns of the Iroquois, but personal circumstances caused him to seek the diversion that this particular campaign offered.

For ten years Ghonka had wanted a son who would someday join him at the Council of the Strong, but for ten years his dearest wish had been frustrated. His first squaw had given birth to a daughter, but both mother and child died in the epidemic of heat sickness that swept across the land.

Then, two years in the past, Ghonka had taken a new squaw, Ena, many years his junior; because he loved her, he was sure the god of fertility would shower him with blessings, and at the start of the harvest season, when all the signs and portents were favorable, Ena gave birth to a son.

Before the Seneca could rejoice, however, the infant died, and Ena almost lost her life, too.

On that very day, Ghonka received word from the Mohawk of their dispute with the Ottawa, and he left at dawn the next morning, placing himself at the head of a band of warriors three hundred strong, marching alone, a bearlike man with a thick chest and broad shoulders, the five feathers of his high rank protruding from his scalp lock.

The Ottawa paid a terrible price for the Great Sachem's grief, for Ghonka attacked their main town, taking the defenders by surprise, and burned it to the ground, killing more than 150 braves while his own forces suffered only a few casualties. Then he razed two smaller Ottawa villages as his foes fled before him, and drums spread the word through the vast forests of the wilderness that Ghonka was on the warpath.

He turned eastward and marched his men for forty-eight hours without pausing to rest. The warriors, accustomed to harsh discipline, did not complain. On the contrary, they enjoyed themselves thoroughly.

They maintained their usual silence as they made their way through the forest of pine and cedar, spruce and hickory, but occasionally they exchanged broad grins. They were the most feared and respected warriors in all the land, and they liked nothing better than showing off their prowess.

Only Ghonka remained gloomy. He set a blistering pace, sometimes taking a few mouthfuls of the parched corn and smoked venison he carried in his pouch, pausing only briefly at rivers and brooks for a swallow of water. Ottawa scalps decorated the loincloths of his warriors, but Ghonka carried none. He needed none to demonstrate his stature.

The drums carried the news of impending doom into the territory of the Algonquian, whose chiefs and senior warriors convened in haste if not in dignity. It was true they had given their pledge to help the Ottawa in their war against the Mohawk, but the Ottawa had suffered ignominious defeat, and now the Algonquian stood alone. Had they faced the Mohawk, they might have been inclined to honor their obligation to the Ottawa, but as one of the oldest braves, a wizened man of eighty summers, pointed out to the members of the council, the Algonquian had no quarrel with the Seneca.

And no sensible nation went to war when Ghonka himself led his warriors.

The Algonquian heeded the elder's advice and promptly sent a delegation to meet the Seneca. The braves unstrung their bows and removed their war paint to prove their peaceful intentions.

The two parties met beside the shores of Lake Winnipesaukee in the land that the men with pale skins were calling New Hampshire, and there they treated with each other.

The Algonquian offered five hundred strips of wampum, each heavy with the shells of clams and oysters, in return for peace.

The Seneca, being an inland nation, placed great value on this special wampum, but Ghonka exacted a higher price. Even his own senior warriors were surprised when he demanded seven hundred strips of wampum and one hundred necklaces of scallop shells, but the Algonquian sought peace so desperately that they agreed, and that night the two parties smoked the pipe of peace and feasted together.

Ghonka remained apart, still brooding as he stared into the fire.

When the feast ended, the Algonquian departed, and the Seneca made camp for the night. Ghonka continued to sit before the fire, his body motionless, his arms folded across his chest. The fire died down, and his closest subordinates, who had the privilege of sleeping nearest him, were awakened by the sound of his voice.

The Great Sachem was intoning something, his cadence rhythmic but his words unintelligible.

The senior warriors closed their ears, for only Ghonka and the chief medicine man had the right to speak directly to the Great Spirit, the god who was the father of all manitous, and it would have been unseemly to eavesdrop. Besides, the warriors had no desire to invoke the wrath of either the Great Spirit or Ghonka. None were sure which was the more ferocious.

His prayers ended, Ghonka slept for a time. But he awakened when the first light appeared in the sky, and soon the Seneca began the long journey home.

They marched due west from Lake Winnipesaukee until they came to the Connecticut River, and because it was easier to walk along the bank than to thread a path through the forest, Ghonka indulged his braves by allowing them to follow the river as it flowed southward. They had performed well and they deserved the reward.

Thus it was that the Seneca came upon the tiny town and fort called Fort Springfield.

One of the scouts in the advance party doubled back to tell the Great Sachem that a town of the pale skins lay ahead, guarded by a large fort made of logs, its walls so high that it was not possible to determine how many men might be defending the town.

Ghonka had no quarrel with the pale skins, who had not dared to establish homesteads and build villages in the land of the Seneca. Lesser tribes had suffered, but his territory had not been violated. It so happened, however, that he knew the worth of their belongings because both English and French traders had come to him with gifts in recent years.

The hatchets of the pale skins were made of a hard metal that could be honed to a fine edge, and the knives of these intruders from the far side of the great sea were superior. They also had firesticks that could kill or maim from great distances, although Ghonka wanted nothing to do with these weapons. The arrows and spears of his ancestors had made the Seneca preeminent in war, and he had no desire to experiment with new weapons.

Nevertheless, he coveted the other belongings of the pale skins. Perhaps, if he acquired these riches, the emptiness inside him caused by the death of his infant son would begin to dissipate. Ghonka's victory over the Ottawa had whetted his appetite for further triumphs, and the craven submission of the Algonquian had denied him the opportunity to win more glory.

He halted his warriors, and they took up hidden positions in the forest while they awaited the coming of night.

For two long weeks, Jed Harper had been too busy to celebrate the birth of his first child, a son. He had brought his wife, Minnie, to Springfield so the fort's doctor could attend her, and since the child's birth she had remained in the doctor's care because of complications that had set in.

Jed had been forced to return to his farm five miles away. The harvest couldn't wait, so he had labored from sunrise to sunset, bringing in the melons and pumpkins, corn and onions and peas that would provide his little family with staple foods during the long winter ahead.

His work done, he had come to Springfield to bring his wife and baby home, but the doctor insisted that Minnie stay in her room at the fort for another day or two, so Jed decided to remain in town.

It was his bad luck to draw militia duty at the fort, although he really couldn't complain. There had been no Indian raids on the fort for more than two years, and he had only to stand at his post in the watchtower, now and then looking out through a knothole to see if there was any activity in the woods beyond the town. The night was dark, with banks of heavy clouds obscuring the moon and stars, so he couldn't see much of anything even when he tried.

This was a perfect time to celebrate, and Jed had brought a jug of rum to the watchtower with him. Rum was a sure cure for the dreary boredom of sentry duty, and Jed and his friends were delighted to pass the time toasting the arrival of his baby son.

The militiamen scarcely knew what hit them.

Jed sensed something moving behind him and turned in time to see a husky Indian warrior, naked to the waist. Then a stone hammer descended, crushing Jed's skull, and he knew no more.

The efficient Seneca went about their task silently. One group neutralized the fort while another moved from house to house. Ghonka had ordered that no prisoners be taken and no survivors left, and his men obeyed him to the letter.

They were directed to take only cooking utensils and blankets, hatchets and knives. This was the purpose of the raid, and the braves were permitted to snatch only the personal trinkets they saw in passing. No time was to be wasted gathering frivolous items.

In all, 189 men, women, and children died in the slaughter, which would be recorded as the worst raid in Springfield's forty-year history. For years thereafter, no settler, militia officer, or official of Massachusetts Bay knew the identity of the raiders, and no one suspected the Seneca because their homeland was so far away—near Lake

Ontario in the western portion of the unsettled area claimed by New York Colony.

Ghonka seemed to be everywhere. He sped up and down the town's three streets making certain that his instructions were followed and that no man took more than he could carry comfortably on the long march home.

Hurrying on to the fort, Ghonka was gratified to note that there was no sign of resistance. His braves were moving from chamber to chamber, silently dispatching the pale skins.

Ghonka came to a small chamber where a young woman had just died in her bed, her blood staining the sheets. The young warrior who had killed her raised his stone hammer to destroy the infant who lay beside her.

Minnie Harper had been changing her son's diaper when the attack had come, so the baby was naked. Ghonka saw that the child was a sturdy, well-formed boy, and on sudden impulse he ordered, "Stay your hand!"

The young warrior lowered his hammer.

Ghonka approached the bed and looked down at the infant.

The baby returned his gaze, and the Great Sachem was astonished to note that there was no hint of fear in the infant's eyes.

Ghonka could not help laughing aloud.

The baby smiled and gurgled at him in return.

That settled the matter. Ghonka picked up the infant and clumsily wrapped him in a blanket. The son he had so desperately craved. Now Ena would have a child to hold in her arms and the future of his dynasty would be assured.

He would call his son Renno, after the god of

fertility, whom he would honor for the rest of his days.

Less than a half hour after the raiders struck, they departed as silently as they had come, and the only survivor was the infant who would be known as Renno.

Chapter II

Most of the Seneca lived in longhouses made of clay-chinked logs covered with thick elm bark. Clan members or relatives lived in clusters of such communal dwellings. But the Great Sachem, Ghonka, although a member of the Bear Clan, lived separately with his family, as befitted his rank.

His house, a miniature version of a longhouse, was twenty-five feet long, nineteen feet wide, and had a hide of elk skin covering the entrance, beside which the emblem of the Bear Clan was carved and painted red.

In the stone-lined pit in the center of the dwelling burned a fire that was never extinguished, night or day, no matter the season. The smoke escaped through a hole cut directly over the fire in the center of the roof, and above the hole stood a platform, supported on four legs, that kept out rain or the heavy snow that had been falling regularly in recent weeks. The wind was mild, so the smoke escaped freely and the interior was clear.

A double row of bunks lined one wall, each made of a slab of wood; those on the bottom were covered with skins and furs and used as beds, and those above were used as storage space for clothing, weapons, tools, and other private belongings that were not suspended from the pegs on the other walls.

Renno's bed was only half the size of those used by his father and mother because he would remain under their roof only until his seventh summer, when he would be moved to the longhouse of the boys. Even now he enjoyed no special privileges, just as Ghonka and his wife, Ena, had few prerogatives of rank. A square of burnished metal hanging from a wall peg, which Ghonka had brought with him from the town of the pale skins two years earlier, was the only visible luxury.

Ena saw to it that Renno slept beneath a soft blanket made of the marvelously warm cloth taken from the pale skins' town. But there were disadvantages to the use of the blanket, too, the worst being the cold shock he felt when he was removed from his bed.

Ena placed Renno in the backsack used for the exclusive purpose of carrying him out of doors, and he relaxed again. The outer portion of the container was tough bearskin, itself warm enough for older people, but the inner layer was composed of the deliciously warm fur of the silver timber wolf, which lay next to Renno's skin.

As his mother moved out into the open, Renno snuggled into the fur, trying to bury his face in it.

The air was so cold that his cheeks burned and his nostrils stung, but the discomfort soon eased and he was enveloped by the warm cloud.

He was incapable of remaining quiet for very long, and his normal and powerful two-year-old curiosity had him wriggling in his wrappings until he could peer out and watch the scenery.

His mother's beaded leggings flapped as she walked with purposeful strides, plowing through the deep snow. Soon they were joined by another woman, similarly laden, the mother of his friend Anowara, who was slightly younger and smaller.

The two women exchanged greetings, then walked out past the stockade that surrounded the Seneca town, and after a while they caught a glimpse of their destination.

Renno saw it, too, and promptly ducked back into the warm fur. He hated this place, and he braced himself for the ordeal.

His mother began to sing. In a low melodic chant she called on the spirits of the wilderness, the manitous, to give her child strength and courage. Renno's skin prickled. Ena was a medicine woman renowned for her ability to communicate with the spirits, and Renno felt their presence in the towering trees, and he could imagine them listening to her, then whispering to each other in the wind. Perhaps they were even whispering to him.

"Be strong," they told him. *"Be brave."*

The women, both singing, walked slowly onto the frozen surface of a small lake, and Renno and Anowara were placed carefully on the ice, still wrapped in their furs.

The boy watched as his mother hacked at the ice with a small stone hatchet she took from her belt. A hole had been broken in the ice earlier in the day, but the cold was so intense that a new skin of ice had already thickened. Ena cleared it away, then plucked the child from his cocoon and held him high over her head.

The air numbed Renno as it struck his naked body, but he did not struggle, and his face remained impassive.

"Manitous, make Renno strong!" Ena cried. "Sky-woman, see your child and make him hardy!"

Renno folded his little arms across his chest, as he had been taught, then sucked in his breath.

Holding him tightly and maintaining her firm grip, his mother plunged him into the icy water and held him there.

Renno bit back the cry that came to his lips. Silently he endured the heart-stopping shock of the freezing water, the almost warm feeling of the air as his mother removed him from the lake, then the renewed sting as he was plunged below the surface a second time.

Anowara, younger and less sturdy than Renno, began to weep as her mother performed the same ritual. The woman clamped a hand over the child's mouth to stifle her sobs, then continued to hold her hand there until it seemed that the baby would choke. The hand moved briefly to allow the little girl to gulp in a short breath, and the process was repeated until Anowara gained control of herself.

Her mother spoke gently. "Do not cry, little turtle. A Seneca never cries. You will be a strong woman, a brave woman. You will not be one who cries!"

"Look at Renno," Anowara's mother said. "He knows the wisdom of silence. One day he will be a great warrior."

Ena smiled.

Even though she made no comment, Renno knew

she was pleased with him as she dried him and wrapped him in his furs. Curling up in this warm place, he willed himself to stop shivering.

His mother looked at him with approval. That was his reward, and he wanted nothing more.

Renno, who grows up to be the strongest, bravest and wisest of Seneca warriors, is suddenly plunged into the turbulent world of the white settlers where he must make a decision: is he white or Indian?